COUNTRY

OF

ORIGIN

ALSO BY DON LEE

Yellow

COUNTRY

OF

ORIGIN

A NOVEL

DON LEE

W. W. NORTON & COMPANY / New York / London

Manufacturing by Quebecor World, Fairfield
Book design by JAM Design
Production manager: Anna Oler

Library of Congress Cataloging-in-Publication Data
Lee, Don, 1959–
Country of origin : a novel / Don Lee.— 1st ed.
p. cm.
ISBN 0-393-05812-3
1. Young women—Crimes against—Fiction. 2. Police—Japan—Tokyo—Fiction. 3. Sex-
oriented businesses—Fiction. 4. Americans—Japan—Fiction. 5. Missing persons—
Fiction. 6. Tokyo (Japan)—Fiction. 7. Diplomats—Fiction. I. Title.
PS3562.E339C68 2004
813'.6—dc22

2004004722

W. W. Norton & Company, Inc., 500 Fifth Avenue, New York, N.Y. 10110
www.wwnorton.com

W. W. Norton & Company Ltd., Castle House, 75/76 Wells Street, London W1T 3QT

1 2 3 4 5 6 7 8 9 0

For David and Bethany Daniel
and the extended Pappalardo family

COUNTRY

OF

ORIGIN

O N E

TOM HURLEY dove into the embassy pool, slipping into the hush and cool of the water. On the other side of the world, it was day 226 of the Iran hostage crisis, but here in Tokyo, on June 17, 1980, it was placid, quiet, and, at six in the morning, already hot and a little sticky. Tom was a week into his tour to Japan as a Junior Foreign Service Officer, and for some reason he had yet to adjust to the time change, waking up at ungodly hours. Antsy and wired, he had taken to swimming laps before work.

The pool was directly behind the Grew House, the largest of the three low-rise apartment buildings on the American Embassy housing compound, all of them drab concrete-and-steel structures, designed when stripped-down industrial functionality was actually an architectural choice. Tokyo itself wasn't any prettier. Indeed, given the refinement and delicacy of the Japanese culture, the general ugliness of the city had surprised Tom, offices and stores and houses jammed haphazardly into every available inch of space. No, what distinguished the compound, which sat on a hill near Roppongi, within walking distance of the embassy, was its size, its expanse, twelve full acres of wide, green sweeps of lawns and trees, the pool and tennis courts and parking lots, everything so *big,* an excess that the Japanese must have found typically arrogant, the way Americans always seemed to spread out and take more room than was necessary.

Yet that morning, Tom was enjoying—quite guiltlessly—the roominess of the twenty-five-meter pool, which he had all to himself, no one else there other than the college-age lifeguard. In high school, Tom had been on the swim team, and when the topic arose, he sometimes implied that he might have competed collegiately if he had attended someplace smaller than UCLA. It was quite an exaggeration, on several levels. He could be terribly vain. Thirty-one, single, in his prime, he worked hard to keep fit and trim and tan. He was tall—he told people six-foot even, although he was a bit shy of that—and he had those mixed-blooded *hapa haole* features that women liked: thick, wavy black hair, a straight nose, angular cheekbones and jaw, long, girlish eyelashes. He was half-white and half-Korean, but when asked about his ethnicity, he always said Hawaiian, a declaration of racial neutrality that, more often than not, let him avoid further inquest.

In the pool, he fell into the rhythm of his strokes, the slight roll of his body between the flutter of kicks. He focused on his technique, trying to perfect something new. As a teenager, he had been taught the standard S stroke for freestyle, keeping his palms flat and pushing back with them like paddles. Recently, however, he'd discovered that world-class swimmers were doing something minutely yet dramatically different with their hands, angling them in during the pull and out during the finishing sweep. Instead of paddling, they were *sculling*. Their hands were acting as airfoils, producing lift, not drag. Tom had become possessed by the technique, buying books on hydrodynamics and Bernoulli's principle and trying to track down Olympic training films. This was how he was. He fixated, he obsessed, he studied and practiced, and then, in short order, he dropped it altogether. He was a dilettante, a self-aggrandizing dabbler, in almost everything he did, not able to follow through to the end with anything, in particular with women.

But it was early still, in the pool he was still infatuated with his *hands,* the way they seemed to propel him, the tiny adjustment of angles making him more efficient, faster, making him fly.

As he headed over the deep end, he heard a splash behind him. He did a flip turn, and, halfway across the pool, he saw another swimmer coming from the opposite direction. It was a woman, wearing a white bathing cap and a dark blue tank suit, cut high on the thighs. She swam well, arms stroking smoothly, long legs kicking with power. Her face was a blur as they passed, a flash of skin amid white-water turbulence. Tom reached the wall at the shallow end and flip-turned, but since he could only breathe on his right side, he lost sight of her for a lap. After he turned around, he met her at the middle of the pool again, and they kept passing each other this way for ten minutes. Two ships.

All at once, Tom noticed something. Almost imperceptible at first. Then he was sure. She was speeding up. Soon, she closed the gap altogether so they were on parallel tracks, side by side. She stayed with him for four laps, matching his position exactly, synchronizing her strokes to his, and they went along at a relaxed pace, as if on a friendly little jog together. Several times Tom had the impulse to wave to her. She edged ahead of him ever so slightly. He picked up his pace, only to have her pull forward again by half a body length. She was toying with him, teasing him, making him chase. Every time he accelerated, she accelerated, over and over, until eventually they were at a full sprint, racing.

His technique broke down instantly. He was trying to quicken his strokes, and, just trying to keep up with her, he forgot all about his hands. This was not fair, he thought, his arms and legs leadening. He'd been swimming for a good while before she had entered the pool. She had caught him when he was tired, out of shape, unprepared.

She was two body lengths in front of him. He forced himself to swim faster, every muscle aching, lungs squeezing, dots flashing in his eyes as he flirted with blacking out. He pushed through it. He was drawing even with her, he was catching up. At the shallow end, they flip-turned at the same time. Tom felt himself cruising now, his strokes and kicks back in rhythm, going fast, unconquerable. But when he turned off the far wall, she wasn't beside him anymore.

He stopped and popped his head out of the water. The pool was empty. She was gone. She must have gotten out while he was on his blind side, breathing to his right. Treading water, Tom looked up at the lifeguard, who was dozing peacefully in his chair.

▪　　▪　　▪

SLEEP. KENZO OTA needed sleep. He had thought it would be so convenient for the supermarket to be next door to his new apartment, but he had not noticed the air-conditioning condenser on the market's roof, eye level with his bedroom, rattling and humming in unpredictable cycles and not allowing Kenzo a decent night's sleep since he had moved in two weeks ago.

The apartment was a ten-minute walk to Musashi-Koganei train station on the Chuo Line, which was twelve stops to Shinjuku, where he transferred to the Yamanote Line, on which he rode four stops to Ebisu, where he switched to the Hibiya subway line, on which he rode two stops to Roppongi, where he got off and walked to Azabu Police Station, where he was a detective—an Assistant Inspector, to be more precise. The commute took an hour and a half each way, actually shorter than before, when he had lived in Fuchu.

This apartment was small: two rooms that were the equivalent of ten and a half tatami mats, plus a bathroom and a kitchen. Sort of a kitchen—a sink and one gas burner and a refrigerator cube in a single modular unit in the hallway which faced the bathroom that was adjacent to the front door. The apartment was on the third floor of a five-story ferroconcrete building, and Kenzo had paid, in advance, the first month's rent, an additional month's as a realtor fee, two months' as a security deposit, and another two months' as *reikin*, key money, which was a nonrefundable gift to the landlady in a show of gratitude for being permitted to dwell in a matchbox of an apartment next door to the sputtering din of a supermarket condenser that was making his ears ring.

He couldn't afford to move out, not with all that *reikin*, so he called the landlady, Miss Saotome, and, after sheepishly apologizing for the bother and explaining about the noise, asked if she had something else vacant in her building. Miss Saotome said no one had ever complained about the condenser before, and then was curious how he could even hear it over his own air conditioner, with the windows presumably closed, and he had to tell her that he didn't like air conditioning at night when he slept, choosing not to reveal that he had some sort of dermatitis or psoriasis, they couldn't figure out what it was, and that he was quite possibly *allergic* to air conditioning, because it made his skin feel funny—tingly and itchy—not adding further that even with the air conditioner on, he would have *still* heard the supermarket condenser, such was its volume, its tinniness, its *irregularity*.

On the telephone, Miss Saotome was silent for quite a while, thinking—Kenzo was sure—that he was neurotic or homosexual, but finally she said yes, there was one apartment available on the fourth floor, No. 401, on the other end of the building, with the exact same layout and rent as his present apartment, but he would have to see it the next day, since she was going out of town the following evening, and, furthermore, he would have to make a decision immediately, since she knew a realty agent was bringing in several clients to look at the place that week.

Just the apartment number, 401, made Kenzo jittery, the Japanese word for four, *shi,* being unlucky, as it was associated with the word for death, but the following day at noon, he met Miss Saotome—young, painfully skinny in her chic French designer dress, with her hair died *chapatsu,* tea-color—in front of the building. They rode up the elevator together, and she let him inside the sweltering apartment, not bothering to take off her high heels at the door, plainly in a hurry, not in the greatest of moods. She slid open the window in the living/dining room and said, "*Hora. Nanimo kikoe masen.*" See? You can't hear a thing.

And other than the faint registration of cars and trucks and buses going by, an occasional siren, dogs barking, a plane overhead, bicycle bells, and the ambient hum of twenty-five million people living and working in the vast, gray, cramped megalopolis that was the Kanto Plain, Kenzo couldn't hear a thing. He looked out the windows—just rooftops, antennas, telephone poles and wires, power lines—and opened the closet door, eyed the floors. "Is it a little smaller than the other apartment?" he asked.

"It's exactly the same. Everything's exactly the same."

He could, he thought, live with this, maybe. But what if the supermarket condenser was in a rest cycle right now? What if there was something else that would rear up when they departed? A transformer buzzing, a nest of crows, wind chimes, the flush of pipes, a neighbor who played disco on the stereo late and loud into the night?

"Is it possible for me to stay here for twenty minutes? Maybe thirty?" he asked Miss Saotome.

"What?"

"I think I'll take it," he said. "I just want to make sure."

She looked at her watch, sighed. "I have to go to the post office. Knock yourself out," she told him, then, under her breath, said, "*Henjin.*" Freak.

He squatted down on the floor in the bedroom where his futon would be and closed his eyes, listening carefully for sounds from the windows. But instead of anything from that side of the building, almost immediately he heard a distinctive *ding* from the other side, the side with the outdoor walkway that led to the stairs and—he realized now, as he jumped out of the apartment—to the *elevator.* He pushed the DOWN button and waited for the tiny elevator to return. When it did—*ding*—the doors opened with a bell ringing. Why hadn't he noticed it before? He had come up the elevator with Miss Saotome, and they had exited right in front of No. 401. For a police inspector, he had very poor powers of observation, he had to admit. He took that back. They were not poor. They were sometimes heightened, electrified, excruciatingly sensitized, but, alas, *misplaced.* Had he not observed the checkered linoleum floor in the humid, stifling elevator, the squashed, dried remnant of gum near Miss Saotome's shiny black left high heel, her trim, shapely ankles and calves encased in pantyhose? Had he not noted her perfume, the smell of her shampoo, baby powder, the heat and proximity of her body next to his?

He pressed the button on the console for the third floor, stepped off the elevator, and, after letting it begin its descent, pushed the DOWN button to retrieve it. He went inside No. 401, closed the door, and waited. Soon enough, he heard it. *Ding.* He tested it again and again, listening from the hallway kitchen, the bathroom, the living/dining room, the bedroom. There were six other apartments on the fourth floor, a maximum of three tenants in each, an average, say, of 1.4. That would mean a minimum of 16.8 dings coming and going on weekdays, many more on weekends. Would he get used to the noise? Which was the lesser evil, the elevator or the condenser? At least he would only have to deal with the condenser for half the year, when it was warm enough to require the windows open, whereas the elevator would continue all year long, every day and night.

And did he really want to go through the hassle of moving again? Once more, he would have to change his address at multiple ward offices, transfer the gas, electricity, water, telephone. It had been so stressful moving two weeks ago, beginning life anew in a different neighborhood. He had been in his last apartment, the one in Fuchu, for fourteen years, but the building had been sold to convert into condominiums, and he had been unable to find anything else in his price range in the area. Before then, he had lived with his wife, Yumiko, in a comfy little house for four years until she had summarily kicked him out. Up to that point, Kenzo had never been on his own. He had lived with his parents, then in one of the Metropolitan Police Department dormitories, then with Yumiko. As in most Japanese households, she had handled all the financial and domestic details. He hadn't known how to open a bank account, how to cook or clean or do laundry, how to go about buying furniture or dishware. It had been humiliating. He had worked very hard to become self-sufficient, developing routines until he was completely independent. But now, at thirty-eight years old, all that familiarity and comfort was gone, and he was comparing the relative disadvantages of dings and drones and questioning whether it would be outlandish to ask Miss Saotome, who would be back any minute now wanting his decision, if he could spend a trial night in No. 401. He couldn't make up his mind—

about anything. He wished he could take a nap, or maybe go for a long walk. Perhaps at the Inogashira zoo, to see the monkeys.

■   ■   ■

MONKEY. LISA COUNTRYMAN heard her say it—*saru*, monkey— and she thought at first that the girl was talking about her. But no, the Japanese schoolgirl and her friend, who were sitting opposite Lisa on the subway, hands covering their mouths as they giggled, were looking down the car at an African man in a dashiki. *Saru mitai*, they whispered. He looks like a monkey.

It had been years since anyone had thought definitively that Lisa was part black. Not since junior high school, really. Before then, she had heard it all, from whites and blacks alike, neither of whom had cared for her peculiar mulatto mix: gook monkey, bamboo coon, chigga jigaboo, dim-sum casco yellowbone chinkamo slope-head nine-iron UFO ping-pang yangmo buckethead. They knew her mother was Japanese, but her father's muddied origins could only be conjectured: Creole and/or Bahamian and/or Mexican and/or German and/or Dutch.

Yet when Lisa had hit puberty, something had happened. Her skin became lighter, her hair straighter, her nose narrower. Her Negroid and Asiatic features blended together and repudiated each other, fading both ethnic distinctions, and she became nice and light, almost white, high, high yellow. People now mistook her for Italian, Israeli, Hawaiian, French, Native American, Russian, Lebanese—*some*thing, some sort of exotic dark mixture, but not really dark, not a real darkie, not—God forbid—black. When people presumed to ask, "What are you?" they discounted black, they didn't want to believe black, because black was too threatening, too uncomfortable, it wasn't a *fun* color.

Before getting off the subway car at Akasaka-Mitsuke, Lisa detoured in front of the Japanese schoolgirls and said, "*Nande sonna-koto iun-dayo? Shine, baka.*" Loosely translated: Why the hell are you talking like that? Fuck you. The girls were quite speechless.

Outside, it was near dusk, and muggy. It was past rush hour, but there was still quite a bit of pedestrian traffic as she walked toward the Hotel New Otani. She should have taken a cab, she thought. She was late and perspiring lightly in her cocktail dress when she entered the lobby of the hotel, but Mojo, who was fanatically punctual, refused to let her apologize. He wouldn't hear of it. It was *his* fault, he insisted. He should have sent his car for her. He was sweating, too, but not from the heat outside or from exertion. He was nervous. They had seen each other many times before during working hours, but this was their first *dohan,* their first outside date. Mojo blotted his brow with a folded handkerchief and ushered her to the express elevator, which whisked them straight up the forty-story tower to the Rainbow Lounge.

When the elevator doors opened with a soft, pleasant ding, they were greeted by four tuxedoed waiters and the maître d', all of whom bowed and said, "*Irasshaimase*"—Welcome. Lisa and Mojo were led to the table with the best view in the restaurant, breathtaking, the State Guest House below and the skyscrapers of Shinjuku beyond.

"Okay?" Mojo asked as they were seated.

"Wonderful," Lisa told him.

"I am sorry so not special. No time to arrangement," he said, anguished.

They always spoke in English, although Lisa could have run circles around Mojo with her conversational Japanese. Some customers liked that she knew the language, others did not. Mojo—which was a *nom de guerre,* his real name a mystery to her—claimed he wanted to practice his English, and she didn't challenge the assertion. She had learned that it was less intimidating to older Japanese men if she played dumb.

They ordered drinks—Maker's Mark with water for Mojo and a Stoli gimlet for Lisa. It was her third drink of the evening. He wasn't the only one who was nervous. She had stopped by a bar on her way to Akasaka, wanting to loosen up, to gather courage. She owed it to Mojo to at least pretend as if she were having a good time. He was, after all, going to be dishing out several hundred dollars for this dinner, and then giving her, if she kept her nerve and went through with the plan, a $10,000 cash "gift."

But first he handed her a small *presento,* a token memento of the evening—a brooch with red gems of indeterminate origin, ostensibly arranged to look like a ladybug, but which regrettably resembled a sunburned cockroach. "*Domo,*" Lisa said. "Gosh, a little bauble."

"Bubble?" Mojo asked.

"Bauble."

"Bobble?" He juggled his hands.

"Bauble. A geegaw. Or is it gewgaw?"

Mojo stared at her, thoroughly confused.

"A pretty-pretty," Lisa said, slurring a little.

"Ah," he said, brightening, "you think pretty?"

"Yes, very pretty."

He smiled at her and mopped his forehead and then, noticing her half-emptied glass, frantically motioned to the waiter for another round.

They made a few excruciating passes at small talk, but mostly stared out the windows at the view—a convenient reprieve from conversation. When his châteaubriand and her coq au vin were served, they sliced and forked and chewed with great deliberation, as if the act of eating the meal required the utmost focus. They each had another drink, split a bottle of Merlot, then had a snifter of X.O. with their cherries jubilee.

"Good? *Oishikatta?*" Mojo asked her when the bill came.

"*Oishikatta,*" she said.

He wiped his brow, happy.

Laughing, they teetered to the elevator, stumbled across the lobby, then hung on to each other for balance at the hotel entrance, waiting for his car. When they were tucked into the black Toyota Crown, Mojo asked where he should direct his driver, the club or his *mansion*.

"*Mansion,*" Lisa giggled.

Beaming, Mojo clutched her hands in his. "Thank you, thank you," he said.

They drove onto one of the elevated expressways and shot through the city, neon blurring past the windows of the car. Lisa was drunk, terribly, terribly drunk, and also a little stoned. Before leaving the restaurant, she had gone to the bathroom and gulped down a Quaalude. She had never taken a Quaalude before. She hardly ever did drugs—well, okay, she had also ingested one Percodan that morning, but it had been purely medicinal, a salve for her hurt ribs, one of which might have been broken—and, combined with the booze, the pills were affecting her quickly.

Mojo lived in an exclusive residential neighborhood called Denen-Chofu. It was only twenty-five minutes from Akasaka, but it seemed a world apart. Ginkgo trees lined the streets, and it was quiet, as if they had been kidnapped to the country.

Mansion was a misnomer, just a name for a nicer apartment. This building, the Homat King, was one of a string of fancy abodes that catered to rich Japanese and foreigners. Still, Mojo's place was palatial: four bedrooms, a garden patio, more space than he knew what to do with. He was a widower, and his children, he said ruefully, did not visit often.

Lisa sank into the couch, head spinning. Mojo made drinks for them, but she worried suddenly that he might not be able to perform, which would embarrass them both and lead to all kinds of awkwardness, such as the question of whether she would still receive her gift, or if they would have to try again. She didn't care about the money. She wasn't doing this for money. But the money was important to stamp the evening as an official transaction. If she was going to be accused of being a whore, she wanted to do this right.

Mojo began dancing. He had some god-awful disco on the stereo, and he had taken off his suit jacket and rolled up his shirt-sleeves and unclipped his tie. He was loose, flying, making funny gyrating movements with his hips, arms akimbo. He wasn't a bad man, he was actually quite nice, he was rather sweet. And not frightfully ugly. No, he might have been short and squat and big-bellied, face pancaked as to be featureless except for one eyelid that drooped, and he might have been unctuous, a font of secretions, sweaty, hair greased with rank-smelling ointment, skin oily and shiny and pungent with cologne, but he wasn't entirely repulsive.

Wanting her to dance with him, he tried to lift Lisa off the sofa, but he didn't leverage himself properly and fell face-first into the cushions, which broke the two of them into hysterics, until Lisa, swallowing a hiccup, farted. It wasn't a huge fart—*chisai desho*—and it wasn't long, but it was a watery fart, a short, powerful splutter, a moist punctuation of air that horrified Lisa and shocked them into momentary silence, mouths yawned open. But then Mojo began guffawing, and Lisa did, too. He had a high-pitched, keening, hyenic laugh, and Lisa's was a deeper, slower rumble, and the two of them—convulsing, shrieking, moaning—harmonized into a sound that was an ornithological abomination, a cross between a turkey buzzard and a titmouse on speed.

Flatulence was a time-honored tradition in Japan. Lisa had seen farting contests on TV, participants imitating animal noises, farting

along to popular songs, lying on a table, knees to chest, a labora-
tory tube stuck up their ass, attempting to blow out candles. Mojo
now tried to eke out his own fart, squeezing his face tight, grunting,
holding his breath, but he was having trouble. He grabbed Lisa's
palm and slapped it against his sweaty forehead, pressing hard. It
was a childhood game played by Japanese boys to induce farts, but
to Lisa it felt evangelical, like a tent-top preacher laying hands.
"*Heal,*" she said, and gripped Mojo's head harder. "I command
you to receive the power of the Lord and say unto you, demons
asunder, let's hear that bunghole thunder!" She pushed Mojo's head
against the back of the sofa. "I anoint you and compel you to blow
a gasket, give me some almond toast." She rose onto her knees on
the sofa and shoved her hand down on his forehead. The movement electrified the pain in her ribs and made her throw up a little
in her mouth, but she swallowed it back down. "I call on the bene-
diction of God to empower you, toot the chute, shoot the monkey."
She was floating upward, lifting. "I want spark plugs!" she
shouted, hovering near the ceiling. "Ringo vapor! *Koita, koita!*
Anus evacuas, fanny fumigatorio!" She was so dizzy, red and green
lights popping in her eyes, the room darkening. "Fart for me, my
sweet methane prince. Fart for Mama."

She wouldn't have sex with Mojo, she decided. It would prove
nothing. She would be punishing no one other than herself. It was
stupid to have even considered it. She resolved to leave Japan, to
go back to the States. She didn't belong here.

And then she awoke in the dark. She was lying on her back in a
bed. The lights were off, but the curtains weren't drawn, and the
moon was seeping into the room—one of the bedrooms in Mojo's
mansion, she gathered. She was alone. She still had her clothes and
shoes on. But why did she feel so groggy and heavy?—oh,
molasses. She couldn't move, her arms and legs were dead weight.
She could barely turn her head. What had happened? Had she

fallen asleep? Passed out? Where was Mojo? She was very cold, and her face and neck felt wet. Her throat and chest hurt. Her ears were plugged, as if she were on an airplane on a steep descent. The pressure was unbearable. She tried to swallow, but the pain in her ribs and also her chest got worse, her lungs seared. Something was wrong. She wasn't breathing. Her airway was blocked. Oh, God, she wasn't breathing. She tried to cough, to get up, to grab her throat, but she could do nothing, she couldn't move, she was already losing consciousness. The cold wet on her skin—she had vomited. She had been passed out on her back, and she had vomited from all the drinks and the Percodan and the Quaalude, and she was now choking on her own vomit.

This can't be happening, she thought. I can't die like this, not like this. The pain in her chest began to ease, but she instinctively knew that this meant neither relief nor rescue, but finality. She was sinking. She was drowning. She felt embarrassed, and stupid, and terrified, and very, very alone. She had no family, no one who would really miss her. Was she really going to die like this? She wondered what would happen to her body, where she would be buried, if anyone would claim her. She was not quite twenty-five years old.

TWO

THE FIRST call came on July 10, 1980, at 2:35 a.m., the message taken by the overnight embassy duty officer. A woman named Susan Countryman from Richmond, Virginia, was trying to locate her younger sister, Lisa, in Tokyo. She hadn't been able to reach her for over a month.

After his morning coffee, Tom Hurley called the number the woman had left, but her daughter, who couldn't have been more than twelve, said she was at work. Tom asked the girl to have her mother contact him at the embassy, explaining that Tokyo, accounting for Daylight Savings Time, was thirteen hours ahead of the East Coast. When he hung up, he worried for a moment that the girl hadn't understood what he'd meant about the time difference, but promptly forgot about it.

The embassy was abuzz with Jimmy Carter's visit. The President had come to Tokyo for Prime Minister Ohira's funeral, and this morning he was meeting with China's Premier Hua at the Hotel Okura. There was so much going on in the world that year: the hostages in Iran, the Soviet invasion of Afghanistan, the Olympic boycott, Cyrus Vance's resignation, Kim Dae Jung's sedition trial and the Kwanju riots, the strikes in Poland. Here in Japan, there were the Lockheed and KDD scandals, the no-confidence vote against Ohira, his heart attack, the subsequent elections for both houses in the Diet, and the trade war with the US over everything from cars to rice to telecommunications equipment.

It was an exciting time to be a diplomat in Tokyo, and Tom was privy to none of it. As a Junior Officer in American Citizens Services, the most delicate issue he faced these days was fetching Jujyfruits for a pothead in jail. Benny Daws and Jorge Hernandez, two veteran Consular Officers he had befriended, weren't any better off.

"It's because we don't have last names for first names," Jorge said that night. "If you really want to belong to the Yankee establishment, you need a good Eastern Seaboard, old-money first name like Ellsworth or Thorne."

They were drinking beers in a pub in Akasaka. Benny waved over the waiter and asked for another round of bottles, then said, "Of course, along with the name, it helps to be Ivy League."

"And then there's that other thing," Jorge told him.

"Hm?"

"Seals the deal if you're tidy-white," said Jorge, who was Chicano.

"Oh, yes, there is that little thing," said Benny, who was black.

"Please," said Sara Sobeske, who was Polish. "Can't we go one night without talking about race? Night after night. I'm bored out of my tree."

Tom began, "How do you get a one-armed Pollack out of a tree?"

"Don't you dare," Sara said.

"Wave at him," Tom said. "How did the Pollack break his leg raking leaves?" He had dozens of these jokes memorized. He had found a book of them.

"Shut up!"

"He fell out of the tree," Tom said. "How many Pollacks—"

"Stop!" Sara cried.

They had been going out for a couple of weeks—nothing serious. She was a secretary in Admin, and she was leaving for the US next Friday, quitting the State Department for good. She hated being a secretary, and Tom couldn't blame her. The hierarchy in the department was rigid and clear. At the top were Foreign Service Officers, FSOs, in the Political and Economic sections. At the bottom were the secretaries and FSNs—Foreign Service Nationals—locals who were saddled with all the shit work. Languishing in between were the FSOs in the Administrative and Consular sections. Every Junior Officer had to spend his first tour or two as a Vice Consul, but to get stuck in Consular meant the death of one's career before it began. It was a repository for flunkeys, hacks, washouts, and layabouts. It was also, by a remarkable coincidence, where most women and minorities ended up.

Jorge refilled everyone's beer glasses. "It's curious to me how you can be so cavalier all the time," he said to Tom.

"I've got no complaints." In ACS, Tom mostly pushed paper— renewing passports, certifying births and deaths, handing out absentee ballots and tax forms—but he was, in his opinion, doing relatively well. He was in Tokyo, after all, a coveted post, rather than in Africa or on the Cucaracha Circuit, and he was no longer stamping visas—unlike Jorge and Benny, who had three graduate degrees and twelve years of Foreign Service experience between them.

"Exactly my point," Jorge said. "I don't know what it is. Maybe you're charmed, maybe the gods have anointed you, but somehow you lucked into this cushy gig—"

"Who'd you pay off, anyway?" Benny asked. "Who'd you sleep with?"

"I'll never tell," Tom said, winking.

"You shouldn't be content with where you are," Jorge said.

"Ouch," Benny said.

"You should demand more of yourself."

"Had to take it up the ass, huh?" Benny said.

The three men made for an odd trio. Benny was bandy-legged and small-shouldered, with a supple, light step, but he had a loose, rumpled quality about him. Jowly face. Jiggly gut. Always the joker. Jorge, on the other hand, was thin and edgy and cantankerous, a bit of a subversive, sinister-looking with his gray-tinted eyeglasses. Jorge had dubbed them the Triplets of Token, the Three Mudketeers, the Rainbow Brethren, and, like an older brother, he was always riding on Tom.

Sara's apartment in Perry House was unnavigable with moving boxes, so she and Tom went to his place in Harris House, the middle of the three buildings on the embassy compound. His apartment had steel doors and linoleum and a concrete balcony, and it was outfitted with standard government-issue furniture that evinced the American penchant for plaid, but it had a ridiculous amount of space for a single man: two floors with two huge bedrooms upstairs. That night, however, Sara was partial to the sofa in the living room downstairs, a lovely wine-and-green-tartan monstrosity with matching chair and ottoman.

"Two Pollacks are walking through a field," Tom said.

Sara snapped her head around and glared at him. "I—am—"

He grabbed her hips in his hands and pulled her toward him, staring down at her ass, which was, all in all, quite a lovely sight. "They come across a sheep with its head stuck in a fence."

She expelled a soft moan. "—going—"

"One of the Pollacks drops his pants and fucks the sheep."

She closed her eyes and bent down farther. "—to—"

"Then he turns to his friend and says, 'Okay, your turn.' "

"—kill—"

"His friend says, 'Fine,' and sticks his head in the fence."

"—you."

They changed positions, Sara rolling onto her back on the sofa, Tom kneeling on the floor between her legs. "Are you going to miss me?" she asked, looking up at him.

"Of course," he told her.

"Why do I even bother to ask?" she said. "You know, Jorge doesn't get it. You don't care about delivering demarches or getting on the country team, because the work itself doesn't really interest you. You just want to travel and get laid. It's all a lark to you. They love people like you, people who'll just go along with whatever's decreed."

Trying to distract her, he kissed her neck, nibbled her earlobe.

"You don't want anything to ever get too serious," she said. "You don't want to have to feel or *think* about anything."

Tom brushed her hair off her forehead with his fingers. Everything she was saying about him was essentially true. He was weak and acquiescent, and he was superficial. He didn't work very hard, and he wasn't very ambitious. But not for the reasons she presumed. In any case, he knew she wasn't trying to be mean or recriminatory. She was young—twenty-three. She had become more affectionate for him than the situation, with her imminent departure, had warranted, and he was touched by her peevishness. "I really will miss you, Sara," he said.

She turned away from him. "I'm sure you will."

■   ■   ■

LISA COUNTRYMAN had not registered with the embassy, which wasn't unusual in Tokyo. Most expats didn't think it necessary to keep their local contact information up to date or to specify emergency next of kin, since Japan was hardly Third World and the city was virtually crime-free. But not registering also meant that Lisa Countryman had not signed a Privacy Act Waiver, and therefore, by law, there was only so much Tom could disclose to her sister about her welfare and whereabouts.

"What does that mean?" Susan Countryman asked when she and Tom finally spoke on the telephone.

"This will sound silly," he said, "but it means that even if we find her, there's a limit to what we can tell you without her written consent."

"What?"

"We can't reveal her location, welfare, intentions, or problems unless she specifies we can." Tom had never handled a missing-persons case before, and he was reciting straight from the FAM, the Foreign Affairs Manual. "Some people disappear by choice," he said, "which is their legal prerogative."

"Look, I'm her sister," Susan Countryman said, betraying a faint Southern accent.

"I understand," he said.

"I just want to know if she's safe." There were children screaming in the background. She explained that she was a nurse in the burn unit at Richmond Memorial, and she had just finished a twelve-hour night shift, and now her three kids were awake and demanding breakfast.

"Mrs. Countryman," Tom said, doodling on a notepad, "I assure you we'll do everything we can to help you."

"Ms.," she corrected. "Let's say you find her but she doesn't give you consent. You'll at least tell me you found her?"

Tom set down his pen, mildly interested. "Is there some reason she might not want to talk to you?"

"No. Of course not. I'm just asking. You're the one who brought up the possibility."

He slid the FAM closer and paraphrased Section 135 of Subchapter 7. "We can only give you negative information. We can tell you that a careful search has failed to reveal any information that she is or was in the consular district. We can tell you she departed the district and left no forwarding address. But we can't tell you she's in the district if she doesn't want that revealed, and we can't give you her forwarding address unless she expressly said that we could. All we can do is inform her that you're trying to locate her and forward a message to her."

"This is ridiculous," Susan Countryman said. "Okay. Fine. What do you need from me?"

Tom pulled out Form FS-118, Report of a US Citizen Missing Abroad. "Her full name?"

"Lisa Marie Countryman."

"Date and place of birth?"

"September 14, 1955. Yokohama."

"She was born in Japan?"

"Yes."

"Your father was in the military?" Tom asked. He himself was an Army brat, born in Heidelberg, Germany.

"Navy."

"Don't suppose you have her passport number."

"No."

"That's all right. Is she married? Any dependents?"

"No."

"Last known address?"

"Hold on," Susan Countryman said, shuffling papers. "8-15-12 Higashiyama, Meguro-ku, Tokyo."

"Phone number?"

"I don't have one."

"You don't?"

"I've been trying to send her telegrams."

"When's the last time you actually spoke to her?"

"In March—when she left for Tokyo."

"You haven't talked to her since she came to Japan?"

"I just said that."

"Was she here to go to school or to work?"

"She was going to teach English, but I'm not sure where."

"You don't know any friends or colleagues she might have had here, do you?"

"No."

"What message would you like us to relay?"

"I have some documents for her to sign. Legal documents."

"That's your emergency?"

"They're very important."

He asked Susan Countryman to mail some recent photographs of Lisa to him, and promised he would report back to her soon.

▪ ▪ ▪

THE ADDRESS turned out to be a *gaijin* house, a boardinghouse for foreigners. It was a rat hole, chock-full of Brits and Aussies, one of whom answered the door in his skivvies. Mrs. Fujiwara, an FSN Tom had taken along in case he needed an interpreter, discreetly turned away.

"Never heard of her," the Aussie said. It was two in the afternoon, but it seemed he had just woken up, still drunk.

"How long have you lived here?" Tom asked.

"End of May?" he said, unsure himself.

"Is there someone who's been here longer? She arrived in March."

"Hang on," the Aussie said, and slunk into the house.

There was hardly a clear patch of floor on which to stand in the foyer. It was crammed with shoes. Just beyond the entranceway, on top of a table, was a huge disorganized pile of mail, and underneath the table was a plastic crate stuffed with letters and papers. No doubt Susan Countryman's telegrams were in that crate.

"Yeah, I remember Lisa," a Brit named Tony Somers said.

"Did you know her well?"

"Not really. Only spoke to her once or twice. She didn't last long here. A bit of a prima donna, if you ask me. She moved out in April."

"Toward the beginning or the end of the month?"

"Beginning," Somers said, scratching his left armpit.

"Do you know where she went?"

"I heard she got a private *apaato* from the same bloke who owns this shithole." Somers fished through the mail pile on the table and found a namecard: Teiji Takagi, Friendship Guest Home Co.

"She was teaching English?" Tom asked.

"A novel concept, eh?" In Tokyo, the vast majority of *gaijin* in their twenties taught conversational English, or *eikaiwa*, to support themselves. "I think she was originally with an outfit in Shimbashi called Rocket America, but I heard she punted out of there right quick. I knew when I first laid eyes on her she was gutless, know what I mean?"

In the taxi back to the office, Mrs. Fujiwara studiously ignored Tom, plucking pieces of lint from her skirt. She had nineteen years of experience in the Consular Section, and she had no patience for JOs like Tom, with whom she was unfailingly polite and respect-

ful, doing everything he asked, but never anything more, convey-
ing an ever-present if passive hostility.

From Tom's office, she called Teiji Takagi, who volunteered to
come to the embassy. She then dialed Rocket America. After a
minute, Mrs. Fujiwara set the phone down, looking shaken.

"They hung up on you?" Tom asked.

She nodded.

"Did they tell you anything at all?"

"The director said she quit after two weeks," Mrs. Fujiwara
told him. "He was very rude."

An hour later, Teiji Takagi walked into the office, carrying a large
cardboard box. "*Chotto shitsurei,*" he said. "*Koko de ii desu ka?*"

Dressed in gray coveralls, he was a cheerful man, with none of the
anti-*gaijin* sentiments of most landlords, and he spoke some
English. He said Lisa Countryman had rented a room at the Meguro
house in March, and then had moved to one of his furnished studios
in Nishi-Azabu in April, where she had stayed until the night of June
18. That was when Lisa had called him to say that she was leaving
Japan for Hong Kong and wouldn't be returning.

"I go next day *apaato*? Typhoon!" Takagi said.

She had left the place a mess, everything strewn on the floor, as
if hit by a tropical storm. Obviously she had been in a great rush.
Takagi had collected her abandoned personal effects and kept
them in the cardboard box, which he, Tom, and Mrs. Fujiwara
examined now. Cassette tapes, books, towels, sheets, miscella-
neous kitchenware, some large envelopes—she had dumped her
clothes and toiletries into her suitcases and deserted the rest.

"You take box, okay?" Takagi said to Tom.

The box was neatly labeled with Lisa Countryman's name and
the apartment address. Despite the chaotic condition of his rental
property, Takagi appeared to have been fretting over Lisa's possessions. Was he this conscientious with all of his tenants' detritus?

Tom picked up one of the envelopes and opened the flap. It contained sundry papers, but on top were two small identical photographs.

"Is this her?" Tom asked.

"*Hai,* Lisa-san," Takagi said. "Pretty girl. Nice girl."

She was pretty, Tom had to agree. The passport-size photo was a formal head shot—perhaps for an Alien Registration Card, a visa to another country, or an international driver's license—but she was very striking. Her face was both hard and soft, a juxtaposition of opposites, with a strong jawline, enormous green eyes, brown hair, a slip of a nose, her skin whitewashed in the glare of the flash. A Caucasian mongrel, maybe Irish and Italian. Tom pulled out the other contents of the envelope, and lo and behold he found a half dozen telegrams from Susan Countryman, all addressed to the Meguro house, asking Lisa with increasing urgency to call her.

"Before same," Takagi said. There had been two telegrams earlier that month which he had personally given to Lisa, who, it was now apparent, had been intentionally dodging her sister.

■　　■　　■

THEY NEEDED bodies for the party. Sara Sobeske's best friend at the embassy, Marly Hughes, was the secretary for Jay Steiner, the cultural attaché, and at the last minute he had asked her to set up a reception for a sculptor visiting from New York. Marly was afraid no one would show up, and she had enlisted Sara to bring Tom, Jorge, Benny, and anyone else they could think of.

The party was in the lounge on the top floor of the Grew House. Enough people were there to make it respectable, but overall it had the feel of a perfunctory official function, replete with the usual soggy hors d'oeuvres, like the shrimp Tom was forking onto a plate.

"You're fast, but not fast enough."

There were so many sensations. First the voice—contralto, slow, confident, thrilling with its implied history of naughty behavior. Then her smell—a rich perfume, yet faint and elusive, even at this distance, the perfect distillation. Then the hair and face—wavy and blond, shoulder-length, high forehead with thick eyebrows arching over blue eyes and aquiline nose and large smirking mouth, crooked left incisor, lipstick, lambent skin. "Excuse me?" Tom asked.

"In the pool," she said.

She was his age, he guessed. She was wearing tan Capri pants and a white silk blouse, top three buttons undone, a sneak of breast. With her heels, she was the same height as Tom, and she was slender, lean.

"Wasn't that you I passed in the pool?" she asked. "Or was that a log held stationary by an anchor?"

"You caught me on an off day," Tom said.

"Oh, *really?*"

"I had the flu."

"I see. The flu. That seems to be going around. And let me guess. You were also still suffering from the effects of malarial shigella."

"How did you know?"

"I couldn't miss with that jaundiced pallor."

They smiled. "You never came back to the pool," Tom said.

"Were you looking for me?"

"No, not at all," he told her. After that morning, the rainy season had begun in earnest, and it had poured almost every day since. Tom had gone to the pool for six straight mornings, looking for her, and then had given up. It had been wretched swimming in the rain.

"I think you're lying," she said. "In fact, I'm sure of it."

"You're rarely unsure of anything, are you?"

"It makes life much simpler."

Her name was Julia Tinsley. She was an artist, a photographer. Now and then, she said, she helped Jay Steiner out with the artist exchange program.

"Where are you from?" she asked.

"Everywhere. Nowhere," he told her—the standard answer. "I was an Army brat."

"What are you? Half-*nisei*?"

"I'm Hawaiian," he said.

"What does that mean?"

"Sorry?"

"You're native Hawaiian? You have Hawaiian blood?"

He looked at her, trying to determine if she was being combative or merely curious. She was asking all the questions he normally despised—*Where are you from? What are you?*, code for *You don't look like a real American*—but he decided to give her the benefit of the doubt. "I'm half and half," he said. "White and Korean. I grew up in Hawaii."

"Which island?"

"Oahu."

"Did you surf? You look like a surfer."

He laughed—it was such a stereotype. "Yeah, I surfed."

"Which breaks? Town or country?"

Startled she knew enough to ask, he said, "All the ones near Haleiwa. Lani's, Jocko's, Leftovers. Sometimes in the summer we'd drive into town to Kaiser's and Bowls. Did you live in Hawaii? Did you surf?"

"No, it's just something I've always loved to watch. An old boyfriend. Were you any good?"

"I ripped. I was a fucking marvel."

"Oh, you like yourself, don't you?" she said. "I can tell you're trouble."

He snagged two glasses of wine from a waiter passing with a tray and gave her one. She took a sip, grimaced, and set the glass down on the buffet table.

"What about you?" he asked. "Where are you from?"

"Boston."

"Ah," he said. He knew Boston, and an image of Julia Tinsley began to coalesce before him, an Eastern Seaboard, old-money image of private schools and Block Island vacations and Brahmin privilege.

"Did you know we're being surveilled?" she said. "Rather intently, I might add."

He thought she meant Jorge and Benny, who were standing in the corner, but she was referring to Sara and her friend Marly, who were across the room.

"The blonde your girlfriend?"

"I wouldn't call her my girlfriend," Tom said.

"Does she know that?"

"We've been going out a little. Very casually. She's leaving for the States in a couple of days." Across the room, Sara waved to Tom unhappily, and he waved unhappily back.

"She doesn't at all seem like your type," Julia said.

"What's my type?"

She looked at him, sizing. "I don't know. You're not one of those men who gets all tender and sentimental, are you?"

"No."

"Good. I hate those kind of men. No, I think you like women who give you a hard time, who are a bit mean and unpredictable. You're a lot like my husband that way. You see him in the corner? The forlorn one?"

Tom was disappointed to hear she was married. She wore two modest silver rings on the right hand, one on the left, but none had

been immediately recognizable as a wedding ring. He looked to
the corner of the lounge, and he was surprised to see her husband
was Japanese. He was a handsome, thin man, and he did look forlorn—absolutely miserable.

"I better get back to him," she said. "Although I don't think he's
missed me."

Tom watched her move across the floor, everything about her
unhurried, long, and athletic.

Jorge joined Tom beside the buffet table with Benny in tow. "Sara
hasn't left yet, and here you are, trolling already," Jorge said.

"I like to be prepared."

"What is it with you and blondes, *primo*?"

"It happens to be my favorite color."

"She's married."

"I know," Tom told him. "Her husband's a *nisei*?"

Benny, eating Tom's forgotten shrimp, said, "*Sansei*. His name's
Vincent Kitamura." They watched Julia Tinsley and Vincent
Kitamura exit the lounge and make their way toward the eleva-
tors. "He's a spook in Econ," Benny said, which was not terribly
shocking news. Other than in Moscow, there were more CIA officers in Tokyo than at any other post, most of them posing as FSOs
in the Economic and Political sections.

"If you're smart, you'll stay away from her," Jorge said.

It was sensible advice, and, left to his own devices, Tom might
have listened to it, despite being more than a little intrigued with
Julia Tinsley. She was spirited and intelligent. She bristled with all
kinds of potential for fun and unbecoming conduct. She was
everything someone like Sara was not. She had mystery about her.
Sophisticated and cultured. Maybe a little spoiled. She was also
beautiful. But Tom told himself he would, for once, behave. He
would, for once, check his impulse for self-sabotage. He would,
for once, keep out of trouble. It was a fine commitment, a very

honorable resolution, that fell apart immediately at the end of the month, when he came home to his apartment in Harris House and found a handwritten note under his door. "Let's go out for a drink sometime," Julia Tinsley had scrawled, "before the whole summer slips away."

THREE

THE FIRST thing Kenzo Ota noticed was the refrigerator. It had been turned off when he had inspected No. 401, but the next weekend, when he moved into the apartment, he turned on the refrigerator, and it whirred and cranked to life with an awful racket. He was flabbergasted. It had a *compressor.* Yet this refrigerator was identical to the one in the other apartment on the third floor, and he hadn't noticed it at all. The compressor kicked up in twenty-minute cycles with a loud click, then kept getting louder with weird whizzes and buzzes and whines for seven minutes, then shut off with another click. It was clearly defective. He called Miss Saotome.

"The previous tenant never made a complaint about it," she told Kenzo.

"I'm very sorry," he said.

She agreed to have a repairman come over for a look, and the next night, when Kenzo got home, he found a maintenance report taped to the front of the refrigerator. He was pleased the problem had been addressed so quickly, until he read the report. The repairman wrote that he had checked the compressor and the evaporator fan and the condenser and the coils, and had concluded that everything was "normal."

"If I may be presumptuous," Kenzo told Miss Saotome on the telephone, "I don't believe the repairman was here long enough. You know how these repair people can be. He probably didn't have time to wait for the compressor and the fan to go on."

"It's such a small refrigerator," Miss Saotome said. "How noisy can it be?"

"My point *exactly*," Kenzo said, a little too excitedly. "There must be something wrong with it."

She would send for the repairman again, she said.

The following night, there was another maintenance report taped to the refrigerator, with the same diagnosis: "normal."

"I was with the repairman in the apartment this time," Miss Saotome told Kenzo when he called to protest.

"You waited for the compressor?"

"Twice."

"You didn't think it was noisy?"

"No."

"You didn't hear the buzzing and whining?"

"Those are normal refrigerator sounds," she said. "Refrigerators make noise."

"The refrigerator in the other apartment didn't make those noises."

She was silent for a good ten seconds. "Mr. Ota," she said at last, "perhaps this building location is bad for you?"

"Excuse me?"

"Perhaps you would be happier somewhere else with a more convenient location?"

Shut up or move out, Kenzo understood her to be saying. "The location is fine."

"You like the apartment in general, then?"

"Yes."

"I'm so glad," Miss Saotome said. "Sometimes it's unsettling, being in a new place, but you get used to things. Air conditioners, for instance, or refrigerators. It may seem abnormal now, but I'm sure you'll get used to it. Wouldn't you agree?"

"I suppose," he said, not agreeing with her at all.

"Are you recently divorced, Mr. Ota?"

"Yes," Kenzo said, although it had been fourteen years since Yumiko had left him. It was such a stigma—divorce. In Japan, the divorced were called *batsu-ichi*. One strike against them.

"Ah, I see now," Miss Saotome said. "And you don't have a girl-friend?"

"No."

"Perhaps you need a hobby," Miss Saotome said. "Do you have any hobbies?"

"No." This was not entirely true. He did not have any *current* hobbies, but over the years he had made dozens of attempts to acquire one, hundreds of hours spent in *bunka* or culture centers, taking one class after another: golf, drawing, painting, piano, guitar, tennis, cooking, rock climbing, wine appreciation, ballroom dancing.

"I'll try to think of something suitable for you," Miss Saotome said.

■   ■   ■

IT WAS amazing that *gaijin* could not smell themselves, the *bataku-sai*—butter stink—they emanated from eating so much dairy. The odor overwhelmed Kenzo as he stepped through the security door of the American Embassy in Toranomon. The Marine guard, a massively built, pink-faced jarhead who was the offending source, handed him a visitor's pass, and Kenzo hurried off to the Consular Section, trying to suck in fresh air. Only there wasn't any fresh air in the nine-story building, just recycled air conditioning, which made his skin prickle and itch.

A Mrs. Fujiwara greeted him at the American Citizens Services desk, and then he was led into an interior office and introduced to Tom Hurley, a young bureaucrat who didn't know any Japanese and who looked too dumb and pretty to do anyone any good. What was he? An *ainoko*—a half-breed? Hawaiian? A surfer, no doubt.

There was some initial confusion. Hurley kept speaking to Mrs. Fujiwara and waiting for her to interpret his remarks into Japanese for Kenzo, until finally Kenzo explained that his English was proficient enough to make out what Hurley was saying. The three of them had a little chuckle over the misunderstanding, although Kenzo remained puzzled. He was certain that he had dealt with Mrs. Fujiwara several times before, and she should have remembered him, saving them the embarrassment.

Tom Hurley had called the Metropolitan Police Department about a missing American girl named Lisa Countryman. "There doesn't seem to be anything out of the ordinary," Hurley said. "In all likelihood she simply decided to skip out of town. But we checked with all the airlines, and she wasn't on any of the flights to Hong Kong that week—or to anywhere else."

"Maybe she depart later or take ferry, or maybe ship freight. You said you call Immigration?"

"They found a record of entry at Narita on March 13, but no record of departure for her."

Kenzo wasn't surprised. The departure cards collected at ports weren't usually inputted onto the Immigration Bureau's computer systems for quite a while. He had become familiar with the workings of the Immigration Bureau of late. "She was on ninety-days tourist visa?" he asked.

"Yes."

"Time make sense, yes? She leave Japan almost exact time visa expire. She is require to leave."

"Well, not everyone does what they're required to, do they?" Hurley told him.

The Japanese—the vast majority of them—did, Kenzo thought, but not Americans. *Gaijin* always tried to skirt the rules, and Americans were the worst, believing they were above Japanese laws. "You think Lisa Countryman still in Japan? You think something happen to her?"

"No, nothing like that," Hurley said. "I'm sure she took off to Hong Kong. I just wish we had some confirmation. I'd like to square everything away and close the file."

"You know young people. They come and go with freedom. Maybe confirmation never be possible."

"I suppose that's true," Hurley said.

They rose and shook hands and bowed.

"There doesn't seem to be a case here, does there?" Hurley said.

"No," Kenzo said happily. "I do not think so."

■　　　■　　　■

HE WAS an Assistant Inspector in Criminal Investigations, but he got all the cases that no one else wanted, all the shit cases involving foreigners—petty thefts and drunk-and-disorderlies and runarounds like this one involving Lisa Countryman, who would unquestionably turn up safe and sound somewhere in a few months, another globe-trotting American white-girl slut in search of sex and adventure with no regard to anyone else—he got these cases because he had spent three years in America and his English was fluent, absolutely flawless. Or so he believed.

From age eleven to fourteen, Kenzo had lived in St. Louis, Missouri. In 1953, his father, a chemistry professor, had taken his wife and young son with him to Washington University on an extended research fellowship, and Kenzo's years there had been the most miserable of his life. The American schoolkids had teased him mercilessly about his broken English and his slanty-eyed dogeater tapehead Jap looks. "We dropped the bomb on you," they had gloated. Moreover, his parents had not gotten along. Something had happened—a secret they never revealed to Kenzo—but in St. Louis, his mother had mysteriously disappeared for two months, and Kenzo always suspected she had left his father for another research fellow, Stewart Lavallee, carried away by some half-baked notion of romance and passion until she came to her senses and returned to them.

They moved back to Japan, but the damage was irreparable. His parents didn't speak to each other for weeks at a time. The tension was often more than Kenzo could bear, halting whenever he heard the slightest noise. He waited for an argument, waited for one of them, his mother, his father, to leave for good, for them to separate, divorce, yet they never did. They aged quickly—they looked so *old*—and both died prematurely at sixty-two and fifty-nine.

Reentering the Japanese educational system in Kobe, Kenzo had been ridiculed more than he had been in America. He now spoke Japanese like a *gaijin*. He had difficulty catching up in school, despite attending *juku,* cram school. He wasn't at all dumb, but he wasn't book-smart with all the rote memorization required for the college entrance exams, so after high school, he went straight into the police academy in Tokyo, and he advanced steadily from Patrolman to Sergeant to Assistant Inspector.

Ironically, his English got him the elite assignment to Criminal Investigations and transferred to Azabu-sho, where so many foreigners resided and congregated, but soon afterward his career stalled, other detectives continually promoted ahead of him. He didn't know exactly why—maybe his divorce, his childless state. The final indignity had come this past April, when his section chief, Inspector Shiro Kunichi, had asked him to move to a window desk, relegating him to *madogiwazoku,* one of the "window people."

In Criminal Investigations, as in most Japanese offices, your status determined where you sat in the room. The OLs, or office ladies, were closest to the door. The detectives were in the center around gray metal desks that were bunched together—the farther from the door, the higher the rank—with the section chief at the head of the room. But there was a tributary to this flow, a shameful eddy into which those who were being bumped off the promotion ladder settled. These lost souls were condemned to dishonorable idleness near the windows, so isolated they could stare outside all day long if they wished.

Kunichi had moved Kenzo aside to make room for a new Assistant Inspector, Iso Yamada, a slick, cocky, good-looking college kid who was an intolerable show-off. He instantly became everyone's best friend, the section's favorite son. Kenzo despised him. He despised his witty repartee and his goofy imitations and his stupid jokes. Kenzo couldn't tell a joke to save his life—not that he hadn't tried to learn. He had gone to joke school, ten sessions with a bunch of hapless salarymen who glumly recited mimeographed jokes as if delivering eulogies.

Kenzo didn't have a sense of humor—he knew this. His wife, Yumiko, had continually reminded him of the deficiency. His other failing was alcohol, or his inability to drink it. He had the flushing response, which afflicted half of the Japanese population in various degrees of severity, due to a missing enzyme. Kenzo's flushing response was aggravated by allergens. One or two small glasses of beer, and his face would flame beet-red, his heart would palpitate, he'd sweat, he'd become nauseous, his head would pound, his skin would bump into hives, and his lips and throat would swell. One time at a bar with a group of detectives, while trying to tell a joke from his joke-school repertoire, Kenzo had vomited on himself—a lush stew of soybeans and fried eel and rice—and then, aghast, knowing this would happen but unable to stop it, he had turned and thrown up on Inspector Kunichi's lap.

Thereafter he would limit himself to a few sips and just *pretend* to be drunk, but the other detectives could easily tell he was faking it, and gradually he was no longer invited out with them. Getting drunk together was essential to building a bond of friendship and obligation. The Japanese were *yasashi*, wet. They stuck to one another in tribes like wet, glutinous rice. They were warm, gentle, emotional, whereas Westerners were dry and hard and individualistic, like their rice, which fell apart into solitary grains. Why would anyone choose to be like that? Kenzo always wondered.

Yet Yumiko had chafed at the strictures of Japanese society, and she had said Kenzo epitomized all that was wrong with the country, calling him a humorless, passionless, sexist wimp. She loved America and its supposed ideals, and immediately after their divorce she immigrated to Los Angeles in pursuit of them. Equality. Independence. Individualism. A load of crap, Kenzo thought. If the American Dream was so wonderful, why was there so much crime in the US, and drugs, and racism, and divorce? Everything was corrupt, the people self-centered, lazy, mean, *nihirisuto*, nihilistic. Kenzo often thought how lonely it would be to be an American, and he was terrified of such a fate. He longed to be wet again, part of the tribe. He didn't want to be different. He wanted, more than anything, to be accepted as *hei-bon*—normal.

■　　　■　　　■

HE NEVER heard from Yumiko, didn't know what had become of her, until this past May. He saw a woman who looked exactly like her—older, sure, but a dead ringer—in the window of Charleston & Sons, a restaurant in Roppongi down the alley from Tony Roma's. Dressed nicely, she was having coffee with several *gaijin* women, shopping bags at their feet.

Kenzo checked with the Immigration Bureau. Was it really possible that Yumiko had returned to Japan? Was she visiting, or had she come back for good? It wasn't easy finding out, because she had changed her last name. She was no longer using Kenzo's name, Ota, nor her maiden name, Tanizaki. She was using an American name, Marabelli. According to Immigration, Yumiko Marabelli was an American citizen from Atlanta, Georgia, and she had been issued a one-year work visa under the category of Legal/Accounting Services. She put in three days a week as an accountant, a CPA, for IBM. She was married to Doug Marabelli, who had a one-year work visa under the category of Investor/Business Manager. He was a development director for Procter & Gamble. Appended to Yumiko and Doug Marabelli's applications was one for Simon Marabelli, who had been issued a one-year dependent visa under the category of Unmarried Minor Child.

But Simon Marabelli was not, as expected, a *haafu*, Kenzo saw as he stood outside the Marabellis' *mansion* in Higashi-Azabu one day. He looked to be full-blooded Japanese, about thirteen years old. Doug Marabelli was not the father. After verifying Simon's birthday, Kenzo had a very good idea who the father might be.

Simon was born seven and a half months after Yumiko had left for the United States, almost nine months to the day after Kenzo and Yumiko had last made love, on his final night in their house, a terrible, shameful night during which he had begged and tormented her into having sex with him. Unless she had had an affair—and he was certain she had not, for he would have surely known about it—Simon was his son.

The resemblance was really uncanny. Simon had the same narrow, long face, the same high forehead, the same widely spaced eyes. He was already relatively tall, like Kenzo, and he had Kenzo's lanky limbs. He was the spitting image of his father, except for one rather large, glaring difference. Kenzo had always been rail-thin, as was Yumiko, but Simon was fat. Roly-poly, flesh-bobbling fat. Trundling, waddling fat. Wheezing, heaving, lard-ass fat. American fat. What had they been feeding him over there in Atlanta, Georgia? Kenzo could only imagine. Mounded, gelatinous meals, like chicken-fried steak, mashed potatoes, white biscuit gravy. Kenzo had a complex about fat people, developed during his years in Missouri. He was afraid of fat people. He was also afraid of loud people, and uneducated people, and black people.

Simon needed discipline, the kind of discipline only a father could provide. Obviously Doug Marabelli—with his laid-back inattention, his bland, corporate American good looks, his colonial fetish for Oriental women—was worthless as a role model. Simon needed Kenzo to teach him about self-control, courage, strength, denial, all the things that he would require to protect himself from being taunted and bullied and outcast. This was why Yumiko had brought him to Tokyo. Kenzo was sure of it. This was why she had chosen Higashi-Azabu, just blocks from the police station, for them to live. She wanted Simon to find the proper direction for his life, learn where he came from, who he was. She wanted Simon to meet his father and get to know him.

Of course, she had yet to contact Kenzo, and he could understand her trepidation. It was monumental, what faced her, informing Kenzo that he had a son, and who knew what she had told Simon up to this point, or Doug Marabelli, for that matter. Yet Kenzo was surprisingly calm about the situation. He felt a certain inevitability that everything would come together, that there was no reason to force things.

So he stood across the street from the Marabellis' *mansion* only two or three times a week during lunch, and only two or three times a week after work, and only every other Saturday and Sunday, and only for five or ten minutes at a time, a mere flyby, very casual, nothing obsessive, just to see if by chance he could catch them coming or—even better—going, and if by chance he did, he would follow them.

One rainy Saturday afternoon, he happened to spot Yumiko and Simon walking out of their apartment building and scurrying up the hill under umbrellas. Simon was carrying a tennis racket and a duffel bag, going to tennis lessons, apparently. There were indoor courts at the posh, members-only Tokyo American Club in Azabudai, near the base of the Tokyo Tower, right next door, in an ironic coincidence, to the Soviet Embassy. At the entrance to the club, Yumiko said goodbye to Simon. She was going shopping, most likely. She had always been something of a clotheshorse, and she had transferred her preoccupation with fashion onto her son, dressing him in a pink Lacoste polo shirt, khaki pants, and Topsiders. It wasn't a good look for him. The shirt was bursting at the seams. He had breasts, and his nipples were visible. He was perspiring heavily just from the short walk to the club.

Yumiko tugged on the collar of his shirt so it stood upright, kissed him on the cheek, and turned him toward the door. After he entered the lobby, she marched off. A minute later, Simon emerged, checked that his mother was gone, and then, with almost a spring in his step, walked up Gaien-Higashi-dori to the

Roppongi Plaza Building, where he took the elevator to Nicola's, an Italian restaurant on the third floor.

There, Kenzo watched Simon, his poor, neglected boy, raid the buffet table. It was all-you-can-eat at Nicola's, and he loaded piles of pasta and veal marsala and meatballs and lasagna on his plate. He slurped and chewed, and the look on his face—red sauce smeared around his mouth—was nothing short of ecstasy. It broke Kenzo's heart.

▪   ▪   ▪

ALL OF a sudden, Kenzo could hear the people above him in No. 501. He could hear them—very distinctly, unmistakably—fucking. He first noticed them one night at 1:33 a.m., when he was lying on his back on his futon, sweating from the humidity, kept awake by the hums and buzzes and whines of the refrigerator, audible even with his bedroom door closed. There were some soft thuds from the ceiling, innocuous in the beginning, they could have been anything, then they got faster, harder, quite undeniably this was fucking, no-amateurs-allowed, slap-belly, sopped-juiced, eye-white, plunge-and-lunge, arrive-alive fucking, and it kept going, and going—how long could they keep this up? Were they machines? Were they some sort of *über*-copulators? Finally, he heard a woman moan—*uh, uh, uhhhh*—and then it stopped. Only to begin again the next morning at seven a.m. on the dot, apparently commencing with the alarm clock. "Are you *kidding* me?" Kenzo said to the ceiling.

Those weren't the only noises. Over the next few nights, he could also hear footsteps, heels clacking. It seemed that No. 501 had hardwood floors instead of the linoleum and tatami in Kenzo's apartment. The slightest impact resonated, and there were plenty of them, thumps and smacks and squeaks that sounded like marbles or billiard balls dropping and rolling, bricks being laid, furniture being dragged, lumber being hammered and sawed. What were they *doing* up there? It was maddening. It was unbearable.

"No one's ever complained about it before," Miss Saotome said on the phone.

"I'm very sorry," he told her, peeved by the difficulty he had had reaching her. Her old number had been disconnected. She had moved to a new house without informing her tenants, it seemed.

"It's curious to me, because the building is made of concrete," she said. "You shouldn't be able to hear anything. Can you hear the person next door to you?"

"No."

"Only above."

"Yes."

"And just footsteps and objects knocking and rolling and such, no stereo or TV, no voices, nothing like that?"

"That's correct," he said.

"Are you sure?"

"Yes." It seemed indelicate to say he heard sex noises.

"I see," she said. "Mr. Ota, I sense that you are under a great deal of stress. Do you feel you are under stress?"

"Not particularly."

"I feel you must be. You might not even realize it, how stressed you are. But fortunately there are methods to relieve a man's stress. As a detective, you must be familiar with some of these methods."

"Excuse me?"

"Would you like me to arrange something for you?"

"Excuse me?" What was she proposing? A prostitute? Was she insane?

"It would be no trouble for me," she said.

He hung up the telephone, and within seconds he heard a

machine gun firing a fusillade of shots. No, not a machine gun. His upstairs neighbors were ripping apart the floor with a jackhammer. No, it was tap-dancing, no, the *flamenco*. He was sure of it. He had almost taken a class in the flamenco at the *bunka* center. Who *were* these people? He had to find out. He needed to know what they *looked* like.

The next Sunday, early in the morning, he climbed the stairs of the adjoining building and found a spot on a walkway where he had a vantage of No. 501. Foolishly he didn't bring anything to read, or to eat, or to drink, and once in a while he needed to go to the bathroom, so there were times, as he went back and forth to his apartment, when his neighbors could have ducked out on him. He waited all day, a deadly boring stakeout, during which he had the opportunity to consider many things, including the fact that Yumiko had been his last lover, so, unbelievably, it had been fourteen years since he had had sex. Finally, at sunset, he saw who it was who was living above him, making all that noise, fucking and dancing. It was a woman— young, skinny, stylishly dressed, with puffed and layered *chapatsu* hair. It was Miss Saotome. That was why her phone number had been changed. She had moved into No. 501.

He watched her take the elevator down just one floor to the fourth floor, his floor, and he could hear the elevator *ding* all the way from the adjoining building. He saw her slip something under an apartment door, his door. After she left, Kenzo ran down the stairs of the adjacent building and up the stairs of his apartment building. Under his door, he found a namecard: "Keiko Saotome," it said. "Romance Consultant," and underneath, in English, "Vital Energy Health Prana Renew."

▪ ▪ ▪

A FEW evenings later, Kenzo stood outside on his apartment walkway with a bundle of dried reeds. It was *Bon,* the Buddhist Festival of the Dead, in Tokyo. By tradition, you were supposed to return to your hometown for *Bon,* pay your respects at the family grave, then go to the family house with your relatives and reunite with the spirits of your deceased ancestors. But Kenzo never went back to his hometown of Kobe anymore. Few of his relatives were still in the city, the family home had been sold, and the crowds on the trains and planes and roadways made the trip excruciating.

Kenzo believed in traditions, however. As a small compensatory gesture, he lit his bundle of reeds on the walkway and let them burn for a few minutes—a *mukaebi,* a welcoming fire. Then he went inside his apartment and waited for the arrival of the souls of the dead.

FOUR

EVERYTHING WENT wrong from the beginning. The
flight on March 13 from San Francisco to Tokyo had
been interminable, fourteen hours, and then at Narita Airport,
bleary-eyed and jet-lagged, Lisa Countryman said the wrong thing
to the immigration official. He asked where she would be staying
in Japan, and she forgot. She had been told that specifying a *gaijin*
house was a dead giveaway she planned to work illegally in the
country, and she had written the name of a modest hotel on the
entry card, but she had forgotten its name.

They took her to a side room, where two immigration officials
kept asking her, "What purpose you come to Japan?" and she kept
repeating, "Vacation. Tourist," until at last she remembered the
name of the hotel, and they let her go to baggage claim, where she

waited forty-five minutes, only to glean that her two suitcases were missing.

She caught a bus to Tokyo Station, and by then it was past two in the morning and the trains and subways had stopped. She had to flag down a taxi, and the driver got lost going to the Friendship Guest Home in Meguro. When they finally found it and she trudged inside, exhausted, just wanting to collapse into a bed and sleep, no one was there to greet her. Lisa didn't know which room was hers. She tried to fall asleep on a frayed couch in the lounge, huddling underneath her coat, but people—drunk, cavorting— kept banging into the house into the wee hours, and then soon after daybreak another crew of residents awoke and began kicking around the kitchen.

Lisa forced herself to get up—at least she could find out from the early birds where the house manager was—but by then it was too late. Everyone had already left for work. She went into one of the bathrooms, took a shower, using someone's shampoo and soap, and then dried herself with someone's towel, which reeked, and then, reluctantly, brushed her teeth with someone's nubby toothbrush, and then dressed again in the same clothes she'd worn for twenty-nine straight hours.

From the pay phone in the hallway, she called the airlines, who told her that her suitcases were presently in Minneapolis, but should be delivered within forty-eight hours.

She took a walk around the neighborhood, strolling down winding, narrow back streets that could barely accommodate the widths of cars, and then ventured out to the main boulevards, which were not that different from avenues in any other big city, buildings and traffic and stores, all homogenized and sanitized and Americanized, with more Kentucky Fried Chickens and McDonald's than she could count. Yet she was exhilarated. She could read the *kanji* and *hiragana* on signs. She could converse with shopkeepers. All the Japanese classes she had taken were no longer abstractions. It seemed a miracle, almost a transmigration. She was actually in Japan.

Despite her excitement, jet lag overcame her, and she returned to the *gaijin* house and took a long nap on the couch, a deep, dreamless, black slumber. It was still daylight when she awoke, and a man was staring at her. He was sitting in a chair opposite the couch, eating a bowl of cereal. He was around thirty, she guessed, with a ruddy face and long brown hair parted in the middle.

"Hello," he said. British accent.

"Hello."

"What's your name?"

She told him, and then asked, "Yours?"

"Tony Somers," he said.

The possessive TS, she thought. In the bathroom, several ablutionary items had been labeled with pieces of paper and tape, marked "TS" or, more insistently, "Hands Off!—TS!" She had used TS's shampoo and conditioner—nice, sweet-smelling, expensive stuff. He clearly had a thing for his hair, which she had to admit was in grand shape, lots of body and shine.

"You're American?" he asked.

She nodded.

"Native American?"

"What?"

"You got a little of that Rita Coolidge thing going for you. What are you? Part Cherokee?"

"Sure," Lisa said, irritated. Whatever floated his boat. It was easier not to argue. "Do you know where the house manager is?"

"Quit. Had a bit of a nervous breakdown. Come on, I'll show you what's free."

He had her follow him upstairs, and he slid open the doors to two empty rooms, telling her to take her pick. The owner, Takagi, would probably be by later that night to collect her rent. In the meantime, was she hungry? Did she want to join him for a bite?

He took her to a restaurant called Tonki's near Meguro Station, a cheap, popular *tonkatsu* place with a line of customers waiting on the staircase, from which they could watch cooks in the open kitchen, dipping the pork cutlets in batter and flour. The *tonkatsu* came with shredded cabbage and rice and *miso,* all for nine hundred yen, and it was delicious. Lisa was tempted to have another plate, but Tony Somers was filling her up with beer, ordering bottle after bottle.

He was trying hard to chat her up. He told her he was from Leeds, and he was in Tokyo freelancing as a computer programmer for buckets of yen, and also, he said, picking up occasional jobs as a model, which Lisa found difficult to swallow, since he was not exactly good-looking. And he had a nasty smell—what *was* that?—and then she remembered a bottle of cologne—no, it had been a *can,* an aerosol can—in the bathroom labeled "TS." How could someone so particular about his hair be so cheap with his cologne? Really, though, she was too tired and unattracted to him to care. She nodded and smiled while he chattered away, and after they paid the check, she asked to go back to the *gaijin* house.

Once there, they ran into Teiji Takagi, the owner, who was jovial and enterprising. For a small deposit and a monthly service fee, he lent her a towel and freshly laundered sheets and a comforter for her futon. When he noticed she didn't have any bags, he unlocked a closet and let her select a few items of clothing from the stacks of neatly folded garments on the shelves—discards from previous tenants, evidently—selling them to Lisa at bargain-basement prices. His own little thrift shop.

She washed up in the bathroom—at least she had been able to buy a toothbrush and paste and shampoo during her morning walk—and although it was early still, not yet nine o'clock, she went to her room and laid out her bedding. The tatami room was ridiculously small, but she was happy to be settled finally, thinking that maybe things would work out for her in Japan, maybe she would find what she came for, and she slept soundly for the next fifteen hours.

▪   ▪   ▪

THE STOREFRONT for Rocket America was plastered with posters of young Japanese tourists at famous US landmarks: Waikiki Beach, the Golden Gate Bridge, Mount Rushmore, the Statue of Liberty. It looked very much like a travel agency, which was not accidental, Lisa soon discovered.

On the Monday after her arrival, she reported to the school director, Seiji Waru, who openly appraised her body, staring at her breasts and legs. "You'll do very well here, I think," he said. "You'll be very popular."

She gave him a copy of her passport, her college diploma, her transcripts, and two passport-size photos—all the things the recruiter in California had told her to bring. Seiji Waru would take the documents to the Immigration Bureau and sponsor her application for a work visa. In about three weeks, Waru told Lisa, her Certificate of Eligibility would be approved, and then she could take the weekend ferry from Fukuoka to Pusan, South Korea. This was the process, as silly as it seemed. Companies didn't want to go through the visa application procedure until potential employees were actually in the country, but once foreign workers were in Japan on a tourist visa, they had to leave to a Japanese consulate in a third country to get a work visa issued.

They each signed two copies of her employment contract, and then Waru told her she would start teaching the next morning.

"But I don't have my visa," she said.

"Oh, that's just a formality," he said. "We do it all the time. We just call it training. You're training. No one will be the wiser. Tell me, though, do you have any shorter skirts?"

She got the gist of Rocket America's rinky-dink operations soon enough. The school was a scam. Whenever anyone wandered into Rocket America, usually to inquire about round-trip airfares and package deals, the poor sap was seated at one of the two front desks and subjected to a hard-core two-hour sales pitch from Seiji Waru or his assistant. They tried to get people to buy as many lesson tickets in advance as possible, and one of their tactics was to offer an introductory course at a discount. Lisa and another *gaijin* girl, a leggy American blonde named Harper Boyd, taught these introductory lessons, which amounted to nothing more than following a series of exercises from an expensive textbook, practicing tourist scenarios at airports, hotels, stores, and restaurants. Harper Boyd was some sort of ringer, brought in before the real term began. She was indifferent toward Lisa, not saying a word, really, other than suggesting that she tone down her Japanese. Lisa began to understand that her Japanese wasn't as good as she had believed, that it sounded peculiar—an amalgam of stiff college Japanese and baby talk from when she was four, the last time she was in Japan. Owing to politeness, no one thus far had corrected her. Anyway, Harper Boyd said, Lisa didn't want the students to think she was a non-native English speaker, to whom they would be unwittingly reassigned once the introductory period was completed, once they had bought six months of lesson tickets. At that point, they would likely be given a Malaysian, Filipino, or Hindi teacher, someone who should have been enrolled in concomitant ESL courses. The old bait and switch. If students quit at that point, it was fine with Seiji Waru. He *wanted* people to quit. The lesson tickets were nonrefundable.

For three weeks, Lisa played along, teaching her classes. As unnecessary as any experience proved to be, she was actually a good instructor, having run several discussion sections of her own as a TA at Berkeley, where she was a Ph.D. candidate in cultural anthropology. She was in Tokyo—at least this was what she told people—to do research for her dissertation, which didn't quite have a topic yet, something or another about Japan as a patriarchal society and the subjugation of women, the dismissal of individual worth over the cohesion and homogeneity of the group, the sad, brutal reign of conformity.

She didn't make any friends at Rocket America, and she stuck to herself at the *gaijin* house, where she remained one of the few women. She had to get out of there soon. Teiji Takagi had yet to hire another house manager, and the place was getting dirtier and more chaotic by the minute. Plus, Tony Somers had not been so paranoid after all with his little labels. People were always pilfering her toiletries in the bathroom and her food in the kitchen.

Walking around Tokyo was her only recreation, trying to become familiar with the city and its rhythms, taking photographs of what she found odd and exceptional. Ironically, what ended up drawing her eye were phrases of English—or approximations of English, hilariously mangled snatches of near-English, which *gaijin* called Engrish. They were everywhere. On billboards, clothing, vending machines. Slogans with wonderfully incoherent syntax, garbled spellings, and inadvertent double entendres. Lisa began a photo collection: *Spanking by the Sea* (a pencil case). *Snot House* (a T-shirt). *Hide with Spread Beaver* (a band name). *Boneractive Wear* (a store name). Once in a while, Lisa found not just phrases but whole paragraphs that were strangely profound: *Frais Espece. Formidable the rising ear. Be indignant. Perplexity. Be amazed* (a denim jacket). *As you, who has everyday vivify like a new air of a new epock. On your evertime of rest, let's stay by you* (a bakery wrapper). *Floated on the water. This form visited at the time of sleep, with one drop of a sweet tear, one day decaying into the soil* (a postcard).

She was often moved by these poetic pronouncements. Lately she had become perplexingly maudlin, given to sudden soil-decaying tears, reduced to the snot house, and as the cherry trees bloomed, the news showing maps of the blossoms approaching from the south like foliage, she succumbed to the Japanese proclivity for melancholia—*Join Melon Collie* (a pet store)—as they both celebrated and mourned the fragility of the flowers, their temporality. The Japanese believed in *mono no aware,* the essential sadness of things—that was how they defined their national character—and it made Lisa even more lonely. But she told herself she was used to loneliness. Besides, she wasn't in Japan to have a good time. She had work to do.

■   ■   ■

SHE CAUGHT the Keihin-Tohoku Line at Shinagawa and rode the train southwest to Yokohama. From the station, she took a taxi to the main gate of the Navy base, where she was met by the Public Affairs officer, a balding black man in his thirties. He asked her to fill out several visitor forms, and then put her in his car and drove her to North Pier.

"I'm afraid you're going to be disappointed," he told her. "All the port operations were handed over to the Army in 1978."

Lisa's father, Richard Countryman, had worked for the Navy's MSTS, the Military Sea Transportation Service. While stationed in Yokohama, he had been a logistics supply management specialist, responsible for the flow of cargo, troops, and equipment through the port. North Pier had been a key hub for supplies to Korea and then later to Vietnam.

They didn't bother getting out of the car at North Pier. The officer—his name was Omar Johnson—drove slowly through the installation, passing cargo ships, loading docks, cranes, petroleum tanks, warehouses, stacks of containers. Not much to see. Then he swung the car around and took them on a tour of the Navy base. "Everything's really at Yokosuka now," Omar said. "The Yokohama detachment's just housing. You remember where you used to live?"

She looked at him blankly.

"Negishi? Area Two? Bayside Courts?"

"I don't know."

"How old were you when you left?"

"I'd just turned four."

"This is your first time back to Japan?"

"Yeah."

"So nothing looks familiar."

"Not really."

They rode by houses and barracks, the base exchange, commissary, and cafeteria. They rode by the chapel, golf course, and baseball field, the bowling alley, library, and garage. Omar kept up a running patter on the landmarks: Lou Gehrig Stadium, the Bluffs, Bayview, Fire Engine Hill, Byrd Elementary. Nothing rang a bell. They were just names to Lisa—meaningless, a blur.

"You look sad," Omar said. "Don't be sad. I see this all the time. You're feeling a little lost these days. You were hoping, since you were born here, that visiting would give you a little insight, the whole *Roots,* Kunta Kinte thing. But the problem is you're a Navy brat, a Third Culture Kid. Every base was exactly like the last one. Like I said, I see it a lot. It's a common syndrome."

She stared at him. "What you're saying, then, is I'm a cliché."

"I'm sorry," Omar said, smiling. "I didn't mean to be presumptuous. Have you eaten lunch yet? There's actually a fantastic Chinatown here. My treat."

Lisa looked him over. He was average height, average weight, his only distinctive feature a regal ridge, like the top of a pitched roof, running down the middle of his bald head. She did find him presumptuous. He knew nothing about her, why she had come to Japan, why she was in Yokohama.

"Are you married?" she asked. She hadn't had any boyfriends in high school, and her relationships at university had been short and intermittent. Only recently, venturing outside academe, had she begun to attract the attention of older men, and she wasn't accustomed to it yet, suspicious of their intentions. It made her nervous and self-conscious, wary—as she had been all her life—of betrayal.

Omar kept smiling. "No," he said, "I'm not married."

"Oh."

"You almost sound disappointed."

"Are you just being friendly, or are you asking me out?"

"I guess I'm asking you out."

"Why?"

"What?"

"Why do you want to go out with me?"

He laughed helplessly. "Well, I think you're pretty. I think you're interesting."

"No, I'm not. I'm a blank page. You said so yourself. You said I don't know who I am. You said I'm lost, and I'm sad. By deduction, the only reason you'd want to go out with me is out of pity or exploitation."

"I don't think that's what I said. That's not what I meant, in any case. Is it because I'm black?"

Lisa was taken aback. "I'm part black," she said, depressed he couldn't tell.

"Really?"

"Yes."

"I'd never have guessed."

"My mother was Japanese."

"I'd never have guessed that, either."

"Now you're the one who sounds disappointed," she said.

"No, of course not."

"I need to get back to Tokyo," she told him.

The conversation left her quite sad. She was never black enough, or Oriental enough, or white enough, and everyone always felt deceived if she didn't announce her ethnic taxonomy immediately upon meeting them, as if not doing so were a calculated sin of omission, as if she were trying to pass. But just as often, when she did claim racial solidarity with a group, people didn't believe her, suspecting she was merely trying to appropriate the radical-chic color of the month.

For a while on the Berkeley campus, some biracial student activists had campaigned for miscegenation as the country's only hope and, with great merriment, had handed out leaflets that crooned "Cross-Fuck for a Better World!" They could joke, because they were blessed. They at least *looked* like they were mixed. They were identifiable as something. They could seek membership in a tribe. Multiple tribes. Lisa—appearing absent of color—was excluded from even applying.

■   ■   ■

SEIJI WARU called Lisa into his office. Her Certificate of Eligibility had finally been processed, and she could go to Pusan anytime to obtain her work visa, but they had had to make a few small, last-minute changes to her employment contract.

"This is very difficult for me to admit," he told her, "but the school is in a little money trouble. A temporary situation, I'm hoping, but it was necessary to cut some corners."

Lisa read the amended one-year contract. Waru had simply stapled the original last page with their signatures to two revised pages, but all three pages had now been stamped by the Immigration Bureau and therefore were unalterable. The number of hours per week she was guaranteed and her hourly wage had been reduced, and she was prohibited from taking on private students or any other part-time teaching work.

"Are you *joking*?" Lisa said.

"I hope you will appreciate the delicacy of the—"

"You can't get away with this."

"We really had no choice in the matter."

"I quit," Lisa said. "Effective immediately."

"Oh, I don't think you want to do that," Waru said. "The hiring season is over. All the schools have already started. It would be very difficult to find another position, you see."

He was probably right, which infuriated her even more. She desperately needed money. "I want to get paid for the classes I taught."

"Unfortunately you just missed the monthly pay cycle. If you continue, you'll be fully compensated with the next pay cycle."

"I'll go to the authorities."

"No, you won't. You've been working without a visa. You'll be deported. And if you think the authorities will side with you over me, you don't know Japan at all."

Lisa knew he was right about this, too, but she couldn't accept this, being trapped, manipulated, oh, the humiliation, and she said, "Fuck"—she held up the Certificate of Eligibility and tore it in half—"you"—and then she ripped the employment contract in half. It was the wrong thing to do, and it was irrevocable, but if nothing else, she could always be counted on, at every given opportunity, to do exactly the wrong thing.

▪   ▪   ▪

SHE WANTED to go out. She wanted to get drunk. She saw Tony Somers at the *gaijin* house, and asked if he wanted to accompany her.

"You'll have to twist my arm," he said.

He took her to Henry Africa's, across the street from the Roi

Building in Roppongi. It was a fern bar with a brass rail and a toy train that revolved on tracks near the ceiling, and it was filled with *gaijin,* excepting the odd pairs of Japanese girls.

"*Gaijin* groupies," Tony said.

"What?"

"It's a status symbol for Japanese girls to fuck a *gaijin.* You can be a complete wanker at home, but here, as long as you're a *gaijin,* you're a god."

"Oh, yeah?"

"Absolutely."

"You know this for a fact?"

"Bloody right. I'm a fucking god."

"I'm going to need more drinks," Lisa said.

After several more rounds, he convinced her to go to a disco nearby called Fou-Fou, a little hothouse painted all black with flashing strobes and a pumping bass, and she actually had fun there, dancing with Tony, high on the booze, the beat, momentarily released from her panic over how she would make enough money to stay in Japan, which led with some sort of far-fetched logic to lying in her room in the *gaijin* house with Tony on top of her, his mouth in a slobbering suction lock over hers, his hands jammed up the back of her shirt, furiously trying to unclasp her bra.

"Need some help there?" Lisa asked.

Grunting from the effort, he kept tugging and pulling.

"Are you sure you've done this before?" she laughed.

He gave up on undressing her and began undressing himself.

"So serious," she said. "Talk to me. Say something sweet."

"Shut up," he told her.

" 'Shut up'?"

He dropped his pants and yanked down his underwear, and the sight made her gasp. "Oh, my," she said. "What *is* that?" It was the strangest-looking erection she had ever seen, about eight inches long but only the width of a finger, sloped like a fillet knife, and pink, preternaturally smooth, nary a wrinkle or hair. "Is that *human*?" Lisa asked. "Did you get that in a transplant?"

Immediately his erection wilted. "Fucking slag," he said, slipping his pants back on.

"Oh, come on, I'm sorry," she said. "That was mean of me. I apologize. Come here. Just be sure to turn off the lights," she giggled.

"You're part wog or Paki, aren't you? Fucking wog," he said. "You piece of shit. You goddamn Paki tom."

"Hey," she said.

With difficulty, he stood up, brushed back his hair, and then spat at her, spray and spittle landing on her comforter and clothes and a little on her right chin.

"Hey!" she said.

He stumbled out into the hallway, bumped into the walls, and slammed shut the door to his room.

She had to get out of here. Find somewhere else to live. She went into the bathroom and washed her face. What was she going to do? she wondered. Where was she going to live? How would she find another job? What would she do for money? In the mirror she saw Tony's bottle of conditioner with its taped label: "TS." She took the conditioner downstairs to the kitchen and poured some cooking oil in it. She got a staple and bent it straight and in the bathroom tamped it down deep into his deodorant stick, and then borrowed his shaving cream and cologne and put them in her backpack with a sack of flour and a handful of large manila envelopes.

Tipsy, she walked across town to Shimbashi, losing her way several times but finally arriving outside of Rocket America. She pulled out one of the envelopes, filled it halfway with flour, slid the open flap underneath the front door, and stomped on the envelope with her foot, poofing a fine, powdery, messy mist into the office, covering the desks, the floor, the walls, the shelves. Beautiful. Like virgin snow. Then she took another envelope and sprayed shaving cream into it, flavored it with a dash of the awful cologne, slid it beneath the door, and stomped. Oh, it was like the backwoods of Vermont! So pretty! Shaving cream drooped and blooped over everything. She kept going, switching between the flour and the shaving cream, thinking about Seiji Waru opening the door in the morning, about Tony in the coming weeks, wondering why his hair was so lank, so flat, so greasy, why his armpits were itching and burning—pranks she had learned from her sister, Susan, who had inflicted them upon Lisa with gleeful malice, the bitch. She stomped, and stomped some more. This was terribly immature of her, she knew, but it made her feel better. It did.

CAFÉ NOUS was a *kissaten,* a coffeehouse, one of over ten thousand in Tokyo where you were welcome to linger the entire day over a single cup of coffee. This *kissaten* in Shinjuku was famed for the five hundred cup-and-saucer sets they displayed in illuminated cases on the wall, elegantly numbered and labeled with discreet signage. Royal Copenhagen, Meisen, Spode. You chose a number, and your coffee—Blue Mountain from Jamaica was the prized blend—was then served in the selected cup and saucer with pomp and precision.

What Tom needed, though, was a drink, not coffee. He was still shaking from the drive over. Julia Tinsley had an Alfa Romeo Spider, a zippy little green convertible, and she didn't seem to be familiar with the concepts of lanes and turn signals, whipping

between cars at will, racing through intersections, scaring the beje-
sus out of him.

"They don't serve alcohol here?" he asked.

"Sorry." She shook out her hair, which had been in a ponytail.
There was a light evening drizzle outside, another dreary, coolish
night, but she had kept the convertible top down. Her cheeks were
pinkened from the wind, and her skin was dewed. She looked
quite lovely. She had her own clean, classical sense of fashion,
wearing a sleeveless sage shirt and a tight gray skirt and black
pumps, allowing Tom a peek at her legs, which were trim, muscu-
lar, and tan.

"Do you always drive like that?" he asked.

"Like what?"

An old joke. They sat back and watched their waitress serve
their coffees. Julia asked her for two glasses of water, and then she
and Tom settled in at the table, stirring cream and sugar into their
cups.

"How long have you been in Tokyo?" he asked her. He was
nervous, a familiar state of agitation he'd become adept at hiding.

"Two years," she said. "Before this, we were in Paris for five."
She dropped sugar cubes into her coffee with the tiny silver
tongs—by the time Tom thought to begin counting, she had put in
at least four. The front door opened, and he caught a draft of
Julia's perfume, the same perfume she had worn at the reception,
and his head momentarily swirled. He breathed in to smell it
again, but it had already disappeared.

"*Je t'envie*," he said to her. "*Vôtre francais doit être très bien
maintainent.*"

She nodded, impressed by his fluency. "*Je le parlais couramment
avant que jáille là bas. Le vôtre n'est pas mal.*"

"*Je le peux truquer s'il faut*," he said. "I was a language major
in college."

"What else do you speak?" she asked, lighting a cigarette.

"Spanish, Portuguese, Italian, a little German. No Asian languages, which is why, of course, in their infinite wisdom, they transferred me here. I was supposed to have gone to Europe. Was it difficult to learn Japanese?"

"Oh, I don't know Japanese."

"But you were talking to the waitress."

"I just start everything with *excuse me—sumimasen—*and close with *please—kudasai—*and in the middle I transliterate English words. You just have to remember a few basic rules: turn your *l*'s to *r*'s and stick a vowel after each consonant. So *glass* becomes *gurasu,* and *blacklist* becomes—are you ready?—*burakku-risuto.*"

"That's funny."

"The numbers always throw me off, though. I said *gurasu futatsu* to the waitress, but I think I should have said *nisatsu* or *nihai.*"

They talked for a while about Tokyo, Julia giving him pointers on what to see and do, and then the conversation wended to a variety of subjects: the seasons, parks, Paris, architecture, swimming. She had been Ivy League champ in the 200 free at Princeton, where she had met Vincent Kitamura her senior year.

"He's always been CIA?" Tom asked.

"What do you mean? He's an Economic Officer," she said, then smiled. "He takes the whole thing very seriously—his oath of secrecy, his cover. People will call in the middle of the night, and whatever *nisei* name they ask for—Peter Okada, Bob Sasaki—I have to say, 'Just a minute, please,' and get Vincent. He goes out in disguise sometimes. He has a wig and makeup. He's out three or four nights a week. I only get to see him on Sundays."

"What does he do when he goes out?"

"A lot of drinking, from what I gather. Only Peter Okada never gets drunk. Peter Okada will pretend to be as looped as you are, and he'll get you to talk, but he'll be stone-sober and remember everything you say. Not that Vincent's ever told me a thing about what he actually does. I've had to piece together everything for myself."

"Do tell," Tom said, although, like everyone in the Foreign Service, he was already well versed with the CIA, no longer perplexed by the nonchalance—even boastfulness—with which spooks divulged their *modi operandi*.

"First of all," Julia said, "you know, don't you, they're called case officers, not agents? Agents are the people they recruit, who can be anyone, not just communists and politicians, but also business executives and journalists, even entertainers. They cast an indiscriminate net, get as many people in their pockets as they can, and hope a few of them will pay off. There's no master plan. The CIA's not particularly organized, you know." She cited Vincent's cover as an example. He was supposed to be an Economic FSO, yet they lived in a private apartment in Omotesando, not in the Grew House, and they had white civilian license plates on their cars instead of blue diplomatic ones. The covers were a joke, Julia said. If anyone really wanted to figure out who the spooks in the embassy were, all they had to do was check the embassy telephone directory. All these supposed FSOs had extensions with a prefix that didn't belong to the Economic or Political sections, wired as they were into the locked, unmarked doors on the sixth and seventh floors, where cameras were bolted overhead and you had to be buzzed in to gain entry.

"What do they do to recruit the agents?" Tom asked.

"They prey on people's vulnerabilities. They figure out where you're weak and what you covet. They flatter and cajole, they do little favors for you and give you gifts, maybe money. Once they gain your trust, once you're dependent on them, they begin asking for a little favor in return, or information, or a document. Not unlike a pimp or a drug dealer. It's very much a seduction."

"It must be hard to live a lie all the time. Betray people," Tom said.

"He's gotten very good at it," Julia said. "He's one of the most charming men I've ever met."

It was peculiar, the way she spoke of her husband, with both pride and resentment. Tom couldn't read her clearly, but there was an undeniable intensity of emotion there, and in his experience, that sort of attitude wasn't conducive to an inconsequential affair. Indifference was what he had been looking for.

He asked about her photography, and he quickly gathered that she was quite the star, not another embassy housewife indulging in a cute hobby. She taught at the ISA, the International School of the Arts, in Takadanobaba. She had gotten her master's of fine arts degree at the Rhode Island School of Design while Vincent had been at Harvard for grad school. In Paris, she had apprenticed with Jeannot Magritte, and she'd had two solo exhibitions there and one in Tokyo already, with another in the works for October.

Tom had little to say about his career in turn. After graduating from UCLA, he told her, he had taught high school French in the San Fernando Valley for three years before joining the Foreign Service, then had spent his first tour in São Paulo.

"How was that?" Julia asked.

"Terrible. Terrible. Did I mention terrible?"

But he loved Tokyo. Everything in Japan was so clean, modern, the people so polite. If anything, the country was *too* orderly and safe, Amcits—American citizens—rarely getting into real trouble. His biggest case thus far was turning out to be Lisa Countryman, and he told Julia a bit about it, although there hadn't been any recent developments. Hong Kong had ended up to be a dead end. Her sister, Susan, kept calling, and Tom kept apologizing to her, saying there wasn't much more he could do, it wasn't within his power, wasn't his job, to be an investigator. Whose was it? Susan

Countryman had asked. Tom had given her Kenzo Ota's phone number.

Tom's supervisor in ACS, Kimball Reeves, didn't want him to waste any more time on the case. Initially, he had asked, "Is her family well-to-do?" Tom had said he didn't know, and Reeves had said, "Countryman—that's a German name. Or maybe Pennsylvania Dutch. Probably not well-to-do," and then had instructed Tom to contact the police, but only as a formality.

Reeves would be deciding Tom's tenure in the Foreign Service in eighteen months, which was somewhat problematic, since he had been disinclined toward Tom from the start, skeptical about his fast-track transfer from São Paulo, how he had been able to breeze through two weeks of cursory ACS training in Roslyn, exempt from Japanese language classes. Reeves made no bones about his belief that Tom was benefiting from some sort of affirmative-action largesse. His response had been to ordain Tom as his personal minion, giving him all his work while he sequestered himself in his office all day long, chain-smoking and doing crossword puzzles. When things got slow, he liked to saddle Tom with one laborious task after another, making him compile statistical reports and procedural manuals that no one would ever open, much less read.

Tom revealed none of this to Julia in the coffeehouse, of course, just the barest facts about Lisa Countryman, so he was surprised when she showed interest in the case, asking, "You really don't have any leads?"

Tom shook his head.

"What was she doing in Tokyo?"

"Nothing, from what I can tell," he said.

"It doesn't look like there was any foul play involved?" she asked.

"No, nothing like that," he said. "I told you it wasn't very interesting."

The waitress brought her another coffee, and Julia dropped six sugar cubes into it. "I had a close friend who disappeared," she said. "A girl I knew at Princeton, Vicky Crow. One night, she didn't come back to the dorm. She just disappeared. There was an investigation, but they never found out what happened to her. No clues, no body, no witnesses. I don't know if she was murdered or if she ran off on her own. To this day, I keep expecting her to show up somewhere. It's not knowing that eats away at you."

Julia drove him back to the Grew House. In the parking lot, as they were saying their goodbyes, she squeezed Tom's hand, brushed a kiss across his cheek, and said, "Please let me know if anything turns up about the missing girl. It feels important for me to know."

■   ■   ■

THAT SUMMER, no one could stop talking about the weather, for while a brutal heat wave had choked the US for much of June and July, killing over twelve hundred people, here in Japan the temperature had been well below normal—the coldest summer in seventy-five years—and the rainy season had extended well into August. Some forecasters surmised that volcanic ash from Mount St. Helens was to blame, and others attributed the unusual weather to a persistent high-pressure system over the Sea of Lkhotsk. Whatever the case, the collective mood in Tokyo was getting gloomier with each cool, dank day.

Tom was in a funk himself. He kept thinking about Julia Tinsley. After the coffeehouse, he had seen her only once more, when she had taken him to Akihabara, the shopping haven for electronic goods and appliances, to buy a portable cassette player. Otherwise she seemed content to confine their relationship to the telephone, calling him at random times, occasionally late into the night, shooting the breeze and asking, incidentally, if the Lisa Countryman case was going anywhere.

Tom began to understand that the query was a psychological vehicle for her—a justifiable excuse for talking to him, a way to traverse the guilt of attraction. Undeniably, he thought, she was attracted to him, for right away she seemed to attach a gloss of secrecy to their association, a need to be surreptitious. He sensed, for instance, that it wasn't safe for him to call her in the evenings and on weekends, when her husband might answer, so he only tried to reach her during the workday or at her studio at the ISA, never leaving a message. Mostly, he waited for her to call him, and he tried not to sound overly grateful when she did.

He hung out with Jorge and Benny—more so now that Sara had left Japan. They went to movies at the Sanno Hotel, watched fireworks along the Sumida River, cruised Omotesando-dori, a wide, tree-lined boulevard that was often compared to the Champs-Élysées. And on his own, Tom embarked on a new project: architecture. In passing, he had told Julia he was a devotee of architecture, but when she'd asked about his favorite architects, he had been unable to name a single one, because, in truth, he knew nothing about architecture. He scoured bookstores in Jinbocho and set about memorizing a few bon mots like "articulated space" and *"béton brut"* and "neo-Aristotelian," should the subject ever arise again.

Anyone who saw him would have assumed he had been a diligent student, that he was a motivated autodidact, and this might have been so, were it not for his extremely short attention span. Yet he was good at mimicking a certain level of superficial competence—a Cliffs Notes approach to self-improvement—acquiring just enough to impress people, as long as he didn't take things too far, as long as he didn't, as he was strangely wont to, profess expertise when he had absolutely none. It was a compulsion that baffled him. Always he felt like a fraud. Always he felt on the verge of being exposed and thrown out the door.

He didn't really understand himself, his impulsiveness and coincident passivity. Occasionally he thought what had happened in São Paulo had changed him, had disrupted his development from the person he had wanted to be into the person he was now, but this seemed fallacious, or he would not have accepted the outcome that he had there.

Sixty percent of São Paulo's population had been mired in poverty, living in the *favelas,* the slums, from which many residents were willing to do almost anything to escape. More than once at the consulate, Tom had had women slip photographs of themselves, nude, to him underneath their visa applications. There had been four of them on the Non-Immigrant Visa line, two FSOs and two JOs, Tom and Roberto Ramirez. They had to go through an average of five hundred NIV applicants a day, which meant they could spend no more than two minutes per interview. Awful, dispiriting work. Their job was to assess the likelihood that the person would return to Brazil when his or her visa expired, and they based their judgments on the person's solvency and ties to the community—a good job, a family, property, money.

Yet the Consular Officers knew that the documents they were offered as proof were often forgeries, so they had to rely on their instincts and take whatever shortcuts were available to them, one of which was an informal five-page manual that the FSOs had devised with the Consul General. Most of it consisted of procedural tips and reminders, but there were also alerts about current fraud patterns, particularly about third-country nationals— Koreans, Chinese, Filipinos, Arabs, Nigerians—who were reportedly being smuggled through Brazil into the United States. The manual also advised them to use a series of two-letter codes in reviewing people: LR for "Looks Ratty," TP for "Talks Poor," SR for "Smells Rank," BT for "Bad Teeth," CH for "Coarse Hands." None of the codes were explicitly associated with the applicants' skin color or racial features, but it just so happened that the majority of applicants whose visas were denied were either black or Asian or Arab.

"Come on, you know it's racist," Ramirez told Tom. The Consul General and the FSOs were white. Ramirez, whose family had immigrated to the US from Santo Domingo when he was six, was black—a *prieto*. Ramirez kept complaining about the manual and its policies, refusing to follow them, and the Consul General gave him a highly unfavorable candidate evaluation report, which ensured that Ramirez would be bounced out of the Foreign Service. He appealed to the Grievance Board, which declared that such a manual, without question, would be unconstitutional, that they would absolutely not tolerate the systematic discrimination of visa applicants on the basis of race, color, class, socioeconomic status, national origin, or appearance. Only, how could they know for sure Ramirez wasn't just a disgruntled employee, crazily making false accusations in an attempt to salvage his career? Where was his evidence? Copies of the supposed manual and a folder of visa applications with the Consular Officers' alleged notes and codes had mysteriously disappeared, lost with his luggage when he left São Paulo. And there was also the suggestion—magnanimously omitted from his evaluations but implied during the inquest—that Ramirez might have succumbed to the stress and temptations of the job and traded visas for sexual favors.

Ramirez's only hope was to obtain the corroboration of the people he had worked with in São Paulo. To a man, they denied the existence of the manual. When it came time for Tom to be deposed, the Consul General told him, "You do what you have to do, but you should know, we take care of our own in the Foreign

Service," and then had hinted he'd heard of an opening in Vienna, another in Madrid.

Under oath, Tom had said he knew nothing about a manual. He had never seen a manual.

■   ■   ■

AN AMERICAN—a nineteen-year-old coke addict—was being held for purse theft, and Tom went down to the Metropolitan Police Department's new headquarters, an eighteen-story, ivory-white building across from the Imperial Palace, to interview him. The inspector who had arrested the boy told Tom that they'd discovered something in his locker at the youth hostel where he'd been staying. Two duffel bags, inside of which were dozens and dozens of wallets and passports. One of the passports belonged to Lisa Countryman.

He called Julia, and they met in a little bar called Flashbacks in Iidabashi, a faux-hippie artists' hangout where customers could go up to the record collection and pick out albums to play: Dylan, Hendrix, Jefferson Airplane. The entire place was made of varnished pine—walls, ceiling, floor, booths, and tables—a tiny tinderbox that was dimly lit, windowless, but homey. On the table of each booth was a candle, a ceramic ashtray shaped like a gnome, and a brass bell with a wooden handle. ("Whatever you do, don't touch that," Julia had told him when they sat down.)

"She couldn't have left the country, not without her passport," Tom said to Julia. "That's probably why she had those two photos. She was going to apply for a replacement passport."

"So she's either alive and still in Japan," she said, "or she's dead. But either way, there's been a cover-up. Someone tried to make it look like she left Japan."

"Yes."

"What happens now?"

"We've filed an official missing-persons report. Now the police have to actively investigate the case."

The bar's ponytailed owner, Yoshi, who taught at the ISA with Julia, brought over two beers and a tin can with different colored felt pens.

"What are the pens for, Yoshi?" Tom asked him, trying to be friendly.

"Draw," he barked, and walked away.

Tom raised his eyebrows. "He has a problem with *gaijin*?" he asked Julia.

"He has a problem with you—with any man I happen to be with. He's always been in love with me." She picked up the can and offered Tom a pen. "Here, draw something."

The tables were covered with disposable sheets of paper. "I can't draw," he said.

"You must be able to draw something. A cartoon?"

"No, but I have a special talent. Sign your name here," he said, pointing at the corner of the sheet. She did, and he reached over, tore off the corner, and turned it around. Then he took a pen in each hand and copied her signature, tracing a very good forgery with his right hand and simultaneously creating its mirror image with his left hand, the pens dancing apart in synchronicity.

"That's a pretty neat trick," Julia said. "Do you have any other special talents?"

The music in the bar abruptly stopped, and the twenty or so customers let out a chorus of groans and boos. Apparently a fuse or a tube in the amplifier had blown out. Yoshi frantically began dismantling the stereo. Without music, the whole rhythm of the place had been thrown off, as if in the relief of lights, and some people left. The remainder fidgeted. "What's everyone supposed to do now? *Talk*?" Julia said. "Poor Yoshi." Carole King's *Tapestry* had been on the turntable before the amp had fritzed, and Julia hummed the melody to "Way Over Yonder." Quietly she sang the first lines to Tom, then suddenly rose and belted it out, stepping from the booth to the head of the room. She had a terrible voice, hardly able to carry a tune, but she made up for it with verve, *into* it, swaying, eyes closed, arms outstretched, delivering a rousing, soulful performance.

She received an ecstatic ovation, and, amid the applause, Tom whistled and picked up the brass bell from the table and waved it in the air, clanging it in appreciation.

Everyone in the room turned to him. "Ahhhh!" they exclaimed, and laughed and clapped.

"What?" he asked Julia.

"I warned you not to touch that," she said. "You just bought the house a round of drinks."

Yoshi ran up to him with a Polaroid camera and snapped a picture, and then tacked the Polaroid on the wall next to the stereo, Tom's face joining a hundred other befuddled philanthropists', his mouth crooked with a reluctant smile as he looked at Julia, already half in love with her.

SIX

THERE WERE many possibilities, Kenzo thought. She was in an accident of some sort. She was hiking in the woods and fell into an abandoned well and died of exposure and starvation. She had amnesia. She tripped off a curb and smacked her head and couldn't remember a thing about her life. She was a *johatsu-sha,* an evaporation. She had a married lover, and they had decided to run away together and absconded to Hokkaido with the help of *yonige-ya,* an overnight "furniture removal" company. She committed suicide. She took a train to the sea and sequestered herself in a cave underneath a bluff and swallowed cyanide. She was kidnapped. She was snatched off the street and injected with heroin until she turned into an addict and was now a sex slave. She was murdered. She owed a gangster money from gambling and was shot and thrown into Tokyo Bay.

Kenzo ran through some of these scenarios—minus the fanciful descriptions and elaborations—during the morning *chorei,* or daily meeting, at Criminal Investigations. With the discovery of Lisa Countryman's passport, he was now convinced that her disappearance was not another dead-end nuisance case after all. He thought it could be something big, something that would impress his section chief, Inspector Kunichi, and allow Kenzo to reclaim his seat at a center desk, away from the window. But Iso Yamada, the slick new Assistant Inspector, undercut Kenzo immediately.

"Ota," he said, "you've really got quite the imagination. Or maybe you've just been reading *Fancy* too much." The other detectives at the meeting laughed.

Fancy was a weekly magazine that carried excoriating commentary on the ruling Liberal Democratic Party in the front, vitriolic reports on the Yomiuri Giants in the back, and titillating true crime stories in the middle, usually involving the rape, bondage, and strangulation of OLs and prepubescent schoolgirls—stories replete with glossy photographs, most of which were staged. The magazine had a circulation of two million.

A wildly popular series last winter had featured the case of a Hokkaido divorcée who had had an affair with her daughter's junior high school teacher, who was married. The girl discovered them in bed one afternoon, and they bound and gagged and blindfolded her after making her swallow sleeping pills, trying to stall and figure out what to do. (Here, *Fancy* took some liberties, suggesting with color reenactments that the couple had fondled the girl and inserted ben-wa balls and other implements into her vagina and anus, when there had been absolutely no evidence of molestation of any kind.) But they had gagged the girl too tightly, and she suffocated to death, whereupon the couple panicked and dismembered her—dismemberment was almost a criminal tradition in Japan—and made numerous trips to the countryside to bury the body parts. A farmer's dog sniffed out the right arm, and other dogs, special earthquake-rescue canines, found the torso, thighs, and feet as the search area was widened. The couple, knowing they would soon be arrested, tried to commit *shinju,* double suicide, another revered tradition. First they went to a seaside cave and had sex repeatedly and tried to drink poison at the exact moment of simultaneous orgasm, but they failed to die. Then they fed a hose from the exhaust pipe of his car through the rear passenger-side window and tried to inhale the carbon monoxide fumes at the exact moment of simultaneous orgasm, but they failed to die. And then they decided to crash his car and tried to ram into a concrete support column underneath a highway bridge at the exact moment of simultaneous orgasm, but they failed to die. They were captured that way, naked, bloody, barely alive with massive internal injuries, the woman straddling the man in the driver's seat, *in flagrante delicto,* which was depicted by *Fancy* in extensive color reenactments.

"I'm afraid I agree with Yamada," Inspector Kunichi said to Kenzo at the meeting. "There are probably more reasonable, mundane explanations for the girl's disappearance, the most likely of which is that her visa was expiring, and she went underground to evade the immigration authorities."

"What do they always say?" Yamada interjected. "Follow the money. If Ota can find out what she was doing for money, where she worked after the *eikaiwa* school, he might be able to locate her."

"Yes, yes, that's very logical," Kunichi said. "What do you think, Ota?"

Kenzo wanted to tell him, You presume I'm an idiot? You're actually commending Yamada for stating something so obvious?, but instead he said, "Yes, that sounds logical." He looked at Yamada, so cocky in his Armani suit—what color was that? Mauve? How was it, anyway, that he could afford an Armani suit? And his car, a gleaming, piss-yellow, souped-up, custom-bodied

Datsun 280Z. Who did he think he was with such a car? *Bosozoku? Yakuza?*—and he looked at Kunichi, who beamed at Yamada as if he were in love with him, and Kenzo vowed to keep his mouth shut from now on. He wouldn't utter a word, not a peep, until he was close to cracking the case and proving that something amiss had indeed happened to Lisa Countryman.

■　　■　　■

THE PROBLEM was, he had no one to ask the usual questions that would have been asked in a missing-persons case. Basic questions, like: Exactly when did Lisa Countryman disappear? Where was she last seen? With whom? What was her behavioral, professional, personal, emotional, financial, and medical situation at the time? Had she ever disappeared before? Was she depressed or ill? Did she have cause to run away? Did someone wish her harm? An abusive relationship? A stalker?

Kenzo couldn't ask her friends or colleagues or lovers—and subsequently compile a list of suspects—because he didn't know who they were. All he had was her sister, Susan Countryman, who was calling him twice a week now, badgering him for information, implying he wasn't doing his job.

"Did she ever break bone?" Kenzo asked during their most recent phone conversation.

"What? What's that got to do with the price of eggs?" Susan Countryman asked.

"Maybe important."

"She broke her arm a couple of Christmases ago. She tripped off the front stoop. I can't tell you how klutzy she is."

"Please have hospital send X-ray and type blood. Also dentist with teeth X-ray."

"Why?" she asked, then said, "Oh. I understand. In case you need to identify her body. Wait. Have you found a body?"

"No," Kenzo said. He had checked every hospital and morgue in the vicinity and had come up with nothing—no unidentified bodies, or body parts—but he felt it prudent to ask for these things now, in case something emerged.

"Somewhere is Lisa's fingerprints?" Kenzo asked.

"I wouldn't think so."

"No police arrest one time?"

"Not that I know of."

"She have birthmark? Scar?"

"Not really."

"Tattoo?"

"No, not that I know of."

"Did she have money?"

"What do you mean, money?"

"Did she have many savings?"

"No, she was as broke as I am. Worse. College loans."

"Maybe your father give her money?"

"No."

"Maybe she have family money?"

Susan Countryman paused, as if to think about it. "No."

"No inherit money?"

"No," Susan Countryman said. "Look, you're getting awfully personal here."

Yamada and Kunichi were both right and wrong: the key question was the money—what was Lisa Countryman doing for money?—but she had no reason to go underground, even if she had been working illegally, because no one had been looking for her, the Immigration Bureau had not been seeking her.

He called her landlord, Teiji Takagi, and had him meet Kenzo at the furnished studio apartment that she had rented from him. Unfortunately, a new tenant had moved in, and the crime scene, if a crime had been committed here, had already been compromised.

It was useless to look for fingerprints or forensics in the apartment, which was even smaller than Kenzo's, just one room, but more modern and with a great location in Nishi-Azabu. Takagi conceded that the rent was outrageously high, but said his transient tenants thought it was an agreeable trade-off, since he didn't require them to pay him key money.

Takagi didn't know much about Lisa at all, it turned out—where she was working, with whom she was acquainted, if she had a boyfriend.

"Did she pay her rent by cash?" Kenzo asked.

"Of course. What, you think I'd take a check?"

Japan was a cash culture. No one used personal checks. The crime rate was so low, people could keep and carry bundles of ten-thousand-yen bills without fear. "Did she have a phone?" He thought he could get her phone records from NTT, Nippon Telegraph and Telephone.

"No," Takagi said. "I told her I'd help her set one up, but she said it'd be a waste, she didn't have anyone she wanted to talk to."

"That's a strange thing to say."

"I thought so, too."

"She was a loner, then?"

"I guess. I didn't see her too often, only when I got her rent, a couple of times on the stairs. Oh, once I came to fix her toilet. She never had any company."

"But you talked to her enough times to recognize her voice."

"Yes, I think so."

"And you're sure it was her on the phone on June 18th, when she said she was going to Hong Kong."

"Yeah, pretty sure."

"But it's possible it could have been someone else?"

"I don't think so," Takagi said. Then he reconsidered. "Well, I guess it's possible. There was something odd about that phone call."

"Yes?"

"She spoke to me in English."

"So?"

"Her Japanese was pretty decent. She always spoke to me in Japanese before."

Who was it that might have called Takagi, then? Who had tried to make it look like Lisa Countryman had left Tokyo, and why?

Kenzo canvassed her apartment building, first going to her downstairs neighbor. The soundproofing was more than adequate, evidently, for the man said he had never been cognizant of any noises from Lisa's apartment, and couldn't say, even, what sort of hours she had kept. Her other neighbors and the local shopkeepers, though they recognized her, were equally unaware of Lisa's movements and appearance. She was quiet and nice and always alone, they said. She blended in. Despite being a *gaijin,* she had faded into the background. She had become a ghost.

He kept trying to follow the money. He stopped by all the banks and post offices near Nishi-Azabu and Meguro, particularly those on the way to the subway, asking if Lisa had had a savings account. One woman at a bank thought she remembered a *gaijin* who resembled Lisa cashing traveler's checks in April.

"She was with a *kokujin,*" the woman whispered. A Negro.

"Are you sure?"

"Oh, yes," she said, but Kenzo doubted her. If what she was saying were true, other people would have mentioned it, everyone would have remembered. It would have been very noticeable, an interracial *gaijin* couple, especially a black man with a white woman.

Kenzo dropped in on Rocket America in Shimbashi and talked to the director, Seiji Waru, who immediately denied that Lisa Countryman had ever worked there.

"You told the woman at the embassy, Mrs. Fujiwara, that she quit after two weeks."

"She must have misheard me. We were in the process of obtaining a Certificate of Eligibility for her, but she decided before the application was completed that she didn't want the job. As you know, it would have been illegal for her to have done any work for us without the proper paperwork."

Just then, a tall, attractive blond woman entered the school, and Waru stiffened. His eyes flickered toward her, as if to signal her, then came back to rest on Kenzo nervously.

"I'm interested in a ticket to New York," the woman said in English.

"No airplane here," Waru said.

"This isn't a travel agency?" she asked.

"No. Sorry."

But instead of leaving, the woman walked farther into the office. "What the heck is this place, then?"

"School," Waru said, startled. "This is school."

"It sure *looks* like a travel agency. Are you trying to run some sort of scam or something?" she said. She had extraordinarily long, beautiful legs.

"Go away, please," Waru said, standing up.

"*Excuse* me?"

"Go away. Busy."

"Why, I never," the woman said. "With manners like that, the way you treat people, it's a wonder your office hasn't been *vandalized*." As she turned to leave, she smiled and winked at Kenzo.

■　　■　　■

THIS TIME, during his lunch hour, Kenzo followed Simon to Harajuku, trailing the boy as he took the subway and train by himself. Once he got to Omotesando-dori, Simon went straight to Shakey's Pizza, where he devoured a large pepperoni, washing it down with multiple Coca-Colas. When he finished eating, he stepped outside to the street, dug two one-hundred-yen coins out of his pocket, dropped them into a vending machine, yanked the lever for a pack of Seven Star, tore off the cellophane wrapper, and lit a cigarette. Kenzo was mortified. He was only thirteen! But Kenzo was a bit reassured when Simon began to cough and grimace. After a few more distasteful tokes, he squashed the cigarette out with his sneaker. It looked like he was merely experimenting—a youthful rite of passage that he could now put behind him.

His next stop was the Oriental Bazaar, a store for tourists, filled with antiques, lacquerware, *happi* coats, and other *omiyage*. A boring store for kids. Simon left quickly and walked down the block to his true destination, every boy's true destination in Harajuku, Kiddy Land, a five-story toy mecca. With delight, Simon roamed through the cramped aisles, touching everything, the action figure dolls, the games, the little cars and spaceships. He was having enormous fun, Kenzo could tell. He was just a boy, after all, and Kenzo felt a surge of paternal affection toward him. Simon picked up a toy car, a spiffy red convertible, and put it in his right pants pocket. He lifted a tiny yellow dump truck and inserted it into his left pants pocket. As he turned around, something fell out of his waistband and clattered to the floor. It was a miniature *katana* sword, most certainly from the Oriental Bazaar. Without the slightest bit of panic, Simon retrieved the sword and stuffed it back under his shirt. Kenzo watched him in horror. His son was a juvenile delinquent.

■   ■   ■

HE DECIDED to backtrack. Once again, he sifted through the box of Lisa's possessions that Takagi had collected. Nothing very helpful. He carefully read the telegrams from Susan Countryman. Why had Lisa been avoiding her sister? He listened to the cassette tapes. Second-rate *enka*. Odd that she had liked such traditional Japanese music. He flipped through the handful of books. Very heady stuff. *Man and His Symbols,* Jung. *The Will to Power,* Nietzsche. *Three Essays on the Theory of Sexuality,* Freud. There were notations in the margins in barely decipherable handwriting, a tiny, cramped chicken scratch: "And this led to selective breeding how?" "Why, you dirty old perv."

He went down to MPD headquarters and interviewed the American purse thief again, but he was useless, a stoner who couldn't distinguish any of the women he had robbed, there had been so many.

Kenzo signed out the thief's duffel bags from the evidence room and laid out all the unclaimed items on a table. The thief hadn't kept any of the purses or briefcases or totes, had simply dumped the contents into his duffel bags, so everything was jumbled together. Kenzo was looking for an address book, an organizer, an appointment calendar, a diary or journal, something that would point to Lisa's acquaintances and assignations. He spent a good hour sorting through the articles, along with the wallets and keys and compacts and hairbrushes and birth control pills, and then he found something—a tiny, spiral-bound, dog-eared notebook with a distinctive, nearly illegible chicken scratch.

■　　■　　■

HE DIDN'T understand the notebook at first. It took him quite some time just to unravel the handwriting, and when he did, the words didn't make sense to him. It seemed to be a list of English phrases: Red New Art, DX Night, Ten Carat Gold, Wild West Wow, Splash Poodle, Private Cat, 21 Cup, Mona Lisa Honey, Jungle Hot. There were almost a hundred more phrases, each with a two-letter code beside it in parentheses: PS, IC, SL, NP, SM, NT, PR.

Kenzo thought it was a list of mangled English phrases that *gaijin* called Japlish or Engrish, yet Lisa's additional comments next to some entries confused him further: "transvaluation," "hegemonic instead of ideological," "fetishization," "cultural narcissism," "gender power differential," "capitalistic phallicism." There were also occasional references to Marcuse, Lacan, Foucault, Barthes—whoever they were. It was all gibberish to Kenzo.

Two days later, he was stuck on his morning train commute between Koenji and Nakano. It ended up to be a fifty-three-minute delay, caused by a suicide at Okubo Station. A twenty-six-year-old woman who worked as an elevator operator at Isetan department store had leapt in front of an inbound train, becoming the 652nd jumper of the year.

Kenzo didn't have anything to read on the train, and he was sneaking peeks at the magazine held by the salaryman sitting next to him—an issue of *Frank,* a sleazy, bad imitation of *Fancy.* As the salaryman flipped to a back page, Kenzo saw an ad for Wild West Wow. Of course. How could he have been so stupid? The notebook wasn't a list of Japlish. It was a list of businesses in what was sometimes euphemistically referred to as *mizu shobai,* the water trade, and sometimes more directly referred to as *shasei sangyo,* the ejaculation industry.

That afternoon, Kenzo went to Kabukicho, the red-light district in Shinjuku. Wild West Wow was in an eight-story corner building stacked with bars, discos, and nightclubs. The place was empty. Kenzo should have known it would be at two in the afternoon. The *tencho,* the manager, was the only person there, and he wasn't talkative.

"Have you seen this *gaijin* woman?" Kenzo asked, showing him Lisa Countryman's photo.

"No."

"You could at least pretend to look."

He didn't pretend to look.

"What time do the girls who work here come in?"

"Don't bother coming back," the *tencho* said. "They won't talk to you."

He was right: they wouldn't talk to Kenzo. The girls and the rest of the staff denied ever having laid eyes on Lisa, and it was clear they would have lied to him if they had. He would never get anywhere identifying himself as a cop.

He killed some time eating dinner at a *soba* restaurant, and afterward played *pachinko* for an hour. When he came back out to the street, Kabukicho had been transformed. Now that it was evening, everything was alive, cacophonous, ablaze in neon. The alleyways were crowded with men, many of them already drunk, and touts directed a steady banter at them from doorways, promising beautiful young girls.

The entrance fee for Splash Poodle was five thousand yen before eight p.m., eight thousand yen after. It bought you one drink and thirty minutes of "play time" with a "splash girl" chosen for you. However, for an additional three thousand yen, you could pick your own splash girl from the Polaroids tacked to the wall just inside the entrance. Kenzo carefully examined each Polaroid, taking so much time, one of the doormen said, "Come on already. You're not picking a wife."

Kenzo finally selected one of the younger splash girls, a wide-eyed girl who looked naïve and malleable, someone he might be able to get to talk.

He was led to a small curved booth and was immediately attended to by a waitress, who set down a dish of peanuts on the table and gave him an *oshibori*—a wet towel—to refresh himself. She asked him what he wanted to drink.

"Coca-Cola," he said.

"Coca-Cola? You get one drink for free, you know."

"Okay, a rum and Coke," he said. It was too troublesome to explain that he couldn't drink alcohol.

The booths were lined in rows with unusually high seatbacks, so he couldn't get a view of the other patrons. It was too dark, anyway. He could barely see his hand in front of his face. The waitress used a penlight pointed at the floor to guide her way back to his table with his rum and Coke. Kenzo could hear things, though. Soft murmurs and wisps of conversation. And there were smells: cigarettes and perfume and something else, something sharp and acidic. Disinfectant?

He wondered why Lisa Countryman had been interested in nightclubs such as this one. Had she been that desperate for a job, for money? What else could the notebook have been for? He hardly knew anything about how the sex industry operated. Somehow he had gotten to the age of thirty-eight without ever having stepped into a strip bar. But he assumed the girls at these clubs were prostitutes. He imagined they chatted men up at the tables, and if the men desired, they went to a back room to have sex for an agreed price. And he also knew that Kabukicho was heavily controlled by the *yakuza*, the Japanese mafia. If Lisa had been working in a place like this, it was very conceivable she had fallen in harm's way.

His splash girl slid into the booth, carrying more *oshibori*.

"Wanna another drink?" she asked, not noticing that he hadn't touched his first one. He couldn't tell in the darkness if she was the girl in the Polaroid he had picked, couldn't tell if she was young or old, pretty or ugly. Her Japanese was clipped and accented—foreign. Was she Chinese?

He pulled out the photo of Lisa from his suit pocket. "Let me ask you something. Do you recognize this American woman?" he said, but then realized she couldn't see. "Do you have a lighter? Or maybe we could ask the waitress if we could borrow her flashlight."

He felt the girl grab his zipper.

"*Nanda-yo?*" he asked. What're you doing?

She fished her hand through the fly of his pants and then his boxer shorts and then located his penis and fished it out.

"*Shitsukoi dayo.*" Stop that.

She took an *oshibori* and cleaned his penis, rubbing it very roughly, and, despite himself, he got an instant and insistent erection.

"*Kuso, mate, mate.*" Damn it, wait, wait.

She began pumping him up and down with her hand.

"*Yamero-yo.*" Don't do that.

She dove her head down and took his cock into her mouth.

"*Kuso! Iikagen ni-shiro, yariman!*" Shit! Leave me alone, you whore!

He pushed her off and stood up and stepped away from the booth while trying to tuck his penis inside his pants. He knocked over the table with his rum and Coke and peanuts and the *oshibori,* and then he tripped, falling to the floor. The doorman and the waitress ran over, both pointing their flashlights at him. As people rose from their booths to see what was going on, as his splash girl laughed, Kenzo flopped and wriggled on the floor, desperately trying to zip up his pants.

SEVEN

ER FIRST night at Musky Club, Lisa was paired with another American girl, Rebecca Silo, and told to keep quiet and observe. The first group of men arrived at eight, and after they were seated, given *oshibori,* and had ordered their drinks, Rebecca and Lisa joined the four men at their table. When everyone had introduced themselves, Kazuo asked Rebecca in tentative English, "Where are you from?"

"I'm from Chicago," she said, drawing out the middle syllable.

"Ah, Chicago!" Kazuo said, as if this were a wondrous, serendipitous coincidence. Everyone waited for him to follow with a relevant comment about Chicago, but none was forthcoming, and there was an uncomfortable silence.

Chitoshi blinked and sat upright with an idea. He enunciated to

Lisa, as though she were the one who couldn't speak English, "Where—are—you—from?"

"Berkeley," she said.

"Ah, Berkeley!" the four men said at once.

"San Francisco!" Nobu said.

"Golden Gate Bridge!" Hiro said.

"Cable car!" Kazuo said, and they all chuckled, relieved by this brilliant conversational breakthrough.

"You wanna light?" Rebecca asked Hiro.

He frowned, not understanding. "Excuse?"

She sparked her Bic lighter in the air and nodded at Hiro's cigarette, which he dangled from his mouth.

"Ah, yes, please," he said, and she lit his cigarette for him, whereupon the other three men hurriedly tamped out cigarettes from their packs of Seven Star and waited for the same courtesy from the girls, as if this were a special treat, a fabulous and rare luxury they couldn't let pass unexploited. The same was true with their drinks. The girls poured the men's drinks, continually keeping their glasses full to the brim with beer from the big bottles. These two touches of *sabisu,* service, along with the girls' company and their engagement in halting, stultifying, excruciatingly banal conversation, were what these men—all in their forties and from the same advertising company—were paying an exorbitant amount of money for, and it utterly mystified Lisa.

"How long you in Japan?" Chitoshi asked her, with Hiro looking on.

"Six weeks," she told him.

"Ah. You like Japan?"

"Yes, I do."

"You have boyfriend?" Hiro chimed in.

"No, not at the moment."

"You have ever Japanese boyfriend?"

"No, I haven't."

"You no like Japanese boy?"

"It's not that—"

"You maybe have Japanese boyfriend someday?"

"Sure, I don't see why not."

"*Subarashi!*" they said. Wonderful!

There were three more groups of men that night, each hardly distinguishable from the next.

"That wasn't too bad," Lisa said to Rebecca at the end of the night, although she was exhausted. Her face hurt from smiling so much, and her mind was fried from trying to think of things to say.

"Oh, you had it easy. These guys were cupcakes," Rebecca said. "Consider your cherry still intact."

The next night, Naoko, the thirtyish mama-san, or proprietress, handed out the weekly payroll, giving each of them an envelope of cash. All told, Lisa had made almost twenty-five thousand yen the night before, or a hundred dollars for five hours of work, based on an hourly wage, tips, and a commission on drinks and snacks sold. In the future, Naoko told her, she would also get a bonus for *shimei*—specific requests by returning customers for her company.

Lisa hadn't known you could make so much money in these clubs, and she needed the money. She had funded this trip to Tokyo with yet another college loan that she had no hope of ever repaying, and she was already up to her neck in credit-card debt. True to Seiji Waru's prediction, it had been too late to find another teaching job, and, without a visa, she'd had no luck landing more conventional forms of employment. She had nearly tapped out her savings, right at the moment when her expenses had increased dramatically, having moved out of the *gaijin* house and into Teiji Takagi's outrageously expensive furnished studio in Nishi-Azabu.

After looking for two weeks, she had been ready to accept almost any job, but never imagined she'd end up working in a hostess club. She had been doing some side research on the sex industry for her dissertation, making lists of places and dropping by random establishments without an appointment, hoping to interview the female workers. No one had been particularly receptive to her, and she was afraid she would have to give up soon and go home empty-handed, having failed, even, to gather any useful fieldwork. By the time she had walked into Musky Club in Roppongi, she had been at the end of her tether. "Excuse me," she had said to Naoko in her most polite Japanese. "Could I talk to you for a few moments?"

"Turn around," Naoko said.

Lisa assumed she was being peremptorily kicked out of the club, and she began to walk out. "Where are you going?" Naoko said. "I just want to look at you. Spin around for me."

Lisa did. "But I just want to—"

"You're a little chunky," Naoko said, "but you'll do."

"Pardon?"

"Your Japanese isn't bad, but don't use it with the customers. This is known as a *gaijin* girl club. Men come here to meet *gaijin* girls, understand? It's part of the fantasy. Just act like a dumb American, and you'll do fine."

■   ■   ■

SHE FOUND herself praying. It was strange. She didn't think of herself as at all religious, although she had been a regular churchgoer as a child. Wherever they had been stationed, whatever port of call, her parents, Richard and Lenore, had become active in the Baptist church community on the naval base: Subic Bay, Pearl, San Diego, Naples, Portsmouth, Norfolk. God had not drawn Lisa to church, but singing had. Her parents had been musicians. Her father had played guitar, her mother the piano and organ. They had billed themselves as Pea Coat and Lenny, a semi-professional lounge act specializing in ballads and torch songs, and Lisa had loved watching and listening to them sing. Her best childhood memories were of them performing in NCO clubs and church choirs.

On Sundays, she began going to Tokyo Union Church on Omotesando-dori. She would attend the morning service and sing with the rest of the congregation—not an entirely satisfying experience, since there was no band, no solos, just restrained Protestant hymnals. Afterward, she would stroll to Yoyogi Park and witness the strange spectacle of hundreds of Japanese youngsters dancing on the closed-off street. In groups of four to ten, they generally cleaved to Ziggy Stardust or Elvis, platform shoes and eye shadow and red-tinted spiked hair, or leather jackets and hoop skirts and ducktails. Blaring music from portable sound systems, they enacted highly choreographed routines of the shuffle or the twist with an utter lack of irony—dour, really, never acknowledging the half-bemused, half-astonished crowd.

And then Lisa discovered something quite wonderful in her own neighborhood. In Nishi-Azabu, beside the Fuji Building, there was a Zen temple, Chokoku-ji, and once a week, the monks let laypeople meditate inside. There were three buildings at the temple: the Hon-do, the main hall; the Kannon-do, which housed a forty-foot wooden statue of the Buddhist goddess of mercy; and the Zen-do, which was the actual meditation hall.

On a Monday evening, Lisa showed up at the reception area of the Hon-do and put her shoes on the rack. She knelt on a cushion and wrote down her name and address in a guest book on a low table, then dropped a one-hundred-yen coin into the small offertory box. She was led by a monk to another room, where she was asked to remove her socks and belt and any other articles of clothing that might be constricting. Several other visitors were doing stretching exercises, and Lisa, the only *gaijin,* imitated their movements. Then they were all taken into a tatami room and told to line up in front of a row of black round cushions, whereupon a monk instructed them on the proper *zazen* seating position, eyelids half-closed, breathing through the nose.

Finally they were brought into a cavernous tatami room in the Zen-do, in which a number of monks were already meditating. Along with the other visitors, Lisa sat on the cushions facing the wall, and tried to settle into *zazen.* The point was for the mind to go blank, but the task seemed impossible. All sorts of thoughts flitted in and out of her head, the most mundane thoughts, laundry to do, a boy she had liked in high school, the hostages in Iran. What did they do all day long? Were they allowed to roam around at all, or were they bound in a room, forced to sit like this, made to suffer the tyranny of their solitude? She was so *uncomfortable.* Her knees were in severe, scintillating pain. Slowly, her breath quieted, and remarkably the pain became less noticeable, her body warm, atingle, irradiated from the center of her body to her limbs. But instead of thinking of nothing, she began thinking of Kannon, the goddess of mercy in the other building, and she prayed to her.

She prayed to be delivered from her aloneness. She felt herself choke up and start to cry. Ridiculous. Why was she crying? Why was she feeling sorry for herself? She had promised herself she wouldn't. She couldn't stop. Sobbing, she prayed. She prayed to be led somewhere, to something. She prayed for someone to save her.

■   ■   ■

OMAR JOHNSON, the Public Affairs officer who had given her the tour in Yokohama, was waiting for Lisa outside her apartment that night. He had flowers for her.

"I wanted to apologize," he said. "I didn't mean to insult you. I really didn't."

He was dressed in a button-down shirt and pressed jeans. He had gone to the address she had written down on her visitor form, the *gaijin* house in Meguro, and had waited all day for Takagi to show up to find out where she had moved.

She had been thinking about Omar, had felt bad about the way she had treated him. She smelled the flowers. Yellow roses. They were heavenly.

"Can I take you out to dinner?" Omar asked her.

She took his hand. "I don't need to be courted," she said, and led him up the stairs to her apartment.

■　　■　　■

IT GOT worse, much worse, at Musky Club. Apparently she had begun the job during an unusual lull of gentility, and now the customers reverted to the rude, crude, lewd, and lascivious behavior that was their norm, behavior that was tacitly condoned at Musky Club. As a trio of customers concluded one night, this was not a first- or even second-rate club: the décor was cheap, the girls were not very pretty, they didn't dress well, and they were old— *kurisumasu keeki.* In Japan, they called unmarried women who were over twenty-five Christmas cakes, because they were no longer fresh.

"It's a reflection of Naoko's lack of class," one man said.

"Yes, she might be Korean," the second man said.

"She might even be *burakumin*," the third man said, referring to a caste of people who were, although pure Japanese, outcasts, delegated the most menial, onerous jobs.

"You know, her voice is so low, I wonder if she's even a woman!"

This elicited peals of laughter.

"Maybe she's a man! Like the tennis player, Renee Richards! Maybe she's had a sex change operation!"

And then their evaluative attention turned to Lisa. They were aware she spoke some Japanese, but that didn't stop them from openly assessing her attributes in front of her.

"Nice face, but hardly any tits," the first man said.

"Yes, it's true," the second man said. "I need a magnifying glass to find her tits."

"She's big-boned, almost fat," the third man said. "And she has a wide ass, don't you think?"

"And pudgy arms."

"Although her torso is slender. Legs are adequate."

"Paradoxically she has a skinny person's neck and wrists and ankles."

"I like her eyes."

"But her nose is too broad and flat."

"Almost like a black person's, wouldn't you say?"

"Lips, too. Negroid lips."

"She looks old. She said she's twenty-two? Are you sure she's not lying?"

"What do you make of her overall facial structure? Surprisingly delicate."

"Hm, nothing is quite in proportion."

"I see what you mean. She's misshapen."

"Her tits are a real tragedy. As you said, they're almost non-existent."

"Do you think it might be the blouse? Maybe there's something underneath there, after all. It seems impossible to be so flat-chested."

This sort of objectification was degrading enough—particularly since much of it was erroneous—but the customers could be more infuriating, asking Lisa direct questions: How tall was she? What color was her pubic hair? How wide was her vagina? Two fingers, three? Did she have big nipples? Were they pink or brown? Did she fart a lot? There was a rumor that some women had an orgasm when they urinated. Had that ever happened to her?

In the course of these conversations, Lisa picked up all kinds of words: *oppai*—breast; *omanko*—vagina; *ososo*—the residual drops of urine on a woman after she peed. Japanese men seemed quite fond of the scatological. Once, when Lisa returned from the restroom, a customer asked, "*Fukimashitaka?*" Did you wipe?

How many boyfriends had she had? they asked. Did she sleep with all of them? Any of them Japanese? Japanese men were not as large as *gaijin* men, that was true, they said, but they were harder, they lasted longer, they could go all night, many times a night.

"How big is your penis, Hayashi?"

"Fifty centimeters."

"Fifty! You're tiny. Mine's as long as my arm."

"Mine's as long as my leg."

"Mine's so long, it could be used as a jump rope. I have to tie it in a series of knots in order to walk, or else it drags on the ground."

And then the pawing would begin. A hand casually resting on her knee, patting her thigh, creeping up. An arm casually stretched across the back of the booth, around her shoulders, the hand creeping down. Lisa would push and swat their hands away. "*Dame,*" she would say, stop that, which would only make the men laugh and try again several minutes later.

The other girls at the club taught her tactics to occupy the men, like getting them to pose for Polaroids (for which the girls received a commission). A waiter would snap the photos and then hand them over with a flashlight for the men to inspect. Mindless drinking games were also a favorite distraction. There was the Yamanote Line game, in which everyone clapped in 4/4 time and took turns trying to the name the twenty-nine stops on the train loop in the correct order: Mejiro, clap, clap, Ikebukuro, clap, clap, Otsuka, clap, clap. There was the Pin Pon Pan game, in which the first person shouted, "Pin," and pointed at someone across the table, who had to bellow, "Pon," and point at someone else, who had to retort, "Pan," and point at someone else, whose neighbors had to raise their arms and yell, "Woo!" Sophomoric. If all else failed, they played rock, paper, scissors, *jan-ken-pon,* with the loser having to chug a drink.

Fortunately Lisa had the tolerance of a Marine. She could get drunk if she felt like it, but she could just as easily drink and drink and stay sober, although it was hard to do the job sober. Other girls coped with medicinal supplements. Speed was big, as was coke. Lisa would walk into the ladies' room and find Rebecca Silo snorting a line from the lid of the toilet tank. "You wanna line?" she would giggle. Later, after work, Rebecca and her friends would take the edge off with poppers of amyl nitrite and go dancing at Juan Juan, the hot new disco across the hall whose mammoth sound system was making Naoko crazy.

All night long, the beat seeped into Musky Club, the bass pounding relentlessly, shaking the walls. "We Are Family," "Don't Stop Till You Get Enough," "Call Me," "Heartbreaker." The noise, the vibration, was killing her business, Naoko said. It was driving away her customers. She had complained to the disco's owners, who told her she needed better soundproofing. Incensed, Naoko took her frustrations out on the girls, making them call clients during the day at their offices, begging them to come to the club that night, saying there was going to be a "party" (every night, of course, was a party). Naoko also instituted a new *dohan* rule. A *dohan* was an arranged outside date, usually for dinner at a fancy restaurant, after which the girl was to bring the customer back to the club. Sex wasn't supposed to be involved, but the possibility of sex, the potential for sex, the obligation of sex, ratcheted up considerably with each *dohan,* with each tip and gift. Naoko insisted the girls go on at least one *dohan* per week.

One customer in particular, a construction executive, took a liking to Lisa and kept asking her for a *dohan.* He became increasingly aggressive, his hands patting and probing, trying to cop a feel. One night he pretended to be reaching for the ashtray and brushed his palm against Lisa's breast. She slapped his hand and said, "*Yamete-yo.*" Don't.

But Naoko happened to be walking by their table at that moment, and she swooped down upon them. "Don't be rude," she told Lisa. She grabbed the man's hand and planted it on Lisa's left breast. "In Japan, it's considered a compliment."

Both Lisa and the man were so shocked, they stared dumbly at Naoko, the man's fingers laid stiffly over Lisa's breast.

"No, it's not," Lisa said at last, removing the man's hand.

Naoko reached down and flung his hand back upon her breast. "Yes, it is."

Lisa stood up, squared up to Naoko, and said, "Fuck"—she threw a glassful of water in her face—"you."

"You're fired!" Naoko sputtered, leaking water from her mouth.

Lisa gathered her things, and as she walked out of the club, Naoko said to her, "You fucking *gaijin,* you think you can do anything you want. You think you own us. I hate *gaijin.*"

At the elevator, Lisa pressed the DOWN button and put on her coat. "Good Girls Don't" by the Knack was blasting from Juan Juan. This is getting old, Lisa thought. It was the second job she had gotten herself fired from in three weeks.

The elevator doors opened, and Lisa looked down at ten beautifully lacquered red toenails in strap high heels, from which rose a pair of statuesque legs. "Well, well, if it isn't our juvenile delinquent," the legs said.

It was Harper Boyd, the blonde from Rocket America. She was headed into Juan Juan. "You were working in Musky Club? That dump?" she asked. "Are you stupid or just unlucky?"

"I can't tell anymore," Lisa said.

"Were you really the one who vandalized the school?"

"The school was vandalized?"

"Come on."

"I don't know what you're talking about," Lisa smirked.

Harper Boyd puffed out a short laugh. "There's more going on there than I thought," she said. She hooked her arm inside Lisa's and led her toward Juan Juan. "It's against my nature, but I'm going to help you," she said, just before they entered the roar of the disco.

EIGHT

THE END of August, Julia phoned and said she had a surprise for Tom, what was he doing that day? Nothing, he said, and she told him to pack a bathing suit, she would pick him up in twenty minutes at the usual corner—they had a corner now in Akasaka, a few blocks away from the Grew House.

It was, for once, a nice day—humid, but sunny—and as they sped southwest on the expressway, Tom thought Julia was taking him to the beach—the first time he'd get to see the ocean since arriving in Japan. Instead, they wound up in Yokohama, and Julia got lost in the port city, making turn after wrong turn in an industrial section.

"Where are you taking me?" he asked.

"Just wait."

Tom was beginning to feel carsick from the frequent and unexpected lefts and rights, until Julia skidded to a stop, backed up the car, spun forward into an alleyway, and announced, "We're here." Just before they dipped into an underground parking garage, he glimpsed a gargantuan warehouse with a sign that said "Island Blue."

Island Blue was the largest indoor pool complex in the world, an aquatic paradise with water slides, hot tubs, saunas, tanning booths, and restaurants, all festooned with happy Polynesian decorations. The main pool was bigger than a football field, and it swelled and undulated via a state-of-the-art wave machine that produced, if one was extremely kind in describing it, rideable surf.

"Does it feel just like home?" Julia laughed.

Both of them took in the spectacle, amazed. It was a perfectly sunny, warm day outside, with many miles of agreeable coastline nearby, yet Island Blue was packed with over a thousand splashing, cavorting Japanese beachgoers. Only, the beach was indoors, and it was completely fake—a huge rubber mat sculpted and colored and texturized to resemble sand. Everything in Island Blue, including the palm trees, tropical flowers, and lava boulders, was fake, made of Styrofoam or plastic or rubber, the entire vista climate-controlled with a pleasant trade-wind breeze, equatorially bright with stadium lights, and fragrant with the smells of anthuriums, orchids, chlorine, and mildew.

Tom shook his head. "The Japanese are a very strange people," he told Julia. The Japanese preferred their simulations, their imitations, to the real thing, happy to accept sacrifices in translation as long as they were made in favor of convenience and predictability, like the orderly, patient fashion with which everyone waited in lines—lines for everything, interminable lines for the pineapple *hanbaga,* for the restrooms, for the surfboard rentals, for the waves, even. A line to get into the lineup. Throughout the day,

Island Blue ran half-hour periods of designated "Wave Time" in which surfers and boogie boarders could, one by one, hop on a waist-high wave and ride it to the beach mat.

"So, come on, get a board," Julia said.

"What?"

"I want to see you surf."

"What?"

He tried to get out of it, but Julia was relentless. He found himself going one step further, hoping he would think of something before he had to take another, until he was actually standing in line, holding his rental board with a hundred other surfers, all of them tricked out in fancy Day-Glo rashguards and OP shorts and puka shells.

What was he going to do? he wondered, panicking. Julia—comely even in her conservative one-piece Speedo—reclined on one elbow on the beach, reading a book, waiting to see him rip it up on the water. But as he watched the surfers in front of him, he began to relax. The wave machine pumped out a wave every thirty seconds. Theoretically, sixty of them should have gotten a turn with each half hour of Wave Time, yet it was more like twenty. People fell. They didn't paddle into position quickly enough. They chickened out and let a wave pass. Even if Tom kept his place in line, it would take at least three hours before he reached the head of the line.

Three chirpy tones from an electronic bell rang through Island Blue, followed by an announcement that this particular Wave Time was *owari*—over. Tom dropped out of the line and walked over to Julia.

"This is ridiculous," she said. "I want to see you. There's got to be something we can do."

"I don't mind," he told her, lying down on a towel beside her. "I'm happy to sit here with you."

She thought for a second. "You look a little like Gerry Lopez, don't you?"

Gerry Lopez was a professional surfer, a superstar on the circuit. Tom occasionally studied surf magazines. "I don't look anything like him."

"I'll be right back," Julia said, and she hopped up and approached one of Island Blue's employees, a girl bedecked in a lei, hula skirt, and coconut bra, and then to a man in an aloha shirt, flip-flops, and a cowboy hat, apparently a manager, whom she brought over to where Tom lay.

"*Kochira wa* Gerry Lopez-*san desu*," she said. "Gerry Lopez, *wakarimasu ka?*"

"*Ee, domo. Dozo yoroshiku onegai shimasu*," the man said, bowing and bowing, ever so pleased to meet the great Gerry Lopez. He barked a string of instructions into his walkie-talkie, and within minutes the staff had cleared the swimmers from the water.

"You've got the pool to yourself for half an hour," Julia said.

Word quickly spread that the champion surfer, the grand master of the Banzai Pipeline, was on the premises, and spectators were already ringing the pool, pointing at Tom, cameras flashing. He began to sweat. He leaned toward Julia and whispered, "There's a slight problem."

"What kind of problem?"

"I sort of exaggerated my surfing skills."

"So you're no Gerry Lopez. That's all right. Trust me, no one will say a peep. They'll believe what they want to believe."

"It's not going to work."

"Why not?"

"The truth is, I never actually learned to surf."

Julia stared at him, not understanding. "What do you mean?"

"I can't surf. I don't know how to surf. At all," Tom said, petrified. "I lied."

She looked at him blankly, then burst out laughing. "Well, fuck me dumb and call me Molly," she said. "Did you ever live in Hawaii?"

"No."

She laughed again. "Well, fuck me running backwards. How about UCLA? Did you go to UCLA?"

"No."

"Well, fuck me sideways," she said. Then, startling him, she exclaimed, "I love this! Is your name really Tom Hurley?"

She thanked the manager but said that Gerry had changed his mind, his back was acting up, and then she and Tom lay on the beach and talked, interrupted only intermittently by requests for photos and autographs.

She made Tom tell her everything. "Why Hawaii?" she asked, and he told her he had passed through Hawaii on vacation in his early teens, and it had been the one place he'd ever visited where he hadn't had to explain himself, where it had seemed possible to be both Asian and American at the same time. When people asked what he was, he found it simpler, and more appealing, to say that he was Hawaiian, and then a personal mythography, one that included surfing, had evolved.

His father, a GI from South Boston in the Seventh Infantry, had been part of the occupation forces in Korea after World War II. He had met Tom's mother in Seoul, where she was working in a music store, and he had gotten her pregnant. Like a good Irish Catholic boy, he had married her and taken her to his next PCS in Germany, where Tom was born. They spent five years in Europe—Heidelberg, Ausburg, Chievres, Vicenza—and the next six years in the States, shuttling to eight different Army posts: Fort Jackson, Fort Riley, Fort Ord, Fort Campbell. The list went on, broken by one overseas assignment, a year back in Seoul on Yongsan Eighth Army base, when Tom was twelve.

After Korea, they spent six months in Fort Devens, and then his father left for Fort Leavenworth, Kansas, while Tom and his mother stayed behind in Massachusetts. For a short time, they were helped out by his father's family in Southie, a lending hand that was swiftly withdrawn when his father filed for divorce. From there, he and his mother lived in a series of one-bedroom apartments, eventually landing in a public housing project in Brockton, a factory town twenty miles outside of the city. His mother worked two jobs, manning an industrial sewing machine at a shoe factory during the day and cleaning offices at night. Tom worked, too— supermarkets, fast-food restaurants, hardware stores, anything he could find. He had time for little else. No steady girlfriends, no *leisure* activities. He was briefly on the swim team at school, but he missed so many practices, the coach cut him. After high school, he painted houses, installed fences, moved furniture, dropped in and out of Massasoit Community College, thinking at any moment he would be drafted and sent to Vietnam. Then, out of the blue, he received an inheritance. His father's aunt, the one relative who'd ever been kind to Tom, had made him the beneficiary of her life insurance, ten thousand dollars. He gave half to his mother and took the other half to move cross-country to Southern California, where he got his degree from Cal State, Northridge.

"When did you see your father last?" Julia asked.

"When I was thirteen, fourteen. I heard he served two tours in Vietnam and got a Purple Heart. I don't know where he is now. I'm sure he got remarried to a nice girl from Southie and had a boatload of kids."

"I think the last time I saw my father was when I was two. I don't remember him. He was number three."

"Number three?"

"My mother was married seven times. I have nine half-brothers and -sisters. She used to joke that at least none of us was born on a pool table."

He was perplexed. "This was in Boston?"

"No. Port Arthur, Texas."

"But didn't you grow up in Boston?"

She cocked her head at him. "Boston's just the last place I lived in the US, when Vincent was at Harvard."

"But you said—" Tom tried to remember what she had said. He had pictured her in Chilmark and Chestnut Hill and the Buckingham School, but now he couldn't recall if she had ever mentioned such places.

"I suppose we're a lot alike," Julia told him. "I say things that can be misconstrued."

"You're not well-to-do?"

"What a quaint phrase, well-to-do. No, I come from a long line of white trash—deep-fried and double-wide," she said, slipping for a second into a Texas accent. "I busted my ass to get into Princeton so I could marry a Yankee blue blood, and what did I do? Idiot that I am, I fell in love with a Jap. Oh, Vincent has some money. His family owns a paper manufacturing plant in Aberdeen, Washington. But he has this stupid patriotic streak and joins the CIA. Have you ever heard of anything so silly? He knew what he'd be going up against, but he didn't care."

"What's he up against?"

She smiled. "This is what I like about you."

They hit traffic going back to Tokyo. At first, it was clear sailing. They were laughing, roaring down the expressway with the top down, and Tom felt released. He and Julia were more alike than he could have ever imagined. He felt he could tell her anything now, and she would not judge him. They put their heads back and enjoyed the wind, bathed by bands of crimson and magenta from the sunset, a fiery sky made more eerie by the blur of smog. But then it was bumper to bumper for miles, and with each minute stuck in the crawl of cars and trucks and buses, the warmth and cheer of the day seemed to bleed away.

"I can't stand this," Julia said. She honked her horn pointlessly, and the people in the adjacent vehicles glanced over at them, miffed. This was a country in which drivers switched off their headlights at intersections as a courtesy. "Let's *move*," Julia said, and she kept changing lanes, trying to find a faster flow. Two and a half hours they were trapped in the traffic, and there was no rhyme or reason to it. It was a Saturday, so it wasn't rush hour; there were no ball games or special events, there wasn't an accident, nothing to rubberneck.

The last kilometer was the worst. They could see the off-ramp to Roppongi in front of them, but the closer they got to it, the slower they seemed to go. At long last they reached the turnoff, and Julia whooped. "Free at last!" she screamed, and she floored it, zooming down the elevated expressway to the parallel surface road, carving between the concrete support columns from the outside lane to the faster one underneath the expressway, and then swinging left onto a narrow street that was a shortcut to Akasaka. She didn't make the turn. She hit a woman riding a bicycle. Julia was almost able to avoid her, but she didn't. She clipped the back wheel of the bicycle, causing the woman to jerk up into the air, twirl in an awkward helicopter spin, and land on her back, after which Julia sideswiped a parked red car, gouging the door panel with her bumper before coming to a rest.

They looked behind them at the woman, who was motionless on her back for five horrifying seconds. Then she slowly sat up, and—the oddest of things—she raised her hands and adjusted her hair clips.

"Thank God," Julia said.

"Go," Tom whispered.

"What?"

"Go!" he yelled.

After a moment's hesitation, Julia sped away. She stared ahead and drove, her hands white-knuckled on the steering wheel. A mile or so away, she abruptly parked at a curb and shut off the engine. "Oh, God!" she cried. "Did we really do that?" She sat quietly for a second, then looked at Tom, grabbed his head with both hands, and kissed him rapaciously.

When she let go of him, she appeared as shocked as Tom by her impulsion. She dug into her purse for a cigarette and lit it. "We have to go back," she told him.

"I don't think she ever saw us," he said. "The woman. She was always facing away. Do you think anyone else saw us?"

Julia's hands were shaking. "I don't know," she said. "Jesus! What am I *doing*!"

"She didn't look like she was really hurt."

Eyes closed, she expelled a long cloud of blue smoke. "I don't know," she said morosely. "Maybe not."

"I don't think she was. And the car we hit—we didn't do that much damage, did we?"

She turned to him. "No," she said, and the import of the word—such a simple, prosaic word—hung between them.

"We can't go back," Tom said. "There'd be no point now."

Julia leaned forward and pressed her forehead against the steering wheel. "Let's go somewhere," she said quietly.

▪   ▪   ▪

THEY DROVE to a *rabu hoteru*, a love hotel, in Ikebukuro. Hundreds of these hotels dotted Tokyo, renting rooms by the hour, rooms that were paeans to kitsch, done up in campy, lurid themes: Arabian harems, alpine chalets, tiki hut delights. On a lark, Tom had gone to one in Shibuya with Sara Sobeske once, the building designed to resemble the Taj Mahal. This one in Ikebukuro was fashioned after a Scottish castle and was called, aptly enough, Loch Love.

The hotels were always new, immaculate, and extremely discreet. As soon as Julia parked her convertible in the underground garage, an attendant—a skateboarder in a track suit—rolled over and clipped a plastic placard over her license plate. On the way to the hotel, Tom and Julia had checked her car for damage. The left corner of the bumper was crumpled from hitting the parked car, but that was all. Nothing remarkable, hardly worth mentioning. Even the attendant didn't seem to notice.

Inside the small, elegant lobby, only the desk clerk's hands were visible through a gap for the exchange of cash and keys. No names, no registration. On the adjacent wall were photos of the rooms. If a photo was illuminated, the room was available, and they could press one of two buttons for the desired duration, either the two-hour "Rest" or the overnight "Stay."

"Which room do you want?" Tom asked.

"I don't care," Julia said. "You choose."

There was one with a bed shaped like a space capsule, another like Cinderella's glass slipper. There was a Roman bath, a Texas rodeo. Tom chose the most sedate-looking room, "Bunny Hop," which turned out to be a tacky approximation of a seventies bachelor pad, an homage to Hugh Hefner. Rotating circular bed, fully mirrored ceiling, everything draped in shag. Inside the doorway of the room, Tom flicked a switch, and recessed lights illuminated fluorescent black velvet wall paintings of naked women.

"Uh, no, I don't think so," Julia said, and turned off the black lights.

He kissed her, tasting residual chlorine from the pool, exhaust smoke from the expressway. He began undressing Julia, unbuttoning her blouse and unclasping her bra. Kissing her neck, he cupped her breasts, slid down to suck lightly on her nipples, then undid her pants, slipped off her shoes, and rolled down her underwear. He rose back up, fingertips trailing along the backs of her thighs, caressing her buttocks, and kissed her again, mouth opening wider, tongue mingling. He pulled off his shirt, unbuckled his belt, and tucked his erection between her legs and rubbed it along the blond, warm furrow of her flesh.

He picked her up and carried her to the circular bed, kissed and licked and stroked her entire body, taking his time. He spread open the hood over her clitoris and flicked his tongue on it ever so gently, and when he felt her tensing, he inserted a finger into her vagina and curled it up so her hips rose and she grabbed his head and tugged hard on his hair and moaned.

Eventually, he swam up and kissed her again, and then leaned back on his knees. He held his cock and slowly traced the tip along her genital lips, and then dipped his penis—just the head of it—inside her for a second, and then withdrew.

"Just do it," Julia whispered.

He entered her fully and stayed there awhile, pressing his pelvis into hers, moving in small circles, steadily widening the radius and slipping in and out, shallow thrusts, interspersed by a deep, long one. Hooking his arms under her knees, he lifted her legs, squeezing them against her chest, then, holding one calf in the air, he twisted her around, flipping her onto her stomach while he was still inside her, as if she were on a spit, never losing his rhythm, and fucked her from behind.

"There's something very professional about this," she said. "Were you ever a gigolo?"

At first he took the question as a compliment, but later he wondered: Had his lovemaking been that clinical? He had made her come, but the entire evening, she appeared at a remove, as if she herself were a professional, doing a job. They dressed and rode the elevator to the lobby, got in her car, and drove away from Loch Love, and all the while Julia did not speak to him. She looked very, very tired.

When they arrived at the usual corner in Akasaka, she told him, without a hint of affection, "No one can ever know about this."

▪   ▪   ▪

NIGHTS AFTERWARD, the image of the woman they'd hit—floating in the air, slowly spinning—kept returning to Tom, and he kept asking himself why he had forced Julia to leave the scene. He thought perhaps he had been seized by a moment of hysteria, worried how they would explain being together in her car. Nothing between them had yet happened, but the mere appearance of impropriety would ensure that nothing ever would, and he had wanted something to happen. Perversely, a part of him, a manipulative part he hadn't known existed, had instinctively sensed that the accident would help him. It would bind them together. It would be their secret, their shared burden. It would make Julia beholden to him.

▪   ▪   ▪

HE SEARCHED the English-language newspapers for a report of a hit-and-run, but there was none. Gradually, he stopped fretting about it, thinking they had been right, the woman on the bicycle had not really been hurt.

Nonetheless, as if to avoid incrimination, Julia edged away from Tom. Instead of embarking on an affair in earnest, as he had hoped, she made vague excuses for why she couldn't see him, abruptly cutting off their phone conversations by saying, without explanation, "I have to go."

Tom began pestering Kenzo Ota for updates on Lisa Countryman, reaching for a pretext to see Julia.

"Why you so interest now?" Ota asked him. "You not care so much before."

He didn't get anywhere with Ota on the telephone, so he went to the police station in Roppongi to talk to him in person. They sat in an empty interrogation room with cups of cold tea in front of them on the table. "Look," Tom said, "you're supposed to give me your full cooperation, and that means full disclosure."

"I tell you everything," Ota said. "Nothing new."

"Then why do I get the feeling you're holding out on me? What have you been doing? Have you been doing anything?"

The question was a mistake. It gave Ota the opportunity to regale him with a recitation in his rotten English of his every investigative move in the most detailed, boring, painful fashion imaginable: his interviews with Takagi and Waru, with apartment building neighbors and shopkeepers and bank and post office clerks.

"And you've come up with no leads?"

"Nothing," Ota said.

"I find that hard to believe. What about the purse snatcher?"

Ota shrugged. "Nothing."

"Are you sure you're not leaving anything out?"

"No."

"No, you're not sure, or no, you're not leaving anything out?"

"Not leaving."

"What about putting out posters? Or broadcasting announcements on TV and radio?"

Ota frowned. "Maybe not necessary?"

"Why not?"

Ota didn't answer him.

"Oh, I get it," Tom said. "She was working in Japan illegally, so you figure whatever happened to her, she got what she deserved. You're only going through the motions."

Ota looked at him impassively. "I call you when something new."

■   ■   ■

THE SUMMER was winding down. The Lockheed trial had begun again. Ambassador Mansfield met with a group of top LDP officers at the embassy to discuss the car trade issue and wider access to the telecommunications market. Hua resigned. Nicaragua's Somoza was assassinated. The ROK found Kim Dae Jung guilty of sedition and sentenced him to death. Khomeini seemed to soften the terms for the release of the hostages in Iran.

"They'll never be released before the election," Jorge said.

They were at the Grew House pool—Jorge, Tom, and Benny— sitting on lounge chairs near the deep end, all three wearing sweaters over their shorts. It was downright chilly, but it was the last day the pool would be open, and they'd thought they should take advantage of it.

"Reagan's tapping into this jingoism and xenophobia that's been repressed for years," Jorge said. "After he gets elected, it'll be lone-cowboy time, and fuck the rest of the world. Every single social and civil rights gain we've made in the last twenty years will be repealed."

"You're not being just a little pessimistic?" Benny asked.

"No."

"You're a communist, aren't you?" Benny said. "I don't know why it's never occurred to me before."

Tom saw Julia walking down the other side of the pool with two couples. He knew who they were, he'd seen them before. They were fellow spooks, Pete and Betty Congrieves, Brady and Joanna

Keliher. Congrieves was the DCOS, Deputy Chief of Station, the CIA's number two man in Tokyo. He and Keliher stood out, both tall and athletic and aggressively handsome. Apparently they had been teammates on the basketball team at Yale, members of Skull and Bones.

"Look at those fuckers," Jorge said, and Tom knew exactly what he meant. Somehow, merely by the way they walked and talked—their good looks and affability, the ease of their gestures and their lack of self-consciousness—they seemed to flaunt their ownership of the world, the absolute surety that they were kings.

"Tell the truth," Jorge said. "Deep down, don't you think they're all racists?"

"Those two?" Tom asked.

"All of them. Whites."

"Come on."

"Your problem is you think you can straddle the line," Jorge said. "You think you can be both."

Maybe for a time, growing up, Tom had thought he could be both. At each new post or town or city, he had just tried to blend in, not bring attention to himself, but it had never quite worked. His mother, his Asianness, always seemed to single him out as different, as other. On Yongsan Eighth Army base in Seoul, she had been called a moose—the white wives' epithet for any local girl who bagged a GI. Everyone had assumed she was a hooker from Itaewon, as did most Koreans. Her family had disowned her long ago, when she had first gotten pregnant with Tom.

Julia and her friends had settled around a table near the shallow end of the pool, and they were setting up a picnic. From a cooler, they pulled out wedges of cheese and grapes and crackers and chilled martini glasses, along with a thermos of premixed martinis. Julia, wearing a gauzy wraparound dress over her bathing suit, walked to the edge of the pool. She had not looked across the water to Tom yet, had not acknowledged him, and he thought she was stepping away from the group to wave, or maybe even talk to him. Why couldn't they talk to each other? Why couldn't they be casual acquaintances? They had met swimming laps, spoken at the reception, found they had common interests, once in a while got together for coffee.

She slipped off her sandal and dipped her toe in the water, and Pete Congrieves came up from behind her, and with one arm over her ribs—was his hand on her *breast*?—he casually lifted her in the air and swooped her over the water, as if he were going to drop her in. Julia faked a squeal and, once back on the ground, spun around and punched Congrieves's chest and chided him, and the two of them joined the rest of the group at the table.

Tom kept staring at them, trying to will Julia to glance his way. She was holding her martini, laughing at something Brady Keliher had said. Look at me, look at me, Tom implored her. She put her martini down on the table, extracted a tube of lotion from her purse, and extended her right leg. She bent over and, with both hands, massaged the lotion into her calf. Her hair fell forward into her face, and she used her pinkie to hook it behind her ear, and then she turned her head and stared directly at Tom, giving him a look that stopped time, expressionless, unsmiling, but thoroughly wicked, brazen in her complicity, her open declaration of an adulterous heart.

"Holy shit," Benny said.

"What?" Tom said, riveted.

"Did you see that?" Benny said.

"What have you been doing?" Jorge said. "Have you been fucking her? You have, haven't you?"

"I refuse to answer on the grounds it may—"

"You dumbfuck. I wouldn't be so pleased. You're playing a dangerous game."

Julia had turned away and resumed talking to her friends. The moment had gone unnoticed over there. They drank their martinis, laughed lightheartedly at their jokes and gibes. On Yongsan, the embassy housing compound had been next door to the Army base, and Tom remembered looking across the fence at scenes like this, scenes of bourgeois comfort and glamour. It had seemed to Tom the best life imaginable.

THE FUCKING noises had stopped. It had gone on unabated for a week, the sex noises from No. 501, the apartment above, and then they had mysteriously ceased. Nonetheless, Kenzo had taken to wearing earplugs—first cotton balls squeezed into his ears, secured by Scotch tape, and then foam plugs he found at the drugstore. There was still the refrigerator compressor to contend with, and the footsteps, and the odd thumps and smacks.

He hadn't spoken to Miss Saotome since discovering she was his upstairs neighbor, so when he called, she assumed he had another noise complaint.

"What is it now?"

"Your namecard," Kenzo said.

"Mm, yes?"

"I've been thinking about your services," he said.

"Ah, I thought you might."

"Could we talk, please?"

The next night, they met at the coffeehouse around the corner from the apartment building. Miss Saotome was impeccable in another stylish designer dress, her *chapatsu* hair in a bob. It was the first time Kenzo had had the chance to examine her face closely, and he had to say that she was actually quite plain, with bad teeth, and she was much older than he had believed—a *kurisumasu keeki*.

"Why don't you tell me the type of girl you're looking for?" she said.

"That's not why I called you."

"Don't be shy. I'm sure I can find a match for you. The important thing is to be up-front from the beginning about your likes and dislikes. Now, I assume you want her young, which I can accommodate to a certain point. Do you want a city girl or a country girl?"

"I'm not looking for myself."

"Excuse me? I don't think I understand."

Kenzo shifted in his seat. The plastic chairs in the coffeehouse were uncomfortably hard. "I'd like your help in a police investigation."

"An investigation?"

From his inside suit pocket, he pulled out five sheets of paper, on which he had copied the names of all the nightclubs from Lisa Countryman's notebook, with the two-letter codes in parentheses: PS, IC, SL, NP, SM, NT, PR. "I need to find out what kind of establishments these are, what happens at them."

"What sort of investigation is this? Is this an official investigation?"

"You'll be paid for your time at your usual rates, if that's what you're wondering."

"Oh, I see. Not quite official."

"What, by the way, are your usual rates?"

She stared at the pages. "This wouldn't fall under the usual services. I'll have to think about it."

"You'll assist me, then?"

"I don't know," Miss Saotome said a bit churlishly. "This isn't my forte."

"You would be a great help to me," Kenzo said.

He didn't want another embarrassment as at Splash Poodle. He didn't want any more surprises. He could have tried to locate a sex guidebook, he supposed—there had to be things like that, secret, underground guides with ratings and maps—or combed through porno magazines, but he didn't know where to begin. He certainly couldn't ask anyone at Criminal Investigations. Yamada would have had a field day with the revelation that Kenzo was so ignorant about such matters.

There was also another factor, which was that ever since Miss Saotome had slipped her namecard under his door, he had been thinking about her. He was intrigued. She didn't look like a prostitute or a madam, but she clearly was. Those had obviously been clients visiting, making all those sex noises. Now that it appeared that Lisa Countryman had gone to work as a prostitute, it would be beneficial to learn the mind-set of a prostitute. Miss Saotome could be a convenient resource.

More and more, Kenzo sensed that he was onto something fairly big with Lisa Countryman, which had somehow become apparent to the young bureaucrat from the US Embassy, Tom Hurley, who had had the temerity to show up at the station and question his dedication. A little bit of Kenzo felt almost sorry for him. Handsome or not, it couldn't have been easy for Hurley, being a *haafu*. From personal experience, Kenzo knew about the state of racial equality in America. It was sound in theory, but not in practice. It was a glorious dream, but just a dream. It would never work. It had never worked—not anywhere, not anytime in history—and the US was the only country foolish and hypocritical enough to try.

Like the rest of the world, Japan prized its homogeneity. It was all very orderly and predictable, unambiguous, and very reassuring, the dictates of the group, the importance of tradition, the building of *seken*—consensus. Without *seken*, there was anarchy, the disintegration of society, such as what was happening in America today, beginning with the assassination of John F. Kennedy, the race riots, the sixties, hippies, free love, marijuana, rock and roll, the assassinations of Martin Luther King and Robert Kennedy, Vietnam, Nixon, Watergate. Now there was inflation, skyrocketing interest rates, recession, unemployment, servility to OPEC. What had they expected, with their self-indulgence and immorality and rampant consumerism? Look what they had done to Kenzo's son. Look what they had done to Kenzo's wife, his mother. Now they were trying to export their depravity to Japan, bringing in their McDonald's and Kentucky Fried Chicken and Shakey's Pizza. The Americans couldn't kill them with their radiation, so now they were trying to kill them with their fat and grease, their music and movies, their brands and pop culture, Coca-Cola, Marlboros, Ritz crackers, Planters peanuts, Levi's—the ubiquity of American products was overwhelming. That was what Doug Marabelli was doing in Tokyo, trying to infect the Japanese with more toothpaste and shaving cream and hair lotion. And these *eikaiwa* schools—they were bastardizing the Japanese language into Japlish. It was an assault on all fronts, a coordinated campaign to corrupt the Japanese soul and enslave them with American values. It was another Occupation.

And the Americans thought they were entitled to whatever they wanted, because ultimately they believed they were better. They believed Asians were beneath them. Imperialism never changed in that respect. Now that Japan was fighting back, the Americans were whining about nontariff barriers and trade deficits and defense spending. They were picketing with signs to "Buy American." Their weakness and dissolution was matched only by their arrogance.

Secretly Kenzo was happy about the hostages in Iran, pleased that Americans were getting a taste of the humiliation they deserved, the humiliation they had inflicted upon so many other countries. It was only the beginning, Kenzo believed. Japan, with its economic might, would, in due time, crush the United States.

■   ■   ■

THE FOLLOWING afternoon, Miss Saotome called him at the station. "How did you know which station I work at?" Kenzo whispered, cupping the phone and turning his back to the other detectives.

"It's on your rental application."

"Oh."

"You're a lousy detective, aren't you?"

"Have you decided?"

"I'll help you, but only because I'm curious myself."

She told him to meet her in the lobby of the Shinjuku Prince Hotel that night, but at the appointed hour, nine o'clock, he couldn't find her. She had either backed out or was delayed.

"*Ima nanji?*" Twice before, this fellow, who was loitering nearby Kenzo in the lobby, had asked him for the time. It seemed he was being stood up, too. But then the fellow said, "Miss Saotome sends her regards."

Kenzo looked at the man. He was in a baggy blue suit and had a strange mop of hair that Kenzo could now see was a wig, and his skin was smooth and hairless.

"It's me," Miss Saotome said.

"What are you doing?"

"I'm in disguise."

"I can see that," Kenzo said. What a strange woman, he thought.

"A lot of these places don't allow in women."

"But we're not going inside anywhere. I just want you to explain them to me, tell me how they operate, what goes on in them."

"Where's the fun in that?" Miss Saotome said. "Come on. We'll discuss it over a cup of coffee."

The coffeehouse she took him to was very brightly lit, which wasn't very flattering for Saotome, who had no makeup on. She didn't seem to care. She was practically bouncing out of her seat with excitement. She laid out the sheets he had given her on the table. "I took your list," she said, then unfolded some more papers, "and sorted them according to the codes." She pointed to the group of names under the label PS, one of which was Splash Poodle. "These are 'Pink Salons,' " she said, pronouncing the phrase in mellifluous English. "*Pinku saron.* They have booths there where girls"—she leaned closer to him and whispered—"play the *shakuhachi*." The *shakuhachi* was a traditional Japanese bamboo flute, and it was a common euphemism for fellatio.

She showed him the page with the SL code. "These are 'Soaplands,' *sopurando*. They used to be called Turkish baths, but the Turks took offense. The girls will start out with *shakuhachi*, and then will soap the man up and lie on top of him and give him the, eh, human sponge treatment and get him *very* clean." She put her hand over her mouth and giggled.

Kenzo stared at her. "Have you been drinking? Are you drunk?"

"I just had one drink to calm myself. Okay, maybe two drinks."

She identified more categories—PR for "Peeping Rooms," HC for "Hostess Clubs"—but Kenzo became preoccupied with the noises in the coffeehouse. People kept dropping things onto the linoleum floor, spoons, pens, the impacts making him jump, just as the sounds from Miss Saotome's apartment did. He turned around, looked across the room, and noticed three things. One, all the customers were men. Two, the waitresses wore extremely short miniskirts. Three, whenever a waitress approached or passed, the men dropped items and bent down to retrieve them, falling in succession like dominoes, lingering in that twisted-sideways position and staring upward.

"What's going on here?" Kenzo said.

Miss Saotome smiled and tapped on the list under the code NP. "We're in a 'No-Panty' coffeehouse, *no-pan kissa*. The waitresses don't wear underwear."

Kenzo looked across the room again and saw an older man who was clearly a veteran. To save himself the trouble of bending over, he had brought along a hand mirror, which he held beside his chair and angled strategically.

"Let's go to another place," Miss Saotome said.

"Absolutely not."

"Oh, come on. I'll never have the opportunity or courage to do this again."

"No."

"Just three more places from the list."

"No."

"Two, then. Just two."

Kenzo considered it. Weirdly, he thought he would feel safer and less embarrassed going to these establishments with Miss Saotome, and he knew he wouldn't have this opportunity again, either. "Only places where we can watch. No touching," he said. "I don't want to be touched."

■   ■   ■

RED NEW ART was an IC, an "Image Club," or *imekura*, where there was a choice of fantasy rooms, including a fake office in which salarymen could indulge in *sekuhara*—sexual harassment—with office ladies, coming up to the pretend OLs from behind as they stood at mimeograph machines and pressing against their buttocks and squeezing their breasts. Red New Art did not allow *shakuhachi* or penetration of any sort—just one-way male-to-female molestation. Most of the rooms featured *rori-kon*—Lolita complex—girls who dressed in schoolgirl outfits. There was a whole industry built around *rori-kon*, including the sale of girls' used underpants in vending machines on the street, but the fixation, as long as it remained within limits, didn't necessarily carry negative connotations in Japan. It wasn't considered pedophilia. It was considered almost normal.

At the Red New Art, they had a classroom where schoolgirls wrote characters on a blackboard, waiting for "teachers" to walk in and rip their panties down (for an extra charge, the panties could be taken home as souvenirs). The train room, however, was by far the most popular. It was designed for closet *chikan*—gropers—simulating a commuter train with benches, strap handles dangling from rods, and a soundtrack of train noises.

Kenzo and Miss Saotome stood to the side and watched several men eyeing four schoolgirls who stood hanging on to the straps, oblivious. Everyone, including Kenzo and Miss Saotome, soon fell into the rhythm of the soundtrack, unconsciously swaying with the clacking of the train as it rolled over the track seams. Slowly, surreptitiously, the men crept closer to the girls until they were beside them, and then they flicked their hands out for a quick grab of ass cheek. The girls gasped and spun around, and the men—staring off in opposite directions—pretended to be innocent bystanders. A few minutes passed, and it began all over again.

"You know what I used to do?" Miss Saotome said as they walked out of the room. "Whenever I rode a train during rush hour, I carried a safety pin in case I needed to defend myself."

What was extraordinary about the image club was how quiet and well-behaved the men were. Miss Saotome decided this was too tame; they needed to go to a real strip bar.

Mona Lisa Honey was an NT, a "Nude Theater," or *nudo gekijo*. Kenzo and Miss Saotome sat in the back, and she began ordering *mizuwari* after *mizuwari*, whiskey and water, complaining to him that there was hardly any alcohol in the drinks. Kenzo nodded, wondering how much the final bill would be. She had told him she would not charge him for her tour-guide services tonight, but he had to pick up all the expenses.

The preliminary shows were pretty straightforward. Women dressed as stewardesses and nurses dancing and stripping onstage. One woman with an aloha skirt, shorts, and Day-Glo green lipstick came out with a surfboard and pretended to ride waves, windmilling her arms to keep her balance, which made her breasts spin very impressively in contrapuntal circles. Kenzo realized that it was the first time he had ever seen a live naked woman other than his wife, Yumiko, but oddly there wasn't much sensual about the experience. Was it because they were sitting so far back? Or was it the lighting, so dark where they were, so bright on the stage, creating a surreal divide?

There were no Christian notions of sin in Japan. Like everyone else, Kenzo was not prudish. He viewed sex as a natural bodily function. He didn't find any of this immoral. Yet, nor did he find it titillating. He felt nothing.

The waitresses were walking around the room with wicker baskets, and men raised their hands and were given shiny chrome implements.

"What are those?" Kenzo asked.

"They're renting magnifying glasses," Miss Saotome said.

"What for?"

"Just watch."

This time the four strippers who stepped onto the stage were all Asian *gaijin*. They looked to be Thai and Filipina, maybe Korean. Apparently they were the main attraction. They did the regular bump-and-grind and disrobed, but then they sat on the edge of the stage, leaned back, lifted their legs, and spread their knees apart. One by one, blue-suited salarymen came up to the women with their magnifying glasses for a scrupulous examination of their genitalia.

"*Nanda-ro,*" Kenzo said.

Miss Saotome looked as unsettled as he was.

The MC appeared and bellowed on the microphone, asking if anyone in the audience was man enough to fuck these beautiful women. Did anyone have the balls?

After much cajoling, four very drunk men were pushed up onto the stage. The women—whose expressions were utterly vacant—pulled down the men's pants, and the MC ridiculed the size of their penises. The women performed *shakuhachi,* and the MC ridiculed the men for not being able to get it up. One man, sweating, shut his eyes and covered his ears with his hands, concentrating with all his might to induce an erection. Another slunk off the stage, flaccid, a failure. The two others were only partially aroused but fumbled to gain entry, anyway. A replacement, a pinch hitter, emerged and unzipped his trousers. Though short and thin and wan, he had an enormous cock that required no encouragement from the stripper. "Can you believe this?" the MC roared. "Where did this horse come from?"

The man knelt between the legs of the stripper and inserted his penis, making the woman wince, and then started whanging away at her mercilessly.

"I have to go," Miss Saotome said suddenly. "I have to go."

Jumping up, she knocked over their table, tipping their drinks and peanuts and *oshibori* to the floor, and ran out of the club. Kenzo, after quickly settling their bill, followed her out to the street. "What is it? What's wrong?" he asked her.

One hand on a telephone pole, she leaned over to the gutter and retched.

"You've had too much to drink," he said.

She vomited again, heaving, then wiped her mouth with a handkerchief. "That was disgusting. Sick."

"It's okay," Kenzo said. "I can't drink, either."

"No, the show. It was horrible."

Kenzo was confused. "But you must be used to such things."

"What?" she said.

"In your line of work."

"What are you talking about? In what line of work?"

"You're a prostitute."

"What?"

"Aren't you?"

"Where did you get that idea?"

"You're not a prostitute?"

"Of course not!"

"But your namecard."

"I'm a romance consultant. A matchmaker. I arrange dates, marriages. I'm a female *nakodo*." A go-between.

"Oh," Kenzo said.

"How could you be so stupid?" She slapped his arm.

"I'm sorry."

"*Baka ja naino*," she said. "How could you think I was a prostitute?"

"Then how did you know about these businesses?"

She dug into her pocket, took out a little black book, and tossed it at him, bouncing it off his chest. He picked it up. *The Tokyo City*

Sex Guide. "You can get it at practically any bookstore, you idiot! Every place on your list is in there. How come you're so clueless? You should know these things."

"What about the noises?"

"What noises?"

"The noises from your apartment. Sex noises."

She slapped his arm again. "Those are from the woman next door to me! She's a stewardess. One week a month when she's back in town, her fiancé comes over."

"Oh."

"I thought you were kind of cute in a blundering, neurotic way, but you're an idiot! A moron!"

"I'm sorry."

She yanked off her wig and pitched it into his face. "*Iikagen ni shite-yo!*" she said—Leave me alone!—and sprinted down the street.

■　　■　　■

The Tokyo City Sex Guide turned out to be very informative. One important fact was that almost all of these clubs admitted only Japanese men and hardly ever employed white *gaijin* women. It was a waste of time, then, to visit anyplace on the lists other than hostess clubs, the one business which did hire *gaijin,* preferably blondes with blue eyes. These hostesses were not necessarily prostitutes, Kenzo noted attentively.

The mama-sans were no more cooperative than anyone else, however, saying they had never seen anyone resembling Lisa Countryman in her photo. He went to a dozen hostess clubs in Roppongi and Akasaka before a mama-san finally said she thought she recognized her.

"Was she looking for a job?" Kenzo asked.

"No. She interviewed *me*. She asked me all sorts of questions."

"What kinds of questions?"

"About my background, how I got into the business. Pretty nosy," the mama-san said. "She wanted to know what I thought about the roles of men and women in Japanese society, stuff like that. She said she was doing research."

"Research? For what?"

"For a book."

The next day, Kenzo called Susan Countryman from the police station. "Your sister is writer, maybe journalist?" he asked.

"No, she's a graduate student. Why?"

"What kind graduate student?"

"Anthropology."

"She study in Virginia?"

"California. Berkeley."

"Why you not tell me this before?"

"Why you not ask me this before?" she said.

He hung up and got the main number for the University of California, Berkeley. From the switchboard operator he was transferred to the registrar, then the graduate dean's office, then the chair of the anthropology department in Kreber Hall, who said, "Well, I can't say I was all too keen on her dissertation subject. I mean, women's studies—it seems like so much fashion. And contemporary Japan? To tell you the truth, I've always resisted the idea of ethnography qualifying as real anthropology. What did you say has happened to her?"

Kenzo returned to the hostess clubs on the list. He didn't know what to think about Lisa Countryman anymore. She was not looking for a job at a hostess club (or as a prostitute), after all? She was doing fieldwork for her Ph.D. in anthropology? In any event, he was about to give up. He was getting nowhere with the mama-sans and hostesses and *tencho*. No one in this business would give him the time of day. Then, finally, as he was leaving a club called the Bogart Den one night, he saw, coming out of the restroom, an attractive blonde with extraordinary legs, a blonde Kenzo was sure he had met before. It was the blonde who had winked at him in the Shimbashi office of Rocket America.

TEN

RIGHT AWAY, Lisa could tell that Rendezvous in Ginza was different. Unlike Musky Club, which allowed anyone to walk in off the street as long as he could pay the entrance fee, Rendezvous was members-only and had the application procedures of a country club—stringent and exclusive. An existing member had to formally recommend the applicant, who was then asked to provide three references who could attest to his character. If admitted, he was required to pay a hefty initiation, including a wildly exorbitant fee for a bottle of liquor to be kept at the club (*botoru-kipu*, or bottle-keep), which was marked with a numbered tag and shelved neatly on an illuminated display behind the bar.

These clients weren't your usual salarymen. They were politicians, ambassadors, famous actors, art dealers, shipping tycoons, scions of society. They were presidents and top executives from major corporations, brokerage firms, and pharmaceutical companies who thought nothing of writing off thousands of dollars for a single night on their expense accounts. In return, they expected and were given the best.

The club was posh, intimate, and elegant. A hand-etched glass partition at the entrance, eight velvet booths, chandeliers, a grand piano, silver Tiffany ashtrays, gold-plated fixtures in the marble restrooms. Instead of a karaoke machine, Rendezvous had a full-time pianist on hand, as well as three tuxedoed waiters, the *chifu*, or chief, who prepared the snacks and drinks, the *tencho*, and the mama-san, Midori, who presided over a rotation of twelve hostesses, all of whom were pretty, young, and educated.

Midori was a petite woman in her late thirties. She exuded a dignified beauty, with each gesture intimating a wealth of manners and poise, and she demanded that her hostesses project a similar nobility.

After Harper Boyd had brought her to the club to be interviewed, Lisa was informed of Midori's very specific rules of etiquette. She couldn't smoke or eat in front of the customers. In general, she couldn't masticate. She was forbidden from biting her fingernails and chewing gum and gnawing on swizzle sticks. Any kind of slouching was a no-no. She had to sit up straight, couldn't put her elbows on the table, her hands in her pockets, or cross her legs more than was absolutely necessary. Expelling anything from the nose or mouth, much less exposing the insides of those cavities, was strictly *verboten*. If she had to blow her nose, she was to go to the restroom. If she laughed, she was to cover her mouth with her hand, but not touch it, her pinky raised slightly. When she bowed, she was to keep both palms flat against her thighs and lower her eyes, and when she held a glass or a cup, she was to use both hands, the left underneath, the right around the side.

There were also the issues of makeup and clothes. Before Lisa was allowed to begin working, she was forced to endure several dress rehearsals with Midori, who twice summarily dismissed her, telling her to go home and change. "Who taught you to dress?" Midori asked. "A street hooker?" Lisa was wearing a low-cut pink angora sweater with a black leather skirt and a macramé belt and vinyl go-go boots, all of which she had bought on an earlier shopping expedition with Rebecca Silo. Simple, understated cocktail dresses or suits, Midori said. No sweaters. No wool, cotton, leather, or vinyl. Nothing loud or see-through or with spots or patterns or plaid. No cleavage, no going without a bra. No slits, no sequins. Nothing fluffy or puffy.

As for makeup, Midori had to give Lisa a full course in cosmetology. She taught her to use astringent to clean her face and then apply, in order: a cold compress to reduce the swelling in her eyes; a water-based moisturizer, always rubbed in upward sweeps; foundation, dotted on, then sponged and blended, making sure there wasn't a foundation line on her neck; concealer for her freckles and any blemishes and dark circles; a comb for her eyebrows; eye shadow; an eyeliner pencil; an eyelash curler; two coats of mascara; a lip pencil; lipstick; and powdered blush—all to the miraculous effect that she wasn't wearing any makeup at all.

"What's your blood?" Midori asked. "French? Italian?"

Lisa shrugged. She was cowed, utterly intimidated, by Midori.

"You have that nice olive complexion, but your hair . . ."

She sent Lisa to her hairdresser, who instantly rid her of her split ends and Farrah Fawcett wings.

Now that she was reasonably presentable, the real test, Midori told her, was to see how well she could mix with customers. Mondays were slow nights—a good night for her to start. The club was open from seven to 11:45 p.m., and Lisa was there promptly at six, the first girl to arrive. Harper Boyd and the other hostesses—all Japanese—trickled in closer to six-thirty. They were pleasant enough toward Lisa, but they seemed to maintain a deliberate distance from her.

"They think of us as novelty hostesses," Harper told Lisa. "The token *gaijin*. Amateurs, in their eyes. They're willing to tolerate us as long as we don't hang around too long and horn in on the fat cats."

Lisa sat with the girls at the bar, waiting for some customers to enter the club, and she learned that this was the most boring part of the job, having to perch primly on the stools, back straight, not allowed to do anything—no eating, reading, smoking, gum-chewing, excessive or animated talking—until Midori called upon them, even though the club didn't really get going until nine o'clock.

Deep into the evening, Midori at last chose Lisa, who was the sole hostess remaining at the bar, save for Emi. Truth be told, Emi appeared to be a hanger-oner, several years beyond the time she should have retired. She was older than the other girls by far, twenty-eight, twenty-nine, and was, in comparison, homely.

"Emi, Lisa, *onegaishimasu*," Midori said when a group of men had been seated at a booth.

Emi grabbed a box of matches and cheerfully sprang up from the barstool. Lisa stood behind her as Emi asked the group if they could join them, and then the two women nestled between the men in the booth.

"It's been so long since your last visit," Emi said to Mr. Kimura, who was a longtime member. "I've missed you so much. Have you forgotten your promise to make me your mistress?"

"Mistress!" a man said. Kimura's guests howled, delighted by the mere suggestion. Kimura, the president of a computer company who was entertaining some parts suppliers tonight, was at least seventy-five years old and decrepit. He didn't seem capable of ambulation, much less sexual activity, extracurricular or otherwise.

"Yes," Emi said, "Kimura-san's prowess is well-known. He's famous for being able to satisfy six, seven women a night."

"Six or seven?" one of the parts suppliers said. "So few?" The others laughed. "I think you're confusing his reputation with mine. If you want a real man, you should join my harem."

"No, I'm devoted to Kimura-san," Emi said, laying her cheek against the old man's shoulder.

A few minutes later, Midori reappeared in the room, having changed into a resplendent kimono. Everyone in the club clapped.

"Oh, she's a true *bijin*," Mr. Kimura said—a traditional beauty. "She has so much class. That's why her club is so well-respected."

Eventually Midori made her way to their table. "Kimura-san," she said, "how is your back?"

"My back?"

"The last time you were here, you were afflicted with back pain."

"That was months ago," he said, astonished she would remember.

"Has it been that long since your last visit?" she said. "No wonder I've felt this vague yearning, as though I were missing something vital to me."

Clearly Midori knew the exact date of Kimura's last visit, and she and Emi were ensuring that there would not be another lapse of comparable length. Midori remembered everything, Lisa would learn— each customer's name, his job, his likes and dislikes—and she molded all interactions according to her customers' preferences. Nothing happened at her club without her explicit choreography.

Emi summarized what they had been talking about thus far, and when Midori heard that Kimura's worthiness as a lover and a patron had been questioned, Midori threw in her own endorsement. "He is so sweet and thoughtful," she said. "Such a gentleman toward his many girlfriends, but a fierce business competitor. He is a man of great integrity. In addition to being virile, he is aristocratic and wise. He will be loyal to you, as long as you are equally loyal to him. I would be honored to have him as my patron."

Kimura beamed, and the parts suppliers were duly impressed.

Midori leaned closer to Kimura to chat with him privately. When Lisa next glanced over to them, they were still huddled together, Kimura appearing as invigorated and enraptured as if he were back in high school, on a date.

He must have known that he was being manipulated, that nothing Midori said or did was sincere, yet he allowed himself to be seduced, to fall under her spell. He looked like he would do anything for her. That kind of power fascinated Lisa, and, at that moment, she became determined to possess it.

■   ■   ■

DURING THE day, Lisa did her research. She went to the library, she took Japanese classes, she conducted interviews. Trying to narrow down her dissertation topic further, she talked to a dozen or so women—housewives, OLs, a doctor, a schoolteacher, a *sopurando* girl—about their ambitions and desires, their thoughts on work and love and motherhood, the Japanese educational system, company life, sexism, conformity, arranged marriages, that awful Christmas cake designation for women over twenty-five. She approached them mostly in coffee shops, saying she was writing an article for *Time* magazine. No one ever asked for credentials, and they seemed quite pleased to be participating in yet another *Nihonjin-ron,* an analysis of what it meant to be Japanese. The Japanese, she had discovered, were endlessly enamored with themselves as a people, with what they saw as their collective uniqueness.

She was busy, and, as the new girl at Rendezvous, she didn't have many nights off, and Omar was getting frustrated. Things were not going well. He was demanding more and more of her, even though she had warned him not to from the beginning. "I'm not good in relationships," she had said. "We're fundamentally incompatible," she had said. "Stop being so nice to me. It'll only drive me away," she had said.

He was too normal for her. He had been born and raised in a little coastal town called Rosarita Bay, just south of San Francisco. Same town, same house, his entire childhood. He came from a big family, five brothers and sisters, both parents loving and attentive, holidays crowded with relatives. He had gone to San Jose State University for his bachelor's in public relations, and he was now earning his master's in management at Yokosuka through Troy State's extension program. He was an Ensign—a commissioned officer. Lisa's father, after thirty-eight years in the Navy, had retired as a Master Chief Petty Officer—an enlisted man.

After Omar fulfilled his Navy ROTC commitment, he planned to return to the Bay Area and work in the personal computer industry, which he predicted would boom. He didn't have a care in the world. Nothing made him doubt himself or kept him up nights. Except for Lisa, that is. Lisa, whom he hardly had a chance to see. Lisa, whose appearance had changed dramatically of late. Lisa, who was so hard to figure, so aloof, who never seemed able to relax or have any fun, who had so much buried hostility, who drank too much, who wasn't neat enough, who didn't seem to care about him one way or another.

It ended soon after she began working at Rendezvous. They were eating lunch at a sushi restaurant near her apartment, and Omar's curiosity was getting the better of him. He kept asking her what happened at these hostess clubs. "Why are you being so secretive?"

"I'm not," she said.

"So tell me."

"I've told you. I've told you everything."

"They pay all that money just to *talk*?"

"What is it that you're thinking? Why don't you just come out and say it?"

He shook his head. "It's your hours, more than anything. We're never together anymore."

"You don't trust me."

"I trust you."

"It's just as well you don't," she said. "You should never trust anyone. You'll end up getting betrayed."

"Are you going to betray me?"

"It's a general comment about the state of the world as we know it."

They settled the bill and walked out to the street. "You're deeply cynical," Omar said. "It's not a very attractive quality."

She stepped off the curb without looking and was almost mowed down by a taxicab. The driver honked and swerved, and Omar yanked her back.

"Jesus," he said, "you have a death wish?"

"You ripped my shirt."

"What's the matter with you? I don't understand you at all. Why won't you let anyone get close to you? Don't you feel anything?"

"I'm not a good person," she said.

"Why do you say that? Of course you are."

"I only bring bad luck to people."

"That's ridiculous."

"You're angry with me."

"No."

She could tell that he was. "Go ahead," she said. "Be angry. I can take it."

"Lisa, I don't know what you want from me," Omar said. "You

want me to treat you bad? Sometimes I think you do. The way you just lie there when we make love. Sometimes I think you want me to degrade you."

"Oh, I see. Is that what you're into?"

"What?"

"Are those your predilections?"

"You're kidding, right?"

"I can't give you what you want. You want the girl next door. The white girl."

"So it's jungle fever now? Make up your mind. I can't keep up with you. I don't even know what we're arguing about."

Her relationships always ended like this, with vague misunderstandings and hurt feelings. She had never been able to sustain anything longer than a few months. She had a special gift, which was the ability to turn nice guys into assholes. On the surface, it seemed she had yet to learn anything about manipulating men, but perversely this was what she wanted, to sabotage things before they got too far, before she became too attached, before she was seen for who she really was. She recognized this about herself. Recognizing it didn't prevent her from doing it. She was tempted to lie to Omar and tell him that she was a prostitute, just to ensure that he would not return, but she had a feeling it wouldn't be necessary, and she was right. He went back to the base that day, and she didn't hear from him again.

■ ■ ■

THE THREE men were telling Lisa that their boss was lazy, ugly, and incompetent. Their boss, Murayama, sat at the table, smiling, soaking up the camaraderie.

"Oh, you guys are so hard on me," he said.

"He doesn't get into the office until eleven-thirty," Uchida said, "and the first thing he does after setting down his briefcase is say, 'Oh, it's lunchtime.' "

"He's always chasing after the OLs," Shimaki said. "He thinks he's a real ladies' man, but the girls are repulsed by him."

"And his golf game!" Ogata said. "I tell you, I've never seen a worse golfer. I'm shocked he's allowed on the course, he's so dangerous. He sprays balls left and right. He has absolutely no control over his shots. Once, I saw him try to hit a tee shot, and the ball went backwards!"

They all guffawed, the boss, Murayama, most of all. This was his doing, the ragging and ribbing. After they had been ensconced in the booth, after the waiter had brought over the boss's bottle-keep of whiskey, a crystal ice bucket, mineral water, *oshibori*, and tiny dishes of soybeans, peanuts, and grapes, after a toast and some nervous chitchat, after Lisa had come to their booth and introductions had been made, Murayama had said, "*Bureiko shimashoka?*"—Shall we take a break?—signaling that the corny, good-natured insults, the nonsensical derision and mockery, the insipid jokes and non sequiturs, the pathetic attempts at wit, the childish shoves and bumps, the drunken giggles and near-pee-in-the-pants convulsions and hysterics over the most unamusing comments, the silly boasts and one-upmanship about who had the biggest dick and was the biggest *sukebei*—lecher—could begin. This was all about male bonding, solidifying group cohesion. They tore into each other and then built themselves back up. For every putdown, there was an equal and opposite homage.

The talk inevitably turned to sex, but these evenings out weren't really about sex. They could have gone to a Pink Salon or a Soapland for that. Hostesses weren't for sale. The better and tonier the club, the more difficult the hostesses were to date outside the club, and of course their unattainability was part of their allure.

The hostesses made the customers believe there was a tiny chance they might sleep with them, and, tantalized, the men kept coming back to the club, spending more and more money. The point was to keep them on a string, keep them spending for as long as possible. A hostess might say no tonight, but if she was good at her job, the man felt charmed, not frustrated, and would go home thinking he might get lucky on another night.

True, the men could become saccharine and obsessive, proclaiming devotion and heartache, but Lisa suspected they secretly enjoyed the teasing, the torture of unrequited love. It was in line with *mono no aware,* the Japanese penchant for poignancy and sadness. It also corresponded to the generally accepted notion that if a hostess—after being plied with gifts and adoration, or after getting a financial offer she couldn't refuse ($10,000 for one night seemed to be the going rate, but a Porsche was not unheard of)—if she succumbed and finally consented to sex, the game would be over. Almost certainly, the man would no longer be interested in the hostess and would stop coming to the club. That was why Midori forbade her hostesses from going on *dohan* with customers. She would fire them if she found out, she said.

Lisa proved to be a good hostess, much to her own surprise, given her distaste for small talk, her unwillingness to suffer fools. She would never admit it, but she began to like the attention she was receiving from the men, as well as their money (she was making three times more at Rendezvous than she had at Musky Club). It was intoxicating, the use of her femininity, the art of flirting, being told she was beautiful. She developed a persona—a club Lisa that was much different from the real Lisa, a livelier, sexier Lisa. She was playing a role outside of herself—in service of her fieldwork, she told herself—and she changed the role to suit the circumstance. If they wanted boisterous, she could be boisterous. If they wanted demure, she could be demure. A large part of being a

good hostess was the ability to evaluate within a matter of minutes
what men wanted from her, listening and watching and picking up
subtle cues, and adapting to them. It was very much like being a
spy, she thought.

Usually her role was to dole out breathless, vapid, hyperbolic
compliments. Oh, you're *suteki*—fantastic. *Iroppoi*—sexy. *Han-
sumu*—handsome. You're so strong. You're very smart. I love your
tie—it's Pierre Cardin? What a beautiful Rolex. You're very fash-
ionable. You look like a Parisian man. She reinforced whatever
image the customer wanted to appropriate for himself, and never
doubted or challenged his authority. No matter how bored or tired
she was, she never appeared less than completely enthralled.

At all costs, she had to keep the conversation going. If there was
an awkward pause, any sort of dead air, it would create great anxiety among the men, and she had to do whatever was necessary to
avert it. This sometimes meant allowing herself to be humiliated,
reminded in no uncertain terms that she was inferior to the men. If
need be, she let them belittle her, criticize her appearance, order
her around, paw her. Such wanton behavior wasn't as forceful or
frequent as it had been at Musky Club, but it still existed at
Rendezvous. She knew how to handle it better now. Instead of
slapping away groping hands, she took them in her own. "Let's
hold hands, okay?" Or she laughed and gently scolded them, "You
bad boy, you," and moved away to reach for the ice, or excused
herself to go to the bathroom.

After two weeks at Rendezvous, Lisa thought she understood
everything there was to understand at the club, but then a trio of
men came in who immediately baffled her. Two of them were in
their sixties and entirely forgettable in their looks, but one was in
his early thirties and almost beautiful.

He was slender, with long, thin limbs, and long, thin fingers, and
a long, thin neck. He seemed almost sickly, he was so delicate and

languid, but on closer examination, Lisa could see that the impression was false. He was watchful and alert to everything that was happening around him. He had thick hair brushed back from his forehead, angular cheekbones, and obtrusive lips. He looked like a Japanese movie star. Perhaps Midori or another hostess would recognize him and tell her later who he was. Obviously, he was someone special, because the expected hierarchy among the men was inverted. By seniority, he should have been the others' subordinate, but he seemed to be the one in charge, the one who commanded deference. Lisa couldn't figure it out. He didn't appear to be a rich entrepreneur, a *wunderkind* whose business the older men were trying to court, and there was too much of an age gap for the men to be friends.

The dynamics were further confused by two other factors. First, the younger man didn't talk. He hardly said two words the entire hour they were in the club. Second, the men identified themselves with pseudonyms: Moe, Larry, and Curly.

"The Three Stooges," Moe said in hesitant English. "You understand Three Stooges?"

"Yes," Lisa said. "Nyuk, nyuk, nyuckleheads."

Apparently this allusion was too far beyond Moe's capacity, for he stared at her as if she were foaming at the mouth.

"Is there a reason why you're using an alias?" she asked Curly, the other older gentleman.

"*Nani?*"

"Why Three Stooges?" she asked a little slower.

"Ah, secret," he said, and tittered.

"We not here," Moe said, and the two of them cackled.

Another of the qualities for which Midori was renowned was her discretion. There were certain customers who, for whatever reason, wanted to maintain their anonymity. Perhaps their dealings with their guests were not wholly aboveboard. Perhaps they were engaging in bribes, back-door deals, kickbacks. Midori accommodated them with accounts that remained nameless, identified only by bottle-keep number—in the case of Moe, Larry, and Curly, No. 397. Tabs were settled at the end of the month in cash, with no paper trails.

"So, Moe and Curly," Lisa said, "you two are brothers?"

"Yes, brothers," Moe said. "Twins!"

It was an unimaginative icebreaker, but it always worked. "I see. And where are you from?"

"Sweden," Curly said. "Stockholm."

"What do you all do for a living?"

"I am sumo wrestler," Moe said. "Curly is Olympic skier. Larry is . . ." They looked at the younger man. "Larry is garbage man."

They laughed, but they hardly got a rise from the silent Larry. He didn't seem irritated. He wasn't sulking. In fact he might have been slightly bemused. Yet he was inexplicably mute, a detached, impassive observer.

"Really we are"—Curly checked and made sure no one was within earshot—"*yakuza,* gangsters."

"*So desu ka?*" Lisa whispered.

"*Honto-ni,*" Curly asserted. "Can you know how old are we?"

This was one of the customers' favorite games at the club. "You are thirty-three," she said to Moe. "And you are twenty-seven," she said to Curly. "And you," she said to Larry, "you can't be a day younger than seventy-one."

Moe and Curly chuckled, pleased by the profoundly clever repartee. They asked all the perfunctory, predictable questions of her: where was she from, what was she (French-Italian, she told them, as she told everyone at the club), why was she in Japan ("Ah, *insei,*" they said—graduate student—nodding), how long had she been here, did she like it, did she like Japanese men, had she ever had any Japanese boyfriends.

By now Lisa had learned that customers weren't really interested in her answers. They didn't want her life story. They wanted entertainment—a peculiar brand of Japanese entertainment that celebrated the baldest, most transparent exaggerations. "I've had one hundred ninety-three Japanese boyfriends," Lisa said, "and I've slept with them all!"

"*Wa, sugoi!*" the two men exclaimed—Incredible!—and hooted.

Midori, dressed in another sparkling kimono, shuffle-stepped to the grand piano at the head of the room and, after a smattering of applause and a short speech of welcome, began singing a famous *enka* song, "Namida-goi."

Enka was a traditional Japanese style of folk ballads that featured drawn-out notes and swelling vibratos. To Lisa, it sounded like warbling, atonal screeching, like an animal dying. The songs were always tragic, nostalgic, melodramatic tributes to love, death, and abandonment, to women, *sake,* and rain. In other words, *enka* was the Japanese equivalent of country-and-western.

Midori did a lovely job with "Namida-goi," and then she invited the customers in the club to come take a turn at the microphone. A few did. One man from the adjoining booth, where Harper Boyd and Emi sat, gave a very accomplished rendition of Don Ho's "Tiny Bubbles," but evidently this was a song he performed repeatedly. He had even come prepared with costume: an aloha shirt. While he sang, his coworkers jokingly stuffed napkins into their ears and held their noses as if he were emanating a stink and dismissed him as "*wan patan*"—one pattern. Some people took voice lessons, Lisa knew, and practiced for these occasions. They urged another man in the group to sing, but he protested vociferously, saying he was *hazukashii* (ashamed), *heta* (bad), *hidoi* (awful). Finally he trudged up to the piano and blinked in the glare of the spotlight. He adjusted the music stand and flipped through the songbooks, and at last launched into Glen Campbell's "Galveston."

It was a pedestrian recital, but his friends clapped heartily, and the man returned to the booth wiping a handkerchief across his brow, immensely relieved. This was another ritualistic initiation: everyone felt closer after a weaker member had endured such a petrifying trial, risking exposure and embarrassment but pulling through with the others' support.

"You sing?" Moe said to Lisa.

"No, no," she said. He was the first customer to ask.

"Please sing," Curly said.

"Oh, I would really rather not, if that's okay." When she was a child, her parents had sometimes tried to get her onstage with them, but she had hated singing in public, convinced everyone in the audience was trying to dissect her features.

"Why you don't sing?" Curly asked.

"Sing," Moe said, more as an order than a request.

Larry looked at her without expression.

She exhaled. "All right." She stood and smoothed out her dress and walked nervously to the microphone. Out of the blue, she decided on "My Funny Valentine," and straightaway, she flubbed it. She was half a beat late entering the song, and had to ask the piano player to start over.

"*Gomen nasai,*" she apologized into the microphone. "*Hazukashii.*"

She took several deep breaths. She told herself to relax, listen to the music. She closed her eyes and began to sing, letting the lyrics come to her.

The four minutes she was up there would remain a blank to Lisa, the moment both interminable and evaporative. She would remember nothing of that first performance, although people would keep talking about it the rest of the time she was at Rendezvous, about the purity of her voice, about her perfect pitch and three-octave range, her slow, melancholy, mysterious phrasing, her haunting timbre, her dramatic use of crescendo and sustain, about the influences and nuances of blues and jazz they heard—Ella Fitzgerald, Aretha Franklin, Billie Holiday, Odetta Felious, even Joan Baez. Most of all, they talked about the overpowering emotion that flowed out of her, the rawness and passion. It stopped them in their tracks. It broke their hearts. It left them so stupefied, they did not clap when Lisa finished the song, and, slinking back to her booth, she was horrified, believing she must have been terrible.

Finally, Moe began clapping, and the applause grew and grew, booming, and Midori, in the back of the room, looked on with a mixture of surprise and mercantile interest, and Emi, from the next booth, glared at Lisa with unadulterated hatred, and Harper Boyd smiled and said, "I knew I'd regret bringing you here."

E L E V E N

I T WAS standing-room-only in P-Moto 180, the gallery in Ginza, for the opening reception of Julia's photography show. The bulk of the crowd was made up of Japanese artists, collectors, and students and colleagues from the ISA, with a small cluster of people from the embassy: Jay Steiner, the cultural attaché, the Kelihers and the Congrieves, and Julia's husband, Vincent Kitamura, who was roaming through the gallery on his own.

Tom squeezed through the crowd to Julia, who was surrounded by Yoshi, the owner of Flashbacks, and some artist friends from his bar. She didn't appear pleased to see Tom. "This is a surprise," she said. She hadn't sent him an invitation.

She had been assiduously avoiding Tom, often not returning the messages he left for her at the ISA, cool and curt when he did happen to catch her. Her aloofness had only made Tom more desperate to see her, and, remembering her show, he had found the time and location in a listing of gallery openings.

She leaned closer to him and whispered, "I can't talk to you here. Do you understand?"

Yoshi said something in Japanese to the group that Tom didn't comprehend, and they all laughed.

"I hope you like the show," Julia said, and turned to greet an elderly patron.

Stung, Tom wandered away from them to look at photographs.

In her artist's statement, Julia referred to the series as guerrilla photography. They were life-size black-and-white enlargements of people, all from the same vantage point. It looked like it was on a street in Shibuya, near Parco or Marui. In the background, there was an intersection painted with zebra stripes, and pedestrians were crossing quickly from all sides with the stoplight—they called it a scramble in Japan. But the subjects in the photographs had lingered. There were twelve of them: a college student, a housewife, a carpenter, an old man, a schoolgirl, an OL, a cook, a salaryman, an elevator girl, a uniformed cop, a train conductor, a *bosozoku*— or motorcycle gang—member. Somehow they had been caught unaware—they hadn't been ready for this, they hadn't expected this—and they were staring at the camera in strangled expressions, frozen in fright or shock or nervous laughter. Their faces were contorted, their limbs bent at odd, dislocated angles, their fingers arthritic. They were eerie pictures, too candid and raw for comfort, almost pornographic in effect. They were really quite beautiful. They changed the way Tom viewed Julia, her talent and art tangible to him now.

"Do you want to know how she did them?" Vincent Kitamura, dressed in a stylish silk suit, was standing behind Tom. "She built a trap," he said.

He described the setup. She convinced a department store to let her use a display window for bathroom fixtures. She positioned a mirror at eye level, tempting passersby to check their makeup or hair as they waited for the crosswalk signal. (Tom now noticed that several of the subjects had a comb or a brush in hand.) But when they took a step toward the mirror, which was in a recessed alcove of the storefront, unbeknownst to them they triggered a light sensor. A beeping sound then began to emit with alarming volume, the mirror panels slowly swung apart to reveal a Hasselblad camera, the bathroom lights swiveled toward the surprised prey, and the shutter snapped automatically.

"That's very clever," Tom said to Kitamura. "I'd think you'd need an engineering degree."

"A friend of mine on TDY built it for her."

Tom had an idea what kind of friend that might have been—an electronics specialist from Langley on Temporary Duty to Tokyo to plant bugs or wiretaps. The CIA had some cutesy name for them. Locksmiths? Plumbers?

They introduced themselves to each other. Kitamura asked Tom where he knew his wife from, and Tom said the reception for the sculptor from New York, at the Grew House. "I believe you were there, too," Tom said.

"Was I? I don't really remember. You're an aficionado, then. Of art."

"I guess I am," Tom said.

"If you want to know the truth," Kitamura said, "I don't really care for it. The *scene*, I mean to say. I find these people incredibly pretentious. I'm proud of her, of course. You know, don't you, how difficult it is for a *gaijin* to get an exhibition like this? Most places are *kashi-garou*, rental galleries. It's almost unheard of for a *gaijin* to land a *kikaku-garou* run by curators."

"She's really very talented."

"Yes," Kitamura said. "It's funny. She didn't have any particular interest in art or photography when I met her, but she discovered she had a unique gift. She could capture people when they were least expecting it, when they were the most exposed—their vanity, their loneliness, their willingness to compromise themselves, whatever haunted them. She could get people to reveal themselves. She learned to manipulate people into giving her exactly what she wants."

They stared at the photograph in front of them. The *bosozoku* with spiked hair and full leathers was clutching his motorcycle helmet to his chest.

"Tell me," Kitamura said, moving closer to Tom, "what is it she's trying to get from you?"

"Excuse me?"

"What do you suppose she wants?"

Tom stepped away from him. "Nothing," he said.

Kitamura turned to the photograph. "Are you sure?"

■　　■　　■

THE NEXT Sunday, Tom followed them, needing to see how Julia and her husband interacted when they were alone, in their own element. She had said once that on most Sundays they went to Harajuku for brunch, and at ten in the morning, Tom stationed himself across from Minami Aoyama Daiichi Mansion, the couple's massive orange-tiled apartment building, and waited for them. It was a cloudy day, but not too cold, pleasant enough to walk, and just past eleven, Julia and Kitamura came out of the building and headed down Omotesando-dori on foot.

They went to Aux Bacchanales on Meiji-dori, a bustling French bakery with a sidewalk café. While they waited for a table, Tom slipped up the stairs to a crepe restaurant across the street. From the second floor, he watched them standing in line, then sitting at a table, then silently drinking coffee, reading the Sunday *Herald-*

Tribune and the *Stars and Stripes,* sharing an omelet and a crois-
sant and a brioche.

After they finished eating, they walked through Takeshita-dori,
a crowded alley of clothes shops. Kitamura stopped in front of a
shirt store, and Julia came up behind him and rested her chin on
top of Kitamura's shoulder, and they stood staring at the shirts.
They continued down the alley, then up to Yoyogi-koen. As they
entered the park, Julia reached out her hand to her husband, and
Kitamura held it, but only briefly, letting go a few paces later to
dump the folded newspapers in his shoulder bag into a trash can.

They found a bench near a pond, and they read for an hour,
both absorbed in their books. At one point, Kitamura lifted his
head and gazed at the pond, and Julia turned to him. Looking at
her husband, she combed her fingers into his hair, the hair above
his nape. She kept looking at him, but he never turned to her. He
went back to his book, and she went back to hers.

Tom couldn't sleep that night, thinking about them. He had
expected the opposite of what he had witnessed. He had expected
Kitamura to dote on her, and Julia to be the one who was remote.
But the casual familiarity with which she had hooked her chin on
his shoulder, the way she had looked at him as she touched his
hair—what Tom wouldn't have given to have Julia look at him
like that.

He lay awake in bed, listening to the stillness of his empty,
unadorned apartment. In the four months he had been in Tokyo,
he had not put up a single decoration, not acquired a single sou-
venir. Nothing in the apartment could be called a personal effect.
He could pack everything he owned into two suitcases in less than
ten minutes. This was how he had always lived, how he had grown
up. His father had bullied him into adopting the nomadic life of a
solider, an infantryman, had warned him not to get too attached to
anything or anyone. The only thing Tom could count on was for

Staff Sergeant Matthew Coghlan Hurley, an NCO but rank and file through and through, to adamantly refuse any assignment of permanence. His father would not, he always vowed, become an REMF—rear-echelon motherfucker.

Yet as much as Tom liked to think of his peripatetic nature as a mark of toughness, he realized it was also a means of self-protection. If he avoided staying in one place too long, if he avoided relying on someone to be there with him, to accept him for what he was and wasn't, to look upon him with complete devotion, he would never get hurt.

■   ■   ■

ANOTHER AMERICAN arrested on a drug charge or a visa violation—that was what Tom thought when he got the call from Kenzo Ota, but when he went down to Azabu Police Station, Ota said he was holding Harper Boyd because she might know something about Lisa Countryman's disappearance.

"She was working as a hostess?" Tom asked.

"Yes."

"And you think Lisa was, too?"

"Yes."

"So Lisa was a prostitute."

Ota laughed. "No," he said, and he seemed to take great pleasure in Tom's naïveté in this matter. He clarified how hostess clubs operated, and he told Tom that Lisa had been a Ph.D. student in cultural anthropology at Berkeley and had been doing fieldwork on the Japanese sex industry.

"She was undercover, so to speak," Tom said.

Confused by the pun, Ota tilted his head at him.

"Never mind," Tom told him.

Harper Boyd wasn't cooperating. She must have known Lisa at Rocket America; she had a legal visa to teach at the school. Ota assumed they had hostessed together, but Harper had only been employed at the Bogart Den, the Roppongi club where Ota had spotted her, for a month, and she wouldn't tell him where she had been working before then. She would admit to nothing. In particular, how she had acquired the ten million yen in cash—over fifty thousand dollars—he had found in her apartment. After Ota had brought her to the police station, she had invoked her right to remain silent and had asked for an attorney and a representative from the US Embassy.

As a Consular Officer, Tom's first responsibility was to Harper Boyd—to check on her health and treatment and apprise her of Japan's legal system, with which she was clearly unfamiliar, for as soon as he entered the interrogation room, she was fulminating about the violation of her rights and squawking about Geneva Conventions. "I haven't seen an attorney yet. I've been here since last *night*," she said.

It was almost noon, and she was still wearing her hostess outfit—heavy makeup, a short, slinky cocktail dress. She was tall and blond, with a nice figure, great legs. Exactly Tom's type, actually.

"I hate to be the one to tell you this," he said, "but there are no such things as Miranda rights in Japan."

He explained that the police could keep her there for questioning for twenty-three days before indicting her or taking her to court. Even longer. They could continue holding her on a variety of pretexts, claiming, for instance, she might destroy evidence, or arresting her on another charge. *Bekken taiho,* they called it—a re-arrest. They didn't need search warrants. There was no bail. She wouldn't be allowed to make phone calls or write letters or accept visitors. She could hire an attorney, but might only see him twice, for fifteen minutes a visit, before the trial. If she couldn't afford an attorney, she could ask for a onetime free consultation from the *toban bengoshi,* the duty attorney, but otherwise, she would not see a lawyer until the day of the trial.

"Where are we? The Soviet Union?" she asked. "I'm an *American*."

She could be interrogated up to twelve hours a day and, during that time, prohibited from standing or sitting or lying down or leaning against the wall. She might be able to bathe only every five days. If she broke down and confessed, as almost all suspects did, the confession did not have to be recorded or videotaped. It would be written by the police and the prosecutor, and she wouldn't get to read it before signing it. The confession might be altered after she signed it, anyway. There were no plea bargains, and there was no jury system. She would be tried by three judges, in front of whom there would be a ninety-nine percent chance of conviction. Trials were based not on physical evidence or the testimony of witnesses, but on reports from the police and the prosecutors and on the supposed confession, the absence of which would ensure a much harsher sentence.

"In other words," Harper Boyd said, "I am fucked."

"I'm afraid you are," Tom said.

"Okay, fine. When do I get deported?"

"It's not that simple."

"Why not? I don't have the proper visa for—what is it?—entertainment work," she said. "They deport me, everyone's happy."

"There's the ten million yen."

"What about it?"

"They want to know how you got it."

"Coupons," she said, smirking. "I'm a hell of a penny pincher."

"Their presumption is that you got the money illegally."

"Let them prove it."

"That's just it," Tom said. "They don't have to prove it. They can hold you on the mere suspicion of illegal activity. You have to prove to *them* that you got the money legitimately."

"This is total bullshit."

"If all else fails, they're going to charge you with tax evasion."

"I *earned* that money," Harper said.

"It doesn't—"

"It's my fucking money."

If convicted, he told her, she would likely be sent to Tochigi Prison, where the conditions were spartan. She wouldn't be able to talk to the other inmates, or even make eye contact with them. There would be no TV, no books, no smoking, no telephone calls, rarely any visitors.

"All right, all right," Harper said. "I get the gruesome picture. What do they want from me?"

"They want to know if you knew Lisa Countryman."

"Why? What's she done?"

"So you did know her."

"Just tell me what this is about, all right?"

"She's disappeared," Tom said.

She didn't seem at all nonplussed by the news. "Yeah, to Hong Kong."

"Who told you that?"

"She didn't go to Hong Kong?"

He filled her in on a few of the details: the phone call to the landlord, the stolen passport. Lisa had either gone into hiding or had been kidnapped or murdered. Ota had given Tom a list of questions to ask Harper: Was there any reason for Lisa to go underground? Was she in some sort of danger? Was she into drugs, gambling? Did she have debts? Who were her friends, her lovers? Where was she working? Where did she socialize? Did she have *shimei* customers who requested her specifically? Were there any who seemed fixated on her? Where and when did Harper see her last? Did Lisa go on a *dohan* with a customer on June 17? Who had told Harper that Lisa had left for Hong Kong?

"And what do I get if I answer these questions?" she asked.

"I told you, there's no plea bargaining here. You can't make a deal. I don't understand why you're being so evasive. Why can't you just say where you and Lisa were working?"

She smiled ironically at Tom. "Why? You can always make a deal. They might say you can't, they might go on and on about rules and regulations, but there's always a deal to be made. Don't you read the newspapers? This is a country that functions on bribes and corruption. The fact that I'm being asked these questions means that what I know has value. There's value in what I'm willing to say, and maybe there's even more value in what I won't say."

"Is that what the ten million yen's about? Have you been paid by someone to keep quiet?"

"That ten million's legit," she said. "I worked very hard for that ten million, and I'm going to keep it."

"I don't think that's very likely."

"No? Are you absolutely sure about that?" She leaned forward and placed her hand on his forearm for a second. "Can't you help me?" she asked. "What's your role here, anyway, Tom? Are you working in my interests, or do you have to report everything I say to that skinny little mouse, Ota? Is there anything like attorney-client privilege between us?"

"Whatever you tell me will be kept confidential," Tom said.

"So I should feel safe with you?"

"Of course."

"You're here to protect me?"

"Yeah, I am," Tom said, fascinated by this undisguised attempt to seduce him.

"It's a bit like we're in cahoots, isn't it?" she said. "Are we in cahoots, Tom? Could we say we're in cahoots?"

"If you want."

"You know, for a bureaucrat, you're not bad-looking."

He gave her a list of English-speaking attorneys and inquired about NOK—next of kin. If she wanted him to notify NOK, he would need her to sign Form DS-93-579, a Privacy Act Waiver.

"Let's see how this plays out before we worry Mommy and Daddy," she said.

He told her he would bring her some reading material next time, and he would ask Ota to fetch a few changes of clothes from her apartment. "Are you going to cooperate with them?" he asked as he was getting ready to leave. "Are you going to tell them anything?"

"Probably not," Harper said. "Not until I'm . . . shall we say accommodated? I'm a very patient person."

∎ ∎ ∎

HE CALLED her at her studio at the ISA. "I need to talk to you," Tom said.

"This isn't a good time," she said.

"I have something to tell you."

"There's someone here," Julia said.

"The police contacted me."

"Look, is this about the missing girl?" she asked. "I've decided I don't want to know. I don't want to hear about it anymore. I thought I did, but I decided it doesn't really matter to me. I don't need to know."

In point of fact, Tom had been planning to tell her about Harper Boyd, about Lisa Countryman working as a hostess to research her Ph.D., but another matter entirely had arisen. "It's about your car," he told Julia.

"What about it?"

"Someone saw the accident."

She didn't want to meet at the usual corner. He suggested Ueno Park, and after work, he got on the Ginza Line subway at Toranomon, and she got on the Yamanote Line at Takadanobaba, and they rendezvoused in Ueno at Shinobazu Pond. Reluctantly she allowed Tom to rent a rowboat for them, and after they set off from the dock, she asked, "What's going on?"

"A cop called the embassy this morning," he said.

When Mrs. Fujiwara had patched the call through, saying it was a detective from Azabu Police Station, Tom had assumed it was Kenzo Ota, but it hadn't been Ota. It had been another inspector named Iso Yamada.

His English, as opposed to Ota's, had been nearly flawless, with a tinge of a British accent. At some point, Tom thought, he must have studied abroad.

"We're investigating an accident," Yamada had said on the telephone. "A hit-and-run. A woman was injured."

She was still in great pain, Yamada said. She had been hospitalized for two weeks with a concussion, a sprained back, a fractured tailbone, and a broken vertebra in her neck. He told Tom that a witness had seen the car from a distance—a green Alfa Romeo Spider—but not the driver or the license plate. They were contacting the owners of all thirty-three green Spiders that were registered in Tokyo. The Traffic Bureau had asked Criminal Investigations for assistance locating one particular owner, an American named Julia Tinsley. She had apparently moved out of her apartment in the Homat Royal in Hiroo in June, but hadn't submitted the proper change of address forms with the Land Transportation Office for her vehicle registration. Even stranger, she hadn't left a forwarding address with the ward office, the Immigration Bureau, the apartment management, the post office, the NTT, or the utility companies. She and her *nisei* husband, Bob Sasaki, seemed to have vanished. Moreover, the Immigration Bureau had no record of a Bob Sasaki in Tokyo, or anywhere else in Japan. Supposedly he was an Air Force civilian working in the PMLD office at Hardy

Barracks in Nogizaka, but they couldn't reach him there. He didn't seem to exist.

"This is very unusual," Yamada had said on the phone. "You can see why the Traffic Bureau referred this inquiry to us."

"Yes," Tom had said.

"Do you have a telephone number or address for Julia Tinsley or Bob Sasaki?"

"I'll have to check," Tom had said, and promised to get back to him the next day. "I'm confused about something, though. Isn't this Inspector Ota's jurisdiction?"

"Ah, Ota," Yamada had said. "We're keeping Ota occupied with other things."

On the rowboat, Tom told Julia that she would have to let the police examine her car. "Are you sure there wasn't any damage other than to the bumper?"

"I don't know," Julia said.

"What about paint scrapes from the other car? It was red."

"You were there. You saw it. We checked it together. You tell me. I never looked at it carefully after that. I didn't think anything would come of it."

"Where's the car now?"

"At school."

"I guess you can't take it to a garage now. They'll be checking garages."

"This is typical of the Japanese," she said. "All this brouhaha over a fender-bender."

"The woman was in the hospital."

"But you said she was okay. She's not going to be paralyzed or anything."

"I guess."

"You have to give them my address?" she asked.

"Maybe there's something we can do."

"What?"

They had reached the far end of the pond on the rowboat. There were a few other couples on swan pedal boats, but it was rapidly getting chilly and dark on the water, and Julia hugged her arms around her chest, cold. She looked wonderful.

"Why have you been avoiding me?" he asked.

"It was a mistake, sleeping with you," Julia told him. "I shouldn't have done it. I didn't mean to do it."

"But you did. As much as you want to deny it, you feel the same way I do."

"Let's not get sentimental."

Tom pulled in the oars. "I've missed you," he said.

"It's getting late," she said. "Let's go in. I'm freezing."

"I think I'm in love with you," he told her.

"Good Lord," Julia said. "Is that why we're on this rowboat? Because you thought it'd be romantic? I thought you were just being paranoid."

"I'm in love with you," he said.

"Stop saying that. You're being ridiculous. We barely know each other. You're a little infatuated, that's all. It'll pass."

"How do you feel about me?"

And here she seemed to soften a bit. "Can't we just say we fucked once, and it was very pleasant, and leave it at that?" she asked.

"I love you," he said.

"You just want me because you can't have me," Julia said. "You don't know me. If you got to know me better, you might not like me very much."

He was aware of how ridiculous he was being. He didn't know her very well, and, yes, part of his desire was that he couldn't have her. If someone—say, Sara—had made these sorts of declarations after what had amounted to a one-night stand, he would have regarded her a fool. Yet he believed he was in love with Julia, that this was what love felt like, the way he thought about her all the time, the way he looked for her wherever he went.

She wouldn't listen to him anymore, but once they had docked the boat and had walked down a deserted path in the park, she let him kiss her. "I don't know what I'm doing with you," she said. "Sometimes I think I have no control." She kissed Tom, and he could feel her giving in to him, more a resignation than a choice— a distinction he was willing to ignore.

"This is the last time we do this," she told Tom as they rode in a cab to a hotel.

Later that night, she would do exactly what he would tell her to do. She would go back to the ISA and pick up her convertible, drive it out to Waseda-dori, and rear-end a van—a minor fender-bender, but one that would conveniently obliterate any evidence of previous front-end damage.

TWELVE

"**L**OOK," INSPECTOR KUNICHI told Kenzo at the morning *chorei,* "we're going to let Harper Boyd go."

Kenzo was flabbergasted. He felt his face get hot, and he was sure it was flushing an embarrassing red. He began to hear ringing. Every day, it was getting worse, this ringing, a faint but persistent sound, like the ringing of a telephone or an alarm clock in the distance. "But why? What about the money?"

"We can't prove she got it illegally."

"But she can't prove she got it legally, either."

"True," Kunichi said. "However, it's up to the prosecutor, and he doesn't think the case is worth pursuing."

"Tough luck, Ota," Yamada said. "We all know you've gotten to be good friends with her."

A couple of the detectives snickered. Kenzo had been interrogating Harper Boyd for six straight days, and, humiliatingly, he had gotten nothing from her.

He went down to the processing room outside the holding cell, where Harper Boyd was being released. She was haggard and a little gamy, but she looked rather smug. She was going to be deported, but she would be able to reclaim all her possessions, including her ten million yen.

"How you do it?" Kenzo asked her.

"Say what?"

"What you promise? Money? Sex?"

"Detective Mouse, it's been a joy to be in your house, but I must, I must, get myself deloused."

"You promise Kunichi, or prosecutor?"

Harper lit a cigarette. "You know, I feel a little sorry for you. Life isn't easy when you're not smart enough to be corruptible. Let me throw you a bone. Would you like that? Would you like me to throw you a bone?"

He didn't understand the expression.

"Your English is terrible, you know," she said. "The laughable thing is, you think it's good."

He didn't respond.

"Okay, you want to know where I was working?"

Kenzo widened his eyes, taken aback by the sudden offer of generosity. "Why you tell me now?"

"Diminishing returns. I've milked this place dry. I've gotten all I can out of it. You want to know?"

"Yes."

"I'm sure you do. I'm sure it'd be helpful to your image here if you made *some* progress in this case. But I might have to see you kiss up to me a skosh. Are you willing to grovel?"

"Excuse?"

"Beg. I want you to beg. Get on your knees and say, 'Ms. Boyd,

I am velly velly solly for keeping you here for six days and only letting you take one shower and driving you insane with the same stupid questions over and over again for hours at a time.' Can you do that for me?"

"I am very, very sorry," Kenzo said, thankful they were alone in the processing room.

"Uh-uh. Word for word. On your knees."

She stared at him coolly. Why were Americans so vindictive? he thought. Why did they have to affirm their dominance in every matter, no matter how trivial or pointless? "No," he told her.

"No? Can you really afford to let me walk away with this information? Your only lead in the case? Okay, see ya," Harper said, picking up her bag.

"Wait."

Harper made two clicking sounds in her mouth, as if she were praising a dog. "There's a good boy."

■　　■　　■

SHE DIDN'T know their names. Just a number. No. 397. The bottle-keep number. Harper Boyd told Kenzo the three men attached to No. 397 had become frequent customers at Rendezvous, and they always requested Lisa Countryman to sit with them. She thought Lisa might have gone on secret *dohan* with the younger man. Yet Harper hadn't had any reason to regard Lisa's disappearance as suspicious. As far as she knew, Lisa had left the country on her own volition, calling the club on June 18 and saying she was leaving for Hong Kong. Except for perhaps one thing, nothing unusual or remarkable had occurred in the days beforehand.

Midori Atsuta, the mama-san at Rendezvous, gave Kenzo the same story when he interviewed her that Wednesday afternoon at her club. They sat in one of the velvet booths, and Kenzo was impressed with the décor and appointments. The club was far fancier than anything to which an ordinary citizen such as himself could ever gain entry.

The mama-san seemed genuinely surprised by the suggestion that something untoward might have happened to Lisa.

"Didn't you think it was strange for her to take off so suddenly?" Kenzo asked.

"Not really," Midori said. "I was a little miffed, but these *gaijin* girls, they're young. They can be very flaky."

"Are you sure it was Lisa who called? Did you recognize her voice? Did she sound like she was under duress?"

"I didn't actually get the call. The *tencho* did."

"I'll want to talk to him."

"Of course."

"And all the hostesses, and the rest of your staff."

"I'm happy to cooperate in whatever way I can," Midori said. "I was quite fond of Lisa. I was sorry to see her go. She was very popular. She had a beautiful singing voice."

"She was a favorite of bottle-keep No. 397's."

Midori did not flinch. "No more, no less than any other customer."

"That's not what Harper Boyd told me."

"Ah, Harper," Midori said. "Harper is not an entirely trustworthy person. You must have sensed that, talking to her. She always has her own agenda, her self-interests, at heart."

"Why did you fire Harper?"

"She was going on *dohan*."

"She said these three men, 397, hoarded Lisa's company beyond the standard thirty-minute *shimei*."

"Oh, maybe once or twice. Lisa was a charming girl."

"They paid extra for such special attention?"

"Maybe a little."

"They had to arrange it with you?"

"I suppose."

"Are they still coming to the club?"

"Now that you mention it, I guess they are not."

"Was it after June 18th that they stopped coming?"

"To tell you the truth, I hadn't really thought about it. Maybe that's correct. It very well could be."

"Don't you think that's quite a coincidence?"

"Well," she said, "customers can be fickle. Who really knows the whys and wherefores of their patronage?"

"But you have to admit it's a curious coincidence."

"Yes, I see your point. I suppose I must agree with you."

"And it has been implied that Lisa was unusually affectionate with the younger man."

"Is that so? I can't say I noticed."

"Harper told me Lisa was in terrible pain the last time she saw her at the club, as if she had been beaten up."

"Beaten up?" Midori said. "I think Harper was having a little fun with you. I'm pretty certain it was premenstrual cramps."

"Cramps?" he said. Or could it have been that Lisa was pregnant? "In any event, you can understand why I must speak to the men."

"Yes. Of course. That's very understandable," Midori said. "Although I'm afraid it might be somewhat difficult." She explained that No. 397 was a cash account, and the men always used pseudonyms: Moe, Larry, and Curly. "It sounds silly, I know," she admitted. "This whole cloak-and-dagger business, it's like little boys playing James Bond. But I never learned their real names. So you see, I have no way of contacting them."

"Hm. But you have a very strict procedure for screening new members, don't you?"

"I wouldn't say I'm any stricter than many other establishments."

"You require personal introductions and references."

"I find they're helpful."

"So you must have known at least one of the men's names."

"Ah, you're right. I must have. But I'm very sorry. I can't seem to recall it at the moment."

"Do you recall who made the introduction?"

"I'm very sorry. I don't think I do."

"Excuse me, but you can see why I would find that difficult to believe."

"Yes, I do. I understand completely. I apologize."

"Well, then," Kenzo said, "I guess I will have to speak to all of your clients."

"Do you really think that will be necessary?"

"I'm very thorough."

She touched his arm briefly. "I can sense that about you. You must be a very good detective."

Kenzo looked at her. Such a refined woman, he thought, a woman of character, educated, with beautiful manners, very pretty, and perceptive. How did she get into this business? he wondered. She could have been a diplomat's wife. "So I will need your client book and all your financial records."

"Are you sure it has to come to that? I would hate to cause my customers inconvenience."

"Otherwise, I might have to ask you to close your club down until the investigation is completed."

"Oh, that would be very inconvenient."

"You did, after all, employ two *gaijin* without the proper visas."

"I'm afraid they misrepresented themselves to me. But you see, I fired Harper Boyd the moment I realized."

"You said it was because she went on *dohan*."

"That, also."

"It appears to me that you are deliberately trying to hinder my investigation," Kenzo said.

"Oh, am I giving you that impression? I'm sorry. I don't mean to."

"So you will give me your client list?"

"It's not a formal list, per se."

"You keep monthly tabs for company expense accounts. You send them bills."

"I'm actually a very disorganized person," Midori said. "It's a miracle I'm still in business. But I will accommodate you the best I can. Could you give me until next Friday to gather the information?"

"I'll give you until tomorrow."

"My records are really such a mess. It's quite embarrassing. Would you allow me until Tuesday, perhaps? I would so appreciate the extra time, Inspector Ota."

She was truly an elegant woman, Kenzo thought. "You'll give everything to me on Tuesday?" he asked her.

She patted his hand. "You're a sweetheart."

■　　　■　　　■

BECAUSE HE had worked a shift on Sunday, Kenzo had Thursday off, and he decided it was time, finally, to make contact with his son. Simon was now attending the American School in Japan, a private, coed, international school in Chofu, near the ICU campus. Kenzo had figured out his train schedule, and on several occasions had watched him at Shinjuku Station.

This morning, he waited for him on platform 10. Simon was late, as usual. In order to get to ASIJ for the opening bell at 8:30, he had to catch the 7:46 limited express on the Chuo Line, which would get him to Musashi-Sakai just before the Seibu Tanagawa train across the platform took off at 8:06. It was the last possible train he could take to go the two final stops to Tamabochi-mae and hoof it—eight minutes, if he was quick—to school. But it was all predicated on making the 7:46 limited express, and here it was, coming into Shinjuku Station just as the Yamanote Line train on which Simon was riding was pulling into platform 13.

Several ASIJ kids scrambled off the train and leapt up the stairs and raced across the overpass and sped down the stairs to the limited express on platform 10, and they held the doors for stragglers from the Yamanote train, the last of whom was Simon, trundling and jiggling down the stairs, trying his best to hurry, slowed by a massive rucksack on his back. "Come on, Simon," the boys yelled, pinning the doors open. The conductor was blowing his whistle, pointing at them to let go. "Come on, Simon!" the boys yelled, and Simon jumped down and wheeled his arms and treadmilled his feet toward the train. The boys, as Kenzo knew they would, released the doors just as Simon reached them. The boys laughed and pressed their noses against the glass and made pig noises as the train rolled out of the station. Oh, his poor boy.

Kenzo waited on the platform behind Simon for the next train, which arrived within minutes, and then took a seat next to him on the bench. The car was uncrowded. They were going against traffic. Kenzo thumbed through a *manga* he had bought from a platform kiosk, then closed it. "*Boku no manga hoshii? Mou yomi owattanda,*" he said to Simon, offering him the magazine of cartoons.

"What?" Simon said in English. There was no recognition on his part. It seemed Yumiko had not described Kenzo to Simon or shown him a photograph. It was very conceivable that she had yet to tell him about Kenzo at all, waiting for the proper moment.

Kenzo repeated the question, speaking slower.

Simon looked at him irritably. "I'm an American," he said.

"*Nihongo ga wakaranaino?*" Kenzo asked.

"What?"

It had never occurred to Kenzo that he might not speak Japanese at all. It was a travesty. "Do you want my *manga*?" he said. "I am finish."

Without enthusiasm, Simon accepted the magazine and idly began flipping pages. This *manga* had a typical plot—a young schoolgirl being violated by an alien invader from another planet—and only after Kenzo had handed it over did he think it might not be appropriate for a boy Simon's age. He had much to learn about parenting.

"You like Japan?" Kenzo asked him.

"It's all right," Simon said, staring at the *manga*.

"You interest in culture?"

"What?"

"Japanese culture."

"It's all right. Except I'm tired of everybody thinking I'm Japanese."

Kenzo detected a Southern twang, not dissimilar to Susan Countryman's, in his voice, which was deep and contemptuous. He was going through puberty early. He had an ugly peach fuzz above his lip. And his smell. Slightly putrid. A definite butter stink.

"Then when you find out I'm American," Simon said, "y'all want to practice your English on me. 'This is a pen,' " he added in a high-pitched nasal wail.

"This is a pen" was the sentence Japanese schoolboys were most apt to scream at *gaijin* to demonstrate their proficiency with the language.

"But this is a new one on me," Simon said, tapping on the *manga*. "This is porn. What are you? A perv? You trying to lure me to a 'party'? You like little boys?"

Kenzo was aghast. "No. No perv."

"You come near me again, I'll call a cop," Simon said. He picked up his rucksack and moved to the next car, taking the *manga* with him.

A bad start, Kenzo thought. This might be more difficult than he had anticipated.

▪   ▪   ▪

HE LEFT her gifts. A candy dish, followed the next day by bon-bons. A vase, followed the next day by flowers. George Benson's *Masquerade* album, followed the next day by two tickets to Benson's concert at the Nakano Sun Plaza. With each gift left at her door, Kenzo included a card: "Miss Saotome, I am deeply, deeply, deeply sorry for offending you." "I sincerely wish I could eradicate all memory of my abominable, inexcusable behavior." "I truly did not intend to impugn your honor." "I am, as you said, an idiot." "I wonder if there is any possible way that you could come to forgive me." Then: "It is completely up to you, of course, how you use the other ticket, but I would be most pleased if I were allowed to accompany you to the George Benson concert."

The last card was quite a gamble, he knew. Quite bold. Outrageous, really. Yet the instructor had emphasized at every turn that women wanted men to be in charge, to take *action*, to show some—"Please excuse my vulgarity," the female instructor had said, blushing and tittering—*konjo*! Balls!

It had been perplexing, this intensive weekend class at the *bunka* center. They called it the "Love Academy," and it was designed to teach men how to be romantic, which was generally a foreign concept to the typical Japanese male. For instance, *redi fasuto*. Kenzo and the other men in the class had been baffled at first. *Redi fasuto*? But apparently women in Japan now preferred this odd Western custom—ladies first—and expected other gestures of chivalry and romance, although most Japanese men were too shy, or too chauvinistic, or too indifferent to make eye contact or engage in spontaneous conversation, much less touch or participate in anything that might pass as a public display of affection.

His reservations notwithstanding, Kenzo had carried out his instructor's prescriptions to the letter, and wondrously they seemed to have worked. He returned from lunch on Friday and saw Miss Saotome sitting at his desk in Azabu Police Station.

For a second, elation turning to panic, he had a terrible thought—that she was here to file a complaint against him, a harassment complaint—but he was reassured when, as she saw him enter the room, she brightened.

"Hello," she said.

"Hello!" he said back, almost shouting. "It's delightful to see you again!" Be enthusiastic, his instructor had told him.

She hesitated, staring at him. Too enthusiastic? he wondered.

"So this is where you work," she said.

"Yes," he said, lowering the volume.

"You have a nice window view," she said.

Was she mocking him? He couldn't tell. He didn't correct her, and neither did the only other detective in the room, old Obushi, who was reading the newspaper and ignoring them, practically deaf, anyway.

"Thank you for your presents and cards," she said.

"Please do not mention it," he said. "It is I who should thank you for even speaking to me again. I am so sorry for my reprehensible behavior." This response had been carefully prepared for him by the class in a group exercise.

"I was on my way to do some shopping, and I thought I would drop by personally and accept your invitation."

"I'm delighted. Thank you," he told her, maintaining a fixed, frozen smile on his face. Smile and laugh, his instructor had said.

"The concert is tomorrow night at seven-thirty?" Miss Saotome asked.

"Yes," he said, and laughed for no reason. "May I pick you up at six-thirty?" Be decisive about what, when, where, and how, the instructor had said. Don't be wishy-washy about making plans.

"That sounds fine."

"Perhaps we could go eat something after the concert?" Always go to the show or movie before dinner, so afterward you'll have something to talk about during the meal.

"I would like that."

It couldn't have been going any better. This instructor is a genius, Kenzo was thinking, as Assistant Inspector Iso Yamada walked into the room, holding a wet paper towel.

"Ah, you're back from lunch, Ota," he said. "Too bad. I was having fun entertaining your friend. I was just telling her how much you remind me of my brother."

Miss Saotome covered her mouth and giggled.

Yamada dabbed the paper towel on the lapel of his suit jacket. "Actually, she was entertaining me. She was making me laugh so hard, I spilled my tea. What a doofus, eh?"

Immediately Kenzo feared that he had been the subject of their amusement. Had she told Yamada about their night in Kabukicho?

"Is the stain coming out?" Miss Saotome asked. "Such a shame. That's a beautiful Armani."

"Ack, I've got a dozen of them."

"You do not."

"Okay, only two."

Again, Miss Saotome giggled. This was funny why? Kenzo asked himself.

She looked at her watch. "If I visit again," she said to Yamada, "you must finish that story about Oxford."

"Oxford?" Kenzo asked.

"Didn't you know?" Yamada said. "I had a fellowship to Oxford for a year."

Bullshit, Kenzo thought.

Miss Saotome rose to leave, and the three of them bowed and

said goodbye. As she got to the door, Yamada blurted out, "Oh, hey? If you guys go out, be sure not to let Ota drink. I hear there's real trouble if he drinks."

Miss Saotome laughed and waved and headed down the stairs.

Yamada lifted an eyebrow and punched Kenzo on the arm. "You devil. Who would have thought?"

■　　　■　　　■

IN THE morning, it was raining to beat the band. Typhoon No. 19, which was packing winds over 165 kph, was hammering Kyushu and was expected to run up Honshu toward Osaka and then hit Tokyo in the morning. Already, numerous flights and express trains had been canceled, and Kenzo worried that the concert might be canceled, too. He called the ticket office every half hour.

He had his usual weekend breakfast of *miso,* a fried egg, and a banana. He cleaned his apartment, listened to NHK radio for updates on the typhoon, made a lunch of *zaru soba,* and watched a *gaman* show on TV. This particular repeat had two endurance games, the first with the university contestants eating curry rice spiked with one hundred twenty times the normal amount of spice, the second with the students doing handstands on sun-baked aluminum foil while the staff held magnifying glasses to their nipples.

Then Kenzo tried to nap. He had hardly slept the night before, not because of any noise, but because of his nervousness about the date. There was so much to remember. During the night, he had kept getting up and looking at his tip sheet. Now, as tired as he was, he couldn't nap. He was afraid he might fall asleep during the date, so he ran across the street to the outdoor vending machines and bought cans of Pocari Sweat, Calpis, and Dark Plussy, a new stamina drink made with caffeine and nicotine. One of the drinks had a deleterious effect. His dermatitis suddenly flared up on his neck, and he frantically rubbed cortisone cream on his skin, which only inflamed it further. He was a wired, itchy, crimson basket case by the time he knocked on Miss Saotome's door.

She looked beautiful. She was already in her raincoat, as if she had been waiting by the door for him. He had been so concerned that she would change her mind about going out with him, that she would use the typhoon as an excuse to bow out, but here she was, ready for their date, happy to see him.

He offered to pay for a cab to the concert hall, but she insisted on taking the train. It was muggy and windy out, the rain flying horizontally, rendering their umbrellas useless. They were soaked from the short walks to and from the train stations, but the torrential weather did give them something to talk about—continually exclaiming, "Can you believe this wind? This rain?"—until the concert was over and they were seated in Lemongrass, one of the restaurants near Nakano Sun Plaza that Kenzo had scouted out the past few nights. Then they talked about George Benson, his guitar playing and voice, his band, the acoustics in the hall, their fantastic seats, front and center, then about the interesting menu at Lemongrass, a fusion of Thai and sashimi from Odawara. Finally they exhausted the topics at hand, and Kenzo had to mentally refer to his tip sheet, dipping into his reserves. He asked about her hobbies, and she told him about her fondness for museums and dancing (the flamenco!), and about her obsession with golf.

"Oh, really? That's fascinating. Tell me more," Kenzo said. Listen. Be attentive. Ask questions, the instructor had said.

She had the best golf clubs money could buy, as well as half a dozen matching ensembles of clothes, and she had taken many private lessons and could now hit her driver straight and true, but she had never been on a golf course, and, what's more, she had absolutely no desire to go on one. She enjoyed going to Pop Swinger in Mitaka, one of the many multitiered, fully-net-enclosed driving ranges in Tokyo. She was very content just whacking one ball after another there, and she couldn't understand why she was expected to "progress" to a real golf course. Why did the driving range have to be a means to an end? Why couldn't it be the end itself?

"Yes, exactly," Kenzo said. "I've never thought of it that way, but you are exactly correct. You are very smart and independent-minded. A maverick, I think." Be complimentary and admiring, the instructor had said.

"Are you all right?" Miss Saotome asked.

"Yes, I'm having a tremendous time." Project a sunny, optimistic disposition. Be someone who is inherently happy. Accentuate your fun qualities.

"Are you sure?"

"Absolutely," he said, spreading his arms and leaning forward. Avoid crossing your arms and legs, and don't fidget. Indicate with your body language that you are open and receptive.

"Because you seem a bit nervous. You're acting a little creepy, in fact."

Whatever you do, do not panic.

"Do you realize you're making little humming noises?"

If you begin to panic, think of your happiest memory. Hang on to that memory for five seconds, and then face her again, happy.

"Can I ask," she said, "what's wrong with your neck? It's so red."

Breathe. Remember to breathe.

And as he breathed, Kenzo looked at Miss Saotome's face, really looked at it for the first time, and things began to slow down, to fall away. He began to relax. It was a simple face—true, not very pretty, but soft, and solicitous, and merciful. "I'm not well-respected at the police station," he told her. "I am *madogiwa-zoku*." The window tribe.

Miss Saotome did not blanch, and she did not scoff, and she did not snicker. What she did was say, "I know," and reach across the table and pat his hand like Midori Atsuta had done. But not really at all like Midori, whose pat had been a manipulation, a deflection, a lie. Miss Saotome's pat was a gesture of humanity, a signal of shelter, a promise that they were akin, and it was as warm and welcoming as an embrace.

Over the next couple of hours—at Lemongrass, and on the train back to Musashi-Koganei, and at the coffeehouse around the corner from their apartment building—they talked. He told her about the investigation, his feeling that he was close to something big, that he was a step away from uncovering some sort of conspiracy. He told her about his marriage, and his childhood, and the sad withdrawal of his parents after they had returned from the United States.

She told him about her marriage to a stockbroker (she was *batsu-ichi* as well), her childhood in Oiso, a beach town seventy minutes from Tokyo, her alcoholic mother, her absentee father, a real estate mogul who had left Miss Saotome three apartment buildings in Tokyo. She had an older brother and sister, but she did not see them much. They were married with children, and she felt excluded from their cozy lives. She felt they judged her as a failure, that they pitied her.

"It's terrible to be a woman alone in this society," she said. "A Christmas cake."

That was why she was continually moving to different apartments in her three buildings, trying to keep stasis athwart, and that was why she was a romance consultant, to help others avoid her *unmei,* her fate, and that was why she was forever acquiring new hobbies—preoccupations like hitting golf balls at driving ranges— that didn't necessitate a group or a lover.

"I golf," Kenzo said as they walked out of the coffeehouse into the torrential wind and rain.

"You do?" Miss Saotome said, turning back to him.

He heard a distant whine, a sputtering din, an approaching buzzing sound not unlike a compressor or a condenser, and he gently grabbed Miss Saotome's arm and pulled her back a step just as a delivery boy on a motorcycle with a rack of *udon* whizzed past the doorway.

"Oh!" Miss Saotome said, then asked, raising her voice over the calamity of weather, "How did you even hear him coming?"

"I, too," Kenzo shouted, "have never been on a golf course."

■   ■   ■

TYPHOON NO. 19 veered to the east on Sunday, never making it to Tokyo, and on Monday morning the sky was a smogless cerulean blue, the air crisp and dry. Kenzo felt alive and buoyant. At the end of their date, he and Miss Saotome had shaken hands, and when he had asked if perhaps they could see each other again, perhaps do something like go to the practice range together, she had said yes. It was too soon to declare triumph, he knew, but everything was going swimmingly. She was almost his girlfriend. He was thinking she would be a wonderful wife, a wonderful mother to Simon. The next time he saw her, he would tell her about Simon. A tide of some sort had turned for him. His life was going to be different. It was, of course, too good to be true.

Inspector Kunichi stopped him in the hallway of the police station and told him to back off Midori Atsuta. She was connected to someone high up who was vouching for her character. She was beyond reproach. There was no reason to question her or anyone at the club any further.

"She's the key to my case," Kenzo said.

"What case? What case?" Kunichi said. "It's a bullshit case. Three months, and you've got zilch. There's no body, no evidence that a crime has even been committed."

"There's been a cover-up."

"You don't know anything. For all you know, the so-called victim went into hiding voluntarily. Forget about it. She was just another *gaijin* working illegally as a hostess. Whatever happened to her served her right."

"I can't forget about it. The Consular Officer from the American Embassy won't let me forget about it. Her sister won't let me forget about it."

"Fine," Kunichi said. "But you're not going to bother Miss Atsuta again."

"How much did she pay you?"

"What?"

"She bribed you, just like Harper Boyd did."

Kunichi slammed the base of his palm against Kenzo's sternum, knocking his wind out and making his chest sting. "You're an embarrassment to everyone here. You're a fool."

Then that evening, as Kenzo trudged home from the train station, he was up the hill from his apartment when he saw, parked in front of the building, a gleaming, piss-yellow, souped-up, custom-bodied Datsun 280Z that he recognized to be Assistant Inspector Iso Yamada's. Kenzo was pondering all the possible scenarios for Yamada being there—to say he had taken over the case, to inform him of an official reprimand—as Miss Saotome stepped out of the lobby and folded herself into the passenger seat of Yamada's car, her laughter abruptly muffled when she pulled the door shut.

THIRTEEN

OE BECAME a groupie. He came to Rendezvous five out of the next eight nights, sometimes with Curly, sometimes alone, but never with Larry—Larry was mysteriously a no-show. Moe always asked for Lisa, and he began bringing a list with him, standards he wanted her to perform: "Melancholy Baby," "Misty," "I Fall in Love Too Easily," "Moonglow." Lisa was familiar with most of the songs. They had been on her parents' playlist, and after she got over her initial stage fright, she found she didn't mind singing at the club. It was less burdensome than trying to converse with the customers, and, as an audience, they were pushovers.

Moe fawned over Lisa and hogged her time, and when he wasn't there, other customers started requesting her company, too, which didn't sit well with the other hostesses, particularly Emi, who was now sometimes left unwanted at the bar for much of the night.

In the women's restroom one evening, as Emi, Lisa, and Harper Boyd were freshening their makeup, Emi glanced over to her and asked, "What's that?"

"What?" Lisa looked in the mirror at her face, thinking she had a zit.

"That. What is that?" Emi asked, pointing her eyeliner pencil at her.

"It's a necklace," Lisa said.

"Where'd you get it? Did someone give it to you?"

Lisa nodded. "Mojo." It was what the girls in the club called Moe now, a name more befitting his droopy eyelid and oily face and high-pitched laugh and large bankroll.

Emi set down her eyeliner and lifted the necklace's pendant from Lisa's chest. It was a single pearl framed by a gold heart. She slipped her hand underneath Lisa's hair, rotated the chain, and examined the necklace's clasp. "This is a Mikimoto," she said. "Do you realize how expensive this is? At least a hundred thousand yen. Mojo gives you this after a week?"

Lisa nodded sheepishly.

"I've never gotten a gift like this so quickly," Emi said. "Never."

"His company probably gets them in bulk," Lisa said, feebly trying to make her feel better. She didn't know what company that might be. Midori was evasive about who Mojo, Curly, and Larry were, not even willing to tell Lisa how long they had been customers.

Emi grabbed her eyeliner pencil and her lipstick and chucked them into her makeup pouch. "Your singing isn't really so hot. These men don't know anything. You do these little tricks with your voice to impress them, and they fall all over you, just because you're a *gaijin*. You're not even that pretty. You're overweight, and you've got no tits. Look at these," she said, and squeezed her breasts. "*These* are tits." She seized Lisa's hands and clutched them to her breasts. "These are real tits. They're natural, big, and they're shaped perfectly. Do you agree or not agree?"

"I, um, agree."

"You can have your Mojo. I don't care. I'm immune to your insults."

She huffed out of the bathroom, and Harper laughed. "You're good at making friends, aren't you?"

She lit up a cigarette, and Lisa bummed one from her pack. She had taken up smoking lately. Japanese men smoked incessantly, and if you didn't smoke yourself, the stink and haze in the club was intolerable.

"You get a lot of gifts like these, I bet," Lisa said.

"I've gotten a few trinkets in my day," Harper told her. "But as far as my objectives go, it's chump change."

"What are your objectives?"

"I'm looking for investors."

Harper pulled out a small photo album from her purse. The photographs were of a cluster of dilapidated bungalows on a beautiful white-sand beach with postcard-turquoise water. It was in Belize, Harper said, a sleepy resort she had visited as a kid. Her plan was to buy the property and develop the adjoining land. She wanted to add tennis courts and a stable of horses, but she wasn't greedy. She just wanted a nice little place, exclusive, classy, that she could run herself with a small staff. She had already done a good part of the legwork on the development—water rights, beach access, construction costs, indemnification, corporate liability. She simply needed to raise about a quarter of a million dollars in cash.

"Have you gotten anyone interested?" Lisa asked.

"I've got a few hooks in the water," Harper said. "What about you? What's your game?"

"What do you mean?"

"What are you trying to accomplish here?"

"I'm doing fieldwork for my Ph.D."

"Yeah, sure," Harper said. "You might get other people to buy that, but not me. You've got something else going on. You're not a partier, you're not a gold digger like me. You sure as hell aren't doing any research that I can see. What are you doing in Tokyo?"

"I told you."

"Come on."

"I interview people. I transcribe. I write. I'm taking Japanese classes. I go to the library."

"What else? What do you do for fun? You only went dancing with me that one time."

Lisa had to think. "I walk."

"Say what?"

"I like to take walks. I like to go to parks."

Unbeknownst to most tourists, there were over seven thousand parks in Tokyo. Lisa's current favorite was the garden of what used to be Prince Asaka's house, now the Teien Art Museum in Meguro. It was there, a few days later, among the landscaped grounds, that she saw Larry again.

He was sitting on a wooden bench, wearing a trim dark blue suit and reading a newspaper. He didn't look up as she approached and passed him, and she kept going a few meters, then turned back and sat next to him on the bench. "Well," she said in Japanese, "if it isn't Silent Larry."

He raised his head, slowly turned to her, and, after a beat, smiled. "If it isn't Sarah Vaughan," he replied in English.

"Ah, what do you know, he speaks."

"I'm actually quite capable of speech."

"And he even sounds like a native English speaker. A *nisei*?"

"*Sansei*."

"So what was that night at the club about? Hardly saying boo. Was that part of the charade?" she asked.

"No."

"I don't get it."

"Bad mood."

"Oh," Lisa said. "I see. But you're in a better mood now?"

"Not really. But I'll fake it for you."

"That's very kind," she said. She glanced at his hands as he folded the newspaper. She had noticed at the club that he wore a ring, but it was on his right hand, not his left. "Are you going to keep faking your name, too, Larry?"

He looked at her a moment, deciding. "David Saito," he said. "But we can keep that between us, can't we?"

"If you insist."

"And you?" he said. "Your real name's Lisa?"

Some girls used pseudonyms. "Yes. What are you doing here in the middle of the day, David? Don't you have a job?"

"I'm playing hooky. I had a meeting nearby and decided to take the afternoon off."

"Where do you work?"

"The US Embassy."

"Doing what?"

"I'm an Economic Officer."

"Are you high up?" she asked, thinking it might be helpful to know someone in the embassy.

"You're not going to ask me to fix your visa, are you?"

"Mojo and Curly are economists, too?"

David laughed. "Something along those lines. You call him Mojo?"

"You're not going to tell me their real names?"

"They're politicians. Good enough?"

"Good enough."

"You have a terrific voice," he said. "I take it you've sung professionally."

"No, I'm really not that good. I just do these little tricks."

"How long have you been at the club?"

"Less than a month."

"As part of your Ph.D. research, I think I remember."

"Sort of," Lisa told him. "It's true that from an anthropological viewpoint, it's been a fascinating place to work, a world unto itself—the whole interplay of gendered roles. I've been taking copious notes."

"I better watch what I say around you. What conclusions have you reached?"

"Well, the more I'm there, the more clarity I see in the way it functions. When I first started, I dismissed everything as sexist and misogynistic, and I was always on the verge of throwing drinks in people's faces. But now that I've learned more about Japan, I know that was too reductive of an approach. I'm finding some parallels to Hegel's master-slave dialectic—you know, *Phenomenology of Spirit*—although certainly I could, like Frantz Fanon, question its relevance in this post-colonial context."

She was babbling, she knew, but she couldn't help herself. She was nervous, and felt compelled to impress him. She kept talking, throwing in as many esoteric theories and highfalutin phrases as possible. She had never had the audience of such an elegant, good-looking man before, and the wonderful thing was that he seemed *interested* in her, tolerating the nonsense she was spouting, asking her questions, asking her to continue. She began to relax and enjoy herself. He had a way of making her feel more assured, more intelligent, more attractive than she really was.

After half an hour—the best half hour she had ever spent with a man—he had to go. "It was nice seeing you again, Lisa," he said, standing up.

She was disappointed he was leaving. "Will you be coming back to the club sometime?"

"I'd like to," he said, "but it's up to Mojo to invite me." He began walking away.

"David," she called to him.

He stopped and turned.

"You're married, aren't you?" she said.

"Yes, I am," he said.

■   ■   ■

SHE FOUND herself looking for him, but he didn't return to the club the next week, nor did he revisit the Teien garden, through which she strolled every afternoon. She asked Mojo if he had seen his friend Larry lately, and he curtly said no, clamming up. Had they had a falling-out? she wondered.

"Why don't you bring him around again to the club?" she said. "I thought he was very funny."

Mojo didn't question how she could have possibly thought Larry funny, when he hadn't said a thing during his one visit to the club. By this point, she knew Mojo would do pretty much anything she asked, anything to make her happy, and sure enough, a few nights later, as she was singing "In the Dark," she saw David Saito entering Rendezvous with Mojo.

She joined the men in a booth. This time, David was almost voluble, and the three of them settled into a nice rapport—quite a hostessing feat, since Lisa had to ensure that Mojo would not become jealous while still being attentive to David.

They discussed tattoos, of all things. That weekend, the biggest, rowdiest festival of the year, Sanja Matsuri, would be taking place in Asakusa, and one of the real spectacles of the festival was seeing the body tattoos of the *yakuza,* most of whom would only be

wearing white loincloths. Any other time, the tattoos were kept
hidden. Besides *yubitsume*—the custom of slicing off one's pinky
finger to atone for an indiscretion—tattoos were the most telling
signs of *yakuza* membership. They often sheathed the entire body,
covering all the skin up to the neck, wrists, and ankles with elaborate murals of tigers, dragons, plants, mountains, abstract whorls,
angry seas. Some public baths and hotels still banned anyone who
bore them.

"First, black ring on arm each time crime," Mojo said to Lisa,
explaining the origin of the tattoos.

"Then they became a test of mettle," David said. "A back tattoo
can take over a hundred hours to complete. It's very painful."

"*Yubitsume* come from samurai," Mojo said. "*Katana*—you
know *katana*?"

"Yes. The long samurai sword," Lisa said. Mojo and David
were speaking Japanese to each other, but English to her, and she
was expected to speak English to them.

"*Katana* you hold small finger most hard," Mojo said, gripping
an imaginary sword in the air with his pinky and thumb. "Finger
next, finger next." He curled his ring finger, then his middle finger.
"Last finger," he said, wiggling his index finger, "do nothing. Most
soft."

"If you lost part of your pinky through *yubitsume*," David said,
"you became a weaker swordsman and were more dependent on
your master to protect you—akin to a Hegelian master-slave
dialectic," and he and Lisa shared a clandestine smile.

"You see man here sometime?" Mojo asked. "White suit? He is
Takahashi-gumi."

Lisa knew whom he meant. The man had a punch perm and
always wore the same outfit: white suit, black shirt, pink tie. A
senior boss in the Takahashi syndicate, he came to the club infre-

quently. Lisa had never talked to him. He always requested one of the Japanese girls, and would even take Emi over Harper and Lisa. Apparently he hated *gaijin*.

Mojo told Lisa about the *oyabun-kobun*—father-child—relationships in the *yakuza*. When a new member was inducted, he promised undying fidelity and obedience to the boss. In return, he was rewarded with the comfort and protection of belonging to a family, to a cohesive whole with a clear purpose and an unambiguous hierarchy. This was the fundamental tenet of Japanese society, Mojo said. Loyalty. Didn't Lisa think loyalty was important?

Lisa nodded, momentarily bewildered, mishearing his pronunciation of "loyalty" as "royalty."

It was the basis of the Japanese economic system, Mojo said, becoming more impassioned. It explained the structure of alliances between governmental bodies and private corporations—the *zoku,* or tribes, of special interests, the *keiretsu,* or networks, of suppliers and customers. It was all about loyalty.

Here, he switched to Japanese and spoke to David directly: "Without loyalty, there is no order, only confusion. This is something Americans cannot seem to understand. When you ask us to open up our markets, you are asking us to undermine our domestic order."

"But your protectionism is at the expense of efficiency, of lower prices," David said.

"We've had this discussion many times."

"It's a discussion worth continuing—for both sides. As a favor to me, I hope we can continue the discussion."

Mojo shook his head and said, "I sometimes ask myself, When is it asking a favor, and when is it coercion? I wonder about these things sometimes, David. Many things. For instance, about your loyalties."

"What do you mean?"

"You are Japanese," Mojo said. "You may be a *sansei*, but you'll always be Japanese. Where are your loyalties? Are you someone I can trust?"

"Of course."

"How do I know that?"

David set down his drink and smiled at Lisa. "Could you let us talk for a few minutes?" he asked.

She left them alone. She went to the women's bathroom and smoked a cigarette, then stepped behind the bar, poured herself a club soda, and took a seat on a stool. Theirs was obviously a complicated relationship, she thought. What was it that David needed from Mojo? What favor? She caught a whiff of a terrible, tart smell. She turned around. Behind her stood Tony Somers, spruced up in a three-piece suit but still oozing his awful cologne.

"I knew you'd end up in a place like this," he said.

"What are you doing here?" It was extremely rare for Rendezvous to have any *gaijin* guests.

"A client brought me," he said, motioning toward a table and wobbling in the process, betraying how much he'd been drinking. He was with Haruki Kimura.

Lisa remembered Kimura was a computer manufacturer, Tony a programmer. "I thought you were lying when you said your services were in such high demand," she told him.

"You've never given me the credit I deserve."

"Still living in the *gaijin* house?"

"Home sweet home."

"Why do you stay there if you can afford an apartment of your own?"

"I like the company. Although it has its disadvantages, like when people fuck with your toiletries. What did you put in my shampoo, anyway?"

"Your shampoo? I don't know what you're talking about."

"Oh, you are clever. And you're looking quite brilliant with your fancy dress and makeup and hair. How much for *your* services?"

Not this again, Lisa thought. Not in front of Midori, not in front of David Saito. "You need to behave here," she told Tony.

"How much?" he asked again. "How much for that doggy in the window?"

Without seeing him approach, Lisa suddenly noticed David Saito at Tony's side, looking friendly and remarkably nonthreatening. "I'm sorry to interrupt," he said, "but we could use your help at the table."

Tony glowered down at him. He had a couple of inches and a good twenty pounds on David. "What are you? Her pimp?"

"I did interrupt something, didn't I? I apologize."

"All right, fun's over," Lisa said, and hopped off the barstool.

"Did I say I was finished with you?" Tony said.

"Cheerio."

"Excuse us," David said.

"Come back here." He grabbed hold of Lisa's bicep and yanked her arm, whirling her back around, but then David did something—his hand reaching in a blur, twisting Tony's fingers off her bicep—somehow making the movement look effortless and gentle. Tony stumbled back, then lurched forward with a punch. David calmly did something else—the result of which put Tony on his back on the floor—but once again with the utmost tenderness, as if he were laying a child to sleep.

The *tencho* and a waiter hurried over to them, but David was already helping Tony up onto his feet and brushing his jacket. "*Daijobu, daijobu. Tsumazuita-dake,*" he said. Everything was all right. He had just tripped. "Isn't that right, you old sod?" he said to Tony. "You just tripped."

■   ■   ■

SHE ONLY accepted because David would be there. Otherwise it could have been considered a *dohan,* and she didn't want to mislead Mojo, who had become a bit more aggressive about asking her out in recent days.

She met David—dapper as usual in a beige linen suit—in the lobby of the Hotel Sky Asakusa, and together they waded through the crowds and stationed themselves on a street bordering the Sensoji temple. Mojo was in a *ujiko* club that would be bearing a portable Shinto shrine, a *mikoshi,* through the streets that afternoon. Some of the *mikoshi* weighed close to a ton and required a hundred men to keep them aloft on wooden beams. The purpose of the procession was to bring luck and prosperity to the neighborhoods from which the *mikoshi* originated, and the more raucous and calamitous the ride, the more generous the deities would be. Mojo had invited Lisa and David to watch, as well as to come to the *ujiko* club celebration afterward. At the last minute, he threw in a special dinner, the details of which he would not reveal, only telling them to bring dress clothes. They could change after the festival at the hotel, in which he had reserved a suite.

It was a wild scene. Lisa realized that most of the *mikoshi* bearers were completely drunk, tossing back *sake* and beer all day long. The *yakuza,* as expected, were the raunchiest, most boisterous crew, stripped down to their loincloths, thrusting their pelvises and clambering up on top of the beams and palanquins, the police futilely pleading through loudspeakers, "Standing on the shrine is not allowed. Do not get overexcited. The parade must proceed."

At last they saw Mojo's gold and black lacquer *mikoshi.* The club members wore matching outfits fashioned after old-time craftsmen: short blue jackets that resembled *happi* coats, headbands, and leggings. They moved slowly in rhythm, bucking the

shrine up and down, jostling it backward, then pitching it forward, chanting, "*Washoi! Washoi!*" while a group of musicians
followed behind, banging out a discordant cadence with wooden
clappers, whistles, flutes, gongs, and drums. There in the middle of
it all, underneath one of the beams, were Mojo and his friend
Curly, smiling and shouting at them. The procession kept going
down the street to circle the neighborhood.

While they waited for Mojo and Curly to reappear, Lisa and
David ate *yakitori* and drank beer at a street stall. Lisa remarked
how much fun she was having. This was proving to be her most
authentically Japanese experience since arriving in the country.

"You know I speak Japanese, don't you?" she asked David.

"So I gathered."

"I was thinking about what Mojo said to you. Do you ever find
it a conflict, being in Japan and being Japanese-American?"

"No."

"Not at all?"

"My grandparents made a choice for themselves and their progeny when they immigrated. Once you make that choice, I don't
think you can be ambivalent about it."

"Don't you feel a visceral connection to the people, the land?"

"I can't really say I do."

"That's hard to believe. You must have relatives here."

"I don't see them much."

"Why not?"

He raised his palm. "Modern life," he pronounced. "Do you
feel ambivalent, with a Japanese mother?"

"How did you know that?"

He shrugged.

"No one can usually tell," Lisa said, staring at him, astonished.

She admitted to David that she had gained little sense of kinship
or community in Japan thus far. Quite the opposite. She had made

no friends, she hadn't gotten to know any of her neighbors. She was regarded as a *gaijin,* through and through. People sometimes changed seats on the subway when she sat next to them.

"Your situation's both different and the same as mine, isn't it?" Lisa said. "Everyone assumes you're Japanese-Japanese."

"Even people in the embassy."

"Do you run into a lot of racism in the State Department?"

"Certainly," he said prosaically.

"Doesn't it bother you?"

"Yes, of course. But in comparison, I don't find Japanese society, or any other country, nearly as tolerant as the US. Do you?"

"Well, at least if the embassy's ever taken over," Lisa said, "you'll be released."

"Hm?"

"Those thirteen hostages in Iran who were let go, back in November—they were all women or black. It goes to show you, doesn't it, what this is all about?"

She was being playful, and he picked up on her whimsical mood and invited her to run with it. "I have a feeling you're going to tell me."

"It's a classic incarnation of Saidian Orientalism, the depiction of Arabs as aliens and fanatics. I mean, come on, all this outrage, the yellow ribbons, the nightly updates—let's get real," she said teasingly. "We're only talking about a measly fifty-two people here. Insignificant, really, in the larger scheme of things."

"I should have known," David said, rolling his eyes. "You're from *Berkeley.*"

She loved that she could banter with him like this. She didn't have to explain herself to him. He *got* her. "Wouldn't you be pissed if you were Iranian," she asked, leaking a giggle, "after twenty years of the US supporting the Shah, especially when it's all been about *oil?*"

"Here we go," David said.

"Power to the people!" Lisa said.

"Do you know who you're talking to?"

"The only solution—revolution!" she laughed.

They left the stall and rejoined the parade, standing alongside the street. Mojo and Curly's *ujiko* club came around again. The men were now in various states of undress, and some were bruised and bleeding, such was the weight of the beams digging into their shoulders. Mojo and Curly were sweating and huffing, their faces flushed. They looked apoplectic, about to drop dead. "Should they still be doing this?" Lisa asked David worriedly. Down the block, Mojo and Curly staggered out of line, exhausted, and their places underneath the shrine were immediately taken up by waiting substitutes. After a short break, Mojo and Curly dove back into the mob. Lisa didn't know where they found the stamina, and the whole undertaking seemed more than a little dangerous to her, an apprehension that was not unfounded, as it turned out, for Mojo walked up to them later and told them that Curly had had a small heart attack.

"He'll be fine," he said to David, "but I must go to the hospital. Could you accompany Lisa to the restaurant? Do you mind? Eiji will take you. It'd be a shame to waste the reservation since it was so hard to come by, and I cannot disappoint the two of you after my promise of a surprise."

"Are you sure?"

"Don't worry about the bill." He took Lisa's hand in both of his. He looked crestfallen. "I am sorry. I am sad to miss with you dinner, but please enjoy. It is very special dinner."

Indeed, it was special. After they changed at the hotel, Eiji, Mojo's driver, a thick-chested man with a handlebar mustache, took them through the cobblestone streets of Kagurazaka and stopped in front of a wooden door embedded in a high stucco wall. It was a quiet residential area, and the door had no sign, no number, just a buzzer and an intercom. After they identified themselves, a woman in a kimono opened the door. She led them down a stone path through a garden, holding a lantern out in front of them to light the way. Except it was a very unique lantern—a cage made of bamboo and glass, filled with fireflies.

They had entered the exquisite, rarefied world of *kaiseki,* the most exclusive dining experience in Japan. This particular restaurant was aptly named Gokuraku. Bliss. Their guest policy was more stringent than Rendezvous's, requiring referrals and reservations months in advance—at least usually. Mojo must have pulled quite a few strings to get them in on such short notice, especially considering the restaurant's obsession with punctuality, each party's arrival timed so they wouldn't encounter any other guests. Privacy was paramount here, the illusion given that no one else was on the grounds except for the staff. They catered to the upper echelons of business and politics, and there was rumored to be an underground tunnel for those needing extreme secrecy. Each party had their own little teahouse with tatami floors, and the houses were situated so they could not see anything but the garden, could not hear anything but leaves, and wind, and water running from bamboo.

"It's really a shame Mojo couldn't come," David said. "He wanted very badly to impress you."

Lisa was thinking exactly the opposite: the day couldn't have turned out any better. She had been happy enough at the festival with David, but this dinner was beyond anything she could have conjured. It was a date, a splendid date.

The maids in kimonos brought in the food on trays and delicately positioned the dishes on the low table. *Kaiseki,* David told

Lisa, had developed as a light meal served in conjunction with tea ceremonies. The name supposedly came from the practice of Buddhist priests in training. As they fasted, they kept warm stones (*seki*) in their robe pockets (*kai*) to stave off hunger pangs. Accordingly, the portions of temple food were small, but there were eleven courses of everything from fresh roots to ginkgo nuts, smoked octopus, pressed mullet roe, and monkfish liver. The meal cost five hundred dollars a person.

While they ate, Lisa and David talked pleasantly, trading polite summations of their lives. He told her he had grown up in Everett, Washington, just outside of Seattle. He'd gone to Princeton and Harvard, joined the Foreign Service straight out of graduate school, and had been posted to Rome and Paris before Tokyo.

"Does your wife work in the embassy?" Lisa asked.

"No, she's a financial consultant," he said.

"How long have you been married?"

"Five years. I met her in Paris."

"She's French?"

"Yes," he told her.

"Any children?"

He shook his head.

"Your father isn't harassing you for progeny?"

"He died before I was born," David said.

His parents—originally from Modesto, California—had been interned at Manzanar, and his father had enlisted in the famous 442nd Regimental Combat Team, made up of Japanese-American volunteers, which became the most decorated unit in US history. Before David's mother had learned she was pregnant, he had shipped off to France, where he was killed in Bruyères, during the rescue of the Lost Battalion. After the internment camp closed, David's mother and her family returned to Modesto and found their stationery store looted and vandalized, "No Japs Wanted" painted on the wall. Seeking a new start, they moved to Seattle, but David's mother fell into a deep depression and never recovered. She had a breakdown, and throughout his youth, she was in and out of institutions, where she still remained. David had been raised by his grandparents.

"That's so tragic," Lisa said, overwhelmed. It was such a sad story. As sad a story as her own. Yet something confused her. She did a little math in her head. "But that would make you at least thirty-six, wouldn't it? How old are you?"

"Thirty-seven."

She had thought he was in his early thirties. "You look so young," she said.

Two geishas came into the teahouse and sang and danced for them. After the twenty-minute performance, they were left alone again, and David asked Lisa about her dissertation.

"I doubt I'll ever start it," she said.

"Why not?"

"I don't really think I'm qualified. Maybe they made a mistake letting me into the program," she said. "I never had my heart in it, anyway."

"You're here, aren't you?"

"It wasn't something I was planning. I was running away."

"From what?"

"Bad luck. I have awful luck." She gave him the short version. She was dating a fellow graduate student, and she found out he was two-timing her with another girl. He left town for a week-long conference, and she decided to exact her revenge by going to his apartment and dialing the number for the correct time—in London—and leaving the phone off the hook. But the gods were not with her. She took her clothes from his apartment and threw them into the trunk of her car, and as she drove away, one of the wires to her taillight dislodged. She looked in her rearview mirror,

and her trunk was on fire. She stopped the car and watched it burn
to a husk on Ashby Avenue.

"You do have bad luck," David said.

"There's more, much, much more," she said. "People hate me.
You know what I'm supposed to look like?" she asked. "I'm supposed to have a kinky fro and slanty eyes. I'm supposed to have a
fat nose and chipmunk cheeks. I'm supposed to be covered with
freckles and patchy orange skin. It's some sort of genetic joke, the
way I look," she said. "I should look ethnic. I should be ugly. I'm a
freak. I've been a freak all my life," she blurted, intending to joke
but speaking in genuine anguish, giving in for a moment to
pathetic, schoolgirl, banal, self-pitying thoughts, thoughts that
were beneath her, that she had worked so hard to keep at bay,
thoughts that she was bad, that she was worthless, that she was
unlovable.

He looked at her with raised eyebrows, thinking—she was certain—she was crazy. She had disclosed too much of herself, and
she was sure he was now revolted by her.

"It's a shame you're so arrogant," he said.

It took her a second to pick up on his tone—gently mocking,
sweetly ironic. "I know, my inflated ego," she said gratefully. "It's
always been my downfall."

"You really need to acquire some humility."

"Get knocked down a peg or two, huh?"

"At the very least."

He made her laugh.

In the car, Lisa felt happier than she could recall being in years.
"That was a lovely evening," she said to David. "That was a lovely
day and evening. Thank you." She wanted to lay her head on his
shoulder, to have him put his arm around her.

"It's Mojo you should thank," he said. "He's very fond of you."

"He's a nice man."

"He talks about you all the time," he said. "He's always saying how talented and beautiful you are."

"That's . . ." She was going to say "nice" again. "I wanted to ask you. What was that you did to Tony at the club? Was that karate?"

"Aikido."

"Are you always so sure of yourself? How do you get to that state?"

As they passed through Kudanshita, near the Imperial Palace, Mojo's driver, Eiji, slowed down, then halted. The cars in front of them weren't moving. Eiji shifted into neutral. Like almost all chauffeurs and cabbies, he wore white cotton gloves.

"*Nan desu ka?*" Lisa asked him.

"*Jiko,*" Eiji said. Accident.

After a few minutes, he put the car back into gear, and finally they began moving again, slowly edging past the accident. From the back seat, Lisa could see a motorcycle lying on its side, its gasoline tank completely dislodged—ripped off its frame. What had separated the tank from the motorcycle was the rider's leg. The *bosozoku* was on the ground, wearing full leathers, not moving. He looked peacefully asleep, not a mark on him, except his right thigh was gone. The femur—fully exposed—was broken and splintered, the meat of his entire thigh torn off. He lay on a shimmering sheet of blood. There was a car, its left front headlight smashed. Either the *bosozoku* or the car had crossed the center line, and they had hit with such force, the motorcyclist's leg had pried off the gas tank.

Lisa began to cry.

"What's wrong?" David asked. "Do you know him?"

She shook her head.

"What is it, then?" When she didn't respond, he put his arm around her and said, "Don't look."

Uniformed patrolmen were talking to witnesses, but no one was tending to the motorcyclist on the ground. "Why aren't they doing anything?" she asked David, sobbing.

"He's dead, Lisa."

She reached up to his face. "Make love to me," she said, weeping. "Please. Take me somewhere and be with me," she said, kissing him.

FOURTEEN

THE POLLS had them tied. Growing desperate, Carter proposed lifting sanctions if Tehran would release the hostages, and Reagan accused him of using the hostage crisis as a political football. Deploring the humiliation and disgrace of the whole situation, Reagan wasn't too charitable, either, about the gasoline crisis and double-digit inflation. He won in a landslide, carrying forty-three states.

Tom and Julia were meeting once a week now, always at a different love hotel. Maybe she had been right before—he hadn't really been in love with her then—but he thought he was now. She warned him not to become too invested.

"This is strictly temporary," she said. "You and I both know it can't last."

"Why not?"

"Trust me."

"You have no affection for me whatsoever?"

"None," she said, "whatsoever," and she bent down and briefly took his penis in her mouth.

"You see, you do like me," he told her.

"Certain parts of you."

They were in the Julius Room of the Plaza T Hotel in Otsuka. Modeled after a Roman bath, the room was decorated with faux-marble walls and columns and divided into a series of closet-size chambers, the first of which was the tepidarium, where Tom and Julia were applying oils to each other's skin.

"You don't want to be in love," Julia said. "Being in love puts you at a terrible disadvantage."

"It sounds like you have a history."

"Doesn't everyone?" She massaged oil into his back. "It's very possible that I'm just using you, you know."

"For what?"

She sucked on his earlobe. "A respite?" she said. "The thing about affairs is they exist in a vacuum. A real relationship is about functioning in each other's worlds, the intersection of your jobs and family and friends. It's about the future you agree to build together, the ambitions you share. You've never experienced any of that, have you?"

"I suppose not."

"Have you ever wondered why?"

They moved into the sudatorium for a sauna, sitting on a bench of wooden slats. Although Julia would not admit it, he knew she was attached to him now, yet each time they saw each other, he worried it might be the last, that she might suddenly decide to break it off. She was still largely a mystery to him. She could be moody and condescending. She carried herself with so much bravado, but he sensed an underlying sadness about her, the source of which he did not fully grasp. After seeing her photography show, for instance, he had kept marveling about her talent, but she had demurred, saying, "I'm not really gifted. You don't know enough about art to differentiate between substance and surface. It doesn't really matter, anyway. I'll always be defined by the man I'm with. That's all I am to people."

In the soft light of the sauna, Tom looked at Julia, wondering how she defined herself with him. All his life, he had been the type of man with whom women had affairs but did not marry— hitherto a comfortable role for him, one he had always sought. "Does your husband ever ask you questions?" he said.

"What kind of questions?"

"Where you've been—things like that. Does he suspect anything?"

"He's oblivious."

"Maybe not," Tom said, and he recounted his conversation with Vincent Kitamura at the art gallery.

"Why have you waited so long to tell me this?"

"I didn't know what to make of it. What would he do if he found out about us?"

"I doubt anything."

"He doesn't love you?"

"Of course he loves me," she laughed. "How could he not love me?"

"Are you still sleeping with him?"

"I'm not discussing this."

"I don't have the right to ask?"

"No, you don't."

"You're still attracted to him." The thought of it—that she still might be sleeping with her husband—was almost more than he could bear.

"Next you'll ask who's better, who's bigger," Julia said.

"So?"

"You know what the difference between you is?" she said. "Vincent has true beauty. You—you have insouciance."

"I don't know what that means."

"That's all you'll get from me."

"No, really."

"Really?" she said. "Okay, let me ask you, why did you join the Foreign Service?"

"To travel, I guess."

"To travel. Not to stem the tide of communism? Not to promote constitutional democracy and the principles of free trade around the globe?"

"That, too."

"Don't you find it ironic that the people who are supposed to represent the United States are the ones who least want to live there?" she said. "It's rather depressing, when you think about it. Do you ever get depressed?"

"Sure."

"I don't think you do. Your lack of self-awareness is quite spectacular." She lightly slapped his face. "That's oddly appealing to me."

They had worked up a good sweat, and they switched to the hot tub in the caldarium.

"If Vincent and I ever had a child, he'd look like you, wouldn't he?" Julia said.

The question surprised him. "I suppose so. Does he want a baby? Do you?"

"Children don't interest me," she said. "Is that a terrible thing to admit?" She splashed cold water from a fountain onto her face. "You've always had white girlfriends, haven't you?"

"No, not always."

"Any Asian women?"

He shrugged.

"Have you been back to Korea since that time you were a kid?"

"No."

"Any plans to?"

"I might visit. I don't know," he said, becoming irritated with the inquisition.

"You ought to go. It'd be good for you. Like a pilgrimage. A group of us went last year. Our guide insisted we visit an orphanage just outside Seoul. I guess there's a new mandate to encourage Americans to adopt, and there were a few Amerasian babies there. They had the kids sing songs for us with hand motions. The staff was so proud of them, but the place was medieval. Positively medieval. Stifling. Filthy. There were pails at the foot of each bed—buckets of slop."

"Of what?"

"*Slop,*" Julia said. "It was gruesome."

When they couldn't stand the heat of the caldarium anymore, they moved into the last chamber, the frigidarium. They were supposed to jump into the cold-water bath to close their pores, but they both hesitated in front of the small pool.

"We could skip this one," Tom said. They were already shivering from the change in room temperature.

"You just want to possess me," Julia said. "That's all men are really interested in. Women are different. This is painful for me. You don't know. Each time I see you, I'm in anguish. It sickens me, what I'm doing. I love Vincent—you'll never know how much— but our marriage is falling apart, and every morning, I wake up in grief."

Tom turned to her. "Are you going to leave him?" he asked.

She stepped into the cold water and sat down in the tiny pool.

"People don't have affairs to get out of their marriages," she said, looking at him mournfully. "They have them to prolong them."

■　　■　　■

WITHOUT NOTICE, Assistant Inspector Iso Yamada dropped by the embassy, strutting into Tom's office in a trendy suit.

"There's been a development in the hit-and-run case," Yamada said. "Do you remember the hit-and-run case? The green Alfa Romeo Spider?"

"Vaguely," Tom said. He had been hoping it had been forgotten. As promised, he had called Yamada and given him Julia's new address at Minami Aoyama Daiichi Mansion, and two patrolmen had gone by to inspect her car, but nothing had happened after that.

"It was quite a coincidence," Yamada told Tom, casually pacing around the room, not bothering to sit. "Ms. Tinsley has an accident the very night I call you about her. She crumples up the front of her car, and we can't tell if it was damaged before. We ask her apartment building security, her neighbors who park next to her— no one can remember if there was damage on her car before. So we can't prove anything, even though it really does seem like too much of a coincidence."

"That's a shame," Tom said.

"Yes, a shame. It's surprising how unobservant people are. But fortunately someone who is a little more observant has come forward. He happened to see our request for information on the bulletin board outside a *koban,* a police box. A young man. He's a parking attendant for a hotel in Ikebukuro called Loch Love. Do you know the hotel?"

The skateboarder in the track suit, Tom thought.

"He remembers a green Alfa Romeo Spider at the hotel just around the time of the hit-and-run," Yamada said. "He remembers noticing damage on the front bumper when he put the cover over the license plate. The driver was a *gaijin* woman fitting Julia Tinsley's description. She was with a man who looked mixed-blooded, *haafu,* in his early thirties, tall, in good shape. I recalled a *haafu* man who came to the station not too long ago to talk to a witness, Harper Boyd. He seemed to fit that description very well. Could that have been you with Julia Tinsley, or is that another coincidence?"

Yamada ran through the various penalties for violating the Road Traffic Law—vehicular assault, leaving the scene of an accident, obstruction of justice, conspiracy. "I'm sure this will not be very good for your career," he said. He turned his back to Tom and stood in the doorway, gazing out at the waiting area for the visa section. "You might have to stamp visas maybe. Is that something you ever have to do?"

"No, not anymore."

"That's too bad," Yamada said, stepping in front of Tom's desk. "Because I have a brother, you see. His name is Masahiro. Masahiro Yamada. He's very stupid. He wants to go to the United States, but his visa application has been rejected."

"He applied here?"

"That's what I understand. I wonder if it's possible for his application to be reevaluated and maybe receive some special consideration this time. What do you think of that? Do you think that's possible?" As Yamada left the office, he placed his brother's passport on top of Tom's desk.

Benny, it turned out, had reviewed the application himself. A JO named Dan Haesler had done the initial interview with Masahiro Yamada, and everything had seemed to be in order. He had filled out Form DS-156, the Non-Immigrant Visa Application, for a B-2 tourist visa, and had included his photograph, his employment and financial history, and his application fee. But, as his brother had said, Masahiro Yamada was an imbecile. He was an apprentice sushi chef, and Haesler had been told to look at food workers with suspicion: not infrequently, they were flown to the States for jobs in Japanese restaurants. So, as a formality, Haesler asked Masahiro Yamada if he planned to work in the US during his visit, and Yamada, the nitwit, said yes. Where do you plan to work? Haesler asked. Yamada proudly named a sushi restaurant in Camden, New Jersey, and then, realizing what he had just done, tried to take it back. Haesler would have none of it. He told Yamada his visa application would be denied, and began gathering the papers on his desk.

"Guess what he did next," Benny said in his office, feet up.

"What?" Tom said.

"He tried to grab his application. Danny got in a tug-of-war with him. Yamada managed to yank a couple of the sheets free, and he balled them up and *ate* them."

They laughed.

"Danny swears he saw a staple go down."

They laughed harder.

"Not the brightest light in the house," Tom said.

"I'll say."

"So you already signed off on the review?"

"Yeah," Benny said, still laughing.

Each visa refusal made by a JO had to be reviewed by a supervisor, who could, at that point, easily overturn the decision. Once the supervisor approved it, however, the refusal took root in the system and was much more difficult to change.

"Well, you know that case I've been working on?" Tom said. "With the missing girl? Lisa Countryman? There's a cop who might be able to help me with the case, but he wants a favor. Yamada's actually his brother."

"What?"

"He says his brother made an honest mistake," Tom said, and launched into the story he had devised. "He's not planning to work. He's chasing after some girl from Rutgers who was teaching English here. He's got a bad case of puppy love. The girl doesn't even know he's alive. The cop says his brother needs to go to Jersey and see for himself what's up. Once he gets his heart stomped on, he'll give up on the girl and come back to Tokyo."

Benny dropped his feet from his desk. "Are you asking what I think you're asking?"

"Benny, he made an honest mistake. He was nervous."

"I don't buy it. He named the restaurant. He gave Danny the address. Samurai Sushi on Route 9."

"This is how it works here," Tom said. "It's all quid pro quo. It's a system of little favors back and forth. As far as trade-offs go, this one's not reprehensible, is it? It's a pretty venial request. It's pretty harmless. Especially for what we'd get in return. We might be able to find out what happened to Lisa Countryman and give her family some peace of mind. We can look away this one time, can't we?"

"Maybe you can, but I can't," Benny said.

"Come on, Benny."

"I can't do it. I can't believe you'd even ask me to do it."

"Benny, it's such a little thing."

"I don't want to talk about this anymore. We're not going to talk about this again. Do you understand?"

He hadn't expected Benny to be so moralistic. Jorge, maybe, but he had hoped Benny would be more flexible. "Listen," Tom said, "the truth is, I'm in a little trouble."

"What kind of trouble?"

"A car accident."

Benny lifted his palms into the air, baffled. "You don't have a car."

"It was a friend's car."

Benny stared at him. "This has to do with that woman, doesn't it?"

"I borrowed her car and got into a little fender-bender."

"That's bullshit. You're covering for her. Were you even *in* the car?"

"Does it matter?" Tom asked. "I'm *involved,* Benny. It's my neck."

"It's your fucking prick," Benny said. "You stuck it where it doesn't belong."

▪   ▪   ▪

IT WAS a cruise ship theme. The room in Hotel Peach Time in Uguisudani was outfitted with brass portholes and a soundtrack of ocean swells, broken occasionally by a foghorn, and there was a heated waterbed that was designed to undulate as if they were on the high seas.

"What's the penalty?" Julia asked Tom, lying on top of him.

"Your license will get revoked for two years. You'll have to pay some fines. And of course restitution to the woman and for the repairs on the other car."

She gently ground her pubis against his cock. "Two years? That long?" she said. She lifted her hips and felt to see if he was hard again.

"Give me a minute," he said. She was so wet. The first time they had made love in Ikebukuro, back in August, she had faked having an orgasm, he realized long ago, because when she came with him now, she forgot herself in a way that frightened him a little.

"What about you? What'll happen to you?" she asked.

"I don't know. It'll be pretty serious."

"Are you sure you won't be able to change your friend's mind?"

"I'm sure."

She subtly arched and unarched her back, her breasts moving up and down his chest. "This is so exasperating. It's all the agency's fault. Why'd they have to make Vincent's cover so complicated? Well, I know why. It's about pedigree. If I had a diplomatic blue plate, this would be irrelevant," she said. "I'm going to have to ask him to fix it."

"How?"

"He'll just do it. He'll make it go away. That's what he does."

"You're missing the point," Tom said.

"What point?"

"The cop was implying he'll tell Vincent about us if his brother doesn't get the visa," Tom said, embellishing.

"Do you really think he'd do that?"

"What would he have to lose?"

Inexplicably the thought of getting caught aroused Tom. He lifted Julia up and positioned his erection underneath her and had her sit down on it, and the delicious heat of her, the slippery, suctioning enclosure, made him gasp. She pulled her knees up and coaxed him upright so they sat straddling each other. The shift in position made the waterbed oscillate. "Wait," Julia said. "All of a sudden I feel seasick." They stayed still for a minute, then she told him, "Okay, I'm okay," and they began moving again.

"I'd like this—us—to last a little longer," Tom said. "I'm enjoying this. What about you?"

"What?"

"Are you enjoying this?"

She opened her eyes. "I'm enjoying this."

"I'm glad," he said. "Because I wouldn't want you to do anything you weren't enjoying."

"I'm enjoying this very much."

When they finished, they lay together on the floor, pulling the sheets and pillows down with them, opting for solid ground. "Couldn't you just issue the visa yourself?" Julia asked. "You're a Consular Officer."

"It's not that simple."

"Why not?"

"It's got to have Benny's signature on it. Or Jorge's. He's the NIV chief."

"You showed me that trick," she said. "You could forge Benny's signature."

He laughed. "You're serious?"

"Would it be that big of a deal?"

"I'd get kicked out if I got caught."

"So don't get caught."

He thought about it, looking at her. "It'd never work," he said.

She rolled onto her side and draped her thigh over his hip and nestled closer to him. "I don't care what happens to me," she said. "I can handle Vincent, and I can live without a car. But this is your career, isn't it?"

Her concern touched him. She had such a sweet, beautiful face. Sometimes it felt as if making love to her was his only reality, and all else was an interruption. "Kiss me," he said, and she did.

■　　■　　■

IT WAS one of the rare times he stayed late at the office. Like every good bureaucrat, Tom was usually out the door at five on the dot, but Kimball Reeves had dumped a last-minute project on his desk. He wanted Tom to update the Earthquake Emergency and Evacuation Plan. A delegation from the Federal Emergency Management Team was visiting at the end of the week to confer with their counterparts in the Tokyo Metropolitan Government, and the Consul General wanted to review the plan first thing in the morning, before the country team meeting.

As everyone left the embassy for the night, Tom sat in his office, checking disaster relief locations for each ward in the city. He assumed Reeves had known for weeks that the plan would need to be updated, but had delayed telling Tom until now just to spite him. Reeves had been complaining about Tom's absences—his long lunches and mysterious errands that took him away from the office for two hours at a time. He needed to sharpen up, Reeves had warned him.

Mrs. Fujiwara stopped at Tom's door and said, "I go now, okay?," and he swore he saw her smirk. Soon, the entire Consular Section emptied, and he was left alone, making up a list of essential supplies: drinking water, packaged foods, baby formula and diapers, a radio, flashlight, extra batteries, medications, feminine hygiene products, eyeglasses, cash, passports.

As the cleaning ladies came in, he was writing a passage about pets: Each pet had to be in an airline-approved container with at least a ten-day supply of food and up-to-date health and rabies certificates from a licensed veterinarian. Even then, their evacuation could not be guaranteed and they might get left behind, in which case they would be destroyed as humanely as possible.

He stepped out into the visa section to get a cup of coffee and clear his head. The cleaning ladies were in the waiting area, vacuuming and dusting, and he thought for a moment about his mother, cleaning offices at night in Brockton.

The door to Benny's office was open. Tom didn't deliberate or hesitate. He didn't think at all. He went inside and plucked the small key stashed underneath Benny's pencil jar and used it to unlock the top left drawer of Benny's desk and picked up Benny's ring of master keys and put it in his pants pocket and returned to his own office.

He waited for the cleaning ladies to leave, wondering if he was really going to do this. He would have to unlock the cabinets and take out Masahiro Yamada's Visa Tracking Card from the Visa Card File, his Visa Refusal Form OF-194 from the Category II Refusal File, his Non-Immigrant Visa Application Form DS-156 from the A–Z File, and his Lookout Entry Card from the Lookout File. He would have to stamp "REF 5A OVERCOME" on all the forms and cards, and then forge Benny's signature on each page, after which he would have to feed Yamada's passport through the Burroughs machine to apply an official visa stamp in red, blue, and green ink. No one would notice, Tom tried to convince himself. The visa would be buried under thousands of applications, Tom told himself.

But when he opened the Visa Card File and flipped through the reference cards to Masahiro Yamada's, Tom discovered he would not have to forge anything after all. He checked the Category II Refusal File to make sure. Benny had already overturned the refusal. He had approved the visa.

Tom finished updating the evacuation plan a little before ten that night. He walked home, starving—he hadn't eaten dinner. On the back street behind the Grew House, he encountered a Japanese man with wooden clappers and a young boy holding a candle-lit lantern. The two of them yelled, "*Hi no yojiri!,*" startling Tom until he realized they weren't speaking to him but chanting the phrase over and over as they ambled down the street. "Be careful of fire," they were saying—a traditional neighborhood fire watch that had somehow survived modernity.

The next morning, he went into Benny's office. "Thank you, Benny," Tom told him.

Benny stared at the paperwork on his desk. "Give me his passport, and I'll have it stamped," he said, and they were both too ashamed of themselves to look at each other.

■　　■　　■

MRS. FUJIWARA told him Susan Countryman wanted to talk to him. "Which line?" Tom asked, glancing at the blinking lights on his phone.

"No," Mrs. Fujiwara said. "She is here."

"Where? In Tokyo?"

"In waiting room."

She was sitting in a chair by the door, her suitcase next to her. Apparently she had come to the embassy straight from the airport.

"Ms. Countryman?"

She stood and turned around, and Tom was bewildered to see that she was black.

She was a small woman, around thirty-five, her eyes hollow. She wore a burgundy polyester pantsuit and hugged her shoulder bag to her chest with both hands. Wearily, she said, "Could I speak to your supervisor?"

In Reeves's office, she produced a letter from her shoulder bag. Reeves read it, then handed it to Tom. The letter was from Congressman Vernon Beard of Virginia, a rabble-rouser if there ever was one, a famous civil rights activist, quick with accusations of racism whenever things didn't go his or his constituents' way. In the letter, he asked the Consular Officers to give Susan Countryman their full cooperation and bring the investigation of her sister's disappearance to a conclusion as quickly as possible.

"I feel like I've been getting the runaround," Susan Countryman said. "I keep getting pawned off to that detective."

Reeves nodded. "What about that, Tom?" he asked in a grave tone that Tom had never heard him use before.

"I'm sorry if it appears that way. I've tried repeatedly to get the police to follow up on the investigation, and I think they've done that, but there hasn't been a lot to go on." He summarized the turning points in the case, more for Reeves's benefit than for hers.

"They found out she was working in the sex industry?" Susan Countryman asked.

He looked at her, still astounded she had come to Tokyo, and still nonplussed that she was black. She was very dark. She didn't seem to be mixed-blooded. All along, he had assumed Lisa—and, in turn, her sister—was white. "It seems so. For research for her Ph.D."

"So it's possible she got involved with organized crime," she said. "It's the same here as it is in the States, right?"

"That's a possibility."

"So she might have gotten in trouble with them."

"We don't really know, to tell you the truth."

"But you and that detective think someone's been trying to mislead you about what happened to her."

"Yes."

"You think she's dead, don't you?"

He stared at her. She looked so exhausted. He remembered they had given the box with Lisa's personal effects to Kenzo Ota. They should get the box for Susan Countryman, he thought. "Yes," he said. "It's been six months."

"Okay, then," she said.

Tom glanced at Reeves, and he knew they were both afraid she might cry.

But she didn't. She took a breath and asked, "If that's the case, could I get a death certificate for her?"

"Excuse me?"

She explained that her parents had been killed in a car accident the year before. They had died intestate, and Susan and Lisa had had to go to probate to claim their parents' assets and property, which was going to be evenly split between them. Yet once the proceedings were finalized, Susan had never gotten hold of Lisa to sign the court papers. That was why she had been sending her telegrams. Now that Lisa was missing, the only way she could take over the estate was to obtain a certificate of death for Lisa.

"I'm a single mom," she said. "I've got three kids. I need to settle this. I can't wait forever for the bureaucracy."

Tom felt disgusted. He was embarrassed for her. She hadn't come to Japan for her sister. She'd come for the money. She was more concerned with money than her sister. "We don't issue death certificates," he told her. "The Japanese authorities have to do it, and by law, there has to be a number of years of continuous unexplained absence—I think it's seven—before they'll issue a certificate."

"Isn't there something you can do?"

"I'm sorry, no."

"Well, there might be something," Reeves said. He pulled out the FAM from the shelf behind his desk. He flipped through the manual and read a passage, then showed it to Tom: Section 235 of Subchapter 7, Presumptive Death.

Reeves said to Susan Countryman, "If we can get the police to submit a written advisory opinion with all the relevant facts and data, stating she was reported missing and is presumed dead, we can give you an amended FS-192, a Report of Presumptive Death of an American Citizen, which might be enough to settle the estate."

"Will the police do that?" she asked.

"I think we can bring it to bear," Reeves told her. "It's not a definitive finding we're asking for."

"Can I ask you a question?" Tom said to her.

She nodded.

"Were you adopted?"

"What? Of course not," she said, indignant. "*She* was adopted."

"She was born in Yokohama. Was her mother Japanese?"

"That's the assumption."

"And the assumption was also that her father was an American in the Navy?"

"Yeah."

"Was he black?"

"Why does that matter? We never knew for sure, okay? The rumor was that he was some kind of mulatto. The mother was a bargirl. Lisa was in an orphanage until she was four, when my parents adopted her."

"Did she ever find out who her birth parents are?"

"No."

"Did she want to?"

She shrugged. "I don't know."

"Hang on," Reeves said. "Can I see her picture?"

Tom had the case file with him. He extracted the passport photo of Lisa Countryman and handed it to Reeves.

"I didn't put it together because I never asked her name," Reeves said. "She came to the embassy in March or April. She was only here two minutes. She was looking for her adoption records, and I told her the US Consulate in Yokohama closed in 1971 and they transferred all their records to Nagoya. I sent her to Nagoya."

Tom looked down at the photograph of Lisa Countryman. Why hadn't he noticed them before, the contradictory facial features, the parts that didn't quite fit together, as on his own face? She was revealed to him now.

"She was here to find her mother," he said.

FIFTEEN

KENZO AND KUNICHI were summoned to the US Embassy, and in a conference room, they met with Tom Hurley, Kimball Reeves, Susan Countryman, and Mrs. Fujiwara, who acted as translator. Both Kenzo and Kunichi kept glancing at Susan Countryman, and Kunichi finally said to Mrs. Fujiwara, voice lowered, "Excuse me, please do not translate this, as I'm sure it would appear rude, but does this mean that the missing woman's biological father was a *kokujin*?" A Negro. Mrs. Fujiwara nodded.

In the car going back to the station, Kunichi told Kenzo to write an advisory opinion that Lisa Countryman was dead.

"What about her birth mother?" Kenzo asked. " It would be negligent not to follow up on her search for her. This woman could've been the last person to see her."

"Yes, okay," Kunichi said. "Make a few inquiries, purely as a formality, then write the report."

"The regulations call for a due and diligent investigation."

"How much time have I allowed you to spend on this case? You're completely incompetent."

"You won't let me talk to the Atsuta woman or any of her hostesses. You won't let me put out posters or even classifieds or ask the newspapers or the TV—"

"You're lucky you still have a job, Ota. Weren't you listening at the meeting? No one in that embassy, not even her sister, gives a shit what really happened to Lisa Countryman. They want to pretend that everything possible was done, but really they just want the case closed. Wrap it up and write the report, or I'll have Yamada do it for you."

Yamada. Kenzo kept seeing Yamada's piss-yellow car parked outside the station, and each time, he felt tempted to vandalize it— scratch the paint or bend the antenna. He imagined Yamada and Miss Saotome were having a good laugh at his expense. He hadn't seen or talked to Miss Saotome since spying her with Yamada. Whenever he left or returned to his apartment, Kenzo had been careful to skulk around corners and dash quickly in order to avoid her.

He wished he had never met her. He had been doing fine before he met her. But it was too late now. She had done a terrible thing to him—the worst thing a person could do to another—and it was now irrevocable. She had awakened the loneliness in him, reminded him of his need for other people.

On the train to Yokohama, he looked over the file from the US Consulate's archives in Nagoya. They had made Lisa Countryman go all the way to Nagoya to fetch the documents, but with a simple phone call, Tom Hurley had been able to get photocopies of the file delivered to the embassy the next morning via diplomatic pouch.

Most of the papers were US immigration forms: Form I-600 Petition to Classify Orphan as an Immediate Relative, Form I-604 Report on Overseas Orphan Investigation, Form IR-3 Immigration Visa Application for Orphans Adopted Abroad.

The only document relevant to Kenzo was the official adoption decree from the Yokohama Family Court. It gave him Lisa Countryman's original Japanese name, Mayu Kaneda; the name of the orphanage where she had lived, Nonohana-no-ie; and the name of the ward in Yokohama that had had jurisdiction over her adoption, Aoba-ku. With those pieces of information, Kenzo thought it would be relatively easy to track down Lisa's natural mother.

In Japan, privacy rights of individuals were superseded by the importance of the family. Until the American Occupation, the family had always stood as a legal unit, liable for any member's actions. Everything that happened in a family was recorded in the *koseki tohon,* the family register, which was kept at the ward office of the family's legal domicile, whether anyone still lived there or not. The *koseki* went back generations and detailed all marriages, births, deaths, divorces, adoptions, criminal convictions, occupations, relocations. Read carefully, the *koseki* could reveal all manner of familial impurities, from alcoholism to congenital defects. Together with *juminhyo,* certificates of current residence, *koseki* made it virtually impossible to hide the whereabouts of a Japanese citizen, which made them very valuable. They were supposedly kept confidential, but lawyers and the police could access them, and, with a little finessing, so could bill collectors, potential employers, and even *nakodo* like Miss Saotome, matchmakers checking for signs of improvidence in the betrothed. Lisa Countryman's *koseki* would have both her adoptive and natural parents' names.

But when Kenzo arrived at the Family Register Subdivision of the Aoba Ward Office, he learned a *koseki* was not going to help him. There was no *koseki* for Mayu Kaneda, or for anyone she might have been related to.

"I don't understand," Kenzo said to the woman clerk.

"I don't, either," she said.

"If her mother was Japanese, even if her father was a *gaijin,* she'd still be a Japanese citizen, correct?"

"Correct."

"Then she should have a *koseki.*"

"Unless," the clerk said, raising her finger in the air, "she was abandoned."

Of course, Kenzo thought. How stupid of him. To bear a *shiseiji,* a love child, who was also *konketsu,* mixed-blooded, especially if some of that blood was black, was extremely shameful. Lisa Countryman had been abandoned.

"But that still doesn't clear up everything," the clerk said.

"No?" Kenzo asked.

"Even if both her parents had been unknown, as long as she was born in Japan, she would have been deemed a citizen. The mayor would've given her a name and started a *koseki* for her."

She suggested Kenzo go upstairs to the Child Guidance Center, where the adoption for Mayu Kaneda had been processed.

"Before I leave, can I ask you," Kenzo said, pulling out Lisa Countryman's photograph, "was this woman here? It would have been sometime in the spring."

She looked at the photo and frowned. "This is supposed to be her?" she said. "She looks white."

"You've never seen her before?"

"No, but maybe Mariko or Miyuki has."

She talked to the other two clerks, and Mariko came over and said she remembered Lisa Countryman coming to the office. "What did you tell her?" Kenzo asked.

"I told her I couldn't help her," Mariko said to him. "She's a *gaijin*. I can't release *koseki* to *gaijin*."

The clerk at the Child Guidance Center, a pudgy young man with greasy hair, was snippy and officious. He told Kenzo to get a cup of coffee, it'd take him a while to retrieve the documents from storage. Kenzo killed a half hour at a coffeehouse, and still he had to wait an additional thirty minutes for the clerk, who finally plunked a thick file down on the counter for him.

Kenzo never imagined so many documents were required for an adoption. Richard and Lenore Countryman had had to submit copies of their passports, military IDs, immigration forms, medical and psychological examinations, police clearances, income tax forms, bank statements, property deeds, and character references. Everything was there—all translated and notarized—except for one thing. "Where's the birth certificate?" Kenzo asked.

The clerk grimaced. He rubbed his eye, then flipped through the file. "Here," he said, pointing to a smudged, blotchy carbon copy.

"This isn't a birth certificate," Kenzo said.

"It's a Certificate of Acceptance of Notification of Birth."

"What?"

"It's what's used when the baby's illegitimate and stateless."

"Stateless?"

"No nationality."

"Who issued this? The hospital?"

"We did."

"How did you determine she was stateless?"

"*I* didn't determine anything."

"You know what I mean."

The clerk peered at the certificate. "There's a reference number here, but it's not one of ours. It's a Registry number. Go back down to Registry."

Kenzo showed him Lisa Countryman's photo. "Have you seen

this woman? Did she ask you or anyone here about Mayu
Kaneda's adoption?"

The clerk barely gave the photo a glance. "No," he said, but
when Kenzo was almost out the door and into the hallway, the
clerk said, as an afterthought, "That wasn't her."

"What?"

"There was another woman asking about the adoption."

"Who?"

"A private detective."

This made sense. Lisa Countryman had known that, as a *gaijin*,
the local government bureaucracy would not release any information to her, so she had hired a private detective. Smart of her.
"What was the detective's name?"

"You really expect me to remember?"

"She didn't give you a namecard?"

"Sure, I keep all of them in a box, organized by—"

"Didn't she have to sign a request form to examine the file?"

"You know the date she was here?"

"No."

"We keep the request forms by date. Unless you can narrow
down the date, it'll take me forever to find it."

"Listen," Kenzo said, "*you're* the one who saw the woman, not
me. *You're* the only one who can narrow down the date."

The clerk looked at him, then laughed uproariously. "Hey,
you're right. But that doesn't help you, does it?"

Kenzo went back downstairs to the Family Register Subdivision
and spoke to the original clerk, who checked the Registry reference number and discovered another file. There was no *koseki* for
Mayu Kaneda, but there was a *joseki*, a canceled *koseki*.

"Okay, it looks like she was first issued a birth certificate at the
hospital," the woman clerk said. "It was assumed her mother was
Japanese, so she was given citizenship and a *koseki*, but then her

legal status was rescinded, and she was disqualified from citizenship. She became stateless."

"Why was she disqualified?"

"It doesn't say. Maybe they'd know something at the children's
home?"

The Nonohana-no-ie Children's Home was a three-story, state-
sponsored orphanage with forty charges, both boys and girls.
Kenzo strolled around the cement playground with the director,
who had run the home with his wife since its inception after the
war. Although he didn't know what had altered Mayu Kaneda's
legal status, he remembered the girl. She had been left at the front
door to the home when she was five days old and had lived there
until she was four years old.

"She was very, very lucky to have been adopted," he said. "She
would have had a very tough life had she stayed in Japan as an
ainoko."

The director told Kenzo it was unlikely she would have found a
sponsor to become naturalized, and, with her black blood, no
Japanese would have adopted her. Stateless, Mayu Kaneda would
have been stuck in legal limbo. Since she wasn't a citizen, she couldn't
get a *koseki*. Since she didn't have a *koseki*, she couldn't get a *juminhyo*, a certificate of residence. Since she wasn't an official resident,
she would not have been eligible for schooling, health care, any kind
of public assistance. As far as the government was concerned, she
wouldn't have had the right to exist. She would have been a social
outcast, shunned and derided. On her eighteenth birthday, she would
have been expelled from the orphanage, left to fend for herself,
almost certain to turn to prostitution to subsist. Sadder yet, she
wouldn't have been able to leave the country, perhaps to America to
seek a better, more equitable life: without a nationality, there would
have been no way for her to obtain a passport.

Several wives from the naval base had volunteered at the orphanage, Lenore Countryman among them. "As I said, Mayu was lucky Mrs. Countryman took an interest in her. This is what she looks like now?" the director asked Kenzo, holding the photograph. "She turned out to be very pretty. She looks white. When she was a baby, her skin was very dark. I wouldn't have recognized her."

"She didn't come to visit the home a few months ago?" Kenzo said.

"No, but I suppose I shouldn't be surprised. She wouldn't have had good memories of this place. Even here, the children taunted her without mercy."

The only place left to go was the hospital where Lisa Countryman had been born, and at the records department, Kenzo encountered another snooty male clerk. After an incessant wait, the clerk excavated Mayu Kaneda's file, which corroborated that the hospital had initially processed a birth certificate for her as an "Illegitimate Child," "Mother: Unknown Japanese," "Father: Unknown Non-Japanese."

"But why was it revoked?" Kenzo asked.

"The mother gave a false name," the clerk said.

"Yes, well, that's obvious, isn't it, since the mother was marked as unknown."

The clerk glared at Kenzo.

"I'm sorry," Kenzo said. "I apologize for my rudeness. Does it say anywhere why she was disqualified?"

"No."

"What about the particulars of the birth?"

"The mother was brought here in an ambulance, and they had to do a C-section in the surgical ward, then she spent two nights in the ICU and another in the maternity ward."

"Who were her doctors and nurses? Are any of them still working here?"

The clerk examined the names and *hanko*—circular red *kanji* stamps—on the charts, cross-referenced them to a directory of cur-rent hospital staff. "There's one doctor and one nurse."

The doctor wasn't on duty, but the nurse was. She had been in the maternity ward at the time, but was now assigned to the pediatrics ICU. She was in her mid-fifties, a strong woman, stumpy, a barrel.

"I already went over all this with the private detective," the nurse said.

"Oh?" The orphanage director and the records clerk had not been approached by the private detective. This lady detective seemed to be two steps ahead of Kenzo. "Please tell me what you told her."

"I remember the baby because she was a *daburu*." Double, half and half. "There weren't very many back then, especially half *kurombo*." Half-nigger. "Now, of course, it's a different story. It's not so unusual to see these *dojin* babies." Earth people. "The whole area is practically polluted with them."

"Do you know what happened with the birth certificate?" Kenzo asked. "Why was the baby denied citizenship?"

"Her mother wasn't Japanese."

"She wasn't?"

"Oh, she did her best to pass herself off as Japanese, but I could tell something wasn't right. Then I heard she was a *zainichi* Korean, a bargirl *yariman*."

"Where did you hear that?"

"I don't remember now. Maybe another nurse."

"That was enough to disqualify the baby? Just a single rumor? No one ever investigated?"

The nurse crossed her thick arms. "Why does it matter? She was half *kurombo*," the nurse said. "What's this about, anyway? The private detective never said."

"Did the private detective give you her namecard?" he asked the nurse, repulsed by her, not wanting to talk to her anymore.

She rooted through a drawer in the nurses' station and produced the namecard: Ako Abe, Abe Detective & Research Office, Tokyo.

■ ■ ■

"YUMIKO."

His wife was standing in the checkout line at the National Azabu Supermarket, and Kenzo could see from her shock, her utter dismay, that she had not expected to run into him like this— not in a million years. She asked him to wait for her next door in the 31 Ice Cream shop while she put her groceries in her car, and when she met him in the ice cream parlor, she was still pale and wide-eyed with dread.

They each ordered a cup of peach melba and sat down at a table. Timidly, they exchanged pleasantries, remarked at how little the other had changed, at least physically—such was the superiority of the Japanese physiology. He asked her questions, and she answered. She spoke softly, her Japanese stilted now as if she were a *gaijin,* just as his had been when he'd returned to Japan from St. Louis.

She told Kenzo that for her first seven years in America, she had lived in Garden Grove, just south of Los Angeles, and had worked as a bookkeeper in a small electronics firm while attending classes at Whittier College, Richard Nixon's alma mater. After finally getting her degree—Kenzo had to admire Yumiko's resourcefulness, going to university and getting a degree as a single working mother—she was offered a job in Glendale at an IBM branch office, moved to an apartment in Silver Lake, and obtained her CPA. Then—here she lowered her eyes—she remarried and relocated to Atlanta, Georgia. Her husband—eyes still lowered—was a *gaijin* who spoke fluent Japanese. He was always traveling to Japan for business, and his company had been pressuring him to live in Tokyo. With several important product launches in the offing, he couldn't really refuse, so here she was, back in Japan for one year.

Kenzo decided to come right out with it. "How has your son adjusted to being here?" he asked.

She gasped.

"It's all right," Kenzo said. "I know all about him."

"You do?"

"I know everything."

She burst into tears. "I didn't know how to tell you," she moaned.

He patted her hand. "It's all right. Please don't cry."

"I'm so sorry. I'm so, so sorry."

"It's all right," he said. "I forgive you." He gave her his handkerchief, and she blew her nose noisily. People were looking over at them, but he did not feel embarrassed. He felt liberated.

"How did you find out?" she asked.

"Well, I'm a cop."

"Oh, yes, of course. You're a cop."

"It must be very difficult for Simon right now. I'm sure he's confused."

"You have no idea. When Doug accepted the assignment, I thought it would be a great opportunity for Simon to learn about his heritage, but he hasn't shown the least bit of interest. He doesn't care. He's refusing to even take Japanese classes at his school."

"He's at that age when all boys begin to rebel, and with all this, on top of everything else, it's understandable why he might act out."

"You're right. You're absolutely right."

He watched Yumiko eat her peach melba. She was relaxed now, her confession after all these years cathartic and invigorating. "What have you told him about me?" he asked her.

"Told who? You mean Doug?"

"No, Simon. Have you told him yet, or have you been waiting to get in touch with me first? Because I'm all right with whatever you want to do. I'll accede to your thoughts on how best to proceed. You know more about these things than I do."

"Huh?"

"One thing I've been thinking about, though, is I'd like to put Simon on my *koseki.* Then we can establish his Japanese citizenship and get a passport issued for him. However, I looked into this, and I found out that he can only keep his dual citizenship until he's twenty-two. At that time, the Ministry of Justice will make him choose a nationality."

"What are you talking about?"

"I know you're worried, but I really think everything will be fine once he meets me. He'll feel legitimized. A great weight will be lifted from him once he knows I'm his real father."

"But you said you knew."

"I do."

Yumiko put down her plastic spoon, squeezed the bridge of her nose between her fingers, and closed and opened her eyes. "Your ignorance has always been your gift," she said. "You're not Simon's father. I had an affair."

"An affair?" It was unfathomable.

"It was a mistake. It was only two times. I was so ashamed."

"Who was he?"

She mentioned the section chief of the billing department where she had worked as an OL, and he had a vague recollection of a tall, heavyset young man. "You're lying," Kenzo said.

"No."

"You're trying to keep Simon away from me."

"No."

He noticed a dot of ice cream on Yumiko's chin. "You never had any integrity," he told her. "You've never known the meaning of duty. Just like my mother."

She sagged her head. "You haven't changed. You were so intolerant. You excluded me. You never let me in."

"How do you know for sure I'm not the father?"

"I'm sure."

"He could be my son."

"No."

"What makes you so certain?"

"I think you were infertile."

"What?"

"I tried to get pregnant with you, Kenzo. I didn't tell you."

"I want a paternity test. The three of us—you, me, and Simon—will go to a clinic and get blood tests."

"What would be the point? You know I'm telling you the truth. Besides, Doug is his father. He adopted Simon."

"If you won't agree, I'll hire a lawyer and go to Family Court."

"Please don't. I beg of you. Please don't." The ice cream was still on her chin.

He stood up, gave her his napkin, and gestured to his own chin. "You've always been such a messy woman," he said.

▪   ▪   ▪

HE DIDN'T hear the alarm, he didn't smell the smoke, he didn't see the flashing strobe lights. He was asleep when the fire broke out, and Miss Saotome shook him awake. He opened his eyes, and she was pushing on his chest and moving her mouth wordlessly. He removed his special earplugs—given to him by the ear specialist he had seen for his tinnitus. "Get up, get up!" she screamed. "There's a fire!"

The clock said 3:53. He spit out his mouthguard—given to him by the dentist he had seen for his teeth-grinding—and ripped off his wrist brace—given to him by the neurologist he had seen for his thumb twitch. He and Miss Saotome ran down the hallway, banging on doors, using her master key to open them and yell inside for everyone to evacuate. They did this on each floor until the building was empty, all the residents on the street, watching the firemen come in their silver suits and hoods to extinguish a small fire in the boiler room.

"Are you all right?" Kenzo asked Miss Saotome, who looked as if she was about to faint. "Here. Come over here and sit down." He led her to a blue Nissan and had her lean her backside against the hood. She was wearing a robe and a San Francisco 49ers jersey, and she was barefoot.

"What's that on your neck?" she asked.

It was the cream given to him by the dermatologist he had seen for his psoriasis. "It's a special moisturizer," he told her.

"What did you do to your room? What was that on the walls?"

He had been hoping that, in the chaos, she hadn't noticed. He had done a little remodeling to his bedroom. He had weather-stripped the windows and door and covered every inch of the ceiling and walls with acoustical tile. "I'm sorry. It's a special wallpaper," he said. At least she hadn't spotted the wig hanging on the hook—the wig she had used to disguise herself as a man and had thrown at him that night in Kabukicho.

"Why do you have my wig on the wall?" she asked.

She was really quite homely without makeup, and her teeth were terrible. "I'm sorry. I was waiting for a good time to return it to you," he said.

"Why haven't you called me?"

"I'm sorry?"

"You never asked me out on another date. Why didn't you call me? I thought things went well. I thought we had a good time."

"But you're going out with Yamada."

"What?"

"Aren't you?"

"Inspector Yamada?"

"Yes."

"Of course not."

"Oh."

"Where did you get that idea?"

"I saw you get into his car."

"He wanted to *hire* me as a matchmaker. For his *brother.*"

"Oh."

"He wanted me to find his brother a *wife,* but his brother refused."

"I'm sorry."

"You're the biggest moron in the world, aren't you?"

"Yes, I am," Kenzo said. "I'm sorry."

"Shut up," she said, and grasped his head with both hands like a melon, and, in front of all the apartment dwellers and neighbors and firemen and policemen, she kissed him.

■   ■   ■

THE ABE DETECTIVE & RESEARCH OFFICE was in Akihabara, on the second floor above a shop that sold blenders—only blenders, blenders of every shape and type. Ako Abe was a cheerful woman in her late thirties, and could have been considered pretty were it not for several large moles on her face.

They compared notes, and Kenzo learned that he had been on the right track. He was sure that, in time, he would have reached the same conclusions that she had.

Ako Abe had found and interviewed the other nurse who had spread the rumor about Mayu Kaneda's mother being a Korean bargirl. The nurse, now retired, admitted the statement had been an exaggeration. The nurse had seen her at a bar, Club Zoo Fly, that was frequented by American sailors, but the woman wasn't a bargirl. The nurse was fairly certain that the woman was a *zainichi* Korean, and although she never knew her name, she was pretty sure the woman worked on the Navy base. Ako Abe did some leg-work and narrowed down the woman's place of employment on the base to the Office of Naval Intelligence.

"She was a spy?" Kenzo asked.

"No, no, a secretary," Ako Abe said. "So then I went to the Human Resources Office at Yokohama Navy Base. All I needed were the names of the foreign nationals who worked in Naval Intelligence in 1955. Anyone would have sufficed. I could track them down and figure out who Lisa Countryman's mother was. She must have taken an unexpected leave of absence that summer. But I got totally stonewalled. I got nowhere with them. They said those records were confidential. National security."

"Your investigation stopped there?"

"I really tried my best. I was very sorry to disappoint Lisa Countryman, but that was as far as I could go."

"When was the last time you saw or heard from her?"

"Sometime at the end of May, I think."

"There's nothing else you can tell me?"

"Hm?" She seemed to hesitate, then shook her head no. "You really don't know what happened to her?" she asked. "Or do you have an idea but won't tell me?"

Kenzo momentarily entertained a wild theory—that Naval Intelligence or the CIA was somehow involved in Lisa Countryman's disappearance—but he dismissed it as ludicrous. Even when he went to the Human Resources Office in Yokohama the next day and, like Ako Abe, was refused the employment records, he understood it to be a matter of bureaucracy, not malfeasance.

He had nothing more to go on, and he was prepared to write the advisory opinion that Lisa Countryman was dead, just as Kunichi wanted. But then he received a phone call from a woman. She said she needed to speak to him, and when he asked her to come to the station, she said she preferred to meet him outside. They agreed on the Almond coffee shop in Roppongi.

At three o'clock, he walked into Almond, and a woman in her late twenties—nicely dressed and made-up—waved him over to her table.

"You're Inspector Ota?" she asked.

"Yes."

"Sit down," she said. After he took a seat, she told him, "My name is Emi Fukuda. I used to work with Lisa Countryman at the club Rendezvous. The man you're looking for, the *nisei* she went on *dohan* with, his name was David Saito."

L ISA HAD been so unprepared for it—the phone call. She had been at her Berkeley apartment, chopping vegetables to make paella. It was four-thirty, a cold but bright Sunday afternoon in September, and the phone rang.

She couldn't understand what Susan was telling her. It was incomprehensible. Not that Susan was being inarticulate. On the contrary, she was calm, coolly professional, the consummate nurse, as if she were breaking the bad news to a patient's relatives. Yet these were her own *parents*. She sounded a little regretful, maybe, but utterly bloodless.

It took some time for the police to piece together what had happened. Richard and Lenore had been at the beach at Fort Story. He was reading a book, and she went in the water for a swim, even though it was near sunset and a bit nippy out. When Richard glanced up and searched for her, he couldn't see Lenore. He rose and looked and looked, and, becoming frantic, paced the sand at the water's edge, calling out for her. It was dusk, and there were no lifeguards—it was after Labor Day—and no passersby except for one woman. "My wife," he screamed to her. "I can't find my wife." Finally he saw Lenore, floating face-down. He ran into the light surf and dove in, and he and the woman carried Lenore out, and once ashore they began performing mouth to mouth and an approximation of CPR on her—he'd never been trained, why hadn't he taken a Red Cross course? "Call an ambulance!" he told the woman, but she didn't move. She knew Lenore was beyond the possibility of revival. She was dead. She had been under too long. In fact, although drowning was the official cause of death, an autopsy would show that she had suffered a stroke while swimming, a massive cerebral hemorrhage from which she would have never recovered. But Richard didn't know that. He lifted her in his arms and carried her to the car and raced down the road for a hospital.

They found the car on Atlantic Avenue, the driver's side crushed and sheared after it had hit a telephone pole. They estimated that Richard had been traveling in excess of eighty miles an hour, and he had died instantaneously. They assumed he had lost control of the car, and said so in the accident report. Maybe he had leaned behind him to check on Lenore, who was laid out on the back seat, and when he turned back around, he saw he was drifting off the road and overcorrected, crossing the center line to the other side. Yet it was mysterious. He had been on a straightaway, and there were no skid marks. Had he intentionally crashed the car into the telephone pole? Lisa tended to believe that he had—not able to bear the thought of living without Lenore.

Lisa flew to Virginia Beach, and almost immediately she and Susan argued. About everything. First of all, what to do about their parents' burial. As retired career Navy, Richard was entitled to a funeral with military honors and interment in Hampton National Cemetery, just across the bridge from Norfolk, and Lenore could be buried with him. Susan, though, claimed that their father and mother had always said they wanted to be cremated and have their ashes spread into the ocean through a burial at sea.

"I never heard them say that," Lisa said. "When did they ever say that?"

But Richard's best friend, another Navy veteran, confirmed those wishes and arranged for the services.

They had to be cremated one by one—two hours at a time, at a temperature of two thousand degrees, cooking them to dust. Lisa and Susan were both there when Richard was placed inside the chamber, but Susan didn't stay for the actual cremation. She had to go home and tend to one of her three kids, who was sick with a stomach virus, she said. Alone, Lisa sat outside the chamber for the entire two hours, oddly feeling the need to be vigilant. She was afraid someone else's ashes might be mixed with her parents', and it frustrated her that, as much as it would have hurt her to witness, she couldn't supervise the sweeping of their bone fragments into the cooling pan, couldn't oversee the processing of their remains into particle.

She called Susan when it was Lenore's turn.

"Ally's really sick still," Susan said. "I don't think I can come. You go on ahead."

Lisa couldn't believe her cavalier attitude. With each day, she became more incensed with Susan and her children. During the burial at sea, she let her kids—her daughter seemed to have made a miraculous recovery from her stomach virus—run around the deck of the boat as if they were on a picnic. During the wake, she let them play games and laugh. How could Susan let her children be so disrespectful? Didn't she care? Didn't she feel anything?

But the real fight was to be over their parents' house in Virginia Beach. Susan said that once the formal legal matters were settled in probate court, dividing the estate among the two sisters, she wanted to sell the house and split the proceeds. Lisa balked at the proposal.

"I don't see why you're sentimental about this house," Susan said. "You've never even lived here."

This was true. After shuttling all over the world, Norfolk had been their father's last active post, and they had been assigned to naval housing on Sewells Point, Lisa attending Maury High School. When she left for UVA, Richard had retired, and he and Lenore had bought the three-bedroom rambler in Virginia Beach. Nevertheless, Lisa had come to the house every Thanksgiving and Christmas and sometimes during the summer for six years. It was the only permanent home she had ever known.

A few days after the burial, she sat with Susan at the kitchen table. "Why don't you move here?" Lisa asked.

"That's preposterous," Susan said. "What am I going to do? Commute a hundred miles each way to work?"

"Why couldn't you get a job here?"

"In this economy? Besides, I'm not going to uproot my kids. They've got it tough enough as it is."

"Let's rent it out, then. Like you said, the economy's lousy. It's not a good time to sell. We should hang on to it for a couple of years and wait for the market to rebound."

Susan picked up their empty coffee cups, poured water in them, set them in the sink, and sat back down. "To tell you the truth, I need the money. Mark's checks have been bouncing. He got laid off, and without child support, I'm deep in shit."

"There's hardly any mortgage on this place," Lisa said. "You could save a lot of money living here."

"What do you know about money? You don't know anything.

You've never had a real job. You've been in school your entire life, paid for by Mom and Dad, thank you very much."

"That's not fair. I've done it all on fellowships and loans."

"They've been helping you out every step of the way. Talk about *child* support."

"Maybe I'll move here," Lisa said.

"What are you talking about?"

"Maybe I'll transfer to Old Dominion or William & Mary." It was an impulsive suggestion. She didn't even know if those schools had Ph.D. programs in cultural anthropology.

"Look," Susan said, "we're going to split everything fifty-fifty, but I think I should have more say in the decision. I'm the oldest."

"And because you're related by blood and I'm not?"

"I didn't say that."

"Because I was adopted?"

"Come on."

"You've always hated me," Lisa said.

"Let's be grown-ups, okay?"

"The shit you used to pull on me."

"Ancient history, Lisa."

"I'm sorry they loved me more."

"What? What did you say?"

"They loved me more. You know they did."

Susan laughed softly. "You're pathetic. If you weren't so spiteful, I'd feel sorry for you."

They did, Lisa thought. They had loved her more. And why not? Susan had been such a cold, joyless child, a mean, misanthropic sourpuss without a generous bone in her body, exploiting every chance to be cruel to her adopted sister. She had been jealous of Lisa, of the way Richard and Lenore had doted on her, jealous of her light skin and straight hair, of her intelligence and voice—a musical talent that seemed inherited, while Susan was tone-deaf, sulking in her bedroom whenever the other three broke into sing-along. Susan had never suspected that Lisa, in fact, had been jealous of her, that she had wanted to look like her, truly and unquestionably black, that she had wished, more than anything, she could call Richard and Lenore her real parents.

They settled nothing about the house that week, or the week after. What they did do was bicker over their parents' possessions—their mementos, clothes, the family photographs, what to give away, what to keep, who would get what. Susan wanted to take some of the furniture right away—a handmade chest from the Philippines, a panel of screens with inlaid pearl from Taiwan—but Lisa said no, and then worried that Susan might rent a van and try to ferret away pieces in the middle of the night. By the time Lisa returned to school and Susan to her job, they were no longer speaking.

They each hired an attorney. There was not an insignificant amount of money involved: Richard's pension, the life insurance, Social Security, their mutual funds and savings, and, of course, the house. Susan's lawyer filed a suit of partition to force a resolution and sell the property. Eventually the court agreed and ordered the sisters to inventory what was inside the house and decide on an equitable distribution of the items. It dragged on for months, dozens of back-and-forths through the attorneys about the dispensation of a vase or a picture frame. Lisa wavered and wrangled over every trivial piece. Susan just wanted it finished. She wanted the money. Finally, it was done. There was nothing more for Lisa to contest. The only thing left to do was sign the papers.

■   ■   ■

IT WAS the brochure that sold her, the English version of the brochure for the Abe Detective & Research Office, which read: "It is the supporter whose truth which is hid is the best. It has already cried, and it falls asleep, unnecessary. It is exactly that it is trouble-some with the knowing cultivated so far, your worry thing. Anything give OK in such cases as the flirtation, conduction, annoyance, missing, stoker measure, fickleness investigation. A new fact may be hidden behind the love. Love is full the vexatious mystery. There are some knots in the life. Trouble thing is done consulting sincerely. Secret strict observance."

Lisa had known it would not be easy to find her birth mother, but she hadn't thought she would be stymied from the start. She had gotten brushed off at the US Embassy in Tokyo, told to go to the US Consulate in Nagoya, and when she got there, the Vice Consul had said before he could give her the records, she had to provide documentation she was Mayu Kaneda. It took weeks for the Commonwealth of Virginia to mail her a certified copy of the circuit court order that had legally changed her name to Lisa Countryman. She took the train back to Nagoya, showed the order to the Vice Consul, and at last was handed the records, but they didn't tell her anything she hadn't already known. She had found the same forms in the file cabinet in her father's study. She did a lit-tle research and learned about *koseki,* went to Yokohama, and was summarily turned away by the Family Register clerk in the Aoba Ward Office. The clerk would not even look at her documents.

She had no idea what to do next, until one night she was riding the subway home, the last train of the night, 12:17. The subway car was empty except for a few drunk salarymen who were passed out on the velveteen benches, their shoes neatly placed on the floor. Lisa was thinking she might have to hire a Japanese attorney and petition to obtain access to the *koseki*—did they have freedom of information laws in Japan? Then she looked up in the subway car and saw an ad for the Abe Detective agency: "We Find Ways When There Is No Way."

The moment she walked through the door of the agency, she felt reassured. Ako Abe was sympathetic and maternal, and she seemed confident she would be able to help Lisa.

"I cannot make any promises, but this should not be impossible," she said. "In Japan, we keep very good records, and, with the right approach, almost everything is available. But I want to give you a piece of advice. I want you to prepare yourself. What if I find your mother? What are your expectations? What is it that you really want from her?"

What was it that Lisa really wanted? She wanted to recognize where she came from. She wanted to know who she was. She wanted to have a history. She had gone to Yokohama and stood outside the Nonohana-no-ie orphanage, and it had only stirred a vague picture of gray walls and dormitory futons and cafeteria meals. She had no recollection, really, of anything before the age of four, arriving in Norfolk, where everything had been so foreign, strange—these black people who claimed to be her parents, the white people on the naval base, this new language. She hadn't known what was happening, or why, yet within a year she was speaking flawless English, and her new experiences, her new family, began replacing whatever memories she had had. She rebuilt her world, her identity, and she forgot about Yokohama, lost her Japanese. Then, abruptly, they were overseas again, in the Philippines, another Navy base, another country.

They seemed to move all the time, and instead of feeling more secure with Richard and Lenore, she felt, with each new post, petrified. She was afraid she might not be good enough, she might do something wrong, and would be left behind at another orphanage. She did her best to be obedient, quiet, studious, neat, but she grew alarmed as she got older and turned whiter. She could no longer pass as black, as Richard and Lenore's own child, and she could sense their embarrassment whenever they were in public, strangers staring at them, wondering what relation she had to this black couple. Unable to conceal that she had been adopted, Lisa began telling other children that her real parents had been killed in a car accident, a more appealing genealogy. Susan would always dispense with that gentle notion quickly enough, braying that Lisa was the illegitimate child of a Jap hooker.

What did Lisa really want? She wanted someone to love her and protect her and never leave her. She wanted to belong somewhere, to someone. She wanted, for once in her life, constancy.

Ako Abe's revelation that she might be *zainichi* Korean was a shock and, to say the least, confused the issue. "I'm not half-Japanese?" Lisa asked.

"I'm still looking into it," Ako said.

"What's a *zainichi* Korean?" she asked.

They were ethnic Koreans who were permanent resident aliens of Japan, remnants of the colonization of Korea from 1910 to 1945. Millions of Koreans had been dragooned to Japan to serve as slave laborers in coal mines, factories, and shipyards—and not a few to work as comfort women. After World War II ended, the majority had returned to Korea, but about a quarter of them had stayed, fearing a worse fate in their homeland. Many of them had been born in Japan and spoke only Japanese. Like their compatriots in Korea, they had been forced to relinquish their language, their religion, their culture, even their names, given Japanese ones. But unless they became naturalized—a virtual impossibility—they lived as second-class noncitizens in Japan. They had to be fingerprinted for Alien Registration Cards, they couldn't vote, they were banned from working as schoolteachers or civil servants and discriminated from most private jobs, branded as inferior, lazy, prone to crime and violence. Consequently, they did everything they could to pass as Japanese, and they lived in terror of being found out.

In that light, it seemed almost charitable that Lisa's mother had left her at the orphanage door. She would have been saddled with the worst stigmas imaginable: a half-breed, a bastard child, a dirty Korean, a nigger.

Ako worked tirelessly, and after a month, tracking down the hospital nurses, the owner and patrons of Club Zoo Fly, civilians who had worked on the Navy base, she narrowed the search down to one woman, a suspected Korean, who in 1955 took a five-month leave of absence from her job in the Office of Naval Intelligence, but that was where she ran into the roadblock about the employment records and, suddenly and dishearteningly, the investigation ended, without her having learned the woman's name.

■   ■   ■

AT LISA'S suggestion, they met at the Stockholm Farm Lounge, a bar in Shibuya that predictably had no associations with anything Swedish or agricultural. It was in the basement of an office building—a small dark room with a slate floor and leather club chairs and an open fireplace in the center. It was the first time she had seen David Saito since the night of the *kaiseki* dinner.

After he had calmed her at the scene of the motorcycle accident, he had asked Mojo's driver to drop him off in Akasaka and take Lisa home without him, and then he had disappeared. Later that week in Rendezvous, she had asked Mojo about Larry, but Mojo had merely said Larry was busy. Once again he invited Lisa out to dinner, just the two of them, and once again she had patted his hand and said, "I can't go on a *dohan* with you, Mojo. You know the rules," to which Mojo countered, "What *dohan*? Just dinner. Friend dinner."

David had not given her a phone number to reach him, but she called the main switchboard of the embassy and was eventually transferred to his office. He didn't react at all to the fact that she was contacting him. No pleasure, no curiosity. "I need to ask you a favor," she had said, and she told him everything. She asked if he could somehow break through the bureaucracy at Yokohama and learn the name of the woman who had worked in the Office of Naval Intelligence, the woman who might be her mother. Lisa had thought of getting back in touch with Omar Johnson for information, but she knew he wouldn't have been able or inclined to help her.

David had told her to give him a few days, and, true to his word, they now sat in the deserted bar in the middle of the afternoon. He handed her an index card with a name and an address on it: Tomiko Higa in Gotanda, three stops away on the Yamanote Line from Shibuya.

"Are you sure this is her? This is my mother?"

"I'm not at all sure," David said. "There wasn't even an Office of Naval Intelligence in Yokohama at the time. But there was a field office for the 500th Military Intelligence Group of the US Army, and she worked there, and she's *zainichi* Korean."

Tomiko Higa was born in Kawasaki, an industrial city between Tokyo and Yokohama. She had grown up in the neighborhood of Sakuramoto, which was inhabited by nearly two thousand Koreans, and both her parents had worked in the Nihon Kohan Steel Mill. Tomiko had had passable looks and only average intelligence and was unremarkable in almost every way except for one thing: her voice. At the rather advanced age of twenty-two, she had broken into the music scene in Tokyo, and for over two decades she had made a career for herself as a ubiquitous, albeit second-tier *enka* singer and celebrity on TV. She was allowed to pass for Japanese, although it was common knowledge that she was Korean. There were hundreds of Korean singers and actors and baseball players in Japan, and everyone pretended not to notice. There seemed to be an unspoken agreement: as long as they stayed quiet, as long as they didn't ask for too much, as long as they never asserted their nationalism, they could partake in a measure of adulation and privilege. But only to a point. Tomiko Higa never came close to being a superstar.

"I don't know how to thank you," Lisa told David.

"You shouldn't get too excited. It might not be her."

They walked out together into the bright sunshine. It was three-thirty, and he said he had to go back to work. She wanted to suggest they recuse themselves to one of the many establishments nearby, on what was known as Love Hotel Hill, where she could properly convey her gratitude, but his decorum didn't lend himself to that sort of proposition.

"I'm sorry I kissed you the other night," she said on the street. "I didn't mean to embarrass you."

"You don't have to apologize. You were upset."

They stopped at a corner and waited for the stoplight. "Can I ask you something?" Lisa said. "Are you happy in your marriage?"

He took a moment to answer her. "I'm trying to be your friend, Lisa."

It wasn't yes, and it wasn't no. He needed time. He was old-fashioned. He believed in fidelity, whatever the state of his marriage, which was why Lisa had asked Ako Abe to do one more job for her—find out about David's wife. A fickleness investigation. Love was full of vexatious mysteries, and there were knots in life. Lisa just wanted a photograph of his wife. She wanted to know what she was up against. She didn't expect Ako to tell her that David Saito's name was not really David Saito, but Vincent Kitamura, and that his wife was not really French, nor a financial consultant, but a photographer named Julia Tinsley.

SEVENTEEN

OMETHING HAPPENED. Julia suddenly retreated from him, saying she needed to sort things out, she needed space, and she asked Tom not to call her or try to see her for a while. It threw him into despair. He wanted to call her. He wanted to go to her studio at the ISA or even to her apartment and see her. But he feared he might alienate Julia if he didn't honor her wishes, and he left her alone.

He distracted himself with work and spent his off-hours with Jorge and Benny, who could, undoubtedly, intuit what was going on but remained silent about it. They were trying to be supportive, and Tom resented them for it, knowing they believed this was what was best for him.

The third week of December, they went to the Sanno Hotel for the Sunday afternoon feature. Usually they avoided the Sanno, the military transit billet in Akasaka. The sprawling white stucco hotel was open for R&R to all ranks, and it had a pool, a bustling arcade of stores, barber and beauty shops, a spa, and several restaurants that seemed to feature continuous buffets with prime rib the size of tree trunks. All of it was staffed by non-Japanese Asians, mostly Filipino and Korean, with a giggling gaggle of non-Japanese Asian women, mostly Thai and Vietnamese, serving as accoutrements, hanging on to the arms of red-faced officers and GIs like so much insignia. The Sanno was an anachronism in modern, cosmopolitan Tokyo, a gauche, Cold War, colonial outpost, but it offered something Tom and his friends could not resist: American movies, only a few months old, projected onto a large screen in the basement ballroom, where the bar was always open and they could sit comfortably at tables and chairs.

It was there, for the four-thirty show of *All That Jazz,* that Tom saw Julia. He was at a corner table with Benny, and just before the lights dimmed, he spied her across the ballroom, slipping into a seat saved for her by Pete and Betty Congrieves.

Everyone stood for the national anthem, and when it ended and the previews began playing, Julia left the Congrieveses' table and headed for the bar. Tom followed her. Jorge was in line for drinks and waved, but Tom ignored him.

"Can we go somewhere and talk?" he asked Julia, and he pulled her out of line to the adjoining lobby.

"What's going on?" Tom asked.

"Nothing's going on."

"Don't do that."

"I'm going through a bad time right now," she said.

"I'm not having much fun, either."

"I think we need to end it."

"Why?"

"I always told you this would be temporary."

"Did your husband find out about us?"

She shook her head.

"Then what? What is it?" he said too loudly. "Why are you being like this?"

"Let's not do this," she said.

"I want to talk about this."

"Well, I don't particularly want to. There's nothing really to say. It was fun, but now it's over. Let's just walk away, all right?"

"Like adults, you mean."

"Yes."

"Like two ships fucking in the night."

They were within earshot of the ballroom, and a couple sitting at a table near the entrance glanced over to them.

"I want to be with you," Tom told her.

"You don't even know what it means to be in a relationship."

"I want to do things with you. Go out to dinner. Take a walk. Wake up in the morning with you."

"God, give me a break."

"Hold your hand," he said, and he grabbed her hand.

She yanked her arm away from him, and she inadvertently smacked her knuckles against a pane of decorative wall glass, sounding a loud, piercing rap and causing her to cry out in pain.

The man from the table by the entrance stood up.

"Are you okay?" Tom asked Julia.

The ticket-taker poked her head around the corner. "*Daijobu?*" she whispered.

"Did you *hit* her?" the man from the table said, approaching.

"Fuck off," Julia told the man, and briskly walked back into the ballroom.

Tom took off the other way, stomping up the stairs.

"Hey," Jorge called to him, and he met him halfway up the staircase. "What are you doing? Do you even know? You're making a fool of yourself."

"I don't need this, Jorge. Not from you."

"I'm trying to help you."

"Like hell."

"I'm trying to be your friend."

"You just want to gloat."

"You will never learn," Jorge said. "You think you're inside, but you'll always be outside."

"What the fuck are you talking about?"

"You're blind to who you are."

"Christ, listen to yourself. What is it with this self-righteous Che Guevara act, huh?" Tom said. "I'm sick of it. I'm sick of you. I can't help it if you hate yourself."

"You're a putz, you know that? Uncle Tom."

Tom shoved him in the chest, and Jorge fell back a step on the stairs before he could catch himself. "Yeah, that's good, *cabrón*," Jorge said. "You're a real man."

He went to the cocktail lounge, where a duo—a man on guitar and a woman on synthesizer, both Filipino—was singing Beatles songs in broken English.

The Soviets were building up forces around Poland. Three American nuns and a lay worker had been murdered in El Salvador. Iran was demanding $24 billion to release the hostages. But all anyone could talk about was John Lennon, shot dead on December 8 by Mark David Chapman.

Tom had always known it might come to this, that inexplicably Julia might decide to cut him off and he would simply have to accept the edict, no matter how cruel or fickle, because he would be powerless to do anything else. She had once said she had no control of her life, but he had even less. What was it he could do?

Three—or was it four?—drinks later, as the duo was butchering "Hey Jude," Tom saw Pete Congrieves passing through the cocktail lounge. He didn't think anything of it until, after a few minutes, Congrieves returned and stood over Tom's table.

"Mind if I join you?"

It was strange—his presumption. He didn't bother to introduce himself or engage in any formalities. He just sat down and flagged over a waitress in a mind-bogglingly short dress.

"Could I get a Chivas and Seven with a twist?" Congrieves said.

The waitress wrote down the order on her pad and looked to Tom to see if he wanted a refill.

"I'm fine for now," he said.

"Get another," Congrieves said. "Bring him another."

"Scotch rocks?" the waitress guessed. She hadn't been taking Tom's orders.

"Yeah."

"*Hanguk pun isimnikka?*" Congrieves asked her in what Tom recognized as Korean.

"*Ne.*"

"*Kurongot katesoyo. Komawoyo, agassi.*"

After the waitress left, Congrieves said to Tom, "You don't speak Korean, do you?"

"No."

"A shame. I'm sure it breaks your mother's heart."

What did he know about his mother? Tom wondered. How did he know he was half-Korean? Had Congrieves done some sort of background check on him?

Even sitting down, Congrieves seemed to loom over him. His thick blond hair was on the longish side, and his skin was ruddy with vigorous health. He looked to be in his early forties. He was powerfully built underneath his sweater, and he had a faraway gaze in his eyes that made him appear as if he were posing for a magazine ad.

"I was stationed in Seoul for two tours," Congrieves said. "The country's still very primitive, but I loved it there. I prefer the Korean temperament to the Japanese. Their emotionality is very raw and open. Everything is on the table. They're a very passionate people. What about you?"

"What?"

"Have you enjoyed living in Japan?"

"Yes."

"You like the Japanese?"

"I suppose I do." Tom was uncomfortable with the unpredictable zigzags in Congrieves's conversation, and he had an inkling that Congrieves was doing it on purpose, keeping him off-guard as a method of establishing dominion.

"There's a term in Korean, *chin-il-pa*," Congrieves said. "It means lover of Japan. It was what they called collaborators during the annexation. Maybe they'd say you're *chin-il-pa*."

The waitress brought over their drinks, and for a while the men said nothing, listening to the duo break into "The Long and Winding Road." Congrieves was staring at the muted TV above the bar, on which the Far East Network was broadcasting the news, showing a mob of Iranians chanting and burning American flags.

"A lovely state of affairs," Congrieves said. "Do you remember Carter's malaise speech?"

"Of course."

"What a yokel. Goddamn peanut farmer. Malaise, my ass. There's no crisis of the American spirit. There's no national psychosis. There's nothing wrong with the American people. We're a great people. Paralysis, stagnation, drift—those were the hallmarks of his administration, not the body politic. Good God, human rights as a tenet of foreign policy? There could be nothing more naïve. There's only one immutable fact of life, and that's the inherent need of one people to assert their superiority over another. It's always brutal, and it's ugly, and it's unavoidable—not for the faint of heart. We shouldn't be trying to impose values. We should impose stability, and that's what we do. We make things better. I'm not going to insult your intelligence and talk about ideology. We know ideology is relative. Today's fascists become tomorrow's allies. It's all very fluid. I might even allow hypocritical. But people are tribal by nature, which is dangerous, because the ineluctable tendency is to want the tribe to be bigger. You draw the lines, and if everyone stays within them, we all benefit. But you waffle, you let them start thinking they can defy you, the paradigm breaks down. It gets all fucked up. Then you have countries you defeated and occupied and redeveloped emasculating you. You have no-name shithole banana republics pissing in your face. You have parasitic ragheads burning your flag."

He downed his drink. "Forgive me. I have a habit of proselytizing. I almost went to divinity school."

"What do you want from me?" Tom asked.

Congrieves said to him, "I'm not only Vincent's boss, I'm his friend. Julia's, too. I want you to stop bothering her. No more little scenes like the one today. Stop embarrassing everyone. She doesn't want to see you anymore."

"Did she ask you to tell me that?"

"I'm acting on everyone's behalf, including yours."

"Go fuck yourself."

"I appreciate the good wishes, but I know you don't mean them. I know about you. I know about Roberto Ramirez and your fun and games in São Paulo. I know what you do when pressed. You do what you're told, like a good little Ricky. You wouldn't want people to hear about São Paulo, would you?"

Tom didn't answer him.

"I thought as much," Congrieves said.

■   ■   ■

KENZO OTA came to Tom's office and asked for his help with a couple of leads, beginning with access to Yokohama's Naval Intelligence employment records.

"I don't know what I can really do," Tom told him. "If they won't give them to you, what makes you think they'll give them to me?"

"You are embassy."

"I don't have a lot of leverage," he said. "Much less than you might think."

"You can try, yes?"

"I'll try," he said.

"I am sorry. One more," Ota said. He explained that he had gotten a tip about a *nisei* named David Saito, but was having problems locating him. The Immigration Bureau mysteriously did not have a record of a David Saito in Tokyo. Was a David Saito registered with the embassy?

"Let me check," Tom said, and he buzzed Mrs. Fujiwara in the next office and asked her to look through the Master Card Index of Registered Americans for a Form FS-176, 176S, or 299 that belonged to a David Saito. While they waited, Tom asked Ota about the tip. "What's his connection to Lisa Countryman?"

"Oh, maybe nothing. I think nothing," Ota said cagily.

"It doesn't sound like you're expediting an advisory opinion on the case. It sounds like you're investigating it more actively."

"No, no," Ota said. "Give opinion very soon."

"That's not what I'm asking. I want you to investigate it."

"Yes?"

"Yes," Tom said. He had been thinking about Lisa Countryman, that it could have just as easily been him, abandoned in an orphanage, and he felt guilty for not having done more on her behalf. "Maybe no one else cares what happened to her," he told Ota, "but I think we owe it to her to find out."

Mrs. Fujiwara reported that a David Saito wasn't in their files, and Ota left the office, letting Tom return to the matter at hand, yet another trivial task, which was to decide about the "Light Up America" vigil.

Back in the States, radio stations nationwide had been urging Americans to burn candles and shine flashlights for precisely 417 seconds on Christmas Eve—a second for each day that the fifty-two Americans had been held hostage in Iran. The White House had just announced that the national Christmas tree, which, except for the star of hope on top, had remained unlit for the second year, would be illuminated for the vigil. Now expats and embassy staffers and their dependents wanted to know how to participate in Japan. They wanted details. Should their vigil take place at exactly the same time, ten p.m., Eastern Standard Time, on Christmas Eve, which meant noon on Christmas Day in Tokyo, or should they do it on Christmas Eve, local time? Where? At the embassy, or at the Grew House? Should something be sung? "America the Beautiful," "God Bless America," Christmas carols? Would someone make a speech or say a prayer? Would it be appropriate to have a reception afterward?

This should have all been the responsibility of CLO, the Community Liaison Office, but the two FSOs there were out—one had the flu, the other was on home leave. The switchboard was now forwarding all questions to ACS, and Reeves had told Tom to make all the arrangements.

He fielded another call—would the embassy be passing out yellow ribbons, or would people have to bring their own?—and then Tom buzzed Mrs. Fujiwara and asked her to take messages for a while, he had a headache. He sat at his desk and rubbed his temples, and he looked down at the name he had scribbled on his notepad, David Saito, and something bothered him about it—an echo of Inspector Iso Yamada's earlier inquiry into the car accident. He picked up the telephone and dialed zero for the switchboard.

"Operator," the woman said, and Tom hung up. No, that wouldn't do, he thought. The operator would see his call was originating from within the embassy.

He grabbed his coat and walked out of the embassy and down the street, searching for a telephone. He always forgot which kind he was supposed to use. There were red telephones, both small and large, and blue telephones and yellow telephones. Some were for local calls, others for long-distance. Couldn't he make a local call from any phone?

He found a small red phone in front of a newsstand, dropped a ten-yen coin into the slot, and dialed the main number for the embassy.

"US Embassy Tokyo," the operator said.

"David Saito, please," Tom said.

There was a pause, and then the operator said, "Please hold." The call was transferred, and after two rings a woman with a deep, flat voice answered by merely saying, "Hello."

"David Saito, please."

A hesitation. "Who's calling, please?" she asked.

"Which section of the embassy is this?" he asked.

"Who's calling, please?" she asked.

Tom hung up. He tried to remember another name, one of the names Vincent Kitamura used as an alias, other than Bob Sasaki, which likely had been pulled from circulation. Tom waited ten minutes, killing time by walking toward the Diet building and back, then dropped another ten-yen coin into the same phone and dialed the main switchboard again.

"US Embassy Tokyo," the operator said.

"Peter Okada, please," he said.

Once more, a pause, "Please hold," two rings, and the same woman answered, "Hello."

"Is Peter Okada available?" he asked, altering the timbre of his voice.

The woman hesitated, and said, "Who's calling, please?"

He returned to his office, looked into Lisa Countryman's file, and plucked out the message of Susan Countryman's first call to the embassy. Unable to decipher the initials on the message, he marched out to Mrs. Fujiwara's desk. "Who took this message?" he asked her.

Startled, Mrs. Fujiwara delicately pinched the message between her fingertips and turned the paper around to read it.

"Who was the duty officer that night?" Tom asked her. "Come on, come on," he said while she pulled out the duty roster and flipped through the sheets.

Mrs. Fujiwara found July 10 and traced her finger across the sheet to the attendant name in the next column. "Jay Steiner," she said. The cultural attaché.

As Tom was about to leave the Consular Section, Benny caught up to him. "Hey, something's going on," he said worriedly.

"What?"

"Jorge's in the Congen's office."

"I don't have time for this right now," Tom said. He climbed the stairs to Steiner's office on the second floor, where Marly Hughes, Sara Sobeske's old friend, was fixing the photocopying machine.

"Did you forward this message to me?" he asked her.

Marly looked at Jay Steiner's July 10 message that Lisa Countryman was missing. She nodded.

"Did you and Steiner talk about it with Julia Tinsley?"

"What? No. Why would we have?"

"Could she have been around the office when you were discussing it?"

"What's this about?" Marly asked, wiping toner from her fingers.

"Did you say the case was being referred to me?"

"No."

"Are you sure?"

"You've been having an affair with her, haven't you?" Marly said. "Sara had a feeling. You could be the biggest shit I've ever met, you know that?"

From his office, Tom tried calling Julia, but she wasn't home. He took a cab to the ISA in Takadanobaba, and from the reception desk he was directed to the faculty lounge, where he saw her colleague, Yoshi, dipping a bag of green tea into a cup of hot water.

"Where is she?"

"Teaching," Yoshi said.

"Which classroom?"

"No, you wait. Outside."

Three students Tom accosted in the hallways didn't understand what he meant by "registrar," yet he came upon a secretary in an administrative office who accommodated him with a class schedule and a building map, and he found Julia at last, manning a slide projector in the back of a classroom. Through the window slat on the door he tried to catch her attention, but she didn't notice him, and he walked into the dimmed room.

"What are you doing here?" she whispered.

Her students turned around and looked at them. "I need to talk to you," he said. She was wearing glasses. He didn't know she wore eyeglasses.

"Wait in my studio. Down the hall to the left."

Some of the photographs from the P-Moto 180 gallery show were in the studio, leaning in stacks against a wall. There were two large tables in the center of the room, both cluttered with supplies and equipment: a paper cutter, mat boards, negatives in sleeves, film containers, grease pencils, dry-mount tissue. The faint smell of chemicals wafted in from the adjacent darkroom.

After forty-five minutes, she entered the studio, carrying a dozen portfolios, which she dropped onto the near table. "Why are you here, Tom?"

"You knew about Lisa Countryman, didn't you?"

"What?" she said, sweeping her hair back with her hand.

"Come on."

She sat on a stool, lit a cigarette, and let the lighter clatter down on the table. "Okay. I did."

"Was she having an affair with your husband?"

"I'm not sure. He denies it."

"What was their connection to each other? Where did they meet?"

"I don't know."

"You must have some idea."

"She was one of his informants. I don't know the details. Vincent wouldn't tell me."

"How did you find out about them?"

She shrugged. "A fluke."

She tugged on one of the flat-file drawers underneath the table and pulled out several black-and-white eleven-by-fourteens and spilled them across the tabletop. The enlargements seemed to be outtakes from the guerrilla photography series, five of the same person, a middle-aged Japanese woman, taken split-seconds apart. Apparently the mechanism at the department store had triggered not just one shot of each subject, but a succession with a motor drive. Some of the prints of the woman were blurry. She had been stepping back, not forward, wandering out of focus. One eye was closed, hand touching her hair. She was slim and well-dressed. "Who is she?" Tom asked.

Julia opened another drawer and slid a magnifying glass across the table. "Not her. Behind her. On the other side of the street."

He peered through the magnifying glass, and there they were, Vincent Kitamura and Lisa Countryman, in the background of the photograph, standing on the sidewalk in Shibuya, waiting for the stoplight to change. He would never have noticed them unless Julia had pointed them out.

"In June, she ran up to me, screaming she was in love with my husband," Julia said. "I thought she was a lunatic. She kept calling him David. Vincent told me she was a hostess he'd been using as an agent and he hadn't seen her in a year and she was delusional, and I believed him until I developed this roll of film. These shots were taken Memorial Day."

"How did you know the case was going to me? Did you hear Steiner and Marly talking about her?"

"I was in Jay's office and had to use the phone, and I saw a carbon of the call log on Marly's desk."

"And it said it was going to me in ACS."

She drew on her cigarette, then said, "Yes."

"What was the point? Why'd you approach me? What were you hoping to learn?"

"I wanted to find out if he'd lied to me, if they'd had an affair. I wanted to know what happened to her."

"You think Vincent had something to do with her disappearance."

"I don't know. Maybe."

"Do you think he killed her?"

She expelled a derisive puff of air. "No, don't be ridiculous," she said. "Nothing like that. He probably just paid her to vanish."

"Then why the cover-up? Why the ruse about leaving for Hong Kong?"

"I don't know."

"You're not actually sure. You think it's possible he did something to her."

"I seriously doubt it."

She was being so cold, unrecognizable, as if nothing had ever transpired between them. "I was in love with you," Tom said.

"Oh, Jesus. Are we really going to have this conversation? You're still under the mistaken impression that this was about *you*. But it never had anything to do with you. Don't you see? I was heartbroken. The thought of it—that he might've been in love with her—it destroyed me. I needed to know. I didn't *plan* to get involved with you. There are things about our marriage—you'll never know what we've been through."

"What kind of things?"

"They're not your concern. They're private."

"You had an affair with Pete Congrieves," Tom said. He realized he had known this all along, but hadn't allowed himself to articulate it until now.

She rubbed her left hand. Several knuckles bore dark bruises from where she had hit the glass in the Sanno Hotel. "We tend to do the things we tell ourselves we'll never do," she said.

"What kind of bullshit is that? Is that supposed to be an excuse?"

"I'm not looking for absolution. I'm not saying any of this makes *sense*."

"Did you start seeing Congrieves again? Is that what's going on?"

"I don't know. I don't know what I'm doing. It's all shit. At a certain point it didn't matter to me what the truth was, what happened with the girl. I couldn't trust Vincent anymore. My marriage was over."

"So the bigger horror is not that Vincent might have killed her, but he cheated on you?"

"Maybe she was jeopardizing some operation of his. Maybe there was an accident. It doesn't really matter now."

"Why didn't you just ask Congrieves about her?"

"I did," Julia said. "Nothing in Vincent's case files mention her."

"You're quite ruthless, aren't you?"

"Tom, you don't know how the world works. No, what am I saying? Of course you do. You've had no qualms cheating and lying your way through pretty much everything. Even with me. Really, who's been trying to manipulate whom? But you've chosen to ignore all that. It makes it very convenient, then, doesn't it? It makes it easy to deny your own complicity."

"You were in love with me," he said.

"No," Julia said, a barely discernible quiver in her voice, "I don't think I ever was."

Outside, it was snowing, the first snow of the season, although nothing was yet sticking to the ground. There were Christmas decorations in the storefronts—red-and-white bunting, Santa Claus displays, canned Christmas songs, "Jinguru Beru." All of it was purely for show, a fabricated commercial occasion. Christmas was like any other day in Japan, without religious or familial significance.

It was four o'clock, the start of rush hour. He took the Tozai Line to Otemachi, then switched to the Chiyoda Line and got off at Kasumigaseki. When he entered the Consular Section in the embassy, Jorge descended upon him. "What did you do?" he said. "How could you have been so stupid?"

"What are you talking about?"

The irregularities with Masahiro Yamada's visa had been discovered. They were blaming it all on Benny. "I know you had something to do with this," Jorge said. "He's covering for you, and you're hanging him out to dry."

"Tell me where they are," Tom said, and Jorge led him down the hall to the conference room, where everyone had assembled.

EIGHTEEN

As IT happened, Emi Fukuda had called Kenzo out of a grudge. Midori Atsuta had let her go, feeling she had gotten too old to be a hostess at the club, and Emi had been seeking retribution, hoping to make trouble, but she hadn't really known that much. She believed the two older men attached to bottle-keep No. 397, Mojo and Curly, were politicians, and she had overheard them one night refer to Larry, the younger *nisei* man, as David Saito. She told Kenzo about the gifts such as the Mikimoto necklace that Mojo had given to Lisa, yet, like Harper Boyd, Emi thought it more likely that Lisa had been going out on *dohan* with Saito. She saw the way they had looked at each other. But Emi didn't know Mojo's real name, and Tom Hurley at the embassy said he couldn't locate a David Saito, and then, without warning, Hurley left Japan. With no further leads,

Kenzo was forced to write the advisory opinion that Lisa Countryman was dead.

"You've done the right thing," Kunichi said. "Now you can
enjoy *shogatsu* in peace."

It was customary in Japan to try to begin the New Year with as
clean a slate as possible, not carrying over any debts or tasks, and
Kenzo had to admit that he did feel better, burying the Lisa
Countryman case once and for all. "I've been wondering, however," he said, "where has Yamada been? Is he working on a special investigation?"

Kunichi's face tightened. "Yamada had to take care of a family
matter," he said. "In fact, he has asked to be permanently reassigned. You won't be seeing him again."

The news heartened Kenzo. That night, he decided it was time
to put his own family matter to rest. He called Yumiko's *mansion*
in Higashi-Azabu. A male *gaijin* answered in English—it could have
been either Simon or Doug Marabelli—and Kenzo hung up. After a
half-hour, he dialed again, and this time Yumiko picked up. Her
husband must have been in the room, for Yumiko, although
speaking in Japanese, pretended Kenzo was a caterer. It seemed she
was planning a New Year's Eve party.

"That's correct," she said, reading off a list, "the melon and
prosciutto."

"I'm not going to hire a lawyer," Kenzo told her.

"And the jumbo shrimp."

"I've decided not to pursue the paternity test."

"The miniature beef Wellington."

"You're right," Kenzo said. "Even if Simon were my son, there
would be no point in disrupting his life."

"The Parmesan puffs."

"He has a home already."

"Vegetable spring rolls," Yumiko said.

"He's an American."

"Scallops wrapped in bacon."

"I'm not going to call you again," he said. "Yumiko, I wish you well. I hope you and your family will be happy and healthy. I'm going to hang up now."

"Mushroom caps," Yumiko said, her voice warbling, "stuffed with crab meat."

The next day, December 30, Kenzo began his holiday, and he busied himself helping Miss Saotome—Keiko; he was still getting used to calling her Keiko—prepare for the New Year, supervising a cleaning crew she had hired to get the apartment building spotless, hanging pine branches and *shimenawa* around doorways to ward off evil spirits, and tidying his own apartment. On impulse, he tore off all the acoustical tiles in his bedroom and repaired and repainted the walls and ceiling. More often than not now, he was staying over at Keiko's apartment, and after their vocal, wall-bouncing, sweat-drenched sessions of sex—boisterous enough to rival the stewardess's layovers next door—Kenzo always fell asleep with ease. He and Keiko were wonderfully compatible. They felt no apprehension with each other. Even the first time, after the fire in the boiler room, they had been somehow free of anxiety. He and Keiko had actually shared a good-natured laugh when he ejaculated prematurely—he had barely penetrated her—but what could be expected after so long of an abstinence? Any different, Keiko had said, and she would have been insulted. She had offered him, to use a golfing term, a mulligan, and he had quickly risen to the occasion. They were like teenagers now. Every day, they fucked morning and night.

On New Year's Eve, they sat in Keiko's apartment and watched *Kohaku uta gassen*, the annual Red and White Song Festival, on NHK-TV. The three-and-a-half-hour variety show featured performances by a slew of pop singers, pitting the men (the White

Team) against the women (the Red Team). Each song was rated by the audience on an applause meter, and at the end of the show, by an unknown process, they totaled the applause and announced the winning team, frequently eliciting howls of protest from viewers and accusations that the show was rigged.

At eleven, Keiko served Kenzo buckwheat noodles for long life and prosperity, and at eleven-thirty, they sang along to "Ode to Joy." A chorus of four thousand singers had gathered at the Kokugikan, the Sumo Hall, for the nationally televised perform-ance. The ten-minute passage in the final movement of Beethoven's Ninth Symphony was an obsession in Japan. Kenzo and Keiko, like millions of Japanese, knew "Ode to Joy" by heart, in German: "*O Freunde, nicht diese Töne! / Sondern laßt uns angenehmere anstimmen / Und freudenvollere!*"

Fifteen minutes before midnight, the bells began tolling. At every Buddhist temple across the country, monks were solemnly swinging logs against cast-bronze temple bells, striking them 108 times, dispelling the 108 evil passions of man. After each strike, the TV switched to another temple or shrine, from Meiji-jingu to Kawasaki-taishi, and Kenzo and Keiko put on their coats and joined the stream of people walking down to the local shrine.

It was a cold night, but pellucid. "Look at the stars," Keiko said, and she hooked her arm around Kenzo's. The skies over Tokyo were always clearest during the holidays, when the factories tem-porarily shut down their industrial discharge.

At the shrine, they tossed money into the offertory box, bowed twice, clapped two times to summon the gods, and bowed once more in prayer. They moved to one of the stalls on the side and bought fortunes from a shrine maiden in a white kimono. From a canister, they shook out a bamboo stick with a number, gave it to the maiden, and were handed a paper fortune that corresponded to the number.

"You first," Keiko said.

Kenzo unrolled the paper and read that his general fate would include *shokichi*—small good fortune—which was a neutral prognostication, nothing ventured or gained.

"Okay, your turn," he said to Keiko, who held her breath as she unrolled her fortune. She looked at the paper and began weeping. "*Daikyo*," she cried. Great bad fortune.

Kenzo put his arm around her shoulders. "It's okay," he said, laughing. "It's meaningless."

"Don't laugh," she said. "It's terrible."

"I think the woman gave you the wrong fortune," he told Keiko. "I think she made a mistake and gave you the wrong number. She gave you someone else's fortune."

"You think so?" she sniffed.

"Come on," he said. Together, they folded the fortune into a long strip and tied it to a branch. The trees around the shrine were brightly leaved with a hundred other bad prophesies, fluttering in the hopes of averting disaster.

■　　■　　■

IT WAS a fluke of luck, a small dispensation of good fortune, that led Kenzo back to the case. On January 20, he received a call from an Inspector at Meguro Police Station, asking for his assistance. They had a burglary suspect in custody who claimed Kenzo could attest to his character.

"Please tell them this is just a big misunderstanding," Teiji Takagi pleaded when Kenzo walked into the interrogation room at the station. A woman in Takagi's *gaijin* house in Meguro had been ripped off, divested of all her cash and jewelry, and she had accused Takagi of being the culprit. It turned out it wasn't the first such accusation from a *gaijin* tenant. Takagi had a criminal record, something Kenzo had neglected to check. He had been convicted

of fencing stolen property. A search of the locked closets and storage rooms in his buildings had revealed a cache of clothes and
linens and personal appliances—electric shavers, tape players,
cameras, blow dryers.

"I didn't steal anything," Takagi said. "You saw me return all of
Lisa Countryman's belongings. These *gaijin* ditch out on me all the
time, you wouldn't believe the stuff they leave behind, but I keep it
all for them for at least a year, I put everything nice and neat in
boxes and label them and keep them in storage in case they come
back. After a year, well, what's so wrong with making a little extra
for my trouble? Can you answer me that?"

"You did it," Kenzo said.

"Did what?"

"You killed her."

"Who?"

"Lisa Countryman."

"What?"

"You killed her for her money."

"No, now wait a minute."

"She must have had wads of cash in her apartment," Kenzo
said. "And gifts. Like her Mikimoto necklace. I'm sure that caught
your eye. You killed her." In fact, Kenzo thought no such thing,
but he had a feeling, an intuition, that Takagi knew more than he
was saying, and Kenzo was playing dumb, the worst kind of
dumb, crazy-dumb with prosecutorial powers, to extract the truth
from him.

"This is insane," Takagi said. "I would never kill anyone."

"What did you do with her body?" Kenzo said, standing and
yelling into his ear.

"You've got this all wrong."

"Did you bury her in the countryside somewhere?"

"No no no."

"Where, then?"

"I didn't do it!"

"You think the judges will believe a thief like you? You know how the system works. If I think you're guilty, you will be convicted. I don't need evidence."

"Please. I'm—"

"No one called you on June 18th, did they?"

"She did. I swear she did."

"You didn't find the apartment ransacked."

"I did!"

"You're lying," Kenzo said.

"No."

"You cleared the place out yourself."

"That's not true."

"Don't lie to me."

"I'm *not*!"

"You wanted to make it look like she split."

"It wasn't me!"

"You think I'm a fool?"

"It was the goon!"

"What?"

"The guy I caught in her apartment."

Kenzo took a seat at the table and nodded. "Tell me."

Takagi got the call from the girl—some *gaijin* girl, he didn't know who—on June 18, as he had said, but he had lied about going to Lisa's apartment the next day. By chance, he had gone there that afternoon, before receiving the call, to tend to the running toilet that Lisa had been harassing him to fix, and he had walked in on a man packing her suitcases. He was Japanese, maybe forty, big, with a mustache. He had said he was a friend of Lisa's, that she'd asked him to pick up her things, which didn't seem entirely implausible, since he had her keys. He told Takagi that Lisa would call him later to explain. In the meantime, he said, he would appreciate Takagi's discretion. The situation was delicate, he said, implying he was married and that he and Lisa were having an affair. Takagi was skeptical. The man was a goon. Cheap black suit, white gloves, probably a chauffeur. Yet half a million yen and a pick of Lisa's things had swayed him into keeping his mouth shut.

"You never talked to him again?" Kenzo asked.

"No."

"That's surprising," Kenzo said. "An enterprising fellow such as yourself. I'm surprised you didn't try to milk him dry."

"I'm an honest man."

"An honest man who's going to be charged with accessory to kidnapping and murder."

"What?"

"Obstruction of an investigation."

"Hey."

"Making false statements to a police officer."

"I took down his license plate, okay?" Takagi said. He slumped in his chair. "I thought it might be useful. I was just waiting for you to find a body."

▪   ▪   ▪

IT CAME together quickly. The license plate belonged to a black Toyota Crown that was an official government car, assigned to Mokichi Shiokawa, the Minister of Posts and Telecommunications, a longtime Diet member of the LDP.

Kenzo showed a file photo of the minister to Emi Fukuda, and she confirmed that he was the customer who had referred to himself as Mojo. Kenzo was surprised she hadn't recognized Shiokawa. He had been in the news quite a bit lately during the final Nippon Telegraph and Telephone negotiations.

Kenzo also got a copy of the license photo for the minister's driver—a beefy man with a handlebar mustache—and Teiji Takagi told him yes, that was the goon in Lisa's apartment. The driver's name was Eiji Tanaguchi. He had no record, no known criminal associations. He lived in an apartment near Korakuen Stadium, a two-room hovel in which Kenzo found him Tuesday night, washing undershirts in his sink.

Kenzo transported him in a patrol car to Azabu Police Station, and he spent the night with him, interrogating Tanaguchi until dawn, wearing him down with threats and suppositions, cajoling one minute, berating the next, repeating the same questions again and again. Eventually he got what he needed from the driver, and by the morning *chorei,* he was able to lay out the case for Kunichi and the other detectives and assert that, for the first time, he had a viable suspect.

"The driver took Minister Shiokawa to the Hotel New Otani on June 17, where he had dinner with Lisa Countryman in the Rainbow Lounge, which the maître d' verifies," Kenzo said. "At approximately ten p.m., he dropped Shiokawa and the girl off at his *mansion* in Denen-Chofu and returned the car to the ministry garage. The girl, he said, seemed quite out of it, as if she had been drugged. Early the next morning, he received a call from Shiokawa, who told him he was sick and wouldn't be going into the office that day and not to bother coming to pick him up. Yet he summoned him later in the afternoon to the *mansion.* He said Shiokawa appeared extremely agitated and nervous, but not ill. The minister gave him the girl's keys and asked him to go to her apartment and get her suitcases, passport, clothes, anything that seemed at all personal. The minister said the girl was going on a long trip out of the country, and to make absolutely sure no one saw him. The driver did what he was told, but he was confused why the girl wasn't going with him to get her things. He didn't see

her in the *mansion* then, nor later when he brought in the suitcases. When Shiokawa asked if anyone had seen him, he lied about
Takagi catching him and said no.

"He denies knowing anything about the phone call later to
Takagi or to the club. He swears he doesn't know what happened
to the girl. He identified Curly as Ichiro Kimoto, a bigwig at NTT,
but he doesn't think he was involved in the girl's disappearance.
He thinks the other man, David Saito, was—if indirectly. He drove
him and Lisa to a *kaiseki* restaurant in Kagurazaka one night, and
he saw them kissing. He didn't say anything to the minister—he
told me if the minister wanted to make a fool of himself over that
'*gaijin* tramp,' that was his business—but I think we can assume
the minister somehow found out about them. It looks to be the
classic love triangle. Lisa had been playing the minister for cash
and gifts while sleeping with Saito. She kept spurning the minister's advances, and when he finally uncovered the truth, he killed
her in a fit of jealous rage."

"How do you know the driver wasn't in on it?" Kunichi asked.

"I don't. He very well might have been. He doesn't have an alibi.
That's why we should continue holding him while we question the
minister."

The idea of it—questioning a top-ranking LDP official about the
murder of a foreign hostess—silenced the detectives. It was a far
bigger case than any of them had ever handled.

"You're not questioning him alone," Kunichi said.

"No, I didn't expect I would," Kenzo said, pleased and surprised.
He had been certain Kunichi would impede him again, just as he
had prevented Kenzo from interrogating Midori Atsuta any further,
just as he had released Harper Boyd without cause. Perhaps there
was too much evidence to ignore now.

"I have to be there," Kunichi said.

"Yes, of course. I understand completely," Kenzo said.

"It could be a total fabrication. The driver could be trying to frame him."

"Yes, I see your point. That's very possible." He had learned a thing or two from Midori Atsuta about the art of negotiation.

"And this other man, Saito. You still don't know who he is. It could have been that the girl left the minister's house that night and met up with Saito and told him she had slept with Shiokawa, and Saito could have been the one who became enraged."

"That's true."

"There are so many holes in your theory," Kunichi said. "For instance, you said Shiokawa never drove himself anymore because one eye's going bad. How did he get rid of the body, then?"

"I've been wondering that myself."

"He must've had help, an old man like that."

"I think you're right. I agree with you completely."

Kunichi chewed on his pen. "But I suppose we must question the minister, since it appears he might have been the last person to see this girl alive."

"Yes, I suppose."

"We'll call his secretary and make an appointment. We'll talk to him at his office at his convenience—you and me, Ota. Does that seem reasonable?"

"Yes, sir."

Kunichi called Shiokawa's office and asked his secretary if they could possibly see the minister sometime that day. He was put on hold, then was asked what they wanted to speak to the minister about. A woman he might have met named Lisa Countryman, Kunichi said. He was put on hold again, then was asked if it could wait until the end of the week. The minister was very busy, with still so many things to attend to after the long holiday. Plus, his driver had disappeared all of a sudden, the secretary said. He was sorry, he was afraid it couldn't wait, Kunichi said. He was put on hold a third time, then was asked to come to the office at seven p.m.

It was the longest day of Kenzo's life. He hadn't gotten any sleep the previous night, grilling the driver at the police station, and he was being carried by adrenaline and euphoria. Not only would he regain his seat at a center desk, he thought, he might be promoted.

But once they entered the austere building of the Ministry of Posts and Telecommunications, once they were sitting in the minister's waiting room, Kenzo began to doubt himself. What if he was wrong? What if he had made another one of his far-flung assumptions? He would face a worse fate than the window tribe. He would be busted down to Patrolman and transferred to a *koban* in the hinterlands. He would be utterly disgraced. Wedged in the upholstered chair in the waiting room, he felt his skin begin to itch and goose.

Kunichi was fidgeting, too. "Will he be much longer?" he asked the secretary.

She had phoned the minister upon their arrival, and it had been twenty minutes now. "He should be with you shortly," she said.

Kunichi flipped through a newspaper, and Kenzo read the headlines: A Nagoya coed had been kidnapped. Eight people had been killed in a snowslide in Niigata. The dollar had fallen to 198 yen.

The minister would simply deny everything, Kenzo decided. He would admit that Lisa Countryman had come to his house, but he would claim that she had left sometime during the night unharmed and he never saw her again. With his position of authority and influence, they wouldn't be able to press the investigation any further. It would all be deflected to the driver.

Another half-hour went by. "Excuse me," Kunichi said to the secretary, chuckling nervously. "He hasn't forgotten about us, has he?"

The secretary, who had been typing memos, glanced at him irritably. She looked at the clock on the wall, then stood and straightened her skirt. She knocked on the door to the minister's office, walked in, and closed the door behind her. After a few seconds, she came back out.

"I'm afraid the minister has stepped out," she said.

"I'm sorry?" Kunichi said.

"I—" the secretary said, disconcerted. "I'm not sure . . ."

Kenzo and Kunichi stared at her.

"There's a back door, you see," she said.

"He left?" Kunichi asked.

"Apparently," she said.

"Oh."

"Would you like to make another appointment?"

Outside the building, Kunichi said, "That was very strange."

"I don't understand," Kenzo said.

"Very unusual."

"Should we try his house?"

"No, that would be inappropriate. We'll give him another chance in the morning."

Kunichi asked if he wanted a ride back to the station, but Kenzo said he would just hop on the Chiyoda Line subway.

As he walked to Kasumigaseki Station, he stopped for a few minutes outside the windows of the MITI building and watched a news report on a bank of TVs in the lobby. The day before, the American hostages had been released after 444 days of captivity in Iran. Their plane had left Tehran minutes after the new US President, Ronald Reagan, had been sworn into office. The TV news kept replaying the video of the hostages arriving at Rhein-Main Air Base in Frankfurt. The fifty men and two women were running off the plane onto the tarmac, waving, embracing, exultant, free at last.

Kenzo descended the stairs to the subway station, bought a

ticket, and waited for the train to Meiji Jingu-mae. As he heard the rumbling clack of the approaching train, he turned and looked down the platform, and he spotted the minister just as Shiokawa jumped in front of the subway cars that were screaming into the station.

NINETEEN

LISA WAS in the American Citizens Services office of the US Embassy again, this time talking to a Japanese clerk about the procedures for replacing her passport.

She had fallen asleep on the subway home from the club, and her knapsack had been stolen. She had been astonished, always thinking Tokyo was so safe. The knapsack had contained her adoption papers, a little notebook with annotations on the sex industry, one of her hostess dresses, makeup, high heels, her subway pass, cash, keys, her camera, and her passport. She had had to call Takagi to let her into her apartment, and he had taken his sweet time getting over to Nishi-Azabu, grumbling about the late hour. He gave her another telegram from Susan and scolded her for not apprising people of her new address, then had demanded a ten-thousand-yen "key duplication fee" from Lisa.

Replacing the passport was going to take a little more work. The embassy clerk told her she would need proof of identity and citizenship, a police report, two passport photos, Affidavit Form DSP-64, and Application Form DSP-11. She left the office with the forms and loitered in the lobby, wondering if she should ask at the main reception desk to see Vincent Kitamura, if that was indeed his real name.

Ako Abe had followed David Saito from the Stockholm Farm Lounge to his apartment in the Homat Royal in Hiroo. Ako had spoken to the apartment security guard, who had said the *nisei* man's name was Bob Sasaki, not David Saito. He worked for the Air Force, and his office was in Hardy Barracks near Nogizaka. His wife's name was Julia Tinsley, and she taught at the International School of the Arts. The next day, Ako went to the ISA, and the dean's secretary told her Julia Tinsley's husband's name was Vincent Kitamura, not Bob Sasaki, and he worked at the US Embassy, not Hardy Barracks.

Did the deception end there? Lisa wondered. Was there yet another alias or cover? But in the embassy lobby, she decided the mystery of Vincent Kitamura could wait. She had to go see Tomiko Higa. By now Lisa had become familiar with almost everything there was to know about the woman. She had scrolled through microfilm of newspapers and magazines at the Metropolitan Central Library, bought cassettes of all her albums. She had even gone to NHK's video vault and watched tapes of her performances on past *Kohaku uta gassen* broadcasts.

Finally, she gathered the nerve to call her. She said she was a reporter for *Time* magazine and was writing a book on women in the Japanese entertainment industry. She asked to interview Tomiko, saying she wanted to hear about her career as an *enka* singer, how she got her start, the barriers she had faced, what sort of fulfillment she derived from her work. Once assured that her identity would be disguised and that nothing from the book would ever be published in Japan, Tomiko agreed to be interviewed.

Now Lisa was standing in front of Tomiko Higa's house in Gotanda, and she rang the bell, and suddenly she was face to face with the woman who was supposed to be her birth mother.

"Come in, come in," Tomiko said.

She thought she would be taller. From the photographs and videos, she had looked to be around Lisa's height, five-six, but in person she was much shorter, and somewhat plump. She was dressed extravagantly in a tight pink brocade dress with a pattern of rosebuds and poofy sleeves, the neck, wrists, and hems sprouted with lace. Her hair was pulled back and to the side, held together by an elaborate clip festooned with glass shoots and petals, and she wore several large gaudy rings on her fingers.

Lisa wasn't prepared for this. She had thought she would be, but now all she wanted to do was flee. She was afraid she might vomit.

"Don't be shy," Tomiko said cheerily. "Come in!"

Lisa took off her shoes and reluctantly followed Tomiko into the living room. Her house was tiny, made even more claustrophobic by the profusion of plants and flowers inside: begonias, spider plants, philodendrons, palms, African violets, dracaenas, geraniums. It was overwhelming, a veritable greenhouse, the air hot and humid in the living room as they sat in a pair of chairs covered in jonquil-patterned chintz. A jungle mutated with Laura Ashley DNA.

"Your plants are beautiful," Lisa said tensely.

"Oh, they're very ugly." Tomiko beamed with great pride. "Would you like coffee?"

She brought out a tray with a small pot of coffee and two gorgeous Spode cup-and-saucer sets. "I have milk instead of cream, if you like," Tomiko said.

"Cream is fine."

"Are you sure?"

"Yes."

"I got some cakes from Anderson's Bakery for when we take a break. Strawberry cakes."

"I'm on a diet," Lisa said, lying for no reason.

"Diet!" Tomiko said. "Why are you on a diet? You have a *lovely* figure."

"No," Lisa said, pleased.

"Yes. You're a beautiful girl."

Lisa blinked and looked at Tomiko, who smiled at her.

"Do you require anything special for the interview?" Tomiko asked.

"No," Lisa said. She pulled out her tape recorder and a notebook from her purse. "I have everything I need."

With little preamble, Tomiko began telling her about her childhood in Kawasaki and her big break in Yokohama, winning a local song contest that had led to an appearance on a once-popular *enka* show on TV, which had then led to a recording contract.

"Didn't you work on the Navy base in Yokohama for a while?" Lisa asked.

Tomiko faltered for a second. "Yes, for a year, as a clerk. How in the world did you know that?"

"I read it in an article somewhere." She asked Tomiko about the first time she had been selected to sing on *Kohaku uta gassen,* soon after the release of her one and only minor hit, "Fall Like the Petals of a Flower."

"I was so honored," Tomiko said. "It was the proudest day of my life."

"It's very competitive to get on the show, isn't it?"

"Yes. They really look at everything to judge your standing and popularity. Even the suggestion of a scandal can affect the decision of the selection committee. Like what happened to poor Hibari

Misora." Hibari Misora was the queen of *enka,* with an enormous following and staggering record sales. Yet she had been banned from *Kohaku uta gassen* because of her rumored association with the *yakuza.* "Now that *enka* is not so popular, I am not invited to appear on every show, but that only makes it even more marvelous when I am invited," Tomiko said. "Yet nothing, of course, can ever match my first time."

She brought out a photo album. "I didn't know what I'd wear," she said, "but then I found a fantastic seamstress who made me this." She pointed to a photograph of herself in a dreadful fuchsia kimono with a huge, lurid pink rose splashed across her breast.

"It's beautiful," Lisa said.

She expected Tomiko to reply with typical Japanese modesty, "Oh, it's very ugly," but Tomiko squealed gleefully, "Isn't it? The kimonos, the flowers, became my trademark. The same seamstress has been making them for me all these years."

"Your handkerchiefs, too?" Lisa asked. In every performance, Tomiko clutched a pink lace handkerchief in her left hand.

"Those are custom-made in London."

She flipped to the next page in the photo album, and the next, and the next, and then she retrieved more albums. For more than an hour, she recounted various concerts and awards and records and shows, welling up with delight and wonder. She talked about her surprising popularity in Taiwan and Singapore, the gratifying ardor of her many fans, some of whom wrote letters begging to be her driver or maid for *free,* just to be close to her. "They love me," she said, choking up.

Pinned in the stuffed chair, Lisa listened to her, unable to relax, constantly shifting the hard, heart-shaped pillows at the small of her back, brushing away tendrils of ivy that tickled her shoulder. It was too hot in the house. It was all too much—the closeness of the room, the flora, Tomiko's perfume, her makeup, her rouge and eye shadow comically applied in feline streaks, her stories and giggles, her cloying sincerity and oppressive cheerfulness. Everything was overstuffed, on the verge of bursting. Lisa had not planned to stay this long. She had wanted their first meeting to be quick—an abbreviated flyby. She hadn't thought she could handle anything more. She had envisioned a series of interviews, during which they could get progressively more comfortable, become friends, even. But Tomiko continued to babble blithely about herself, not allowing Lisa the opportunity for a graceful exit.

Irrationally, Lisa had assumed her mother would be soft-spoken, humble, kind, but Tomiko Higa was a silly woman, a pitiable figure, mawkish and self-absorbed and deluded. Could this woman really be her mother? Lisa didn't recognize herself in her at all. There was no family resemblance. She didn't want there to be a resemblance. She didn't want Tomiko Higa to be her mother.

Lisa let her prattle on for another half hour—an interminable time—but eventually she couldn't take it anymore. "You're famous for something else," she said.

"Yes?"

"Your emotion."

"Ah, my emotion." Tomiko smiled.

"I saw the tape of that first time."

"You did? You should have said. Oh, I was just overcome. I had no idea it would happen."

During her first performance of "Fall Like the Petals of a Flower" on *Kohaku uta gassen,* at the climatic moment of the song when she was quivering about her lover leaving her in the city, alone, homesick, and heartbroken, tears had streamed down Tomiko's face—a moving, spontaneous display of emotion that she was thereafter able to recreate at will.

"Were you thinking of someone in particular?" Lisa asked.

"Sorry?"

"A lover?"

Tomiko covered her mouth and tittered. "No, no lover."

"You've never been married."

"That's right."

"Did you ever have any children?"

Tomiko smiled tightly. "I just told you I never married."

"You never got pregnant?"

"No."

"You never had a child?"

"No."

"You didn't work in the Military Intelligence office in Yokohama and hang out at a sailor bar called Club Zoo Fly?"

"I'm sorry, what is this about?"

"You're not *zainichi* Korean?"

"I most certainly am not."

"You didn't give birth to an *ainoko* baby at Fujigaoka Hospital on September 14, 1955, and then abandon her four days later at Nonohama-no-ie Children's Home?"

"What *is* this? Who *are* you?"

"I think I'm your daughter," Lisa said.

"What?"

"I'm your daughter."

Tomiko stared at her. "But you're not half-*kurombo*."

And this was when Lisa knew that Tomiko was her mother. "I'm part black. I just look white."

Tomiko stared at her, finally speechless.

"I was given the name Mayu Kaneda," Lisa said. "I stayed at the orphanage until I was four, when a black couple from the Navy base adopted me and took me to America with them. They were nice to me. They had a daughter who wasn't so nice to me, but I suppose we can't have everything." This last comment had been written in for a little comic relief, but Lisa didn't smile wryly with its delivery, as she had rehearsed, and Tomiko didn't react to it. Lisa had gone through a dozen drafts of the monologue before translating it into Japanese and committing it to memory. "We lived all over the world—the Philippines, Italy, then Hawaii, California. I graduated as the salutatorian of my high school in Norfolk, Virginia, and I went to the University of Virginia on a scholarship. I'm now a doctoral student in cultural anthropology at Berkeley. Last September, my adoptive parents were killed in a car accident. Ever since, I've felt I have no one, that I'm alone. That's why I decided to come to Tokyo to try to find you. I think I always intended to find you, although I never said so to anyone, even to myself. I've been studying the Japanese culture and language for years. I guess I should have been studying Korean as well. I don't know why I've waited so long. Maybe I was afraid of hurting my adoptive parents, but maybe I just needed the courage to face the question—the question of whether you would be glad to see me. Or not."

Tomiko glared down at the coffee table, shaking her head rigidly as if afflicted with palsy. Then she said, "Who sent you?"

"No one sent me."

"What do you want? Money?"

"No, I don't want your money," Lisa said.

"What are you going to threaten me with? The scandal magazines? *Fancy* or *Frank*? How much do you want?"

"I'm not here to blackmail you."

"I never had a baby. I never had an affair with a colored sailor."

"Tell me about him," Lisa said. "Tell me about my father."

"Someone's trying to set me up."

"Did you love him?"

"Who are you working for? Who's trying to ruin me?"

"He was married, wasn't he? You were having an affair. Was that why you couldn't be together?"

"Why is this happening?" Tomiko said, grasping her head in her hands. "What did I ever do to anybody?"

"Why didn't you get an abortion? Did you want to keep me? Or did he? Did someone convince you that you shouldn't?"

"I don't have much money."

"Did you do it out of love?" Lisa asked, crying. "Did you give me up so I could have a better life?"

"Get out," Tomiko said.

"I don't blame you. You had no choice. It must have been so hard for you, having to conceal your identity, trying to pass for Japanese. I understand. I forgive you."

"I want you to leave."

"Please tell me about the affair," Lisa said. "Tell me who I am." She had imagined they would weep and embrace, that Tomiko would say she had been in agony all these years, tortured she had given Lisa up, and every day she had wondered what had happened to her, had worried about her, maybe even had searched for her, hired a private detective, hoping for a reunion.

Lisa had been a fool. Tomiko had abandoned her for her pathetic singing career. Now Lisa simply wanted to know about her father. Tomiko was her only link to him. "Do you know where my father is?" she asked. "Where was he from? What did he look like? What *was* he? Do you have any photographs of him?"

"Get out," Tomiko said. "I never want to see you again." She grabbed Lisa's arm and pulled her up and shoved her toward the door. "I won't give you any money. I don't care what happens to me. I never had a baby."

"Just tell me his name," Lisa said. "Please. That's all I ask. Just tell me my father's name," she said, as Tomiko pushed her out the door.

■   ■   ■

THERE WAS no logic to it, going to the ISA. She had not planned it. But after leaving Gotanda on the Yamanote Line, Lisa had not gotten off at Meguro to catch the subway home, too numb to disembark, and she had continued on the train, past Yoyogi, clap, clap, past Shinjuku, clap, clap, perhaps thinking she would ride the entire loop of twenty-nine stops around to Meguro again, or perhaps not thinking at all. She found herself shuffling off the train at Takadanobaba and wandering to the ISA campus, where she waited until she saw her coming out of the building and walking down the sidewalk. Lisa ran across the street and called out to her just as she reached a green convertible with the top down.

"You're Julia Tinsley, aren't you?" she said.

She turned around. "You're . . . ?"

"Lisa Countryman." She was much prettier in person than in the photographs that Ako Abe had taken of her.

"Yes?"

"I'm in love with your husband."

Julia stepped back from her. "Excuse me?"

"David doesn't love you. David's never loved you."

"Who the hell is David?"

"I mean Vincent—*Vincent.*"

Julia dumped her bag in the car and got in the driver's seat.

"He loves *me,*" Lisa said. "We've been having an affair. He's going to leave you for me."

"You're insane," Julia said, and started the car and began pulling out into the street.

"He loves me, not you," Lisa screamed, running alongside the car.

"Get the hell away from me," Julia said.

Lisa tried to hang on to the car. "He doesn't care about you!" she yelled. "He's never cared. He's never given you a second thought. You were as good as dead to him." But Julia had driven into traffic and was already gone, and Lisa sat down on the street and wept.

■   ■   ■

MIDORI NOTICED Lisa moving gingerly at the club. "What's the matter with you? Don't hunch like that. Stand up straight."

Lisa thought she might have broken a rib. As she had run after Julia's convertible, she had hit her ribs against the sideview mirror of a parked car. She was in pain all evening, and she barely talked to her customers. Singing, she sounded awful, not able to breathe fully from her diaphragm. At the end of the night, Midori summoned her to her office, and Lisa expected to be reprimanded for doing such a poor job.

The office was a closet, with space only for a narrow counter, two chairs, and a safe, in which Midori meticulously stored the club's receipts, her client list, and her customers' expense accounts.

"Something occurred to me today," Midori said.

"Yes?"

"Your visa has expired."

She was right. Lisa hadn't realized it herself. It was June 16. Her ninety-day tourist visa had expired the previous week.

"What are your plans now?" Midori asked.

"I don't know."

"Are you going back to the States?"

"I don't know. Maybe. There's not much reason for me to stay anymore." She didn't think Tomiko Higa would change her mind anytime soon, although Lisa planned to write to her in a few weeks, asking again for information about her father.

"You're welcome to continue here if you can be careful," Midori said. "The last thing I need is trouble from Immigration."

"That's kind of you."

"I've enjoyed having you here. Despite my initial reservations, it's worked out well."

"Thank you."

"I've become very fond of you. I usually don't have any maternal urges toward my girls, but you've been an exception."

Overwhelmed, Lisa felt her eyes tear. "Really?" she asked, and she embraced Midori.

"Hey, hey," she said. She patted Lisa's back, then disentangled herself from her. "What's wrong with you? Why are you so emotional? Are you having your period?" She handed her a tissue, and after Lisa blew her nose, the two women looked at each other and laughed.

"I'm sorry," Lisa said.

"It's okay. I just wanted to say that if you decide to return home, I'll be sad to see you go."

"That's nice to hear."

"How are you doing for money? I can't imagine you've saved much, living in that place in Nishi-Azabu."

"No, I guess I haven't," Lisa said. She was indeed broke.

"How much are you paying a month?"

Lisa told her, and Midori shook her head.

"I'm afraid your landlord has been taking advantage of you."

Not just Takagi, Lisa thought. Ako Abe's services had been very expensive. In addition to her hourly fees, she had repeatedly asked Lisa for cash to bribe clerks and bureaucrats and security guards, and Lisa wondered if Ako had been swindling her.

Midori pinched an envelope out from underneath a ledger and slid it across the counter. "This is a little something as a token of appreciation."

"This isn't necessary."

"It's nothing."

"Well, thank you," Lisa said.

"I think Mojo would also like to give you a gift."

"Mojo?"

"For treating him so well these past few months."

Lisa watched Midori tap on a calculator and write numbers on an invoice form. "You want me to go out with Mojo?"

"It's entirely up to you. I think he would be very grateful if you did."

"I thought you don't allow *dohan*."

"I don't," Midori told Lisa. "But it won't be a *dohan* if you're no longer working for me."

■   ■   ■

HE WAS waiting for her outside, half a block from the club, on the way to the Ginza subway station. She saw him leaning against a telephone pole, but she didn't stop, kept walking. He fell into step with her.

"You went to see my wife," he said.

"I'm in love with you," Lisa told him, but even as she said it, she knew she was being preposterous.

"We barely know each other."

She looked at him. He was wearing another sleek dark blue suit. He really was a beautiful man. "Does anyone really know you? You seem to be very slippery, David—or should I say Vincent? You seem to change into whatever people want you to be."

"You met with Tomiko Higa, didn't you? What happened?"

"What do you do? Work for the CIA?"

"Something like that. How did you find out?"

"The private detective."

They walked past Matsuya department store, toward Harumi-dori, the streets bright with neon. "Was it a coincidence that we bumped into each other that day in the garden?" Lisa asked him.

"I have to admit, no."

"You were only using me to get to Mojo."

"I don't think I ever tried to conceal that from you. I might have, in fact, been a little obvious about it."

"When were you going to ask me to sleep with him?"

"I wouldn't have done that."

"You wouldn't have minded if I had, though. Made Mojo happy."

"You needed something from me as well," he said. "You know how this world operates. It'd be disingenuous to say you don't."

He did have something of a point. Oddly, she had wanted to become dependent on Vincent, bound to him for his favors. Perhaps it was no accident that she had gotten a job as a hostess, that she had become infatuated with Vincent, a married man, and slept with Omar, a black sailor. She had wanted to put herself in her mother's position—know what she might have felt. Yet Lisa wasn't willing to concede anything to Vincent. "That's your world, not mine," she said. "I would find it very difficult to live in your world."

"It's more reassuring than you might think. It's much easier when you don't have to decide whom to trust."

It sounded like something Lisa herself might have said, trying to appear world-weary and impervious, but under the circumstances, it made her pity him. "You seem like a very sad man, Vincent Kitamura."

They came upon the entrance to the subway station. "Are you going to be all right?" he asked her.

"Of course. What are you imagining? That I might try to hurt myself?"

"It crossed my mind."

She began walking down the stairs, then glanced back at him. "One thing," she said.

"Yes?"

"What you told me about your mother and father—was any of it true?"

Vincent was about to answer her, but she stopped him.

"I don't want to know," she said. She had already chosen what she wanted to believe.

■　　■　　■

AT SEVEN, she was in Nirvana. She was the only customer in the tiny bar in Harajuku. There were no tables, only ten stools, but there were three bartenders on duty, each wearing identical paisley and silk vests, wing collars, and bow ties. When she entered, one bartender had handed Lisa a leather-bound menu of drinks, the second had laid down a coaster and an ashtray, and the third had dangled a steaming *oshibori* towel in front of her.

She ordered a Stoli martini, and she had to say, this was a perfect martini—very dry. She was going to be late meeting Mojo. She still had to hike up the hill to Omotesando and catch the Ginza Line to Akasaka-Mitsuke, then walk to the Hotel New Otani. But she had to have one more martini, and she signaled Bartender No. 2 to make another for her.

That afternoon, she had called Mojo on the private number Midori had given to her. He had been delighted to hear from her, but was agitated by the short notice. How could he arrange something comparable to the *kaiseki* dinner? She told him not to worry, a simple meal at any restaurant would be fine.

Then she had tracked down Rebecca Silo, who was still working at Musky Club. She wanted some painkillers, Percodan or codeine. Ordinary aspirins were not relieving the pain in her ribs. On a whim, she bought a Quaalude from Rebecca. She thought she would need a dependable agent to get her through the evening. She didn't know exactly why she was going through with the *dohan*. Maybe she felt bad, and she wanted to feel worse. Was it as basic as that? It wasn't the cash, although she could have used it. She needed to reestablish her life in Berkeley—rent a new apartment, buy another car, pay her tuition—but she didn't care about money anymore. She had resolved not to take any of Richard and Lenore's estate. She would sign it all over to Susan, and never speak to her again.

She missed them terribly—Richard and Lenore. She tried not to think of them too often, but she did, and the hurt had not dissipated one bit, despite everything she had done—the distance she had traveled—to displace her grief.

Bartender No. 2 served Lisa her martini. "Hot date tonight?" he asked, wiping the counter.

"Yeah," Lisa scoffed.

It was such a cozy bar. The copper countertop shimmered, and recessed lights made the rows of bottles against the wall glow blue. She didn't want to leave.

She would wait one more minute, she decided, count to sixty—one thousand one, one thousand two—and then she would go.

TWENTY

VER TWENTY years later, Tom ran into
Vincent Kitamura at the Royal Hawaiian
Hotel on Waikiki. Tom had just finished dinner with his wife and
his kids and his mother, who was visiting from the Mainland, and
he was strolling through the lobby when he saw Kitamura, who
was as youthful and dapper as ever. It was Tom who had changed.
Kitamura didn't recognize him. His hair had turned completely
gray and was shorn to a buzz cut, his skin was blackened in a deep
tan, and he was—no getting around it—fat. He had let himself go.
Too many plate lunches, not enough exercise.

   He asked Kitamura to have a quick drink with him while his family went for ice cream, and at the Mai Tai Bar, after they had ordered
their drinks—Dewar's neat for Kitamura, a Bud Light for Tom—
Kitamura said, "I heard you left the Foreign Service after Tokyo."

"I did," Tom said.

"Ah," Kitamura said, and Tom wondered what he knew.

Masahiro Yamada himself had forced the issue. His brother had been right: he was a truly stupid man. He had been busted less than two weeks upon his arrival in the States. The INS had been cracking down on undocumented workers in Camden, New Jersey, and he had been caught in a sweep at the sushi restaurant. The matter should have ended right there with a simple deportation, but Masahiro, without any prompting whatsoever, confessed to the INS agents that his brother had arranged for someone in the US Embassy to doctor his records and produce a tourist visa for him. In Tokyo, the Consul General had pulled out the files and seen the visa refusal had been overturned with Benny's signature, and he had accused him of fraud.

In the conference room, Tom had insisted Benny had not been involved. Benny wouldn't overturn the refusal, Tom said, so he had taken it upon himself to forge the documents. "How?" the Consul General had asked, and Tom had said, "Give me two pens."

They remained skeptical. It seemed implausible. It seemed that Tom was trying to take the fall for his friend. It seemed he and Benny were both culpable. But then Mrs. Fujiwara, who had been translating for Inspector Yamada and his supervisor Kunichi, ratted Tom out and rescued him. The night Tom had been working late in the office, Mrs. Fujiwara had, for once, thought of doing something nice for him. She came back to the embassy with a *bento* dinner that she had bought for Tom, and had witnessed him opening the file cabinets in the visa section.

Tom claimed he had simply hoped to curry favors in the Lisa Countryman case, and Inspector Yamada backed him up. Kunichi, Reeves, and the Consul General tried to get them to admit to a more ignoble motive—money, sex—but Tom and Yamada would not budge. The additional wrinkle about the hit-and-run would have helped neither of them. All in all, it had been an extraordinarily bad day for Tom.

He tendered his resignation and received, as it were, an honorable discharge. He flew home to Washington, DC, where he processed out of the Foreign Service and picked up some belongings from storage. He had no clue what he would do next. To bide time, he substitute-taught a few French classes at a high school in Fairfax, Virginia. He was offered a full-time job, accepted, and stayed there for a couple of years, after which he lived in Europe, teaching first at the International School of Luxembourg, and then at the American School of Valencia, and then he moved to Oahu.

He had been in Hawaii for the past decade and a half, "Mr. Hurley-Burly" to the students at Kailua High School, home of the Surfriders. He taught French and Spanish and coached swimming. He lived nearby in Waimanalo and was married to a fellow teacher, a local Filipina-Portuguese-Korean-Scottish woman. They had three boys, aged twelve, ten, and seven.

"It sounds like you found your calling as a teacher," Kitamura said.

"I love it," Tom said.

Kitamura had remained in Tokyo throughout the 1980s. Julia left him in 1982, went to New York, and continued exhibiting and teaching photography. The last he'd heard, she had opened an art gallery in SoHo. With no children to share, there was no reason for them to stay in touch, and they hadn't.

Tom asked him what really happened to Lisa Countryman. He had always been curious; he'd never believed that Kitamura had harmed her. Unfazed that Tom knew of his involvement, Kitamura matter-of-factly told him that she had died of an overdose at the home of the Minister of Posts and Telecommunications. Whether the overdose had been accidental or a suicide, they would never know. The minister had called Kitamura and said there had been an accident, what should he do? He had begged Kitamura for help. Kitamura told him to phone the police. The minister, however, did not phone the police, terrified by the prospect of scandal. A young *gaijin* girl found dead in his bed. He needed to get rid of the body. Panicked, he began dismembering her in his bathtub, hacking at her leg with a saw, but he couldn't go through with it. He fainted, he awoke, he tried again, vomited. He had to find someone to do this for him, and the only person he could think of was the Takahashi-gumi boss from the club Rendezvous. The *yakuza* boss was very accommodating. The next day, the minister ordered his driver to go to Lisa Countryman's apartment and pick up her things, and then the minister paid Harper Boyd to call Lisa's land-lord and the *tencho* at Rendezvous, saying she—Lisa—was going to Hong Kong.

"After that," Kitamura said to Tom, "he had me squeezing him on one side and the *yakuza* boss on the other. The Takahashi-gumi were bleeding him dry."

"For money?"

"Of course."

"What were you blackmailing him for?" Tom asked. "Not money."

"No, not money. Not his, anyway. Do you remember the NTT accord?"

At the time, the biggest trade issue between the US and Japan had been over the procurement policies of the Nippon Telegraph and Telephone Public Corporation. The giant monopoly bought $3.3 billion worth of telecommunications equipment and supplies a year—everything from electronic switching units to poles—and American manufacturers had wanted access to that market.

"It was about telephone poles?" Tom asked, feeling terribly sorry for Lisa Countryman, almost wishing there had been a deeper conspiracy to justify her death.

"It was about a lot of things," Kitamura said. "None of them very good."

Kitamura had never planned anything as crass as extortion. Lisa had been, really, incidental to his strategy, which had simply been to befriend the minister and his cronies at the NTT, wine and dine them, talk to them, do small favors for them, a soft sell to influence their decision.

Tom was surprised he was being so candid, but he supposed it had all happened so long ago. After 1980, everything had changed—decades of solipsism and greed that seemed without end. A malaise. The Cold War was over. The Japanese economic bubble had burst. Countries and civilizations rose and fell. But the great divisions of ethnicity and class and religion raged on, and everything was still, in the end, about money. The world was a much meaner place now, more superficial, more corruptible. There were scandals, but nothing was really scandalous, because the worst things imaginable happened every day and were immediately packaged into entertainment. No one seemed to have any innocence left to lose. Yet, underneath it all, people still lived out a million heartrending dramas of no consequence, searching for love and kinship, finding joy and betrayal. Hostage to their hearts.

Had Kitamura been sleeping with Lisa Countryman? Did his wife leave him for Congrieves? Did he know that Tom had been having an affair with Julia? He must have, but Kitamura was too discreet to say, and Tom was too chastened to ask. They shook hands and said goodbye, and then Tom called his wife on her cell phone, and she told him they were all on the beach, past the Halekulani.

This end of Waikiki, the *ewa* end in front of Fort DeRussy, was always empty, and, following their voices, he easily found his wife and mother in the dark, sitting on the sand.

"Where are the boys?" he asked.

"Swimming," his wife said.

Tom turned and saw his three sons in the water. They were skinny-dipping.

"Hey, Dad," his eldest said, "come on in."

"Okay," he said, and stripped to his underwear.

As he waded into the water, his boys quietly began chanting, "Boom-boom, boom-boom," mimicking the seismic concussions of the big man—the leviathan—lumbering into the sea.

Tom laughed. The water was lovely and warm.

■   ■   ■

THERE WAS an earthquake in Saitama Prefecture, 5.4 on the Richter scale. Not a big quake by anyone's definition, but large enough to crack open a retaining wall underneath an overpass on the Tohoku Expressway, near Kawaguchi, outside of Tokyo.

An inspector checking the structural integrity of the concrete support columns noticed the crack. The columns had been retrofit-ted, but not the thick wall, which was non-load-bearing. The crack drew his attention, and then something else. He didn't know what it was at first. He walked closer, and saw fingers.

Kenzo heard about it on the news. A skeleton had been found in the concrete. More than that, the skeleton was in pieces. The body had been dismembered before being entombed in the wall.

He had one of his Assistant Inspectors confirm what he already knew. The retaining wall had been built in June 1980 by KMT Construction, the executives of which had long ago been convicted for cutting corners on various expressway projects, jeopardizing public safety. The investigation had revealed the company's ties to the Takahashi-gumi and implicated dozens of government offi-cials, exposing years of misappropriations, kickbacks, and bribes.

As far as they could piece together, the skeleton was of a woman, young, around 165 or 170 centimeters. Kenzo asked a

Patrolman to drive him to MPD headquarters, and he went to the records archive and had them pull out the box that contained everything he had compiled about Lisa Countryman when he had been at Azabu Police Station.

He was the head of Criminal Investigations at Ikebukuro Police Station now. He had gotten back his center desk in Azabu after he had acceded to Kunichi and his superiors and declared that Minister Shiokawa had not jumped and committed suicide, but had slipped off the wet subway platform—a terrible, unfortunate accident. Yes, the minister had probably killed the girl, Kunichi had said, and maybe he had even drugged and raped her, crazed by her involvement with David Saito, whom they were never able to locate, but what was the point of disclosing this information to the public, of creating a scandal? The minister was dead.

By agreeing, Kenzo had been assigned better cases, and he had gotten better at his job, becoming a fairly competent investigator, and he had been promoted to Inspector. Then he single-handedly solved a kidnap-murder case that had gripped the nation for weeks, and he was given his own section in Ikebukuro. During all these years, he had never uttered a word about the circumstances surrounding Lisa Countryman's disappearance. Officially, the written advisory opinion still stood: she was missing and presumed dead.

In the Tokyo Medical Examiner's Office in Otsuka, Kenzo handed over the X-rays of Lisa Countryman's teeth and broken arm that he had gotten from her sister in 1980. He hovered as the ME checked them against the X-rays of the skull and bones that were assembled on the gleaming stainless-steel table behind them.

"Is it her?" Kenzo asked.

"It's her," the ME said.

Uncharacteristically, Kenzo took the rest of the day off, and rode seventy minutes on the Tokaido Line out to Oiso. Keiko was pleasantly surprised to see him, and they walked to the beach and sat on a blanket on the sand and watched the surfers.

They had just celebrated their twentieth anniversary—hard to believe. They never had children, but they had been wonderful companions to each other, no complaints at all. They occupied themselves by taking *bunka* classes together, going to concerts, museums, traveling to Europe. They even made it onto a golf course, but only twice; they decided they preferred the driving range. Yet lately Keiko had had a tough time of it. During the boom years of the eighties, she had started a successful business, packaging romance vacations for newlyweds to Hawaii, and she had bought two more apartment buildings in Tokyo. But after more than a decade of recession, her business failed, rents dropped, and the real estate market tanked.

It was such a dismal time in Japan. It almost seemed as if they were dying as a people, their economy in tatters, the population dwindling, the remaining citizens isolated and adrift. Had they been wrong about everything? Kenzo wondered. The power of consensus and obligation, the imperatives of racial purity and harmony?

Keiko had had to sell her buildings for a deep loss, leaving her with just the one in Oiso, into which she and Kenzo had moved three years ago. She began to suffer from depression and stress-related ailments, and then they had a real scare—a lump in her breast. She was lucky. It was caught early, requiring a lumpectomy and radiation, not a mastectomy and chemo, but Kenzo always worried the cancer might return. She was all he had. She was his life. She was his country of residence.

Tonight she was chipper. "What do you want for dinner?" she asked. "*Tonkatsu* or *unagi?*"

"*Tonkatsu*," he said. "What can I do to help?"

After they cooked and ate and washed the dishes, they sat on the couch and watched TV.

"What are you thinking about?" Keiko asked during a commercial. "You seem distracted."

"Oh, nothing," he said, although he was thinking about Lisa Countryman. He wished he had been able to bring her soul some peace and dignity, since her life seemed to have meant so little to anyone. Tomorrow he would arrange for her remains to be put in a coffin and shipped to the US, but he didn't know to where. Was her sister still alive? Would she want Lisa's remains? And then he thought briefly of Atlanta, Georgia, and Yumiko, and Simon.

He and Keiko turned in early. They made love for a sweet, delicious quarter-hour, then climbed under the blankets, both inserting earplugs and biting down on mouthguards and sliding eyeshades on their foreheads. This apartment was roomy, but the building was beside a highway, and noisy.

Fish-mouthing their lips, they kissed, pulled down their eyeshades, and scooted apart on the bed, careful they wouldn't touch during the night, and fell asleep happily.

■   ■   ■

IT WAS a dream, but not a dream. It was more like a film—grainy, off-hue, the motions stuttering, an old home movie that never existed. As Lisa lay on the bed in Mojo's *mansion,* immobile, she felt her heart slow down, then jiggle, and just before it stopped beating, the film began to unreel, and she saw herself as a little girl—the girl, with fate and fortune, she might have been.

She was four years old, and she stood on the deck of the USNS *Hayford* with her parents—her birth parents. They were among the few passengers on the Navy cargo ship for the passage from Yokohama to San Francisco. Despite a stop in Hawaii, it had been a long trip, but they were finally here, the California coast before them.

It was a brilliant morning, the sky so clear and blue, the sun glaring fiercely, everything painfully aglitter. Lisa looked up at the faces of her father and mother—she knew their names all of a sudden, Bobby and Miyako, sweet names for a couple in love—and Lisa thought of something Miyako had once told her. Growing up, Miyako had said, she had repeated a Korean adage to herself, one with which she had promised to live her life: *chi, sun, min.* Truth. Goodness. Beauty. As they passed under the Golden Gate Bridge, Lisa imagined what her mother must have been feeling right then, seeing the United States for the very first time. A land where all was possible, where truth prevailed, goodness was rewarded, and beauty could be found in the meeting of outcasts. Oh, what a sight, Lisa marveled.

We are orphans, all of us, she thought. And this is our home.

AUTHOR'S NOTE

For their editorial insights and support, I would like to thank my friends Katherine Palmer-Collins, Fred Leebron, Lily King, Danzy Senna, and Kathy Herold; my editor, Alane Mason, and, also at Norton, Alessandra Bastagli; my agent, Maria Massie, and my fact-checker, Chikako Atsuta.

Although I did a fair amount of research for this book and spent part of my childhood in Tokyo, this novel should not be considered an accurate representation of Japan. Dramatic licenses were freely taken. For guides and studies of Japan and its people, I referred to books by Rick Kennedy, Elisabeth Bumiller, Peter Tasker, and Ian Buruma. For information on the *mizu shobai,* I relied heavily on Anne Allison's *Nightwork: Sexuality, Pleasure, and Corporate Masculinity in a Tokyo Hostess Club* and *Permitted and Prohibited Desires: Mothers, Comics, and Censorship in Japan,* and Lisa Louis's *Butterflies of the Night: Mama-sans, Geisha, Strippers, and the Japanese Men They Serve.*